Henry James:
Tales of Art and Life

Signature Series
Frank Gado, General Editor

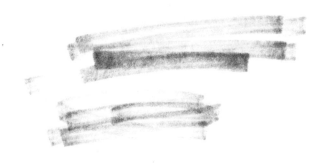

HENRY JAMES

TALES OF ART AND LIFE

Selection and Introduction by
HENRY TERRIE

SIGNATURE SERIES

Union College Press
Schenectady, New York

Tales of Art and Life

Contents

The first of the dates in the parentheses adjoining the James stories refers to original publication; the second, to initial appearance in a James collection.

Introduction

American novelists have tended to write their masterpieces either in early or mid-career and then decline. Hawthorne never matched *The Scarlet Letter*, though he lived another fourteen years. Melville survived his masterpiece by forty years; Mark Twain, by twenty-six. Fitzgerald wrote nothing to equal *The Great Gatsby*, his third novel, in the remaining fifteen years of his short life. Hemingway had done his best work by 1929. Even Faulkner, whose Yoknapatawpha fiction constitutes a remarkably coherent world, had written his best books thirty years before he died.

By contrast no reference to a single masterpiece or to a brief period of explosive creativity invokes Henry James. The publication of his first story in 1864 at the age of twenty-one inaugurated a literary career of fifty-two years. He published in every one of those years: in addition to one hundred twelve stories and twenty novels, he wrote fifteen plays, over two hundred fifty reviews and essays on literature, dozens of art reviews and pieces on the theatre, six volumes of travel literature, two biographies, three volumes of autobiography, and thousands of letters and other miscellanea. At his death in 1916, he left two novels in progress. Slowly and deliberately, in a way virtually unknown to American letters, he built an *oeuvre* in which, to the end, he appears as a gradually developing master of style and form. The eight stories presented in this volume do not proceed in a neat hierarchy of excellence; nevertheless, they reflect the general line of James's growth—from the charming but slight fable of "The Last of the Valerii" to the deep personal confrontation of "The Jolly Corner."

In his autobiography *A Small Boy and Others* (1913), James offers a key to understanding his fictional world. Remembering his youthful introduction to the Louvre during familial wanderings in Europe, he writes,

> I have dim reminiscences of permitted independent visits...during which the house of life and the palace of art became so mixed and interchangeable ... that an excursion to look at pictures would have

but half expressed my afternoon. I had looked at pictures, looked and looked again, at the vast Veronese, at Murillo's moon-borne Madonna, at Leonardo's almost unholy dame with the folded hands ... but I had also looked at France and looked at Europe, looked even at America as Europe itself might be conceived so to look, looked at history ... at society, manners, types, characters, possibilities and prodigies and mysteries of fifty sorts.

Here is the Europe that furnishes so many of James's settings, and the American presence that fired his imagination with the cultural contrasts of the International Theme; the easy transaction between people and the pictures they observe—"the house of life and the palace of art"—so typical of James's narratives; and, most conspicuously, the special concern with style and form that distinguishes James from other American writers of his time. As he says elsewhere in these reminiscences,

> In those beginnings I felt myself most happily cross the bridge over to Style constituted by the wondrous Galerie d'Apollon ... through which I inhaled ... a general sense of *glory*. The glory meant ever so many things at once, not only beauty and art and supreme design, but history and fame and power, the world in fine raised to richest and noblest expression.

Given such "beginnings," it is not astonishing that James found it congenial to live abroad.* Europe nourished a sensibility that expressed itself in stories filled with allusion to the visual arts as well as with direct appeal to the reader's own visual imagination. In every sense, as the eight selections constituting the present volume attest, James wrote tales of art and life.

---

*Born in New York City near Washington Square, Henry James had anything but a conventional American upbringing. James's father, who had expansive, unorthodox ideas about education and about life, saw to it that his children were given wide opportunities for cosmopolitan experience. In the course of their young lives, Henry and his brothers and sister encountered schools and tutors in England, France, Germany, and Switzerland as well as in New York, Newport, and Cambridge in this country. They learned French and German as well as English and went to theatres and art galleries on both sides of the ocean. Henry, after brief flirtations with law and painting, determined to be a writer. In 1869, searching for richer sources of inspiration than he found at home, he began a series of travels in Europe which ended seven years later with permanent residence in England. Thereafter, he came to this country only for short visits at widely spaced intervals.

Perhaps the most important indication in this and other such autobiographical passages, however, is the recording intelligence of James himself. The small boy of James's memory was already characterizing, evaluating, imagining relationships, drawing significance from visual perception. As he was to argue many times in his critical writings, the scene and the characters become interesting only as they are actively observed. "My report of people's experience—my report as a 'story-teller'—is essentially my appreciation of it," he tells us, "and there is no 'interest' for me in what my hero, my heroine or anyone else does save through that admirable process." This principle leads to a central fact about James's short stories: they tend not to be very short. "As soon as I begin to appreciate," he adds, "simplification is imperilled." His notebooks are filled with ideas for stories intended to fit within the limits set by magazine editors. But again and again, "appreciation" swelled five thousand words to ten thousand, and then to twenty thousand. Short story wanted to escape into *nouvelle*; *nouvelle* into novel. "Really, universally, relations stop nowhere," he declares, "and the exquisite problem of the artist is eternally but to draw, by a geometry of his own, the circle within which they shall happily *appear* to do so."

In writing of the short story as a literary form, James distinguished between the "idea anecdotic" and the "idea developmental." Although expressing admiration for the anecdote, the "very short story" he likened to the sonnet in its discipline, he could not resist following his penchant for the developmental mode. The dominant characteristic of the anecdote, in his view, was that it points to and knows a single character; but James always saw one character in relation to another, and once that relation was established, development took over. T.S. Eliot was so struck by this phenomenon in James's fiction that he extravagantly declared, "Compared with James's, other novelists' characters seem to be only accidentally in the same book."

The primary relation in a story is that between the subject and the author. Such authors as Fielding, Thackeray, and Hardy, had adopted a narrative *persona* who operated virtually as a character in the story and yet, at the same time, was allowed the privilege of omniscient commentary. The chief alternative, one designed to remove the author's obtrusive presence and make the fiction self-sufficient, was first-person narration by either the principal fictional character or an eyewitness observer. James adopted this strategy in the majority of his early stories, as in "The Last of the Valerii." After 1880, however, his enthusiasm for this narrative form waned: although he would occasionally resort to it, his interests pulled him in another direction, and in his last twenty stories, written between 1901–1910, he abandoned it entirely.* What he de-

---

*Among James's twenty-two novels, *The Sacred Fount* is conspicuously unique in its first-person narration. He believed that "the first person, in the long piece, is a form foredoomed to looseness"—to what he called "the terrible *fluidity* of self-revelation."

veloped in its stead became the bridge to modern narrative technique, with
its emphasis on direct representation of human consciousness. By effacing the
presence of the author through a third-person narrative seeming to proceed
directly from the thoughts and perceptions of the protagonist, James was able
to dramatize the interior life of his "central intelligence" while maintaining a
strong (if largely unseen) relation to both reader and character. The gradual
refinement of this technique, James's great contribution to making fiction the
shared record of human experience it has become in our time, can be traced
from "Daisy Miller," where the author still shows his hand freely, through
"The Liar," where the author virtually disappears, to "The Beast in the Jungle"
and "The Jolly Corner," where author, reader, and character engage in a
marvelously complex partnership.

Although "The Last of the Valerii," published in 1874 when James was
thirty-one, is simpler and less ambitious than the late masterpieces, it already
shows distinctively Jamesian touches. A way of identifying this characteristic
quality is to compare the story with one of its sources, Prosper Mérimée's "La
Venus d'Ille." In Mérimée's version, the unearthed statue is a Venus who exerts
a baleful influence on a young bridegroom and punishes his infidelity by
crushing him to death on his wedding night. Mérimée's chief interest is in the
supernatural horror of the case, and he plays very skillfully on the reader's
latent susceptibilities. James, on the other hand, is less concerned with the
event than with the response. Thus, although both narrators are artists who
speak in the first person, their roles are quite different. Mérimée's narrator
remains throughout the detached observer—a consciously superior Parisian
watching provincials who simply invites us to share his wonder over what has
happened. In contrast, James's narrator is godfather to the bride, apparently
serves *in loco patris* at the wedding, frequents the Villa Valerio daily, and takes
an almost prurient interest in relations between Martha and Camillo.

Nevertheless, the artist-narrator does not allow this intimacy to blunt his
critical sensibility; significantly, though he professes concern for Martha's welfare, he retreats into objectivity to describe the young couple "from the pictorial
point of view"—*e.g.*, when he notes that her light and his dark hair make a
nice contrast. Equally revealing is the tone he adopts. Observing the early
course of the marriage, he states, with evident condescension: "Their life was
a childlike interchange of caresses, as candid and unmeasured as those of a
shepherd and shepherdess in a bucolic poem." And, despite his affection for
the lovers, he does not shrink from making them appear ridiculous—as in his
mocking the Count's tendency to fall asleep when his wife reads to him: "She
would sit and brush the flies from him while he lay picturesquely snoozing...."
Indeed, when the statue of Juno interrupts this slightly comic idyll, the voy-
euristic narrator virutally enters the nuptial bedroom: "What passed between

them in private, I had, of course, no warrant to inquire. Nothing, I suspected—and that was the misery!" In this wittily patronizing point of view, we find the real force of the tale; for, notwithstanding a touch of melodrama in the Count's bloody worship of his statue and a sentimental appeal in the final reconciliation, the adventure of Martha and Camillo would move us very little on its own. These vapid young people come to life for us by virtue of the narrator's interpreting mind. And it is he who begins to define for us the terms of the International Theme as it was to emerge from James's later works: the clarity and light of the American mind *vs.* the darkness and mystery of the European; the New (as expressed by money and acquisition) *vs.* the Old (as expressed by family tradition and inherited ownership); Protestant vs. Catholic; and marriage as a symbol of the transatlantic encounter. The richness of this Jamesian method is that the meaning of an event always lies in someone's conscious appreciation of it. To understand, the reader must observe the observer.

"Daisy Miller" (1878), James's first popular success and perhaps still his best known story, moves beyond "The Last of the Valerii" in several ways. It leaves the dim world of quasi-supernatural romance for the clear light of everyday reality. It also transcends the pale Martha Valerio with the first truly memorable incarnation of James's great discovery—one might almost say invention—of the American Girl, playing her role on the international scene. (Daisy is the prototype not only of Isabel Archer, Milly Theale, and Maggie Verver in James's own fiction but also of many actual women—like Consuelo Vanderbilt, Doris Duke, Barbara Hutton, and Grace Kelly—who took their money and beauty to Europe, and made the world take notice. Daisy's innocence, her spontaneity, her courage, her confidence, her directness and honesty—all these qualities give her an enormous appeal and lend both dignity and pathos to her death. Yet if she represents the freshness and vivacity of American youth (and of a youthful America), she also stands as an indictment of American carelessness. Daisy is stubborn, willful, reckless—and encouraged to be so by her mother. And as Mrs. Miller abandoned her responsibility for Daisy's social behavior, so her hopeless efforts to control the nine-year-old Randolph indicate another disaster in the making. Both Daisy and Randolph are in many ways prophetic of a future generation's "dropping out" and "doing its own thing."

A third distinction between "Daisy Miller" and "The Last of the Valerii" is the shift in point of view from first-person narrator to third-person central intelligence, which was to become James's dominant method. The ground on which cultures clash in "Daisy Miller" is the puzzled consciousness of Frederick Winterbourne, a decent enough young man whose want of judgment and resolution are attributable to his "Europeanization" (a process with which James

would have been thoroughly familiar). As his aunt warns him, and as he
ruefully admits at the end, he had been "booked to make a mistake." Among
the things he has learned while having "lived too long in foreign parts" is that
unmarried girls do not have unchaperoned meetings with young men—not,
that is, if they wish to be socially acceptable. Thus, Daisy's frankness in offering
to go with him to the Castle of Chillon seems an exciting invitation for a
weekend love affair, but, at the same time, her openness about everything puts
him on his guard against this "extraordinary mixture of innocence and crudity."
The young man's confusion is the pivot on which the story turns; it also
expresses a recurrent motif in James's international stories: the relation between
manners and morals. Winterbourne moves in a society chiefly concerned with
appearance; Daisy, in contrast, reflects the belief that an upright personal
morality gives one leave to behave with complete freedom in public.

     Although James employs Winterbourne's mind to play out this little drama
of appearance and reality and evokes from the reader some sympathy for his
character's uncertainty, he also establishes an authorial intelligence, located at
a distance from both his characters and his setting, to allow for a broader
perspective. This indulgently humorous detachment is readily apparent in the
opening description of Vevay, but it soon reveals its special purpose through
the innuendo in the introduction of Winterbourne: "When his friends spoke
of him, they said that he was at Geneva 'studying'; when his enemies spoke
of him, they said—but, after all, he had no enemies." Subsequently, the reader
learns, as if by hearsay, of Winterbourne's devotion to "a foreign lady—a
person older than himself . . . about whom there were some singular stories."
Lest the reader should miss the significance of these indirections as an ironic
foreshadowing of Winterbourne's later judgments of Daisy, James then slyly
insinuates a remark that Geneva was the home of Calvinism, the foundation
of New England religion. Having thus established his tone and distance (and
invited us to join him), James can lead us on to appreciate the comedy and
pathos of his young couple caught between two worlds. One can hardly fail
to smile at Winterbourne's bewilderment on the trip to Chillon. Nor can one
be unmoved by Daisy's death and Winterbourne's vain regret as he stands
beside her grave, "the raw protuberance among the April daisies." James's
detachment characteristically allows for a free play of both comic and tragic
elements.

     Published a decade after "Daisy Miller," "The Liar" (1888) is clearly a
product of James's middle years, in which the narrative method increases in
sophistication and the penetration of human motive and feeling deepens. Once
again the story comes to us through the mind of a third-person central intelligence, but by this time James has gone far toward surrendering his right of
authorial comment, so that the reader must judge for himself the reliability

of the narration. Granted, a similar problem attaches to first-person narrators, as "The Last of the Valerii" demonstrates. Nevertheless, there is a crucial difference: the first-person narrator must self-consciously *tell* his own story, thereby interposing himself as a barrier between the reader and the events described; the third-person narrator, on the other hand, *experiences* his story without having to talk about it, thus impelling the reader to share directly in the narrator's perceptions. The third-person central intelligence is, to use James's own term, an altogether more "dramatic" form of presentation, one that creates the illusion of unmediated experience. James's great pioneering contribution in this development in narrative art pointed the way into the so-called stream of consciousness technique for writers like Joyce and Woolf and Faulkner. But that was not the way James himself went. In his final period—as "The Beast in the Jungle," in particular, illustrates—James would learn he could recover some of his authorial privilege, without loss of dramatic intensity, by means of subtle shadings and hints.

In "The Liar," then, authorial presence is virtually non-existent (or, at least, invisible): save for two or three faintly editorial phrases, the reader is entirely in the mind of Oliver Lyon as he probes into the lives of Colonel and Mrs. Capadose. Inevitably, such withholding of authorial guidance leads to variant interpretations. Early readers, taking Lyon's views at face value, tended to see the story as a study of Colonel Capadose, whose "monstrous foible" corrupts the once-virtuous Everina Brant. Then, later readers, more alert to Jamesian ambiguity, began to ask, "Who is the liar in 'The Liar'?"; belatedly noting the pun in his name, they shifted the focus to a psychologically perverse and ultimately dishonest Lyon. And, of course, because the ambiguity inherent in James's approach cannot ultimately be resolved, some critics have attacked the story as basically flawed. But if one discounts the need for a single truth, there remains the possibility that James's title is general rather than specific in its reference. Read from this perspective, the story becomes a complex study of lying as a human social phenomenon, a study reinforcing our knowledge that, in the world of Henry James, there are no *a priori* moral judgments: one must rely on sensitive, intelligent appreciation of the individual case.

Two broad views of lying emerge in "The Liar." Sir David Ashmore, a spokesman, of a kind, for the society in which these characters move, sees no moral issue: the Colonel's romancing he dismisses as "a natural peculiarity— as you might limp or stutter or be left-handed"; Everina's practice of supporting her husband's stories he jokingly attributes to a combination of wifely love and female admiration for the art of lying. Lyon, on the other hand, condemns lying as "the least heroic of vices," as vulgar and corrupting for both the liar and the person who condones the lie. Neither of these views, however, allows for the possible range of significance of a lie in its particular context.

At first, Colonel Capadose seems no more than a victim of *pseudologia phantastica*, a relatively harmless compulsion to exaggerate—to tell "fish stories." Indeed, he is so good-humored that he has a Falstaffian ability to join in the laughter when one of his fabrications is shouted down. And at least one of his lies, that concerning the sale of Lyon's portrait of Everina, may be excused as a form of flattery to the artist. Significantly, only on the deliberate provocation by Oliver Lyon does he tell a lie damaging to another person (Miss Geraldine). The reader's moral judgment of Everina should also be tempered by a consideration of the circumstances. When she is driven to lie about the slashing of the canvas, and about her opinion of the portrait, one sees that her choice is between protecting her marriage and giving a useless satisfaction to Lyon. In such circumstances what woman would choose differently?

Oliver Lyon is a more complex case than either of the Capadoses. He does not so much lie as engage in deceitful behavior. He misrepresents his motive for wanting to paint the Colonel, encourages the Colonel to prevaricate, conceals his knowledge of what has happened to the painting, and, in the concluding scene, presses Everina like a prosecuting attorney until she tells the lie he wants. If he is not precisely a liar, Lyon may be something worse: the "father of lies." Nor, in assessing Lyon's behavior, must we forget that he is an artist—and thereby, in a fundamental sense, not altogether unlike the Colonel. Reminding us of his own deep concern with the privilege and responsibility of the artist and with the relation between art and life, he has Lyon say of the Colonel's habit, "It is art for art and he is prompted by love of beauty. He has an inner vision of what might have been, of what ought to be, and he helps on the good cause by the simple substitution of a *nuance*. He paints, as it were, and so do I!"

Although "The Real Thing" (1892) does not represent a forward step in the evolution of James's narrative method, it advances one of his major thematic preoccupations. "The Liar" is a story in which art intrudes on life as Oliver Lyon attempts to use his painter's skill for a selfish purpose; in "The Real Thing," life intrudes on art. Out of a simple idea—two real gentlefolk presenting themselves as the perfect models for illustrations of high society—James's appreciative faculty not only makes a story on imitation, the fundamental unresolved problem in art since the time of Plato and Aristotle; it also sees the problem in distinctively human terms. Not just a representative artist, the narrator is a particular young man of limited talent who aspires to paint portraits from life but who gets on by illustrating works of fiction; that is, he makes imitations of imitations of life. Thus, when Major and Mrs. Monarch arrive in his studio, the question of the "real thing" already has an extra dimension. The Monarchs are recognizable—and gently satirized—types of failed, useless English gentry; but they have a personal history that can be read in their clothes, their manners, and their talk. And they have between them one real thing beyond the power of art: a true marriage.

Here as elsewhere, James sees characters in relation to each other. The human drama over which the narrator rather helplessly presides moves back and forth between art and life. The Cockney Miss Churm and the graceful little Italian Oronte, like the narrator and the Monarchs, also have roles beyond their professional activity. What had been a muted rivalry for modeling jobs becomes personal when Miss Churm resents serving tea to the Monarchs. Later the roles reverse when the Monarchs, mastering their pride, give tea to Oronte. The artistic and the human issues come together for their resolution as the Monarchs watch Miss Churm and Oronte pose for a love scene at the piano. The artist, exhilarated by his recognition that the make-believe lovers are "the ideal thing," discovers that they inspire his imagination as the real thing never could. Even the Monarchs now see the truth: the artist cannot *copy* life, he must *make* it. Their concession to this apparent fact of art is then made manifest in an act of life. Mrs. Monarch, with quiet dignity, ventures to rearrange Miss Churm's hair ("one of the most heroic personal services I've ever seen rendered") and then takes up a dirty rag from the floor. If she is not an ideal model, she is still a real lady—and prepared to be a real servant.

Yet, with his infinite sense of complication, James will not end his story on a note of sentiment, however touching: succumbing to the truth that the Monarchs are no more acceptable as servants than as models, the narrator finally pays them to go away. Predictably, this conclusion produces more questions than answers. By choosing "ideal" rather than "real" models, the artist gets his commission and presumably prospers—though his friend Jack Hawley (himself a mediocre artist) says that, artistically speaking, the Monarchs have done him "a permanent harm." Although the narrator consoles himself with the warm memory of his experience with the Monarchs, the difficulty is that an honest memory could bring very limited consolation. Faced with a problem in real life, the narrator has paid to rid himself of it and turned back to the artificial world where one imagines reality. The inference that the artist must suppress his humanity in the service of art is inescapable. Previously, James had hinted at this separation between art and life with the cold painter's eye of the narrator in "The Last of the Valerii" and the perversion of Oliver Lyon's craft in "The Liar." In "The Real Thing," however, the question, which would remain with James throughout his career, directly invokes the implications of a remark he reportedly made in 1895 to an aspiring young writer: "There is one word—let me impress upon you—which you must inscribe upon your banner, and that, that word is *Loneliness.*"

"Paste" (1899), like "The Last of the Valerii," offers a fascinating opportunity for comparative study. Writing a decade after it appeared, James recalled that he had begun with an idea of reversing the premise of a story by Maupassant, "La Parure" ("The Necklace"). That, in his preface, James remembers the diamond necklace as having been made of pearls suggests not only that he did not reread "La Parure" but also that his indebtedness to Maupassant included another story, "Les Bijoux" ("The Jewels"), in which Maupassant himself had reversed the premise.

In both of Maupassant's stories—very brief, anecdotal narratives emphasizing plot rather than character and relationship—everything leads to the little ironic twist at the end. In "La Parure" the reversal is simple if poignant; the labor has been in vain. The reflective reader might wish to speculate on the character of Mme. Forestier, who deceives her friend with the loan of a fake necklace; or marvel at the dogged bourgeous honesty of the Loisels; or wonder if the Loisels will at least recover the money they have earned so painfully. But these questions are not encouraged: the end of the story is the point of the story. The ironies in "Les Bijoux" are a bit more complicated: first, the shattered smugness of M. Lantin as he learns that his perfect wife has cuckolded him; next, the compensation that his wife's infidelity has made him a wealthy man; and finally, the third turnabout, in which M. Lantin finds that a chaste wife is not what he wanted after all. Yet in this story, too, the ending is closed: the characters have no life outside the particular sequence of events. Both stories are thus little illustrations of the vanity of human aspirations, Mme. Loisel's for a grand life and M. Lantin's for a perfect wife.*

Though very short by James's standards, "Paste" nevertheless stretches roughly twice the length of either story by Maupassant. Indeed, James was probably incapable of writing a story of Maupassant's characteristic length; even in this relatively brief fiction, he develops a set of relations that threaten to break through the boundaries of the short-story form and become a novel. Whereas both of Maupassant's titles focus sharply on the object, the jewelry, James's invites the multiple possibilities in the idea of falseness. A necklace, presumed to be paste, turns out to be genuine. An ostensibly blameless vicar's

---

*Yet another opportunity for comparison of the uses made of permutations in this conceit is presented by "Mr. Know-All," a story by Somerset Maugham (who presumably knew the versions of both Maupassant and James). Here, on an ocean voyage, Max Kelada offends everyone with his officious authority on any subject. He bets another passenger one hundred dollars that pearls worn by the man's wife are genuine. At the point of decision, Max, seeing the wife's distress, chivalrously declares the pearls false and, paying the wager, accepts the scorn of the company. Where Maupassant was concerned with circumstantial irony and James with personal relationships, Maugham is after the revelation of character. By making a false statement, Max Kelada proves himself a truer gentleman than his more genteel companions.

wife seems to have had a passionate love affair during her stage career. Mrs. Guy, who, on entering the story, declares the false pearls to be genuine, acquires the treasure in the end and gives a questionable account of her purchase. Arthur Prime, who declares the genuine pearls to be false and lies to Charlotte about disposing of them, says he is motivated by respect for his stepmother's memory but seems more concerned with his own priggish sense of appearances—and is finally moved by greed. And in the midst of this swirl of dissimulation, there is Charlotte, the central intelligence, who is scrupulously honest while being treated falsely. One marvels at James's ingenuity in exploiting the manifold possibilities of the conceit within his story, yet one feels vibrations of life beyond the ending. Charlotte's final uncertainty reminds one of Joseph Conrad's perceptive statement:

> One is never set at rest by Mr. Henry James's novels. His books end as an episode in life ends. You remain with the sense of the life still going on; and even the subtle presence of the dead is felt in that silence that comes upon the artist-creation when the last word has been read. It is eminently satisfying, but it is not final. Mr. Henry James, great artist and faithful historian, never attempts the impossible.

With "The Great Good Place" (1900), one enters that rare Jamesian territory Frank Moore Colby had in mind when he wrote of traveling "in darkest James." Some readers have found James's late style difficult and the sensibilities of the characters over-refined; others have averred that despite, or perhaps because of, his elaborations and subtleties, these last works succeed in creating a sense of life, a world matched only in the final paintings of Rembrandt or the late quartets of Beethoven—to repeat a phrase from James's memories of the Louvre, "the world in fine raised to the richest and noblest expression." One thing is certain: the James of these works demands attentive readers.

"The Great Good Place" is a tantalizing story in that it so obviously coaxes interpretation yet, at the same time, frustrates the effort. It is clearly enough a variation on the familiar motif of seeking a hidden place of refuge—in the words of George Dane, "a happy land—far, far away"—when one is weighed down by worldly cares. As always with James, however, the value is less in the idea than in the treatment of it—and the treatment here is particularly rich and evocative. In simplest terms, it merely describes George Dane, beleaguered by his very success as a writer, receiving a visit from an ambitious young man, falling asleep in his presence, dreaming of a "great good place" where his burden of cares has been lifted from him, and waking to find that the young man has meanwhile cleared his desk of paperwork. (On this level, the tale will always be an appealing fantasy for anyone who has been over-whelmed by paper—and who among us has not?) An attentive reading of the text, however, quickly reveals suggestions of something more. Rain, which seems to threaten something like T.S. Eliot's "death by water" at the beginning, has been transformed by the end of the tale into a life-giving element. Bells, beginning with Dane's doorbell, signal various stages of the adventure. A succession of handshakes, first with the young man, then with the Brother, and later with the manservant Brown, indicates some communion in progress.

Criticism has produced three main lines of interpretation for this story. One, heavily Freudian, construes Dane's dream as a therapeutic regression to the womb and a rebirth in which his battered ego is healed in a soothing maternal environment ("some great mild, invisible mother who stretches away into space and whose lap is the whole valley"). Reinforcing this notion of a regression is the fact that, when Dane speaks of the "happy land," he "chant[s] it like a sick child." A second reading sees in George Dane's adventure the archetypal pattern of the hero's journey in search of some universal value. After his magical transition from the ordinary world, Dane undergoes a benign initiation into the mysteries of the Great Good Place—with its soothing sights and sounds, its uncoerced rituals of behavior, its merging of identities—and finally achieves a spiritual wholeness. He returns with new vision to the other world where the rain, which had threatened to drown him, is now a pleasant sound, and where his room, which had seemed crowded and stifling, is now "disencumbered, different, twice as large." A third reading gives these personal and archetypal transformations a specifically religious connotation. In this view, Dane's return to the world is a Christian rebirth: by abandoning his old, self-centered identity for an ideal of brotherhood, he finds resources for living. Ample support for this interpretation exists in the many religious allusions: *e.g.*, Dane is moved by the sounds of distant bells and of slow footsteps in "the great cloister" to think of Monte Cassino or La Grande Chartreuse; one of the Brothers compares their experience to a religious retreat and talks of finding, or "getting back," the true self through "material simplification"; and the "wise mind" responsible for the Place has an unmistakable air of divinity.

The systematic reader will have no difficulty in making a case for any of these interpretations; but more important is the fact that there is no necessity for choosing one to the exclusion of the others since the large pattern of disgust, retreat, and renewal remains the same. Indeed, there are many un-certainties, and James carefully multiplies clues to make his reference elusive. Not even the moment when Dane's experience begins is fixed in objective reality. From the outset, an oddity in his perception and his behavior disturbs the reader. Then the doorbell rings, and time blurs: he "never afterward recovered the time taken by Brown to reappear." The name of the visitor "somehow, failed to reach Dane's ear." After a period that, "later on, defied measurement," Dane shakes hands; in the next sentence he has been in the Great Good Place for an indeterminate time. His only account of how he got there is a flashback within the dream. Moreover, the Place itself assumes an amorphous reality: described in religious and psychological terms in some instances, in others, its details half humorously evoke a country house, a gentleman's club, a fine hotel, or even a Swiss *pension.* Mystifying, too, are the curious regular and very precise payments in money. At once familiar and strange, uniquely personal to George Dane and to each reader, the Great Good Place evades definition, and in the final analysis, the story in which it is situated may be regarded as a ghostly tale, sure to haunt the reader's memory. Henry James himself may well have given the only necessary critical instructions in his prefatory remarks: "There remains 'The Great Good Place' (1900)—to the spirit of which, however, it strikes me, any gloss or comment would be a tactless challenge. It embodies a calculated effect, and to plunge into it, I find, even for a beguiled glance—a course I indeed recommend—is to have left all else outside."

Another entry into the psyche, this time with a more chilling purpose, is effected in "The Beast in the Jungle" (1903). One can scarcely imagine a less promising subject than that of this tale about a man "to whom nothing on earth was to have happened"—or conceive of a conventional writer who would attempt it. James not only dared, he fashioned one of the great representations of modern alienation.

The key to his *tour de force* is an interplay between the image of the title, suggesting fierce energy and aggression, and the fact of the content, John Marcher's chronicle of time wasted through steadfast negation. Marcher's expectation of something cataclysmic is "like a crouching beast in the Jungle." Since its spring is "inevitable," marrying May would be like taking "a lady on a tiger-hunt." Then, at the last—in the instant of revelation at May's grave— the Beast rises for the "leap that was to settle him." Opposed to this hallucination of raw, brutal violence is the reality of Marcher's life, in which all vitality is lacking. To appreciate this interplay between image and reality fully, the reader must at once inhabit the central intelligence of John Marcher (significantly, there is no Beast for May; it exists for the reader only insofar as he shares Marcher's consciousness) and, also, maintain enough objectivity for independent judgment.

James creates this opportunity in two ways: through a subtle flow of his own implied judgments, and through the perspectives of May Bartram, which the reader receives in a way denied to Marcher by his egotism. From the first, May furnishes an alternative view of Marcher's situation. His apprehension, she suggests, may be only of falling in love; when he replies that no affair of his heart has been overwhelming, she says, "Then it hasn't been love." As time passes and the intimacy of the two watchers increasingly gives the appearance without the substance of love, May's judgment must recur to the reader. A further separation of perception, or disjunction between metaphor and truth, occurs in the climactic April moment when May hints to Marcher that she knows the nature of his fate. Although she assures him that "It's never too late," Marcher is unable to penetrate the mystery. As James tells us, "She only kept him waiting, however; that is he only waited." All he can see is that his threatened fate is "inordinately soft." Thus, for him, the "leap" of the Beast in this scene is not a leap at all. That is why, after May's death, Marcher feels the Beast has sprung and "stolen away" instead of making a kill, and why he finds himself searching wistfully through his mental jungle, half missing the old sense of danger.

In "The Beast in the Jungle," characteristic of his late narrative mode, James both records the perception of his central intelligence and at the same time encourages objectivity in the reader. Examples of this narrative subtlety occur in virtually every sentence:

"Some such consideration as this was *doubtless* in his mind...."

"Even his original fear, *if fear it had been*...."

"He had kept up, *he felt*, and very decently on the whole...."

"Such, soon enough, *as things went with him*, became the inference...."

(Emphases added.)

One becomes aware, also, that after May's death James begins to refer to his protagonist as "poor Marcher." Thus, while abandoning the posture of omniscience, James quietly retains some of its advantages and leads the reader to a position poised nicely between emotional identification and ironic detachment. The operation of this double consciousness is fully revealed in the conclusion, where the reader, who has long since learned the truth, must examine the nature of Marcher's recognition. Without a measure of detachment, one risks attributing more feeling to Marcher than his capacities warrant; lacking some identification with the protagonist, the reader may feel the pity without the fear.

Often treated as a companion piece to "The Beast in the Jungle," "The Jolly Corner" (1908) represents, almost literally, an excursion into the terrifying chambers of the mind. In this case, biographical facts point that mind as James's own. During the 1890's, James went through troubled times. His sister Alice died of cancer in 1892. In 1894, his dear friend Constance Fenimore Woolson apparently committed suicide (the trauma of which has only recently emerged in Leon Edel's biography). Meanwhile, he had, he declared, abandoned the novel, and by 1895, his efforts as a playwright had failed dismally. Inevitably, as he worked through the last half of the decade to revive his novelist's craft, and approached the formidable age of sixty, James faced doubts about the shape of his life, especially about his early decision to become an expatriate. Although he survived these trials and went on to produce his finest work, he paid a heavy emotional cost. Then, in 1904, he crossed the Atlantic for an extended tour of the United States. One result of that visit would be *The American Scene* (1907), an acute perception of our society in the early years of this century; another, written the following year was "The Jolly Corner." Here, a New Yorker who, like James, has lived many years abroad is haunted on his return by the idea of the life he might have lived had he remained in this country. Through the rooms and passages of his childhood home, he seeks the ghost of that other life, suspended between the aggression of his pursuit and the fear of its outcome. Although, of course, "The Jolly Corner" may be read as a ghost story, the fact that the ghosts are projections of Spencer Brydon's own personality leads into a psychological rather than a supernatural world. One is reminded of Emily Dickenson's quatrain:

> One need not be a Chamber - to be Haunted -
> One need not be a House -
> The Brain has Corridors - surpassing
> Material Place -

As is so often the case in tales where James focuses on the interior life, he dramatizes this life for the reader through imagery of strong or violent action—what one critic has called "the language of adventure." Thus, Brydon thinks of his nightly search in terms of big-game hunting with all its attendant fear and suspense, though he is ambiguous about his precise role. At one moment, he is the stalking hunter taking "the vantage of rock and tree"; at another he feels "like some monstrous stealthy cat." This duality grows out of his sense that he has reversed the usual situation, in which one fears and flees an apparition; instead, anticipating a confrontation, he speculates on which party will most appall the other. Here we touch upon another source in James's own life, a remarkably vivid dream, or nightmare, he recorded in his auto-biography. James remembered desperately holding a door against the attack of some frightful creature when, suddenly inspired, he reversed the pressure and burst through the door in pursuit of the pursuer, who now fled desperately from him. His inspiration consisted in "the great thought that I, in my appalled state, was probably still more appalling than the awful agent, creature or presence, whatever he was." Just so in "The Jolly Corner": Brydon feels he has "turned the tables" (a phrase that occurs in both story and autobiography) on his *alter ego*, who retreats behind a closed door. At this point, however, the parallel with James's dream begins to break down; for when Brydon goes down the stairs and meets a figure at the door, it is he who gives way and falls in a swoon.

In assessing this climax, and the conclusion which follows, the reader faces a number of questions. If, as Brydon assumes, the figure in the doorway is the Brydon who might have been, how has he moved from the closed room above to the front vestibule? And why does he come out of hiding at last? Why is the face Brydon sees "the face of a stranger"? Does this "stranger" represent some self-knowledge which Brydon cannot admit, and is that the cause of his near fatal collapse? And one final question. In the concluding chapter, Brydon experiences a rebirth, in effect, in the lap of Alice Staverton. (Like George Dane in "The Great Good Place," he has become a new man.) Alice seems to have a clearer understanding of this regeneration than does Brydon himself. What is her perception of the stranger's identity, and what is the meaning of her concluding words: "And he isn't—no, he isn't—*you*"?

That the ending to this self-exploration should produce such a barrage of questions is to be expected, and it tells us something about the nature of James's late fictions. Although his aim is not to baffle for the sake of bafflement, neither is it to supply clear, definitive answers. For James, consciousness was life itself, remaining always a mystery; and the experience of that mystery was possible only in a climate of poetry, a poetry not of statement but of reverberation. As noted above, James, as he increasingly internalized the action of his tales, tended to represent that action through elaborate external imagery. One of the most striking images in "The Jolly Corner" may be taken as describing not only the experience of Spencer Brydon entering his house but also that of the reader entering a late James tale:

> ...feeling the place once more in the likeness of some great glass bowl, all precious concave crystal, set delicately humming by the play of a moist finger round its edge. The concave crystal held, as it were, this mystical other world, and the indescribably fine murmur of its rim was the sigh there, the scarce audible pathetic wail to his strained ear, of all the old baffled forsworn possibilities. What he did therefore by this appeal of his hushed presence was to wake them into such measure of ghostly life as they might still enjoy.

The reader who, on entering this bowl, puts aside literal expectations and listens intently will receive strange and wonderful communications.

Henry Terrie
Dartmouth College
Hanover, New Hampshire

THE LAST OF THE VALERII

I had had occasion to declare more than once that if my god-daughter married a foreigner I should refuse to give her away. And yet when the young Conte Valerio was presented to me, in Rome, as her accepted and plighted lover, I found myself looking at the happy fellow, after a momentary stare of amazement, with a certain paternal benevolence; thinking, indeed, that from the picturesque point of view (she with her yellow locks and he with his dusky ones), they were a strikingly well-assorted pair. She brought him up to me half proudly, half timidly, pushing him before her, and begging me with one of her dovelike glances to be very polite. I don't know that I am particularly addicted to rudeness; but she was so deeply impressed with his grandeur that she thought it impossible to do him honor enough. The Conte Valerio's grandeur was doubtless nothing for a young American girl, who had the air and almost the habits of a princess, to sound her trumpet about; but she was desperately in love with him, and not only her heart, but her imagination, was touched. He was extremely handsome, and with a more significant sort of beauty than is common in the handsome Roman race. He had a sort of sunken depth of expression, and a grave, slow smile, suggesting no great quickness of wit, but an unimpassioned intensity of feeling which promised well for Martha's happiness. He had little of the light, inexpensive urbanity of his countrymen, and more of a sort of heavy sincerity in his gaze which seemed to suspend response until he was sure he understood you. He was perhaps a little stupid, and I fancied that to a political or aesthetic question the response would be particularly slow. "He is good, and strong, and brave," the young girl however assured me; and I easily believed her. Strong the Conte Valerio certainly was; he had a head and throat like some of the busts in the Vatican. To my eye, which has looked at things now so long with the painter's purpose, it was a real perplexity to see such a throat rising out of the white cravat of the period. It sustained a head as massively round as that of the familiar bust of the Emperor Caracalla, and covered with the same dense sculptural crop of curls. The young man's hair grew superbly; it was such hair as the old Romans must have had when they walked bareheaded and bronzed about the world. It made a perfect arch over his low, clear forehead, and prolonged itself on cheek and chin in a close, crisp beard, strong with its own strength and unstiffened by the razor. Neither his nose nor his mouth was delicate; but they were powerful, shapely, and manly. His complexion was of a deep glowing brown which no emotion would alter, and his large, lucid eyes seemed to stare at you like a pair of polished agates. He was of middle stature, and his chest was of so generous a girth that you half expected to hear his linen crack with its even respirations. And yet, with his simple human smile, he looked neither like a young bullock nor a gladiator. His powerful voice was the least bit harsh, and his large, ceremonious reply to my compliment had the massive sonority with which civil speeches must have been uttered in the age of Augustus. I had always considered my god-daughter a very American little person, in all delightful meanings of the word, and I doubted if this sturdy young Latin would understand the transatlantic element in her nature; but, evidently, he would make her a loyal and ardent lover. She seemed to me, in her blond prettiness, so tender, so appealing, so bewitching, that it was impossible to believe he had not more thoughts for all this than for the pretty fortune which it yet bothered me to believe that he must, like a good Italian, have taken the exact measure of. His own worldly goods consisted of the paternal estate, a villa within the walls of Rome, which his scanty funds had suffered to fall into sombre disrepair. "It's the Villa she's in love with, quite as much as the Count," said her mother. "She dreams of converting the Count; that's all very well. But she dreams of refurnishing the Villa!"

The upholsterers were turned into it, I believe, before the wedding, and there was a great scrubbing and sweeping of saloons and raking and weeding of alleys and avenues. Martha made frequent visits of inspection while these ceremonies were taking place; but one day, on her return, she came into my little studio with an air of amusing horror. She had found them *scraping* the sarcophagus in the great ilex-walk; divesting it of its mossy coat, disincrusting it of the sacred green mould of the ages! This was their idea of making the Villa comfortable. She had made them transport it to the dampest place they could find; for, next after that slow-coming, slow-going smile of her lover, it was the rusty complexion of his patrimonial marbles that she most prized. The young Count's conversion proceeded less rapidly, and indeed I believe that his betrothed brought little zeal to the affair. She loved him so devoutly that she believed no change of faith could better him, and she would have been willing for his sake to say her prayers to the sacred Bambino at Epiphany. But he had the good taste to demand no such sacrifice, and I was struck with the happy promise of a scene of which I was an accidental observer. It was at St. Peter's, one Friday afternoon, during the vesper service which takes place in the chapel of the Choir. I met my god-daughter wandering happily on her lover's arm, her mother being established on her camp-stool near the chapel door. The crowd was collected thereabouts, and the body of the church was empty. Now and then the high voices of the singers escaped into the outer vastness and melted slowly away in the incense-thickened air. Something in the young girl's step and the clasp of her arm in her lover's told me that her contentment was perfect. As she threw back her head and gazed into the magnificent immensity of vault and dome, I felt that she was in that enviable mood in which all consciousness revolves on a single centre, and that her sense of the splendors around her was one with the ecstasy of her trust. They stopped before that sombre group of confessionals which proclaims so portentously the world's sinfulness, and Martha seemed to make some almost passionate protestation. A few minutes later I overtook them.

"Don't you agree with me, dear friend," said the Count, who always addressed me with the most affectionate deference, "that before I marry so pure and sweet a creature as this, I ought to go into one of those places and confess every sin I ever was guilty of, —every evil thought and impulse and desire of my grossly evil nature?"

Martha looked at him, half in deprecation, half in homage, with a look which seemed at once to insist that her lover could have no vices, and to plead that, if he had, there would be something magnificent in them. "Listen to him!" she said, smiling. "The list would be long, and if you waited to finish it, you would be late for the wedding! But if you confess your sins for me, it's only fair I should confess mine for you. Do you know what I have been saying to Camillo?" she added, turning to me with the half-filial confidence she had always shown me and with a rosy glow in her cheeks; "that I want to do something more for him than girls commonly do for their lovers, —to take some step, to run some risk, to break some law, even! I'm willing to change my religion, if he bids me. There are moments when I'm terribly tired of simply staring at Catholicism; it will be a relief to come into a church to kneel. That's, after all, what they are meant for! Therefore, Camillo mio, if it casts a shade across your heart to think that I'm a heretic, I'll go and kneel down to that good old priest who has just entered the confessional yonder and say to him, 'My father, I repent, I abjure, I believe. Baptize me in the only faith.'"

"If it's as a compliment to the Count," I said, "it seems to me he ought to anticipate it by turning Protestant."

She had spoken lightly and with a smile, and yet with an undertone of girlish ardor. The young man looked at her with a solemn, puzzled face and shook his head. "Keep your religion," he said. "Every one his own. If you should attempt to embrace mine, I'm afraid you would close your arms about a shadow. I'm a poor Catholic! I don't understand all these chants and ceremonies and splendors. When I was a child I never could learn my catechism. My poor old confessor long ago gave me up; he told me I was a good boy but a *pagan*! You must not be a better Catholic than your husband. I don't understand your religion any better, but I beg you not to change it for mine. If it has helped to make you what you are, it must be good." And taking the young girl's hand, he was about to raise it affectionately to his lips; but suddenly remembering that they were in a place unaccordant with profane passions, he lowered it with a comical smile. "Let us go!" he murmured, passing his hand over his forehead. "This heavy atmosphere of St. Peter's always stupefies me."

They were married in the month of May, and we separated for the summer, the Contessa's mamma going to illuminate the domestic circle in New York with her reflected dignity. When I returned to Rome in the autumn, I found the young couple established at the Villa Valerio, which was being gradually reclaimed from its antique decay. I begged that the hand of improvement might be lightly laid on it, for as an unscrupulous old *genre* painter, with an eye to "subjects," I preferred that ruin should accumulate. My god-daughter was quite of my way of thinking, and she had a capital sense of the picturesque. Advising with me often as to projected changes, she was sometimes more conservative than myself; and I more than once smiled at her archaeological zeal, and declared that I believed she had married the Count because he was like a statue of the Decadence. I had a constant invitation to spend my days at the Villa, and my easel was always planted in one of the garden-walks. I grew to have a painter's passion for the place, and to be intimate with every tangled shrub and twisted tree, every moss-coated vase and mouldy sarcophagus and sad, disfeatured bust of those grim old Romans who could so ill afford to become more meagre-visaged. The place was of small extent; but though there were many other villas more pretentious and splendid, none seemed to me more deeply picturesque, more romantically idle and untrimmed, more encumbered with precious antique rubbish, and haunted with half-historic echoes. It contained an old ilex-walk in which I used religiously to spend half an hour every day, —half an hour being, I confess, just as long as I could stay without beginning to sneeze. The trees arched and intertwisted here along their dusky vista in the quaintest symmetry; and as it was exposed uninterruptedly to the west, the low evening sun used to transfuse it with a sort of golden mist and play through it—over leaves and knotty boughs and mossy marbles — with a thousand crimson fingers. It was filled with disinterred fragments of sculpture, —nameless statues and noseless heads and rough-hewn sarcophagi, which made it deliciously solemn. The statues used to stand there in the perpetual twilight like conscious things, brooding on their gathered memories. I used to linger about them, half expecting they would speak and tell me their stony secrets, —whisper heavily the whereabouts of their mouldering fellows, still unrecovered from the soil.

My god-daughter was idyllically happy and absolutely in love. I was obliged to confess that even rigid rules have their exceptions, and that now and then an Italian count is an honest fellow. Camillo was one to the core, and seemed quite content to be adored. Their life was a childlike interchange of caresses, as candid and unmeasured as those of a shepherd and shepherdess in a bucolic poem. To stroll in the ilex-walk and feel her husband's arm about her waist and his shoulder against her cheek; to roll cigarettes for him while he puffed them in the great marble-paved rotunda in the centre of the house; to fill his glass from an old rusty red amphora, —these graceful occupations satisfied the young Countess.

She rode with him sometimes in the grassy shadow of aqueducts and tombs, and sometimes suffered him to show his beautiful wife at

Roman dinners and balls. She played dominos with him after dinner,
and carried out in a desultory way a daily scheme of reading him the
newspapers. This observance was subject to fluctuations caused by the
Count's invincible tendency to go to sleep, —a failing his wife never
attempted to disguise or palliate. She would sit and brush the flies from
him while he lay picturesquely snoozing, and, if I ventured near him,
would place her finger on her lips and whisper that she thought her
husband was as handsome asleep as awake. I confess I often felt tempted
to reply to her that he was at least as entertaining, for the young man's
happiness had not multiplied the topics on which he readily conversed.
He had plenty of good sense, and his opinions on practical matters
were always worth having. He would often come and sit near me while
I worked at my easel and offer a friendly criticism. His taste was a little
crude, but his eye was excellent, and his measurement of the resemblance between some point of my copy and the original as trustworthy
as that of a mathematical instrument. But he seemed to me to have
either a strange reserve or a strange simplicity; to be fundamentally
unfurnished with "ideas." He had no beliefs nor hopes nor fears, —
nothing but senses, appetites, and serenely luxurious tastes. As I watched
him strolling about looking at his finger-nails, I often wondered whether
he had anything that could properly be termed a soul, and whether
good health and good-nature were not the sum of his advantages. "It's
lucky he's good-natured," I used to say to myself; "for if he were not,
there is nothing in his conscience to keep him in order. If he had
irritable nerves instead of quiet ones, he would strangle us as the infant
Hercules strangled the poor little snakes. He's the natural man! Happily,
his nature is gentle; I can mix my colors at my ease." I wondered what
he thought about and what passed through his mind in the sunny leisure
which seemed to shut him in from that modern work-a-day world of
which, in spite of my passion for bedaubing old panels with ineffective
portraiture of mouldy statues against screens of box, I still flattered
myself I was a member. I went so far as to believe that he sometimes
withdrew from the world altogether. He had moods in which his consciousness seemed so remote and his mind so irresponsive and dumb,
that nothing but a powerful caress or a sudden violence was likely to
arouse him. Even his lavish tenderness for his wife had a quality which
I but half relished. Whether or not he had a soul himself, he seemed
not to suspect that she had one. I took a godfatherly interest in what

it had not always seemed to me crabbed and pedantic to talk of as her moral development. I fondly believed her to be a creature susceptible of the finer spiritual emotions. But what was becoming of her spiritual life in this interminable heathenish honeymoon? Some fine day she would find herself tired of the Count's *beaux yeux* and make an appeal to his mind. She had, to my knowledge, plans of study, of charity, of worthily playing her part as a Contessa Valerio, —a position as to which the family records furnished the most inspiring examples. But if the Count found the newspapers soporific, I doubted if he would turn Dante's pages very fast for his wife, or smile with much zest at the anecdotes of Vasari. How could he advise her, instruct her, sustain her? And if she became a mother, how could he share her responsibilities? He doubtless would assure his little son and heir a stout pair of arms and legs and a magnificent crop of curls, and sometimes remove his cigarette to kiss a dimpled spot; but I found it hard to picture him lending his voice to teach the lusty urchin his alphabet or his prayers, or the rudiments of infant virtue. One accomplishment indeed the Count possessed which would make him an agreeable playfellow: he carried in his pocket a collection of precious fragments of antique pavement, —bits of porphyry and malachite and lapis and basalt, —disinterred on his own soil and brilliantly polished by use. With these you might see him occupied by the half-hour, playing the simple game of catch-and-toss, ranging them in a circle, tossing them in rotation, and catching them on the back of his hand. His skill was remarkable; he would send a stone five feet into the air, and pitch and catch and transpose the rest before he received it again. I watched with affectionate jealousy for the signs of a dawning sense, on Martha's part, that she was the least bit strangely mated. Once or twice, as the weeks went by, I fancied I read them, and that she looked at me with eyes which seemed to remember certain old talks of mine in which I had declared—with such verity as you please—that a Frenchman, an Italian, a Spaniard, might be a very good fellow, but that he never really respected the woman he pretended to love. For the most part, however, these dusky broodings of mine spent themselves easily in the charmed atmosphere of our romantic home. We were out of the modern world and had no business with modern scruples. The place was so bright, so still, so sacred to the silent, imperturbable past, that drowsy contentment seemed a natural law; and sometimes when, as I sat at my work, I saw my companions passing arm-in-arm across the end of one of the long-drawn vistas, and, turning back to my palette, found my colors dimmer for the radiant vision, I could easily believe that I was some loyal old chronicler of a perfectly poetical legend.

It was a help to ungrudging feelings that the Count, yielding to his wife's urgency, had undertaken a series of systematic excavations. To excavate is an expensive luxury, and neither Camillo nor his latter forefathers had possessed the means for a disinterested pursuit of archaeology. But his young wife had persuaded herself that the much-trodden soil of the Villa was as full of buried treasures as a bride-cake of plums, and that it would be a pretty compliment to the ancient house which had accepted her as mistress, to devote a portion of her dowry to bringing its mouldy honors to the light. I think she was not without a fancy that this liberal process would help to disinfect her Yankee dollars of the impertinent odor of trade. She took learned advice on the subject, and was soon ready to swear to you, proceeding from irrefutable premises, that a colossal gilt-bronze Minerva mentioned by Strabo was placidly awaiting resurrection at a point twenty rods from the northwest angle of the house. She had a couple of grotesque old antiquaries to lunch, whom having plied with unwonted potations, she walked off their legs in the grounds; and though they agreed on nothing else in the world, they individually assured her that properly conducted researches would probably yield an unequalled harvest of discoveries. The Count had been not only indifferent, but even averse, to the scheme, and had more than once arrested his wife's complacent allusions to it by an unaccustomed acerbity of tone. "Let them lie, the poor disinherited gods, the Minerva, the Apollo, the Ceres you are so sure of finding," he said, "and don't break their rest. What do you want of them? We can't worship them. Would you put them on pedestals to stare and mock at them? If you can't believe in them, don't disturb them. Peace be with them!" I remember being a good deal impressed by a vigorous confession drawn from him by his wife's playfully declaring in answer to some remonstrances in this strain that he was absolutely superstitious. "Yes, by Bacchus, I am superstitious!" he cried. "Too much so, perhaps! But I'm an old Italian, and you must take me as you find me. There have been things seen and done here which leave strange influences behind! They don't touch you, doubtless, who come of another race. But they touch me, often, in the whisper of the leaves and the odor of the mouldy soil and the blank eyes of the old statues. I can't bear to look the statues in the face. I seem to see other strange eyes in the empty sockets, and I hardly know what they say to me. I call the poor old statues ghosts. In conscience, we've enough on the place already, lurking and peering in every shady nook. Don't dig up any more, or I won't answer for my wits!"

This account of Camillo's sensibilities was too fantastic not to seem to his wife almost a joke; and though I imagined there was more in it, he made a joke so seldom that I should have been sorry to cut short the poor girl's smile. With her smile she carried her point, and in a few days arrived a kind of archaeological detective, with a dozen workmen armed with pickaxes and spades. For myself, I was secretly vexed at these energetic measures; for, though fond of disinterred statues, I disliked the disinterment, and deplored the profane sounds which were henceforth to jar upon the sleepy stillness of the gardens. I especially objected to the personage who conducted the operations; an ugly little dwarfish man who seemed altogether a subterranean genius, an earthy gnome of the underworld, and went prying about the grounds with a malicious smile which suggested more delight in the money the Signor Conte was going to bury than in the expected marbles and bronzes. When the first sod had been turned, the Count's mood seemed to alter, and his curiosity got the better of his scruples. He sniffed delightedly the odor of the humid earth, and stood watching the workmen, as they struck constantly deeper, with a kindling wonder in his eyes. Whenever a pickaxe rang against a stone he would utter a sharp cry, and be deterred from jumping into the trench only by the little explorer's assurance that it was a false alarm. The near prospect of discoveries seemed to act upon his nerves, and I met him more than once strolling restlessly among his cedarn alleys, as if at last he had fallen a thinking. He took me by the arm and made me walk with him, and discoursed ardently of the chance of a "find." I rather marvelled at his sudden zeal, and wondered whether he had an eye to the past or to the future, — to the beauty of possible Minervas and Apollos or to their market value. Whenever the Count would come and denounce his little army of spadesmen for a set of loitering vagabonds, the little explorer would glance at me with a sarcastic twinkle which seemed to hint that excavations were a snare. We were kept some time in suspense, for several false beginnings were made. The earth was probed in the wrong places.

The Count began to be discouraged and to prolong his abbreviated siesta. But the little expert, who had his own ideas, shrewdly continued his labors; and as I sat at my easel I heard the spades ringing against the dislodged stones. Now and then I would pause, with an uncontrollable acceleration of my heart-beats. "It *may* be," I would say, "that some marble masterpiece is stirring there beneath its lightening weight of earth! There are as good fish in the sea ....! I *may* be summoned to welcome another Antinous back to fame, —a Venus, a Faun, an Augustus!"

One morning it seemed to me that I had been hearing for half an hour a livelier movement of voices than usual; but as I was preoccupied with a puzzling bit of work, I made no inquiries. Suddenly a shadow fell across my canvas, and I turned round. The little explorer stood beside me, with a glittering eye, cap in hand, his forehead bathed in perspiration. Resting in the hollow of his arm was an earth-stained fragment of marble. In answer to my questioning glance he held it up to me, and I saw it was a woman's shapely hand. "Come!" he simply said, and led the way to the excavation. The workmen were so closely gathered round the open trench that I saw nothing till he made them divide. Then, full in the sun and flashing it back, almost, in spite of her dusky incrustations, I beheld, propped up with stones against a heap of earth, a majestic marble image. She seemed to me almost colossal, though I afterwards perceived that she was of perfect human proportions. My pulses began to throb, for I felt she was something great, and that it was great to be among the first to know her. Her marvelous beauty gave her an almost human look, and her absent eyes seemed to wonder back at us. She was amply draped, so that I saw that she was not a Venus. "She's a Juno," said the excavator, decisively; and she seemed indeed an embodiment of celestial supremacy and repose. Her beautiful head, bound with a single band, could have bent only to give the nod of command; her eyes looked straight before her; her mouth was implacably grave; one hand, outstretched, appeared to have held a kind of imperial wand, the arm from which the other had been broken hung at her side with the most classical majesty. The workmanship was of the rarest finish; and though perhaps there was a sort of vaguely modern attempt at character in her expression, she was wrought, as a whole, in the large and simple manner of the great Greek period. She was a masterpiece of skill and a marvel of preservation.

"Does the Count know?" I soon asked, for I had a guilty sense that our eyes were taking something from her.

"The Signor Conte is at his siesta," said the explorer, with his sceptical grin. "We don't like to disturb him."

"Here he comes!" cried one of the workmen, and we made way for him. His siesta had evidently been suddenly broken, for his face was flushed and his hair disordered.

"Ah, my dream—my dream was right, then!" he cried, and stood staring at the image.

"What was your dream?" I asked, as his face seemed to betray more dismay than delight.

"That they'd found a Juno; and that she rose and came and laid her marble hand on mine. Eh?" said the Count, excitedly.

A kind of awe-struck, gutteral *a-ah!* burst from the listening workmen.

"This is the hand!" said the little explorer, holding up his perfect fragment. "I've had it this half-hour, so it can't have touched you."

"But you're apparently right as to her being a Juno," I said. "Admire her at your leisure." And I turned away; for if the Count was superstitious, I wished to leave him free to relieve himself. I repaired to the house to carry the news to my god-daughter, whom I found slumbering—dreamlessly, it appeared—over a great archaeological octavo. "They've touched bottom," I said. "They've found a Juno of Praxiteles at the very least!" She dropped her octavo, and rang for a parasol. I described the statue, but not graphically, I presume, for Martha gave a little sarcastic grimace.

"A long, fluted *peplum?*" she said. "How very odd! I don't believe she's beautiful."

"She's beautiful enough, *figlioccia mia,*" I answered, "to make you jealous."

We found the Count standing before the resurgent goddess in fixed contemplation, with folded arms. He seemed to have recovered from the irritation of his dream, but I thought his face betrayed a still deeper emotion. He was pale, and gave no response as his wife caressingly clasped his arm. I'm not sure, however, that his wife's attitude was not a livelier tribute to the perfection of the image. She had been laughing at my rhapsody as we walked from the house, and I had bethought myself of a statement I had somewhere seen, that women lacked the perception of the purest beauty. Martha, however, seemed slowly to measure our Juno's infinite stateliness. She gazed a long time silently, leaning against her husband, and then stepped half timidly down on the stones which formed a rough base for the figure. She laid her two rosy, ungloved hands upon the stony fingers of the goddess, and remained for some moments pressing them in her warm grasp, and fixing her living eyes upon the inexpressive brow. When she turned round her eyes were bright with an admiring tear, —a tear which her husband was too deeply absorbed to notice. He had apparently given orders that the workmen should be treated to a cask of wine, in honor of their discovery. It was now brought and opened on the spot, and the little explorer, having drawn the first glass, stepped forward, hat in hand, and obsequiously presented it to the Countess. She only moistened her lips with it and passed it to her husband. He raised it mechanically to his own; then suddenly he stopped, held it a moment aloft, and poured it out slowly and solemnly at the feet of the Juno.

"Why, it's a libation!" I cried. He made no answer, and walked slowly away.

There was no more work done that day. The laborers lay on the grass, gazing with the native Roman relish of a fine piece of sculpture, but wasting no wine in pagan ceremonies. In the evening the Count paid the Juno another visit, and gave orders that on the morrow she should be transferred to the Casino. The Casino was a deserted garden-house, built in not ungraceful imitation of an Ionic Temple, in which Camillo's ancestors must often have assembled to drink cool syrups from Venetian glasses, and listen to learned madrigals. It contained several dusty fragments of antique sculpture, and it was spacious enough to enclose that richer collection of which I began fondly to regard the Juno as but the nucleus. Here, with short delay, the fine creature was placed, serenely upright, a reversed funereal *cippus* forming a sufficiently solid pedestal. The little explorer, who seemed an expert in all the offices of restoration, rubbed her and scraped her with mysterious art, removed her earthy stains, and doubled the lustre of her beauty. Her mellow substance seemed to glow with a kind of renascent purity and bloom, and, but for her broken hand, you might have fancied she had just received the last stroke of the chisel. Her fame remained no secret. Within two or three days half a dozen inquisitive *conoscenti* posted out to obtain sight of her. I happened to be present when the first of these gentlemen (a German in blue spectacles, with a portfolio under his arm) presented himself at the Villa. The Count, hearing his voice at the door, came forward and eyed him coldly from head to foot.

"Your new Juno, Signor Conte," began the German, "is, in my opinion, much more likely to be a certain Proserpine—"

"I've neither a Juno nor a Proserpine to discuss with you," said the Count, curtly. "You're misinformed."

"You've dug up no statue?" cried the German. "What a scandalous hoax!"

"None worthy of your learned attention. I'm sorry you should have the trouble of carrying your little note-book so far." The Count had suddenly become witty!

"But you've something, surely. The rumor is running through Rome."

"The rumor be damned!" cried the Count, savagely. "I've *nothing,* —do you understand? Be so good as to say so to your friends."

The answer was explicit, and the poor archaeologist departed, tossing his flaxen mane. But I pitied him, and ventured to remonstrate with the Count. "She might as well be still in the earth, if no one is to see her," I said.

"*I'm* to see her: that's enough!" he answered with the same unnatural harshness. Then, in a moment, as he caught me eying him askance in troubled surprise, "I hated his great portfolio. He was going to make some hideous drawing of her."

"Ah, that touches me," I said. "I too have been planning to make a little sketch."

He was silent for some moments, after which he turned and grasped my arm, with less irritation, but with extraordinary gravity. "Go in there towards twilight," he said, "and sit for an hour and look at her. I think you'll give up your sketch. If you don't, my good old friend, — you're welcome!"

I followed his advice, and as a friend, I gave up my sketch. But an artist is an artist, and I secretly longed to attempt one. Orders strictly in accordance with the Count's reply to our German friend were given to the servants, who, with an easy Italian conscience and a gracious Italian persuasiveness, assured all subsequent inquirers that they had been regrettably misinformed. I have no doubt, indeed, that, in default of larger opportunity, they made condolence remunerative. Further excavation was, for the present, suspended, as implying an affront to the incomparable Juno. The workmen departed, but the little explorer

still haunted the premises and sounded the soil for his own entertainment. One day he came to me with his usual ambiguous grimace. "The
beautiful hand of the Juno," he murmured; "what has become of it?"

"I've not seen it since you called me to look at her. I remember
when I went away it was lying on the grass near the excavation."

"Where I placed it myself! After that it disappeared. Ecco!"

"Do you suspect one of your workmen? Such a fragment as that
would bring more scudi than most of them ever looked at."

"Some, perhaps, are greater thieves than the others. But if I were
to call up the worst of them and accuse him, the Count would interfere."

"He must value that beautiful hand, nevertheless."

The little expert in disinterment looked about him and winked. "He
values it so much that he himself purloined it. That's my belief, and I
think that the less we say about it the better."

"Purloined it, my dear sir? After all, it's his own property."

"Not so much as that comes to! So beautiful a creature is more or
less the property of every one; we've all a right to look at her. But the
Count treats her as if she were a sacro-sanct image of the Madonna.
He keeps her under lock and key, and pays her solitary visits. What
does he do, after all? When a beautiful woman is in stone, all he can
do is to look at her. And what does he do with that precious hand? He
keeps it in a silver box; he has made a relic of it!" And this cynical
personage began to chuckle grotesquely and walked away.

He left me musing uncomfortably, and wondering what the deuce
he meant. The Count certainly chose to make a mystery of the Juno,
but this seemed a natural incident of the first rapture of possession.I
was willing to wait for a free access to her, and in the mean time I was
glad to find that there was a limit to his constitutional apathy. But as
the days elapsed I began to be conscious that his enjoyment was not
communicative, but strangely cold and shy and sombre. That he should
admire a marble goddess was no reason for his despising mankind; yet
he really seemed to be making invidious comparisons between us. From
this untender proscription his charming wife was not excepted. At
moments when I tried to persuade myself that he was neither worse
nor better company than usual, her face condemned my optimism. She
said nothing, but she wore a constant look of pathetic perplexity. She
sat at times with her eyes fixed on him with a kind of imploring curiosity,
as if pitying surprise held resentment yet awhile in check. What passed

between them in private, I had, of course, no warrant to inquire. Nothing, I imagined, —and that was the misery! It was part of the misery, too, that he seemed impenetrable to these mute glances, and looked over her head with an air of superb abstraction. Occasionally he noticed me looking at him in urgent deprecation, and then for a moment his heavy eye would sparkle, half, as it seemed, in defiant irony and half with a strangely stifled impulse to justify himself. But from his wife he kept his face inexorably averted; and when she approached him with some persuasive caress, he received it with an ill-concealed shudder. I inwardly protested and raged. I grew to hate the Count and everything that belonged to him. "I was a thousand times right," I cried; "an Italian count may be mighty fine, but he won't *wear*! Give us some wholesome young fellow of our own blood, who'll play us none of these dusky old-world tricks. Painter as I am, I'll never recommend a picturesque husband!" I lost my pleasure in the Villa, in the purple shadows and glowing lights, the mossy marbles and the long-trailing profiles of the Alban Hills. My painting stood still; everything looked ugly. I sat and fumbled with my palette, and seemed to be mixing mud with my colors. My head was stuffed with dismal thoughts; an intolerable weight seemed to lie upon my heart. The Count became, to my imagination, a dark efflorescence of the evil germs which history had implanted in his line. No wonder he was foredoomed to be cruel. Was not cruelty a tradition in his race, and crime an example? The unholy passions of his forefathers stirred blindly in his untaught nature and clamored dumbly for an issue. What a heavy heritage it seemed to me, as I reckoned it up in my melancholy musings, the Count's interminable ancestry! Back to the profligate revival of arts and vices, —back to the bloody medly of mediaeval wars, —back through the long, fitfully glaring dusk of the early ages to its ponderous origin in the solid Roman state, —back through all the darkness of history it seemed to stretch, losing every feeblest claim on my sympathies as it went. Such a record was in itself a curse; and my poor girl had expected it to sit as lightly and gratefully on her consciousness as her feather on her hat! I have little idea how long this painful situation lasted. It seemed the longer from my goddaughter's continued reserve, and my inability to offer a word of consolation. A sensitive woman, disappointed in marriage, exhausts her own ingenuity before she takes counsel. The Count's preoccupations, whatever they were, made him increasingly restless; he came and went

at random, with nervous abruptness; he took long rides alone, and, as
I inferred, rarely went through the form of excusing himself to his wife;
and still, as time went on, he came no nearer explaining his mystery.
With the lapse of time, however, I confess that my apprehensions began
to be tempered with pity. If I had expected to see him propitiate his
urgent ancestry by a crime, now that his native rectitude seemed resolute
to deny them this satisfaction, I felt a sort of grudging gratitude. A
man couldn't be so gratuitously sombre without being unhappy. He
had always treated me with that antique deference to a grizzled beard
for which elderly men reserve the flower of their general tenderness
for waning fashions, and I thought it possible he might suffer me to
lay a healing hand upon his trouble. One evening, when I had taken
leave of my god-daughter and given her my useless blessing in a silent
kiss, I came out and found the Count sitting in the garden in the mild
starlight, and staring at a mouldy Hermes, nestling in a clump of
oleander. I sat down by him and informed him roundly that his conduct
needed an explanation. He half turned his head, and his dark pupil
gleamed an instant.

"I understand," he said, "you think me crazy!" And he tapped his
forehead.

"No, not crazy, but unhappy. And if unhappiness runs its course
too freely, of course, our poor wits are sorely tried."

He was silent awhile, and then, "I'm not unhappy!" he cried abruptly.
"I'm prodigiously happy. You wouldn't believe the satisfaction I take
in sitting here and staring at that old weather-worn Hermes. Formerly
I used to be afraid of him: his frown used to remind me of a little
bushy-browed old priest who taught me Latin and looked at me terribly
over the book when I stumbled in my Virgil. But now it seems to me
the friendliest, jolliest thing in the world, and suggests the most delightful
images. He stood pouting his great lips in some old Roman's garden
two thousand years ago. He saw the sandalled feet treading the alleys
and the rose-crowned heads bending over the wine; he knew the old
feasts and the old worship, the old Romans and the old way, and
describes it all! No, no, my friend, I'm the happiest of men!"

I had denied that I thought he was crazy, but I suddenly began to
suspect it, for I found nothing reassuring in this singular rhapsody. The
Hermes, for a wonder, had kept his nose; and when I reflected that my
dear Countess was being neglected for this senseless pagan block, I

secretly promised myself to come the next day with a hammer and deal him such a lusty blow as would make him too ridiculous for a sentimental tête-à-tête. Meanwhile, however, the Count's infatuation was no laughing matter, and I expressed my sincerest conviction when I said, after a pause, that I should recommend him to see either a priest or a physician.

He burst into uproarious laughter. "A priest! What should I do with a priest, or he with me? I never loved them, and I feel less like beginning than ever. A priest, my dear friend," he repeated, laying his hand on my arm, "don't set a priest at me, if you value *his* sanity! My confession would frighten the poor man out of his wits. As for a doctor, I never was better in my life; and unless," he added abruptly, rising, and eying me askance, "you want to poison me, in Christian charity I advise you to leave me alone."

Decidedly, the Count *was* unsound, and I had no heart, for some days, to go back to the Villa. How should I treat him, what stand should I take, what course did Martha's happiness and dignity demand? I wandered about Rome, revolving these questions, and one afternoon found myself in the Pantheon. A light spring shower had begun to fall, and I hurried for refuge into the great temple which its Christian altars have but half converted into a church. No Roman monument retains a deeper impress of ancient life, or verifies more forcibly those prodigious beliefs which we are apt to regard as dim fables. The huge dusky dome seems to the spiritual ear to hold a vague reverberation of pagan worship, as a gathered shell holds the rumor of the sea. Three or four persons were scattered before the various altars; another stood near the centre, beneath the aperture in the dome. As I drew near I perceived this was the Count. He was planted with his hands behind him, looking up first at the heavy rain-clouds, as they crossed the great bull's-eye, and then down at the besprinkled circle on the pavement. In those days the pavement was rugged and cracked and magnificently old, and this ample space, in free communion with the weather, had become as mouldy and mossy and verdant as a strip of garden soil. A tender herbage had sprung up in the crevices of the slabs, and the little microscopic shoots were twinkling in the rain. This great weather-current, through the uncapped vault, deadens most effectively the customary odors of incense and tallow, and transports one to a faith that was on friendly terms with nature. It seemed to have performed this office for the Count; his face wore an indefinable expression of ecstasy, and he was so rapt in contemplation that it was some time before he noticed me. The sun was struggling through the clouds without, and yet a thin rain continued to fall and came drifting down into our gloomy enclosure in a sort of illuminated drizzle. The Count watched it with the fascinated stare of a child watching a fountain, and then turned away, pressing his hand to his brow, and walked over to one of the ornamental altars. Here he again stood staring, but in a moment wheeled about and returned to his former place. Just then he recognized me, and perceived, I suppose, the puzzled gaze I must have fixed on him. He saluted me frankly with his hand, and at last came toward me. I fancied that he was in a kind of nervous tremor and was trying to appear calm.

"This is the best place in Rome," he murmured. "It's worth fifty St. Peters'. But do you know I never came here till the other day? I left it to the *forestieri*. They go about with their red books, and read about this and that, and think they know it. Ah! you must *feel* it, —feel the beauty and fitness of that great open skylight. Now, only the wind and the rain, the sun and the cold, come down; but of old—of old"—and he touched my arm and gave me a strange smile—"the pagan gods and goddesses used to come sailing through it and take their places at their altars. What a procession, when the eyes of faith could see it! Those are the things they have given us instead!" And he gave a pitiful shrug. "I should like to pull down their pictures, overturn their candlesticks, and poison their holy water!"

"My dear Count," I said gently, "you should tolerate people's honest beliefs. Would you renew the Inquisition, and in the interest of Jupiter and Mercury?"

"People wouldn't tolerate my belief, if they guessed it!" he cried. "There's been a great talk about the pagan persecutions; but the Christians persecuted as well, and the old gods were worshipped in caves and woods as well as the new. And none the worse for that! It was in caves and woods and streams, in earth and air and water, they dwelt. And there—and here, too, in spite of all your Christian lustrations— a son of old Italy may find them still!"

He had said more than he meant, and his mask had fallen. I looked at him hard, and felt a sudden outgush of the compassion we always feel for a creature irresponsibly excited. I seemed to touch the source of his trouble, and my relief was great, for my discovery made me feel like bursting into laughter. But I contented myself with smiling benignantly. He looked back at me suspiciously, as if to judge how far he had betrayed himself; and in his glance I read, somehow, that he had a conscience we could take hold of. In my gratitude, I was ready to thank any gods he pleased. "Take care, take care," I said, "You're saying things which if the sacristan there were to hear and report—!" And I passed my hand through his arm and led him away.

I was startled and shocked, but I was also amused and comforted. The Count had suddenly become for me a delightfully curious phenomenon, and I passed the rest of the day in meditating on the strange ineffaceability of race-characteristics. A sturdy young Latin I had called Camillo; sturdier, indeed, than I had dreamed him! Discretion was now misplaced, and on the morrow I spoke to my god-daughter. She had lately been hoping, I think, that I would help her to unburden her heart, for she immediately gave way to tears and confessed that she was miserable. "At first," she said, "I thought it was all fancy, and not his tenderness that was growing less, but my exactions that were growing greater. But suddenly it settled upon me like a mortal chill, —the conviction that he had ceased to care for me, that something had come between us. And the puzzling thing has been the want of possible cause in my own conduct, or of any sign that there is another woman in the case. I have racked my brain to discover what I had said or done or thought to displease him! And yet he goes about like a man too deeply injured to complain. He has never uttered a harsh word or given me a reproachful look. He has simply renounced me. I have dropped out of his life."

She spoke with such an appealing tremor in her voice that I was on the point of telling her that I had guessed the riddle, and that this was half the battle. But I was afraid of her incredulity. My solution was so fantastic, so apparently far-fetched, so absurd, that I resolved to wait for convincing evidence. To obtain it, I continued to watch the Count, covertly and cautiously, but with a vigilance which disinterested curiosity now made intensely keen. I returned to my painting, and neglected no pretext for hovering about the gardens and the neighborhood of the Casino. The Count, I think, suspected my designs, or at least my suspicions, and would have been glad to remember just what he had suffered himself to say to me in the Pantheon. But it deepened my interest in his extraordinary situation that, in so far as I could read his deeply brooding face, he seemed to have grudgingly pardoned me. He gave me a glance occasionally, as he passed me, in which a sort of dumb desire for help appeared to struggle with the instinct of mistrust. I was willing enough to help him, but the case was prodigiously delicate, and I wished to master the symptoms. Meanwhile I worked and waited and wondered. Ah! I wondered, you may be sure, with an interminable wonder; and, turn it over as I would, I couldn't get used to my idea. Sometimes it offered itself to me with a perverse fascination which deprived me of all wish to interfere. The Count took the form of a precious psychological study, and refined feeling seemed to dictate a tender respect for his delusion. I envied him the force of his imagination, and I used sometimes to close my eyes with a vague desire that when I opened them I might find Apollo under the opposite tree, lazily kissing his flute, or see Diana hurrying with long steps down the ilex-walk. But for the most part my host seemed to me simply an unhappy young man, with an unwholesome mental twist which should be smoothed away as speedily as possible. If the remedy was to match the disease, however, it would have to be an ingenious compound!

One evening, having bidden my god-daughter good night, I had started on my usual walk to my lodgings in Rome. Five minutes after leaving the villa-gate I discovered that I had left my eye-glass—an object in constant use—behind me. I immediately remembered that, while painting, I had broken the string which fastened it round my neck, and had hooked it provisionally upon a twig of a flowering-almond tree within arm's reach. Shortly afterwards I had gathered up my things and retired, unmindful of the glass; and now, as I needed it to read the evening paper at the Caffè Greco, there was no alternative but to retrace my steps and detach it from its twig. I easily found it, and lingered awhile to note the curious night-aspect of the spot I had been studying by daylight. The night was magnificent, and full-charged with the breath of the early Roman spring. The moon was rising fast and flinging her silver checkers into the heavy masses of shadow. Watching her at play, I strolled farther and suddenly came in sight of the Casino.

Just then the moon, which for a moment had been concealed, touched with a white ray a small marble figure which adorned the pediment of this rather factitious little structure. Its sudden illumination suggested that a rarer spectacle was at hand, and that the same influence must be vastly becoming to the imprisoned Juno. The door of the Casino was, as usual, locked, but the moonlight was flooding the high-placed windows so generously that my curiosity became obstinate—and inventive. I dragged a garden-seat round from the portico, placed it on end, and succeeded in climbing to the top of it and bringing myself abreast of one of the windows. The casement yielded to my pressure, turned on its hinges, and showed me what I had been looking for, —Juno visited by Diana. The beautiful image stood bathed in the radiant flood and shining with a purity which made her most persuasively divine. If by day her mellow complexion suggested faded gold, her substance now might have passed for polished silver. The effect was almost terrible; beauty so eloquent could hardly be inanimate. This was my foremost observation. I leave you to fancy whether my next was less interesting. At some distance from the foot of the statue, just out of the light, I perceived a figure lying flat on the pavement, prostrate apparently with devotion. I can hardly tell you how it completed the impressiveness of the scene. It marked the shining image as a goddess indeed, and seemed to throw a sort of conscious pride into her stony mask. I of course immediately recognized this recumbent worshipper as the Count, and while I stood gazing, as if to help me to read the full meaning of his attitude, the moonlight travelled forward and covered his breast and face. Then I saw that his eyes were closed, and that he was either asleep or swooning. Watching him attentively, I detected his even respirations, and judged there was no reason for alarm. The moonlight blanched his face, which seemed already pale with weariness. He had come into the presence of the Juno in obedience to that fabulous passion of which the symptoms had so wofully perplexed us, and, exhausted either by compliance or resistance, he had sunk down at her feet in a stupid sleep. The bright moonshine soon aroused him, however; he muttered something and raised himself, vaguely staring. Then recognizing his situation, he rose and stood for some time gazing fixedly at the glowing image with an expression which I fancied was not that of wholly unprotesting devotion. He uttered a string of broken words of which I was unable to catch the meaning, and then, after another pause and a long, melancholy moan, he turned slowly to the door. As rapidly and noiselessly as possible I descended from my post of vigilance and passed behind the Casino, and in a moment I heard the sound of the closing lock and of his departing footsteps.

The next day, meeting the little antiquarian in the grounds, I shook my finger at him with what I meant he should consider portentous gravity. But he only grinned like the malicious earth-gnome to which I had always compared him, and twisted his mustache as if my menace was a capital joke. "If you dig any more holes here," I said, "you shall be thrust into the deepest of them, and have the earth packed down on top of you. We have made enough discoveries, and we want no more statues. Your Juno has almost ruined us."

He burst out laughing. "I expected as much," he cried; "I had my notions!"

"What did you expect?"

"That the Signor Conte would begin and say his prayers to her."

"Good heavens! Is the case so common? Why did you expect it?"

"On the contrary, the case is rare. But I've fumbled so long in the monstrous heritage of antiquity, that I have learned a multitude of secrets; learned that ancient relics may work modern miracles. There's a pagan element in all of us, —I don't speak for you, *illustrissimi forestieri*, —and the old gods have still their worshippers. The old spirit still throbs here and there, and the Signor Conte has his share of it. He's a good fellow, but between ourselves, he's an impossible Christian!" And this singular personage resumed his impertinent hilarity.

"If your previsions were so distinct," I said, "you ought to have given me a hint of them. I should have sent your spadesmen walking."

"Ah, but the Juno is so beautiful!"

"Her beauty be blasted! Can you tell me what has become of the Contessa's? To rival the Juno, she's turning to marble herself."

He shrugged his shoulders. "Ah, but the Juno is worth fifty thousand scudi!"

"I'd give a hundred thousand," I said, "to have her annihilated. Perhaps, after all, I shall want you to dig another hole."

"At your service!" he answered, with a flourish; and we separated.

A couple of days later I dined, as I often did, with my host and hostess, and met the Count face to face for the first time since his prostration in the Casino. He bore the traces of it, and sat plunged in sombre distraction. I fancied that the path of the antique faith was not strewn with flowers, and that the Juno was becoming daily a harder mistress to serve. Dinner was scarcely over before he rose from table and took up his hat. As he did so, passing near his wife, he faltered a moment, stopped and gave her—for the first time, I imagine—that vaguely imploring look which I had often caught. She moved her lips in inarticulate sympathy and put out her hands. He drew her towards him, kissed her with a kind of angry ardor, and strode away. The occasion was propitious, and further delay unnecessary.

"What I have to tell you is very strange," I said to the Countess, "very fantastic, very incredible. But perhaps you'll not find it so bad as you feared. There *is* a woman in the case! Your enemy is the Juno. The Count—how shall I say it? —the Count takes her *au sérieux*." She was silent; but after a moment she touched my arm with her hand, and I knew she meant that I had spoken her own belief. "You admired his antique simplicity: you see how far it goes. He has reverted to the faith of his fathers. Dormant through the ages, that imperious statue has silently aroused it. He believes in the pedigrees you used to dog's-ear your School Mythology with trying to get by heart. In a word, dear child, Camillo is a pagan!"

"I suppose you'll be terribly shocked," she answered, "if I say that he's welcome to any faith, if he will only share it with me. I'll believe in Jupiter, if he'll bid me! My sorrow's not for that: let my husband be himself! My sorrow is for the gulf of silence and indifference that has burst open between us. His Juno's the reality; I'm the fiction!"

"I've lately become reconciled to this gulf of silence, and to your fading for a while into a fiction. After the fable, the moral! The poor fellow has but half succumbed: the other half protests. The modern man is shut out in the darkness with his incomparable wife. How can he have failed to feel—vaguely and grossly if it must have been, but in every throb of his heart—that you are a more perfect experiment of nature, a riper fruit of time, than those primitive persons for whom Juno was a terror and Venus an example? He pays you the compliment of believing you an inconvertible modern. He has crossed the Acheron, but he has left you behind, as a pledge to the present. We'll bring him back to redeem it. The old ancestral ghosts ought to be propitiated when a pretty creature like you has sacrificed the fragrance of her life. He has proved himself one of the Valerii; we shall see to it that he is the last, and yet that his decease shall leave the Conte Camillo in excellent health."

I spoke with confidence which I had partly felt, for it seemed to me that if the Count was to be touched, it must be by the sense that his strange spiritual excursion had not made his wife detest him. We talked long and to a hopeful end, for before I went away my god-daughter expressed the desire to go out and look at the Juno. "I was afraid of her almost from the first," she said, "and have hardly seen her since she was set up in the Casino. Perhaps I can learn a lesson from her, —perhaps I can guess how she charms him!"

For a moment I hesitated, with the fear that we might intrude upon the Count's devotions. Then, as something in the poor girl's face suggested that she had thought of this and felt a sudden impulse to pluck victory from the heart of danger, I bravely offered her my arm. The night was cloudy, and on this occasion, apparently, the triumphant goddess was to depend upon her own lustre. But as we approached the Casino I saw that the door was ajar, and that there was lamplight within. The lamp was suspended in front of the image, and it showed us that the place was empty. But the Count had lately been there. Before the statue stood a roughly extemporized altar, composed of a nameless fragment of antique marble, engraved with an illegible Greek inscription. We seemed really to stand in a pagan temple, and we gazed at the serene divinity with an impulse of spiritual reverence. It ought to have been deepened, I suppose, but it was rudely checked, by our observing a curious glitter on the face of the low altar. A second glance showed us it was blood!

My companion looked at me in pale horror, and turned away with a cry. A swarm of hideous conjectures pressed into my mind, and for a moment I was sickened. But at last I remembered that there is blood and blood, and the Latins were posterior to the cannibals.

"Be sure it's very innocent," I said; "a lamb, a kid, or a sucking calf!" But it was enough for her nerves and her conscience that it was a crimson trickle, and she returned to the house in sad agitation. The rest of the night was not passed in a way to restore her to calmness. The Count had not come in, and she sat up for him from hour to hour. I remained with her and smoked my cigar as composedly as I might; but internally I wondered what in horror's name had become of him. Gradually, as the hours wore away, I shaped a vague interpretation of these dusky portents, —an interpretation none the less valid and devoutly desired for its being tolerably cheerful. The blood-drops on the altar, I mused, were the last instalment of his debt and the end of his delusion. They had been a happy necessity, for he was, after all, too gentle a creature not to hate himself for having shed them, not to abhor so cruelly insistent an idol. He had wandered away to recover himself in solitude, and he would come back to us with a repentant heart and an inquiring mind! I should certainly have believed all this more easily, however, if I could have heard his footstep in the hall. Toward dawn, scepticism threatened to creep in with the gray light, and I restlessly betook myself to the portico. Here in a few moments I saw him cross the grass, heavy-footed, splashed with mud, and evidently excessively tired. He must have been walking all night, and his face denoted that his spirit had been as restless as his body. He paused near me, and before he entered the house he stopped, looked at me a moment, and then held out his hand. I grasped it warmly, and it seemed to me to throb with all that he could not utter.

"Will you see your wife?" I asked.

He passed his hand over his eyes and shook his head. "Not now— not yet—some time!" he answered.

I was disappointed, but I convinced her, I think, that he had cast out the devil. She felt, poor girl, a pardonable desire to celebrate the event. I returned to my lodging, spent the day in Rome, and came back to the Villa toward dusk. I was told that the Countess was in the grounds. I looked for her cautiously at first, for I thought it just possible I might interrupt the natural consequences of a reconciliation; but failing to meet her, I turned toward the Casino, and found myself face to face with the little explorer.

"Does your excellency happen to have twenty yards of stout rope about him?" he asked gravely.

"Do you want to hang yourself for the trouble you've stood sponsor to?" I answered.

"It's a hanging matter, I promise you. The Countess has given orders. You'll find her in the Casino. Sweet-voiced as she is, she knows how to make her orders understood."

At the door of the Casino stood half a dozen of the laborers on the place, looking vaguely solemn, like outstanding dependants at a superior funeral. The Countess was within, in a position which was an answer to the surveyor's riddle. She stood with her eyes fixed on the Juno, who had been removed from her pedestal and lay stretched in her magnificent length upon a rude litter.

"Do you understand?" she said. "She's beautiful, she's noble, she's precious, but she must go back!" And, with a passionate gesture, she seemed to indicate an open grave.

I was hugely delighted, but I thought it discreet to stroke my chin and look sober. "She's worth fifty thousand scudi."

She shook her head sadly. "If we were to sell her to the Pope and give the money to the poor, it wouldn't profit us. She must go back, —she must go back! We must smother her beauty in the dreadful earth. It makes me feel almost as if she were alive; but it came to me last night with overwhelming force, when my husband came in and refused to see me, that he'll not be himself as long as she is above ground. To cut the knot we must bury her! If I had only thought of it before!"

"Not before!" I said, shaking my head in turn. "Heaven reward our sacrifice now!"

The little surveyor, when he reappeared, seemed hardly like an agent of the celestial influences, but he was deft and active, which was more to the point. Every now and then he uttered some half-articulate lament, by way of protest against the Countess's cruelty; but I saw him privately scanning the recumbent image with an eye which seemed to foresee a malicious glee in standing on a certain unmarked spot on the turf and grinning till people stared. He had brought back an abundance of rope, and having summoned his assistants, who vigorously lifted the litter, he led the way to the original excavation, which had been left unclosed with the project of further researches. By the time we reached the edge of the grave the evening had fallen and the beauty of our marble victim was shrouded in a dusky veil. No one spoke, —if not exactly for shame, at least for regret. Whatever our plea, our performance looked, at least, monstrously profane. The ropes were adjusted and the Juno was slowly lowered into her earthy bed. The Countess took a handful of earth and dropped it solemnly on her breast. "May it lie lightly, but forever!" she said.

"Amen!" cried the little surveyor with a strange mocking inflection; and he gave us a bow, as he departed, which betrayed an agreeable consciousness of knowing where fifty thousand scudi were buried. His underlings had another cask of wine, the result of which, for them, was a suspension of all consciousness, and a subsequent irreparable confusion of memory as to where they had plied their spades.

The Countess had not yet seen her husband, who had again apparently betaken himself to communion with the great god Pan. I was of course unwilling to leave her to encounter alone the results of her momentous deed. She wandered into the drawing-room and pretended to occupy herself with a bit of embroidery, but in reality she was bravely composing herself for an "explanation." I took up a book, but it held my attention as feebly. As the evening wore away I heard a movement on the threshold and saw the Count lifting the tapestried curtain which masked the door, and looking silently at his wife. His eyes were brilliant, but not angry. He had missed the Juno—and drawn a long breath! The Countess kept her eyes fixed on her work, and drew her silken stitches like an image of wifely contentment. The image seemed to fascinate him: he came in slowly, almost on tiptoe, walked to the chimney-piece, and stood there in a sort of rapt contemplation. What had passed, what was passing, in his mind, I leave to your own apprehension. My goddaughter's hand trembled as it rose and fell, and the color came into her cheek. At last she raised her eyes and sustained the gaze in which all his returning faith seemed concentrated. He hesitated a moment, as if her very forgiveness kept the gulf open between them, and then he strode forward, fell on his two knees and buried his head in her lap. I departed as the Count had come in, on tiptoe.

He never became, if you will, a thoroughly modern man; but one day, years after, when a visitor to whom he was showing his cabinet became inquisitive as to a marble hand, suspended in one of its inner recesses, he looked grave and turned the lock on it. "It is the hand of a beautiful creature," he said, "whom I once greatly admired."

"Ah,—a Roman?" said the gentleman, with a smirk.

"A Greek," said the Count, with a frown.

DAISY MILLER: A STUDY

In Two Parts

I

At the little town of Vevay, in Switzerland, there is a particularly comfortable hotel. There are, indeed, many hotels; for the entertainment of tourists is the business of the place, which, as many travellers will remember, is seated upon the edge of a remarkably blue lake—a lake that it behooves every tourist to visit. The shore of the lake presents an unbroken array of establishments of this order, of every category, from the "grand hotel" of the newest fashion, with a chalk-white front, a hundred balconies, and a dozen flags flying from its roof, to the little Swiss *pension* of an elder day, with its name inscribed in German-looking lettering upon a pink or yellow wall, and an awkward summer-house in the angle of the garden. One of the hotels at Vevay, however, is famous, even classical, being distinguished from many of its upstart neighbors by an air both of luxury and of maturity. In this region, in the month of June, American travellers are extremely numerous; it may be said, indeed, that Vevay assumes at this period some of the characteristics of an American watering-place. There are sights and sounds which evoke a vision, an echo, of Newport and Saratoga. There is a flitting hither and thither of "stylish" young girls, a rustling of muslin flounces, a rattle of dance-music in the morning hours, a sound of high-pitched voices at all times. You receive an impression of these things at the excellent inn of the "Trois Couronnes," and are transported in fancy to the Ocean House or to Congress Hall. But at the "Trois Couronnes," it must be added, there are other features that are much at variance with these suggestions: neat German waiters, who look like secretaries of legation; Russian princesses sitting in the garden; little

Polish boys walking about, held by the hand, with their governors; a view of the sunny crest of the Dent du Midi and the picturesque towers of the Castle of Chillon.

I hardly know whether it was the analogies or the differences that were uppermost in the mind of a young American, who, two or three years ago, sat in the garden of the "Trois Couronnes," looking about him, rather idly, at some of the graceful objects I have mentioned. It was a beautiful summer morning, and in whatever fashion the young American looked at things, they must have seemed to him charming. He had come from Geneva the day before by the little steamer, to see his aunt, who was staying at the hotel—Geneva having been for a long time his place of residence. But his aunt had a headache—his aunt had almost always a headache—and now she was shut up in her room, smelling camphor, so that he was at liberty to wander about. He was some seven-and-twenty years of age; when his friends spoke of him, they usually said that he was at Geneva "studying." When his enemies spoke of him, they said—but, after all, he had no enemies; he was an extremely amiable fellow, and universally liked. What I should say is, simply, that when certain persons spoke of him they affirmed that the reason of his spending so much time at Geneva was that he was extremely devoted to a lady who lived there—a foreign lady—a person older than himself. Very few Americans—indeed, I think none—had ever seen this lady, about whom there were some singular stories. But Winterbourne had an old attachment for the little metropolis of Calvinism; he had been put to school there as a boy, and he had afterward gone to college there—circumstances which had led to his forming a great many youthful friendships. Many of these he had kept, and they were a source of great satisfaction to him.

After knocking at his aunt's door, and learning that she was indisposed, he had taken a walk about the town, and then he had come in to his breakfast. He had now finished his breakfast; but he was drinking a small cup of coffee, which had been served to him on a little table in the garden by one of the waiters who looked like an *attaché*. At last he finished his coffee and lit a cigarette. Presently a small boy came walking along the path—an urchin of nine or ten. The child, who was diminutive for his years, had an aged expression of countenance, a pale complexion, and sharp little features. He was dressed in knickerbockers, with red stockings, which displayed his poor little spindle-shanks; he also wore a brilliant red cravat. He carried in his hand a long alpenstock, the sharp point of which he thrust into everything that he approached—the flower-beds, the garden-benches, the trains of the ladies' dresses. In front of Winterbourne he paused, looking at him with a pair of bright, penetrating little eyes.

"Will you give me a lump of sugar?" he asked, in a sharp, hard little voice—a voice immature, and yet, somehow, not young.

Winterbourne glanced at the small table near him, on which his coffee-service rested, and saw that several morsels of sugar remained. "Yes, you may take one," he answered; "but I don't think sugar is good for little boys."

This little boy stepped forward and carefully selected three of the coveted fragments, two of which he buried in the pocket of his knickerbockers, depositing the other as promptly in another place. He poked his alpenstock, lance-fashion, into Winterbourne's bench, and tried to crack the lump of sugar with his teeth.

"Oh, blazes; it's har-r-d!" he exclaimed, pronouncing the adjective in a peculiar manner.

Winterbourne had immediately perceived that he might have the honor of claiming him as a fellow-countryman. "Take care you don't hurt your teeth," he said, paternally.

"I haven't got any teeth to hurt. They have all come out. I have only got seven teeth. My mother counted them last night, and one came out right afterward. She said she'd slap me if any more came out. I can't help it. It's this old Europe. It's the climate that makes them come out. In America they didn't come out. It's these hotels."

Winterbourne was much amused. "If you eat three lumps of sugar, your mother will certainly slap you," he said.

"She's got to give me some candy, then," rejoined his young interlocutor. "I can't get any candy here—any American candy. American candy's the best candy."

"And are American little boys the best little boys?" asked Winterbourne.

"I don't know. I'm an American boy," said the child.

"I see you are one of the best!" laughed Winterbourne.

"Are you an American man?" pursued this vivacious infant. And then, on Winterbourne's affirmative reply—"American men are the best," he declared.

His companion thanked him for the compliment; and the child, who had now got astride of his alpenstock, stood looking about him, while he attached a second lump of sugar. Winterbourne wondered if he himself had been like this in his infancy, for he had been brought to Europe at about this age.

"Here comes my sister!" cried the child, in a moment. "She's an American girl."

Winterbourne looked along the path and saw a beautiful young lady advancing. "American girls are the best girls," he said, cheerfully, to his young companion.

"My sister ain't the best!" the child declared. "She's always blowing at me."

"I imagine that is your fault, not hers," said Winterbourne. The young lady meanwhile had drawn near. She was dressed in white muslin, with a hundred frills and flounces, and knots of pale-colored ribbon. She was bare-headed; but she balanced in her hand a large parasol, with a deep border of embroidery; and she was strikingly, admirably pretty. "How pretty they are!" thought Winterbourne, straightening himself in his seat, as if he were prepared to rise.

The young lady paused in front of his bench, near the parapet of the garden, which overlooked the lake. The little boy had now converted his alpenstock into a vaulting-pole, by the aid of which he was springing about in the gravel, and kicking it up not a little.

"Randolph," said the young lady, "what *are* you doing?"

"I'm going up the Alps," replied Randolph. "This is the way!" And he gave another little jump, scattering the pebbles about Winterbourne's ears.

"That's the way they come down," said Winterbourne.

"He's an American man!" cried Randolph, in his little hard voice.

The young lady gave no heed to this announcement, but looked straight at her brother. "Well, I guess you had better be quiet," she simply observed.

It seemed to Winterbourne that he had been in a manner presented. He got up and stepped slowly toward the young girl, throwing away his cigarette. "This little boy and I have made acquaintance," he said, with great civility. In Geneva, as he had been perfectly aware, a young man was not at liberty to speak to a young unmarried lady except under certain rarely occurring conditions; but here at Vevay, what conditions

could be better than these? —a pretty American girl coming and standing in front of you in a garden. This pretty American girl, however,
on hearing Winterbourne's observation, simply glanced at him; she then
turned her head and looked over the parapet, at the lake and the opposite
mountains. He wondered whether he had gone too far; but he decided
that he must advance farther, rather than retreat. While he was thinking
of something else to say, the young lady turned to the little boy again.

"I should like to know where you got that pole," she said.

"I bought it," responded Randolph.

"You don't mean to say you're going to take it to Italy?"

"Yes, I am going to take it to Italy," the child declared.

The young girl glanced over the front of her dress, and smoothed
out a knot or two of ribbon. Then she rested her eyes upon the prospect
again. "Well, I guess you had better leave it somewhere," she said, after
a moment.

"Are you going to Italy?" Winterbourne inquired, in a tone of great
respect.

The young lady glanced at him again. "Yes, sir," she replied. And
she said nothing more.

"Are you—a—going over the Simplon?" Winterbourne pursued, a
little embarrassed.

"I don't know," she said. "I suppose it's some mountain. Randolph,
what mountain are we going over?"

"Going where?" the child demanded.

"To Italy," Winterbourne explained.

"I don't know," said Randolph. "I don't want to go to Italy. I want
to go to America."

"Oh, Italy is a beautiful place!" rejoined the young man.

"Can you get candy there?" Randolph loudly inquired.

"I hope not," said his sister. "I guess you have had enough candy,
and mother thinks so too."

"I haven't had any for ever so long—for a hundred weeks!" cried
the boy, still jumping about.

The young lady inspected her flounces and smoothed her ribbons
again; and Winterbourne presently risked an observation upon the
beauty of the view. He was ceasing to be embarrassed, for he had begun
to perceive that she was not in the least embarrassed herself. There
had not been the slightest alteration in her charming complexion; she

was evidently neither offended nor fluttered. If she looked another way when he spoke to her, and seemed not particularly to hear him, this was simply her habit, her manner. Yet, as he talked a little more, and pointed out some of the objects of interest in the view, with which she appeared quite unacquainted, she gradually gave him more of the benefit of her glance; and then he saw that this glance was perfectly direct and unshrinking. It was not, however, what would have been called an immodest glance, for the young girl's eyes were singularly honest and fresh. They were wonderfully pretty eyes; and, indeed, Winterbourne had not seen for a long time anything prettier than his fair country-woman's various features—her complexion, her nose, her ears, her teeth. He had a great relish for feminine beauty; he was addicted to observing and analyzing it; and as regards this young lady's face he made several observations. It was not at all insipid; but it was not exactly expressive; and though it was eminently delicate, Winterbourne mentally accused it—very forgivingly—of a want of finish. He thought it very possible that Master Randolph's sister was a coquette; he was sure she had a spirit of her own; but in her bright, sweet, superficial little visage there was no mockery, no irony. Before long it became obvious that she was much disposed toward conversation. She told him that they were going to Rome for the winter—she and her mother and Randolph. She asked him if he was a "real American;" she shouldn't have taken him for one; he seemed more like a German—this was said after a little hesitation—especially when he spoke. Winterbourne, laughing, answered that he had met Germans who spoke like Americans; but that he had not, so far as he remembered, met an American who spoke like a German. Then he asked her if she should not be more comfortable in sitting upon the bench which he had just quitted. She answered that she liked standing up and walking about; but she presently sat down. She told him she was from New York State—"if you know where that is." Winterbourne learned more about her by catching hold of her small, slippery brother, and making him stand a few minutes by his side.

"Tell me your name, my boy," he said.

"Randolph C. Miller," said the boy, sharply. "And I'll tell you her name;" and he levelled his alpenstock at his sister.

"You had better wait till you are asked!" said this young lady, calmly.

"I should like very much to know your name," said Winterbourne.

"Her name is Daisy Miller!" cried the child. "But that isn't her real name; that isn't her name on her cards."

"It's a pity you haven't got one of my cards!" said Miss Miller.

"Her real name is Annie P. Miller," the boy went on.

"Ask him *his* name," said his sister, indicating Winterbourne.

But on this point Randolph seemed perfectly indifferent; he continued to supply information with regard to his own family. "My father's name is Ezra B. Miller," he announced. "My father ain't in Europe; my father's in a better place than Europe."

Winterbourne imagined for a moment that this was the manner in which the child had been taught to intimate that Mr. Miller had been removed to the sphere of celestial rewards. But Randolph immediately added, "My father's in Schenectady. He's got a big business. My father's rich, you bet!"

"Well!" ejaculated Miss Miller, lowering her parasol and looking at the embroidered border. Winterbourne presently released the child, who departed, dragging his alpenstock along the path. "He doesn't like Europe," said the young girl. "He wants to go back."

"To Schenectady, you mean?"

"Yes; he wants to go right home. He hasn't got any boys here. There is one boy here, but he always goes round with a teacher; they won't let him play."

"And your brother hasn't any teacher?" Winterbourne inquired.

"Mother thought of getting him one, to travel round with us. There was a lady told her of a very good teacher; an American lady—perhaps you know her—Mrs. Sanders. I think she came from Boston. She told her of this teacher, and we thought of getting him to travel round with us. But Randolph said he didn't want a teacher travelling round with us. He said he wouldn't have lessons when he was in the cars. And we *are* in the cars about half the time. There was an English lady we met in the cars—I think her name was Miss Featherstone; perhaps you know her. She wanted to know why I didn't give Randolph lessons—give him 'instruction,' she called it. I guess he could give me more instruction than I could give him. He's very smart."

"Yes," said Winterbourne; "he seems very smart."

"Mother's going to get a teacher for him as soon as we get to Italy. Can you get good teachers in Italy?"

"Very good, I should think," said Winterbourne.

"Or else she's going to find some school. He ought to learn some more. He's only nine. He's going to college." And in this way Miss Miller continued to converse upon the affairs of her family, and upon other topics. She sat there with her extremely pretty hands, ornamented with very brilliant rings, folded in her lap, and with her pretty eyes now resting upon those of Winterbourne, now wandering over the garden, the people who passed by, and the beautiful view. She talked to Winterbourne as if she had known him a long time. He found it very pleasant. It was many years since he had heard a young girl talk so much. It might have been said of this unknown young lady, who had come and sat down beside him upon a bench, that she chattered. She was very quiet; she sat in a charming, tranquil attitude, but her lips and her eyes were constantly moving. She had a soft, slender, agreeable voice, and her tone was decidedly sociable. She gave Winterbourne a history of her movements and intentions, and those of her mother and brother, in Europe, and enumerated, in particular, the various hotels at which they had stopped. "That English lady in the cars," she said—"Miss Featherstone—asked me if we didn't all live in hotels in America. I told her I had never been in so many hotels in my life as since I came to Europe. I have never seen so many—it's nothing but hotels." But Miss Miller did not make this remark with a querulous accent; she appeared to be in the best humor with everything. She declared that the hotels were very good, when once you got used to their ways, and that Europe was perfectly sweet. She was not disappointed—not a bit. Perhaps it was because she had heard so much about it before. She had ever so many intimate friends that had been there ever so many times. And then she had had ever so many dresses and things from Paris. Whenever she put on a Paris dress she felt as if she were in Europe.

"It was a kind of a wishing-cap," said Winterbourne.

"Yes," said Miss Miller, without examining this analogy; "it always made me wish I was here. But I needn't have done that for dresses. I am sure they send all the pretty ones to America; you see the most frightful things here. The only thing I don't like," she proceeded, "is the society. There isn't any society; or, if there is, I don't know where it keeps itself. Do you? I suppose there is some society somewhere, but I haven't seen anything of it. I'm very fond of society, and I have always had a great deal of it. I don't mean only in Schenectady, but in New

York. I used to go to New York every winter. In New York I had lots of society. Last winter I had seventeen dinners given me; and three of them were by gentlemen," added Daisy Miller. "I have more friends in New York than in Schenectady—more gentleman friends; and more young lady friends too," she resumed in a moment. She paused again for an instant; she was looking at Winterbourne with all her prettiness in her lively eyes and in her light, slightly monotonous smile. "I have always had," she said, "a great deal of gentlemen's society."

Poor Winterbourne was amused, perplexed, and decidedly charmed. He had never yet heard a young girl express herself in just this fashion; never, at least, save in cases where to say such things seemed a kind of demonstrative evidence of a certain laxity of deportment. And yet was he to accuse Miss Daisy Miller of actual or potential *inconduite*, as they said at Geneva? He felt that he had lived at Geneva so long that he had lost a good deal; he had become dishabituated to the American tone. Never, indeed, since he had grown old enough to appreciate things, had he encountered a young American girl of so pronounced a type as this. Certainly she was very charming, but how deucedly sociable! Was she simply a pretty girl from New York State? were they all like that, the pretty girls who had a good deal of gentlemen's society? Or was she also a designing, an audacious, an unscrupulous young person? Winterbourne had lost his instinct in this matter, and his reason could not help him. Miss Daisy Miller looked extremely innocent. Some people had told him that, after all, American girls were exceedingly innocent; and others had told him that, after all, they were not. He was inclined to think Miss Daisy Miller was a flirt—a pretty American flirt. He had never, as yet, had any relations with young ladies of this category. He had known, here in Europe, two or three women—persons older than Miss Daisy Miller, and provided, for respectability's sake, with husbands—who were great coquettes—dangerous, terrible women, with whom one's relations were liable to take a serious turn. But this young girl was not a coquette in that sense; she was very unsophisticated; she was only a pretty American flirt. Winterbourne was almost grateful for having found the formula that applied to Miss Daisy Miller. He leaned back in his seat; he remarked to himself that she had the most charming nose he had ever seen; he wondered what were the regular conditions and limitations of one's intercourse with a pretty American flirt. It presently became apparent that he was on the way to learn.

"Have you been to that old castle?" asked the young girl, pointing with her parasol to the far-gleaming walls of the Château de Chillon.

"Yes, formerly, more than once," said Winterbourne. "You too, I suppose, have seen it?"

"No; we haven't been there. I want to go there dreadfully. Of course I mean to go there. I wouldn't go away from here without having seen that old castle."

"It's a very pretty excursion," said Winterbourne, "and very easy to make. You can drive, you know, or you can go by the little steamer."

"You can go in the cars," said Miss Miller.

"Yes; you can go in the cars," Winterbourne assented.

"Our courier says they take you right up to the castle," the young girl continued. "We were going last week; but my mother gave out. She suffers dreadfully from dyspepsia. She said she couldn't go. Randolph wouldn't go either; he says he doesn't think much of old castles. But I guess we'll go this week, if we can get Randolph."

"Your brother is not interested in ancient monuments?" Winterbourne inquired, smiling.

"He says he don't care much about old castles. He's only nine. He wants to stay at the hotel. Mother's afraid to leave him alone, and the courier won't stay with him; so we haven't been to many places. But it will be too bad if we don't go up there." And Miss Miller pointed again at the Château de Chillon.

"I should think it might be arranged," said Winterbourne. "Couldn't you get some one to stay for the afternoon with Randolph?"

Miss Miller looked at him a moment, and then, very placidly, "I wish *you* would stay with him!" she said.

Winterbourne hesitated a moment. "I should much rather go to Chillon with you."

"With me?" asked the young girl, with the same placidity.

She didn't rise, blushing, as a young girl at Geneva would have done; and yet Winterbourne, conscious that he had been very bold, thought it possible she was offended. "With your mother," he answered, very respectfully.

But it seemed that both his audacity and his respect were lost upon Miss Daisy Miller. "I guess my mother won't go, after all," she said. "She don't like to ride round in the afternoon. But did you really mean what you said just now—that you would like to go up there?"

"Most earnestly," Winterbourne declared.

"Then we may arrange it. If mother will stay with Randolph, I guess Eugenio will."

"Eugenio?" the young man inquired.

"Eugenio's our courier. He doesn't like to stay with Randolph; he's the most fastidious man I ever saw. But he's a splendid courier. I guess he'll stay at home with Randolph if mother does, and then we can go to the castle."

Winterbourne reflected for an instant as lucidly as possible—"we" could only mean Miss Daisy Miller and himself. This programme seemed almost too agreeable for credence; he felt as if he ought to kiss the young lady's hand. Possibly he would have done so, and quite spoiled the project; but at this moment another person, presumably Eugenio, appeared. A tall, handsome man, with superb whiskers, wearing a velvet morning-coat and a brilliant watch-chain, approached Miss Miller, looking sharply at her companion. "Oh, Eugenio!" said Miss Miller, with the friendliest accent.

Eugenio had looked at Winterbourne from head to foot; he now bowed gravely to the young lady. "I have the honor to inform mademoiselle that luncheon is upon the table."

Miss Miller slowly rose. "See here, Eugenio!" she said; "I'm going to that old castle, anyway."

"To the Château de Chillon, mademoiselle?" the courier inquired. "Mademoiselle has made arrangements?" he added in a tone which struck Winterbourne as very impertinent.

Eugenio's tone apparently threw, even to Miss Miller's own apprehension, a slightly ironical light upon the young girl's situation. She turned to Winterbourne, blushing a little—a very little. "You won't back out?" she said.

"I shall not be happy till we go!" he protested.

"And you are staying in this hotel?" she went on. "And you are really an American?"

The courier stood looking at Winterbourne offensively. The young man, at least, thought his manner of looking an offence to Miss Miller; it conveyed an imputation that she "picked up" acquaintances. "I shall have the honor of presenting to you a person who will tell you all about me," he said, smiling, and referring to his aunt.

"Oh, well, we'll go some day," said Miss Miller. And she gave him a smile and turned away. She put up her parasol and walked back to the inn beside Eugenio. Winterbourne stood looking after her; and as she moved away, drawing her muslin furbelows over the gravel, said to himself that she had the *tournure* of a princess.

He had, however, engaged to do more than proved feasible, in promising to present his aunt, Mrs. Costello, to Miss Daisy Miller. As soon as the former lady had got better of her headache he waited upon her in her apartment; and, after the proper inquiries in regard to her health, he asked her if she had observed in the hotel an American family—a mamma, a daughter, and a little boy.

"And a courier?" said Mrs. Costello. "Oh yes, I have observed them. Seen them—heard them—and kept out of their way." Mrs. Costello was a widow with a fortune; a person of much distinction, who frequently intimated that, if she were not so dreadfully liable to sick-headaches, she would probably have left a deeper impress upon her time. She had a long, pale face, a high nose, and a great deal of very striking white hair, which she wore in large puffs and *rouleaux* over the top of her head. She had two sons married in New York, and another who was now in Europe. This young man was amusing himself at Hombourg; and, though he was on his travels, was rarely perceived to visit any particular city at the moment selected by his mother for her own appearance there. Her nephew, who had come up to Vevay expressly to see her, was therefore more attentive than those who, as she said, were nearer to her. He had imbibed at Geneva the idea that one must always be attentive to one's aunt. Mrs. Costello had not seen him for many years, and she was greatly pleased with him, manifesting her approbation by initiating him into many of the secrets of that social sway which, as she gave him to understand, she exerted in the American capital. She admitted that she was very exclusive; but, if he were acquainted with New York, he would see that one had to be. And her picture of the minutely hierarchical constitution of the society of that city, which she presented to him in many different lights, was, to Winterbourne's imagination, almost oppressively striking.

He immediately perceived, from her tone, that Miss Daisy Miller's place in the social scale was low. "I am afraid you don't approve of them," he said.

"They are very common," Mrs. Costello declared. "They are the sort of Americans that one does one's duty by not—not accepting."

"Ah, you don't accept them?" said the young man.

"I can't, my dear Frederick. I would if I could, but I can't."

"The young girl is very pretty," said Winterbourne, in a moment.

"Of course she's pretty. But she is very common."

"I see what you mean, of course," said Winterbourne, after another pause.

"She has that charming look that they all have," his aunt resumed. "I can't think where they pick it up; and she dresses in perfection— no, you don't know how well she dresses. I can't think where they get their taste."

"But, my dear aunt, she is not, after all, a Camanche savage."

"She is a young lady," said Mrs. Costello, "who has an intimacy with her mamma's courier."

"An intimacy with the courier?" the young man demanded.

"Oh, the mother is just as bad! They treat the courier like a familiar friend—like a gentleman. I shouldn't wonder if he dines with them. Very likely they have never seen a man with such good manners, such fine clothes, so like a gentleman. He probably corresponds to the young lady's idea of a count. He sits with them in the garden in the evening. I think he smokes."

Winterbourne listened with interest to these disclosures; they helped him to make up his mind about Miss Daisy. Evidently she was rather wild. "Well," he said, "I am not a courier, and yet she was very charming to me."

"You had better have said at first," said Mrs. Costello, with dignity, "that you had made her acquaintance."

"We simply met in the garden, and we talked a bit."

"*Tout bonnement!* And pray what did you say?"

"I said I should take the liberty of introducing her to my admirable aunt."

"I am much obliged to you."

"It was to guarantee my respectability," said Winterbourne.

"And pray who is to guarantee hers?"

"Ah, you are cruel!" said the young man. "She's a very nice young girl."

"You don't say that as if you believed it," Mrs. Costello observed.

"She is completely uncultivated," Winterbourne went on. "But she is wonderfully pretty, and, in short, she is very nice. To prove that I believe it, I am going to take her to the Château de Chillon."

"You two are going off there together? I should say it proved just the contrary. How long had you known her, may I ask, when this interesting project was formed? You haven't been twenty-four hours in the house."

"I had known her half an hour!" said Winterbourne, smiling.

"Dear me!" cried Mrs. Costello. "What a dreadful girl!"

Her nephew was silent for some moments. "You really think, then," he began, earnestly, and with a desire for trustworthy information— "you really think that—" But he paused again.

"Think what, sir?" said his aunt.

"That she is the sort of young lady who expects a man, sooner or later, to carry her off?"

"I haven't the least idea what such young ladies expect a man to do. But I really think that you had better not meddle with little American girls that are uncultivated, as you call them. You have lived too long out of the country. You will be sure to make some great mistake. You are too innocent."

"My dear aunt, I am not so innocent," said Winterbourne, smiling and curling his mustache.

"You are too guilty, then!"

Winterbourne continued to curl his mustache, meditatively. "You won't let the poor girl know you then?" he asked at last.

"Is it literally true that she is going to the Château de Chillon with you?"

"I think that she fully intends it."

"Then, my dear Frederick," said Mrs. Costello, "I must decline the honor of her acquaintance. I am an old woman, but I am not too old, thank Heaven, to be shocked!"

"But don't they all do these things—the young girls in America?" Winterbourne inquired.

Mrs. Costello stared a moment. "I should like to see my granddaughters do them!" she declared, grimly.

This seemed to throw some light upon the matter, for Winterbourne remembered to have heard that his pretty cousins in New York were "tremendous flirts." If, therefore, Miss Daisy Miller exceeded the liberal

margin allowed to these young ladies, it was probable that anything
might be expected of her. Winterbourne was impatient to see her again,
and he was vexed with himself that, by instinct, he should not appreciate
her justly.

Though he was impatient to see her, he hardly knew what he should
say to her about his aunt's refusal to become acquainted with her; but
he discovered, promptly enough, that with Miss Daisy Miller there was
no great need of walking on tiptoe. He found her that evening in the
garden, wandering about in the warm starlight like an indolent sylph,
and swinging to and fro the largest fan he had ever beheld. It was ten
o'clock. He had dined with his aunt, had been sitting with her since
dinner, and had just taken leave of her till the morrow. Miss Daisy
Miller seemed very glad to see him; she declared it was the longest
evening she had ever passed.

"Have you been all alone?" he asked.

"I have been walking round with mother. But mother gets tired
walking round," she answered.

"Has she gone to bed?"

"No; she doesn't like to go to bed," said the young girl. "She doesn't
sleep—not three hours. She says she doesn't know how she lives. She's
dreadfully nervous. I guess she sleeps more than she thinks. She's gone
somewhere after Randolph; she wants to try to get him to go to bed.
He doesn't like to go to bed."

"Let us hope she will persuade him," observed Winterbourne.

"She will talk to him all she can; but he doesn't like her to talk to
him," said Miss Daisy, opening her fan. "She's going to try to get
Eugenio to talk to him. But he isn't afraid of Eugenio. Eugenio's a
splendid courier, but he can't make much impression on Randolph! I
don't believe he'll go to bed before eleven." It appeared that Randolph's
vigil was in fact triumphantly prolonged, for Winterbourne strolled
about with the young girl for some time without meeting her mother.
"I have been looking round for that lady you want to introduce me to,"
his companion resumed. "She's your aunt." Then on Winterbourne's
admitting the fact, and expressing some curiosity as to how she had
learned it, she said she had heard all about Mrs. Costello from the
chamber-maid. She was very quiet, and very *comme il faut*; she wore
white puffs; she spoke to no one, and she never dined at the *table d'hôte*.
Every two days she had a headache. "I think that's a lovely description,

headache and all!" said Miss Daisy, chattering along in her thin, gay voice. "I want to know her ever so much. I know just what *your* aunt would be; I know I should like her. She would be very exclusive. I like a lady to be exclusive; I'm dying to be exclusive myself. Well, we *are* exclusive, mother and I. We don't speak to every one—or they don't speak to us. I suppose it's about the same thing. Anyway, I shall be ever so glad to know your aunt."

Winterbourne was embarrassed. "She would be most happy," he said; "but I am afraid those headaches will interfere."

The young girl looked at him through the dusk. "But I suppose she doesn't have a headache every day," she said, sympathetically.

Winterbourne was silent a moment. "She tells me she does," he answered at last, not knowing what to say.

Miss Daisy Miller stopped, and stood looking at him. Her prettiness was still visible in the darkness; she was opening and closing her enormous fan. "She doesn't want to know me!" she said suddenly. "Why don't you say so? You needn't be afraid. I'm not afraid!" And she gave a little laugh.

Winterbourne fancied there was a tremor in her voice; he was touched, shocked, mortified by it. "My dear young lady," he protested, "she knows no one. It's her wretched health."

The young girl walked on a few steps, laughing still. "You needn't be afraid," she repeated. "Why should she want to know me?" Then she paused again; she was close to the parapet of the garden, and in front of her was the starlit lake. There was a vague sheen upon its surface, and in the distance were dimly-seen mountain forms. Daisy Miller looked out upon the mysterious prospect, and then she gave another little laugh. "Gracious! she is exclusive!" she said. Winterbourne wondered whether she was seriously wounded, and for a moment almost wished that her sense of injury might be such as to make it becoming in him to attempt to reassure and comfort her. He had a pleasant sense that she would be very approachable for consolatory purposes. He felt then, for the instant, quite ready to sacrifice his aunt, conversationally; to admit that she was a proud, rude woman, and to declare that they needn't mind her. But before he had time to commit himself to this perilous mixture of gallantry and impiety, the young lady, resuming her walk, gave an exclamation in quite another tone. "Well, here's mother! I guess she hasn't got Randolph to go to bed." The figure of a lady appeared, at a distance, very indistinct in the darkness, and advancing with a slow and wavering movement. Suddenly it seemed to pause.

"Are you sure it is your mother? Can you distinguish her in this thick dusk?" Winterbourne asked.

"Well!" cried Miss Daisy Miller, with a laugh; "I guess I know my own mother. And when she has got on my shawl, too! She is always wearing my things."

The lady in question, ceasing to advance, hovered vaguely about the spot at which she had checked her steps.

"I am afraid your mother doesn't see you," said Winterbourne. "Or perhaps," he added, thinking, with Miss Miller, the joke permissible— "perhaps she feels guilty about your shawl."

"Oh, it's a fearful old thing!" the young girl replied, serenely. "I told her she could wear it. She won't come here, because she sees you."

"Ah, then," said Winterbourne, "I had better leave you."

"Oh no; come on!" urged Miss Daisy Miller.

"I'm afraid your mother doesn't approve of my walking with you."

Miss Miller gave him a serious glance. "It isn't for me; it's for you— that is, it's for *her*. Well, I don't know who it's for! But mother doesn't like any of my gentlemen friends. She's right down timid. She always makes a fuss if I introduce a gentleman. But I *do* introduce them— almost always. If I didn't introduce my gentlemen friends to mother," the young girl added, in her little soft, flat monotone, "I shouldn't think I was natural."

"To introduce me," said Winterbourne, "you must know my name." And he proceeded to pronounce it.

"Oh dear, I can't say all that!" said his companion, with a laugh. But by this time they had come up to Mrs. Miller, who, as they drew near, walked to the parapet of the garden and leaned upon it, looking intently at the lake, and turning her back to them. "Mother!" said the young girl, in a tone of decision. Upon this the elder lady turned round. "Mr. Winterbourne," said Miss Daisy Miller, introducing the young man very frankly and prettily. "Common," she was, as Mrs. Costello had pronounced her; yet it was a wonder to Winterbourne that, with her commonness, she had a singularly delicate grace.

Her mother was a small, spare, light person, with a wandering eye, a very exiguous nose, and a large forehead, decorated with a certain amount of thin, much-frizzled hair. Like her daughter, Mrs. Miller was dressed with extreme elegance; she had enormous diamonds in her ears. So far as Winterbourne could observe, she gave him no greeting—she certainly was not looking at him. Daisy was near her, pulling her shawl straight. "What are you doing, poking round here?" this young lady inquired, but by no means with that harshness of accent which her choice of words may imply.

"I don't know," said her mother, turning toward the lake again.

"I shouldn't think you'd want that shawl!" Daisy exclaimed.

"Well, I do!" her mother answered, with a little laugh.

"Did you get Randolph to go to bed?" asked the young girl.

"No; I couldn't induce him," said Mrs. Miller, very gently. "He wants to talk to the waiter. He likes to talk to that waiter."

"I was telling Mr. Winterbourne," the young girl went on; and to the young man's ear her tone might have indicated that she had been uttering his name all her life.

"Oh yes!" said Winterbourne; "I have the pleasure of knowing your son."

Randolph's mamma was silent; she turned her attention to the lake. But at last she spoke. "Well, I don't see how he lives!"

"Anyhow, it isn't so bad as it was at Dover," said Daisy Miller.

"And what occurred at Dover?" Winterbourne asked.

"He wouldn't go to bed at all. I guess he sat up all night in the public parlor. He wasn't in bed at twelve o'clock: I know that."

"It was half-past twelve," declared Mrs. Miller with mild emphasis.

"Does he sleep much during the day?" Winterbourne demanded.

"I guess he doesn't sleep much," Daisy rejoined.

"I wish he would!" said her mother. "It seems as if he couldn't."

"I think he's real tiresome," Daisy pursued.

Then, for some moments, there was silence. "Well, Daisy Miller," said the elder lady, presently, "I shouldn't think you'd want to talk against your own brother!"

"Well, he *is* tiresome, mother," said Daisy, quite without the asperity of a retort.

"He's only nine," urged Mrs. Miller.

"Well, he wouldn't go to that castle," said the young girl. "I'm going there with Mr. Winterbourne."

To this announcement, very placidly made, Daisy's mamma offered no response. Winterbourne took for granted that she deeply disapproved of the projected excursion; but he said to himself that she was a simple, easily-managed person, and that a few deferential protestations would take the edge from her displeasure. "Yes," he began; "your daughter has kindly allowed me the honor of being her guide."

Mrs. Miller's wandering eyes attached themselves, with a sort of appealing air, to Daisy, who, however, strolled a few steps farther, gently humming to herself. "I presume you will go in the cars," said her mother.

"Yes, or in the boat," said Winterbourne.

"Well, of course, I don't know," Mrs. Miller rejoined. "I have never been to that castle."

"It is a pity you shouldn't go," said Winterbourne, beginning to feel reassured as to her opposition. And yet he was quite prepared to find that, as a matter of course, she meant to accompany her daughter.

"We've been thinking ever so much about going," she pursued; "but it seems as if we couldn't. Of course Daisy—she wants to go round. But there's a lady here—I don't know her name — she says she shouldn't think we'd want to go to see castles *here*; she should think we'd want to wait till we got to Italy. It seems as if there would be so many there," continued Mrs. Miller, with an air of increasing confidence. "Of course we only want to see the principal ones. We visited several in England," she presently added.

"Ah, yes! in England there are beautiful castles," said Winterbourne. "But Chillon, here, is very well worth seeing."

"Well, if Daisy feels up to it—" said Mrs. Miller, in a tone impregnated with a sense of the magnitude of the enterprise. "It seems as if there was nothing she wouldn't undertake."

"Oh, I think she'll enjoy it!" Winterbourne declared. And he desired more and more to make it a certainty that he was to have the privilege of a *téte-à-téte* with the young lady, who was still strolling along in front of them, softly vocalizing. "You are not disposed, madam," he inquired, "to undertake it yourself?"

Daisy's mother looked at him an instant askance, and then walked forward in silence. Then—"I guess she had better go alone," she said, simply. Winterbourne observed to himself that this was a very different type of maternity from that of the vigilant matrons who massed themselves in the forefront of social intercourse in the dark old city at the other end of the lake. But his meditations were interrupted by hearing his name very distinctly pronounced by Mrs. Miller's unprotected daughter.

"Mr. Winterbourne!" murmured Daisy.

"Mademoiselle!" said the young man.

"Don't you want to take me out in a boat?"

"At present?" he asked.

"Of course!" said Daisy.

"Well, Annie Miller!" exclaimed her mother.

"I beg you, madam, to let her go," said Winterbourne, ardently; for he had never yet enjoyed the sensation of guiding through the summer starlight a skiff freighted with a fresh and beautiful young girl.

"I shouldn't think she'd want to," said her mother. "I should think she'd rather go in-doors."

"I'm sure Mr. Winterbourne wants to take me," Daisy declared. "He's so awfully devoted!"

"I will row you over to Chillon in the starlight."

"I don't believe it!" said Daisy.

"Well!" ejaculated the elder lady again.

"You haven't spoken to me for half an hour," her daughter went on.

"I have been having some very pleasant conversation with your mother," said Winterbourne.

"Well, I want you to take me out in a boat!" Daisy repeated. They had all stopped, and she had turned round and was looking at Winterbourne. Her face wore a charming smile, her pretty eyes were gleaming, she was swinging her great fan about. No; it's impossible to be prettier than that, thought Winterbourne.

"There are half a dozen boats moored at that landing-place," he said, pointing to certain steps which descended from the garden to the lake. "If you will do me the honor to accept my arm, we will go and select one of them."

Daisy stood there smiling; she threw back her head and gave a little, light laugh. "I like a gentleman to be formal!" she declared.

"I assure you it's a formal offer."

"I was bound I would make you say something," Daisy went on.

"You see, it's not very difficult," said Winterbourne. "But I am afraid you are chaffing me."

"I think not, sir," remarked Mrs. Miller, very gently.

"Do, then, let me give you a row," he said to the young girl.

"It's quite lovely, the way you say that!" cried Daisy.

"It will be still more lovely to do it."

"Yes, it would be lovely!" said Daisy. But she made no movement to accompany him; she only stood there laughing.

"I should think you had better find out what time it is," interposed her mother.

"It is eleven o'clock, madam," said a voice, with a foreign accent, out of the neighboring darkness; and Winterbourne, turning, perceived the florid personage who was in attendance upon the two ladies. He had apparently just approached.

"Oh, Eugenio," said Daisy, "I am going out in a boat!"

Eugenio bowed. "At eleven o'clock, mademoiselle?"

"I am going with Mr. Winterbourne—this very minute."

"Do tell her she can't," said Mrs. Miller to the courier.

"I think you had better not go out in a boat, mademoiselle," Eugenio declared.

Winterbourne wished to Heaven this pretty girl were not so familiar with her courier; but he said nothing.

"I suppose you don't think it's proper!" Daisy exclaimed. "Eugenio doesn't think anything's proper."

"I am at your service," said Winterbourne.

"Does mademoiselle propose to go alone?" asked Eugenio of Mrs. Miller.

"Oh no; with this gentleman!" answered Daisy's mamma.

The courier looked for a moment at Winterbourne—the latter thought he was smiling—and then, solemnly, with a bow, "As mademoiselle pleases!" he said.

"Oh, I hoped you would make a fuss!" said Daisy. "I don't care to go now."

"I myself shall make a fuss if you don't go," said Winterbourne.

"That's all I want—a little fuss!" And the young girl began to laugh again.

"Mr. Randolph has gone to bed!" the courier announced, frigidly.

"Oh, Daisy; now we can go!" said Mrs. Miller.

Daisy turned away from Winterbourne, looking at him, smiling, and fanning herself. "Good-night," she said; "I hope you are disappointed, or disgusted, or something!"

He looked at her, taking the hand she offered him. "I am puzzled," he answered.

"Well, I hope it won't keep you awake!" she said, very smartly; and, under the escort of the privileged Eugenio, the two ladies passed toward the house.

Winterbourne stood looking after them; he was indeed puzzled. He lingered beside the lake for a quarter of an hour, turning over the mystery of the young girl's sudden familiarities and caprices. But the only very definite conclusion he came to was that he should enjoy deucedly "going off" with her somewhere.

Two days afterward he went off with her to the Castle of Chillon. He waited for her in the large hall of the hotel, where the couriers, the servants, the foreign tourists, were lounging about and staring. It was not the place he should have chosen, but she had appointed it. She came tripping down-stairs, buttoning her long gloves, squeezing her folded parasol against her pretty figure, dressed in the perfection of a soberly elegant travelling costume. Winterbourne was a man of imagination and, as our ancestors used to say, sensibility; as he looked at her dress and, on the great staircase, her little rapid, confiding step, he felt as if there were something romantic going forward. He could have believed he was going to elope with her. He passed out with her among all the idle people that were assembled there; they were all looking at her very hard; she had begun to chatter as soon as she joined him. Winterbourne's preference had been that they should be conveyed to Chillon in a carriage; but she expressed a lively wish to go in the little steamer; she declared that she had a passion for steamboats. There was always such a lovely breeze upon the water, and you saw such lots of people. The sail was not long, but Winterbourne's companion found time to say a great many things. To the young man himself their little excursion was so much of an escapade—an adventure—that, even allowing for her habitual sense of freedom, he had some expectation of seeing her regard it in the same way. But it must be confessed that, in this particular, he was disappointed. Daisy Miller was extremely animated, she was in charming spirits; but she was apparently not at all excited; she was not fluttered; she avoided neither his eyes nor those of any one else; she blushed neither when she looked at him nor when she felt that people were looking at her. People continued to look at her a great deal, and Winterbourne took much satisfaction in his pretty companion's distinguished air. He had been a little afraid that she would talk loud, laugh overmuch, and even, perhaps, desire to move about the boat a good deal. But he quite forgot his fears; he sat smiling, with his eyes upon her face, while, without moving from her place, she delivered herself of a great number of original reflections. It was the most charming garrulity he had ever heard. He had assented to the idea that she was "common;" but was she so, after all, or was he simply getting used to her commonness? Her conversation was chiefly of what metaphysicians term the objective cast; but every now and then it took a subjective turn.

"What on *earth* are you so grave about?" she suddenly demanded, fixing her agreeable eyes upon Winterbourne's.

"Am I grave?" he asked. "I had an idea I was grinning from ear to ear."

"You look as if you were taking me to a funeral. If that's a grin, your ears are very near together."

"Should you like me to dance a hornpipe on the deck?"

"Pray do, and I'll carry round your hat. It will pay the expenses of our journey."

"I never was better pleased in my life," murmured Winterbourne.

She looked at him a moment, and then burst into a little laugh. "I like to make you say those things! You're a queer mixture!"

In the castle, after they had landed, the subjective element decidedly prevailed. Daisy tripped about the vaulted chambers, rustled her skirts in the corkscrew staircases, flirted back with a pretty little cry and a shudder from the edge of the *oubliettes,* and turned a singularly well-shaped ear to everything that Winterbourne told her about the place. But he saw that she cared very little for feudal antiquities, and that the dusky traditions of Chillon made but a slight impression upon her. They had the good fortune to have been able to walk about without other companionship than that of the custodian; and Winterbourne arranged with this functionary that they should not be hurried—that they should linger and pause wherever they chose. The custodian interpreted the bargain generously—Winterbourne, on his side, had been generous — and ended by leaving them quite to themselves. Miss

Miller's observations were not remarkable for logical consistency; for anything she wanted to say she was sure to find a pretext. She found a great many pretexts in the rugged embrasures of Chillon for asking Winterbourne sudden questions about himself—his family, his previous history, his tastes, his habits, his intentions—and for supplying information upon corresponding points in her own personality. Of her own tastes, habits, and intentions Miss Miller was prepared to give the most definite, and indeed the most favorable account.

"Well, I hope you know enough!" she said to her companion, after he had told her the history of the unhappy Bonivard. "I never saw a man that knew so much!" The history of Bonivard had evidently, as they say, gone in one ear and out of the other. But Daisy went on to say that she wished Winterbourne would travel with them and "go round" with them; they might know something, in that case. "Don't you want to come and teach Randolph?" she asked. Winterbourne said that nothing could possibly please him so much, but that he had unfortunately other occupations. "Other occupations? I don't believe it!" said Miss Daisy. "What do you mean? You are not in business." The young man admitted that he was not in business; but he had engagements which, even within a day or two, would force him to go back to Geneva. "Oh, bother!" she said: "I don't believe it!" and she began to talk about something else. But a few moments later, when he was pointing out to her the pretty design of an antique fireplace, she broke out irrelevantly, "You don't mean to say you are going back to Geneva?"

"It is a melancholy fact that I shall have to return to Geneva tomorrow."

"Well, Mr. Winterbourne," said Daisy, "I think you're horrid!"

"Oh, don't say such dreadful things!" said Winterbourne—"just at the last!"

"The last!" cried the young girl; "I call it the first. I have half a mind to leave you here and go straight back to the hotel alone." And for the next ten minutes she did nothing but call him horrid. Poor Winterbourne was fairly bewildered; no young lady had as yet done him the honor to be so agitated by the announcement of his movements. His companion, after this, ceased to pay any attention to the curiosities of Chillon or the beauties of the lake; she opened fire upon the mysterious charmer in Geneva whom she appeared to have instantly taken it for granted that he was hurrying back to see. How did Miss Daisy

Miller know that there was a charmer in Geneva? Winterbourne, who denied the existence of such a person, was quite unable to discover; and he was divided between amazement at the rapidity of her induction and amusement at the frankness of her *persiflage*. She seemed to him, in all this, an extraordinary mixture of innocence and crudity. "Does she never allow you more than three days at a time?" asked Daisy, ironically. "Doesn't she give you a vacation in summer? There's no one so hard worked but they can get leave to go off somewhere at this season. I suppose, if you stay another day, she'll come after you in the boat. Do wait over till Friday, and I will go down to the landing to see her arrive!" Winterbourne began to think he had been wrong to feel disappointed in the temper in which the young lady had embarked. If he had missed the personal accent, the personal accent was now making its appearance. It sounded very distinctly, at last, in her telling him she would stop "teasing" him if he would promise her solemnly to come down to Rome in the winter.

"That's not a difficult promise to make," said Winterbourne. "My aunt has taken an apartment in Rome for the winter, and has already asked me to come and see her."

"I don't want you to come for your aunt," said Daisy; "I want you to come for me." And this was the only allusion that the young man was ever to hear her make to his invidious kinswoman. He declared that, at any rate, he would certainly come. After this Daisy stopped teasing. Winterbourne took a carriage, and they drove back to Vevay in the dusk; the young girl was very quiet.

In the evening Winterbourne mentioned to Mrs. Costello that he had spent the afternoon at Chillon with Miss Daisy Miller.

"The Americans—of the courier?" asked the lady.

"Ah, happily," said Winterbourne, "the courier stayed at home."

"She went with you all alone?"

"All alone."

Mrs. Costello sniffed a little at her smelling-bottle. "And that," she exclaimed, "is the young person whom you wanted me to know!"

II

Winterbourne, who had returned to Geneva the day after his excursion to Chillon, went to Rome toward the end of January. His aunt had been established there for several weeks, and he had received a couple of letters from her. "Those people you were so devoted to last summer at Vevay have turned up here, courier and all," she wrote. "They seem to have made several acquaintances, but the courier continues to be the most *intime*. The young lady, however, is also very intimate with some third-rate Italians, with whom she rackets about in a way that makes much talk. Bring me that pretty novel of Cherbuliez's—'Paule Méré'—and don't come later than the 23d."

In the natural course of events, Winterbourne, on arriving in Rome, would presently have ascertained Mrs. Miller's address at the American banker's, and have gone to pay his compliments to Miss Daisy. "After what happened at Vevay, I think I may certainly call upon them," he said to Mrs. Costello.

"If, after what happens—at Vevay and everywhere—you desire to keep up the acquaintance, you are very welcome. Of course a man may know every one. Men are welcome to the privilege!"

"Pray what is it that happens—here, for instance?" Winterbourne demanded.

"The girl goes about alone with her foreigners. As to what happens further, you must apply elsewhere for information. She has picked up half a dozen of the regular Roman fortune-hunters, and she takes them about to people's houses. When she comes to a party she brings with her a gentleman with a good deal of manner and a wonderful mustache."

"And where is the mother?"

"I haven't the least idea. They are very dreadful people."

Winterbourne meditated a moment. "They are very ignorant—very innocent only. Depend upon it they are not bad."

"They are hopelessly vulgar," said Mrs. Costello. "Whether or no being hopelessly vulgar is being 'bad' is a question for the metaphysicians. They are bad enough to dislike, at any rate; and for this short life that is quite enough."

The news that Daisy Miller was surrounded by half a dozen wonderful mustaches checked Winterbourne's impulse to go straightway to see her. He had, perhaps, not definitely flattered himself that he had made an ineffaceable impression upon her heart, but he was annoyed at hearing of a state of affairs so little in harmony with an image that had lately flitted in and out of his own meditations; the image of a very pretty girl looking out of an old Roman window and asking herself urgently when Mr. Winterbourne would arrive. If, however, he determined to wait a little before reminding Miss Miller of his claims to her consideration, he went very soon to call upon two or three other friends. One of these friends was an American lady who had spent several winters at Geneva, where she had placed her children at school. She was a very accomplished woman, and she lived in the Via Gregoriana. Winterbourne found her in a little crimson drawing-room on a third floor; the room was filled with southern sunshine. He had not been there ten minutes when the servant came in, announcing "Madame Mila!" This announcement was presently followed by the entrance of little Randolph Miller, who stopped in the middle of the room and stood staring at Winterbourne An instant later his pretty sister crossed the threshold; and then, after a considerable interval, Mrs. Miller slowly advanced.

"I know you!" said Randolph.

"I'm sure you know a great many things," exclaimed Winterbourne, taking him by the hand. "How is your education coming on?"

Daisy was exchanging greetings very prettily with her hostess; but when she heard Winterbourne's voice she quickly turned her head. "Well, I declare!" she said.

"I told you I should come, you know," Winterbourne rejoined, smiling.

"Well, I didn't believe it," said Miss Daisy.

"I am much obliged to you," laughed the young man.

"You might have come to see me!" said Daisy.

"I arrived only yesterday."

"I don't believe that!" the young girl declared.

Winterbourne turned with a protesting smile to her mother; but this lady evaded his glance, and seating herself, fixed her eyes upon her son. "We've got a bigger place than this," said Randolph. "It's all gold on the walls."

Mrs. Miller turned uneasily in her chair. "I told you if I were to bring you, you would say something!" she murmured.

"I told *you*!" Randolph exclaimed. "I tell *you*, sir!" he added jocosely, giving Winterbourne a thump on the knee. "It *is* bigger, too!"

Daisy had entered upon a lively conversation with her hostess; Winterbourne judged it becoming to address a few words to her mother. "I hope you have been well since we parted at Vevay," he said.

Mrs. Miller now certainly looked at him—at his chin. "Not very well, sir," she answered.

"She's got the dyspepsia," said Randolph. "I've got it too. Father's got it. I've got it most!"

This announcement, instead of embarrassing Mrs. Miller, seemed to relieve her. "I suffer from the liver," she said. "I think it's this climate; it's less bracing than Schenectady, especially in the winter season. I don't know whether you know we reside at Schenectady. I was saying to Daisy that I certainly hadn't found any one like Dr. Davis, and I didn't believe I should. Oh, at Schenectady he stands first; they think everything of him. He has so much to do, and yet there was nothing he wouldn't do for me. He said he never saw anything like my dyspepsia, but he was bound to cure it. I'm sure there was nothing he wouldn't try. He was just going to try something new when we came off. Mr. Miller wanted Daisy to see Europe for herself. But I wrote to Mr. Miller that it seems as if I couldn't get on without Dr. Davis. At Schenectady he stands at the very top; and there's a great deal of sickness there, too. It affects my sleep."

Winterbourne had a good deal of pathological gossip with Dr. Davis's patient, during which Daisy chattered unremittingly to her own companion. The young man asked Mrs. Miller how she was pleased with Rome. "Well, I must say I am disappointed," she answered. "We had heard so much about it; I suppose we had heard too much. But we couldn't help that. We had been led to expect something different."

"Ah, wait a little, and you will become very fond of it," said Winterbourne.

"I hate it worse and worse every day!" cried Randolph.

"You are like the infant Hannibal," said Winterbourne.

"No, I ain't!" Randolph declared, at a venture.

"You are not much like an infant," said his mother. "But we have seen places," she resumed, "that I should put a long way before Rome." And in reply to Winterbourne's interrogation, "There's Zürich," she concluded, "I think Zürich is lovely; and we hadn't heard half so much about it."

"The best place we've seen is the City of Richmond!" said Randolph.

"He means the ship," his mother explained. "We crossed in that ship. Randolph had a good time on the *City of Richmond.*"

"It's the best place I've seen," the child repeated. "Only it was turned the wrong way."

"Well, we've got to turn the right way some time," said Mrs. Miller with a little laugh. Winterbourne expressed the hope that her daughter at least found some gratification in Rome, and she declared that Daisy was quite carried away. "It's on account of the society—the society's splendid. She goes round everywhere; she has made a great number of acquaintances. Of course she goes round more than I do. I must say they have been very sociable; they have taken her right in. And then she knows a great many gentlemen. Oh, she thinks there's nothing like Rome. Of course, it's a great deal pleasanter for a young lady if she knows plenty of gentlemen."

By this time Daisy had turned her attention again to Winterbourne. "I've been telling Mrs. Walker how mean you were!" the young girl announced.

"And what is the evidence you have offered?" asked Winterbourne, rather annoyed at Miss Miller's want of appreciation of the zeal of an admirer who on his way down to Rome had stopped neither at Bologna nor at Florence, simply because of a certain sentimental impatience. He remembered that a cynical compatriot had once told him that American women — the pretty ones, and this gave a largeness to the axiom—were at once the most exacting in the world and the least endowed with a sense of indebtedness.

"Why, you were awfully mean at Vevay," said Daisy. "You wouldn't do anything. You wouldn't stay there when I asked you."

"My dearest young lady," cried Winterbourne, with eloquence, "have I come all the way to Rome to encounter your reproaches?"

"Just hear him say that!" said Daisy to her hostess, giving a twist to a bow on this lady's dress. "Did you ever hear anything so quaint?"

"So quaint, my dear?" murmured Mrs. Walker, in the tone of a partisan of Winterbourne.

"Well, I don't know," said Daisy, fingering Mrs. Walker's ribbons. "Mrs. Walker, I want to tell you something."

"Mother-r," interposed Randolph, with his rough ends to his words, "I tell you you've got to go. Eugenio'll raise—something!"

"I'm not afraid of Eugenio," said Daisy, with a toss of her head. "Look here, Mrs. Walker," she went on, "you know I'm coming to your party."

"I am delighted to hear it."

"I've got a lovely dress!"

"I am very sure of that."

"But I want to ask a favor—permission to bring a friend."

"I shall be happy to see any of your friends," said Mrs. Walker, turning with a smile to Mrs. Miller.

"Oh, they are not my friends," answered Daisy's mamma, smiling shyly, in her own fashion. "I never spoke to them."

"It's an intimate friend of mine—Mr. Giovanelli," said Daisy, without a tremor in her clear little voice or a shadow on her brilliant little face.

Mrs. Walker was silent a moment; she gave a rapid glance at Winterbourne. "I shall be glad to see Mr. Giovanelli," she then said.

"He's an Italian," Daisy pursued, with the prettiest serenity. "He's a great friend of mine; he's the handsomest man in the world—except Mr. Winterbourne! He knows plenty of Italians, but he wants to know some Americans. He thinks ever so much of Americans. He's tremendously clever. He's perfectly lovely!"

It was settled that this brilliant personage should be brought to Mrs. Walker's party, and then Mrs. Miller prepared to take her leave. "I guess we'll go back to the hotel," she said.

"You may go back to the hotel, mother, but I'm going to take a walk," said Daisy.

"She's going to walk with Mr. Giovanelli," Randolph proclaimed.

"I am going to the Pincio," said Daisy, smiling.

"Alone, my dear—at this hour?" Mrs. Walker asked. The afternoon was drawing to a close—it was the hour for the throng of carriages and of contemplative pedestrians. "I don't think it's safe, my dear," said Mrs. Walker.

"Neither do I," subjoined Mrs. Miller. "You'll get the fever, as sure as you live. Remember what Dr. Davis told you!"

"Give her some medicine before she goes," said Randolph.

The company had risen to its feet; Daisy, still showing her pretty teeth, bent over and kissed her hostess. "Mrs. Walker, you are too perfect," she said. "I'm not going alone; I am going to meet a friend."

"Your friend won't keep you from getting the fever," Mrs. Miller observed.

"Is it Mr. Giovanelli?" asked the hostess.

Winterbourne was watching the young girl; at this question his attention quickened. She stood there smiling and smoothing her bonnet ribbons; she glanced at Winterbourne. Then, while she glanced and smiled, she answered, without a shade of hesitation, "Mr. Giovanelli—the beautiful Giovanelli."

"My dear young friend," said Mrs. Walker, taking her hand, pleadingly, "don't walk off to the Pincio at this hour to meet a beautiful Italian."

"Well, he speaks English," said Mrs. Miller.

"Gracious me!" Daisy exclaimed, "I don't want to do anything improper. There's an easy way to settle it." She continued to glance at Winterbourne. "The Pincio is only a hundred yards distant; and if Mr. Winterbourne were as polite as he pretends, he would offer to walk with me!"

Winterbourne's politeness hastened to affirm itself, and the young girl gave him gracious leave to accompany her. They passed downstairs before her mother, and at the door Winterbourne perceived Mrs. Miller's carriage drawn up, with the ornamental courier whose acquaintance he had made at Vevay seated within. "Good-bye, Eugenio!" cried Daisy; "I'm going to take a walk." The distance from the Via Gregoriana to the beautiful garden at the other end of the Pincian Hill is, in fact, rapidly traversed. As the day was splendid, however, and the concourse of vehicles, walkers, and loungers numerous, the young Americans found their progress much delayed. This fact was highly agreeable to Winterbourne, in spite of his consciousness of his singular situation. The slow-moving, idly-gazing Roman crowd bestowed much attention upon the extremely pretty young foreign lady who was passing through it upon his arm; and he wondered what on earth had been in Daisy's mind when she proposed to expose herself, unattended, to its appreciation. His own mission, to her sense, apparently, was to consign her to the hands of Mr. Giovanelli; but Winterbourne, at once annoyed and gratified, resolved that he would do no such thing.

"Why haven't you been to see me?" asked Daisy. "You can't get out of that."

"I have had the honor of telling you that I have only just stepped out of the train."

"You must have stayed in the train a good while after it stopped!" cried the young girl, with her little laugh. "I suppose you were asleep. You have had time to go to see Mrs. Walker."

"I knew Mrs. Walker——" Winterbourne began to explain.

"I know where you knew her. You knew her at Geneva. She told me so. Well, you knew me at Vevay. That's just as good. So you ought to have come." She asked him no other question than this; she began to prattle about her own affairs. "We've got splendid rooms at the hotel; Eugenio says they're the best rooms in Rome. We are going to stay all winter, if we don't die of the fever; and I guess we'll stay then. It's a great deal nicer than I thought; I thought it would be fearfully quiet; I was sure it would be awfully poky. I was sure we should be going round all the time with one of those dreadful old men that explain about the pictures and things. But we only had about a week of that, and now I'm enjoying myself. I know ever so many people, and they are all so charming. The society's extremely select. There are all kinds— English, and Germans, and Italians. I think I like the English best. I like their style of conversation. But there are some lovely Americans. I never saw anything so hospitable. There's something or other every day. There's not much dancing; but I must say I never thought dancing was everything. I was always fond of conversation. I guess I shall have plenty at Mrs. Walker's, her rooms are so small." When they had passed the gate of the Pincian Gardens, Miss Miller began to wonder where Mr. Giovanelli might be. "We had better go straight to that place in front," she said, "where you look at the view."

"I certainly shall not help you to find him," Winterbourne declared.

"Then I shall find him without you," said Miss Daisy.

"You certainly won't leave me!" cried Winterbourne.

She burst into her little laugh. "Are you afraid you'll get lost—or run over? But there's Giovanelli, leaning against that tree. He's staring at the women in the carriages: did you ever see anything so cool?"

Winterbourne perceived at some distance a little man standing with folded arms nursing his cane. He had a handsome face, an artfully poised hat, a glass in one eye, and a nosegay in his button-hole. Winterbourne looked at him a moment, and then said, "Do you mean to speak to that man?"

"Do I mean to speak to him? Why, you don't suppose I mean to communicate by signs?"

"Pray understand, then," said Winterbourne, "that I intend to remain with you."

Daisy stopped and looked at him, without a sign of troubled consciousness in her face; with nothing but the presence of her charming eyes and her happy dimples. "Well, she's a cool one!" thought the young man.

"I don't like the way you say that," said Daisy. "It's too imperious."

"I beg your pardon if I say it wrong. The main point is to give you an idea of my meaning."

The young girl looked at him more gravely, but with eyes that were prettier than ever. "I have never allowed a gentleman to dictate to me, or to interfere with anything I do."

"I think you have made a mistake," said Winterbourne. "You should sometimes listen to a gentleman—the right one."

Daisy began to laugh again. "I do nothing but listen to gentlemen!" she exclaimed. "Tell me if Mr. Giovanelli is the right one?"

The gentleman with the nosegay in his bosom had now perceived our two friends, and was approaching the young girl with obsequious rapidity. He bowed to Winterbourne as well as to the latter's companion; he had a brilliant smile, an intelligent eye; Winterbourne thought him not a bad-looking fellow. But he nevertheless said to Daisy, "No, he's not the right one."

Daisy evidently had a natural talent for performing introductions; she mentioned the name of each of her companions to the other. She strolled along with one of them on each side of her; Mr. Giovanelli, who spoke English very cleverly—Winterbourne afterward learned that he had practised the idiom upon a great many American heiresses—addressed her a great deal of very polite nonsense; he was extremely urbane, and the young American, who said nothing, reflected upon that profundity of Italian cleverness which enables people to appear more gracious in proportion as they are more acutely disappointed. Giovanelli, of course, had counted upon something more intimate; he had not bargained for a party of three. But he kept his temper in a manner which suggested far-stretching intentions. Winterbourne flattered himself that he had taken his measure. "He is not a gentleman," said the young American; "he is only a clever imitation of one. He is a music-master, or a penny-a-liner, or a third-rate artist. D——n his good looks!" Mr. Giovanelli had certainly a very pretty face; but Winterbourne felt a superior indignation at his own lovely fellow-countrywoman's not knowing the difference between a spurious gentleman and a real one.

Giovanelli chattered and jested, and made himself wonderfully agreeable. It was true that, if he was an imitation, the imitation was brilliant. "Nevertheless," Winterbourne said to himself, "a nice girl ought to know!" And then he came back to the question whether this was, in fact, a nice girl. Would a nice girl, even allowing for her being a little American flirt, make a rendezvous with a presumably low-lived foreigner? The rendezvous in this case, indeed, had been in broad daylight, and in the most crowded corner of Rome; but was it not impossible to regard the choice of these circumstances as a proof of extreme cynicism? Singular though it may seem, Winterbourne was vexed that the young girl, in joining her *amoroso*, should not appear more impatient of his own company, and he was vexed because of his inclination. It was impossible to regard her as a perfectly well-conducted young lady; she was wanting in a certain indispensable delicacy. It would therefore simplify matters greatly to be able to treat her as the object of one of those sentiments which are called by romancers "lawless passions." That she should seem to wish to get rid of him would help him to think more lightly of her, and to be able to think more lightly of her would make her much less perplexing. But Daisy, on this occasion, continued to present herself as an inscrutable combination of audacity and innocence.

She had been walking some quarter of an hour, attended by her two cavaliers, and responding in a tone of very childish gayety, as it seemed to Winterbourne, to the pretty speeches of Mr. Giovanelli, when a carriage that had detached itself from the revolving train drew up beside the path. At the same moment Winterbourne perceived that his friend Mrs. Walker—the lady whose house he had lately left—was seated in the vehicle, and was beckoning to him. Leaving Miss Miller's side, he hastened to obey her summons. Mrs. Walker was flushed; she wore an excited air. "It is really too dreadful," she said. "That girl must not do this sort of thing. She must not walk here with you two men. Fifty people have noticed her."

Winterbourne raised his eyebrows. "I think it's a pity to make too much fuss about it."

"It's a pity to let the girl ruin herself!"

"She is very innocent," said Winterbourne.

"She's very crazy!" cried Mrs. Walker. "Did you ever see anything so imbecile as her mother? After you had all left me just now, I could not sit still for thinking of it. It seemed too pitiful, not even to attempt to save her. I ordered the carriage and put on my bonnet, and came here as quickly as possible. Thank Heaven I have found you!"

"What do you propose to do with us?" asked Winterbourne, smiling.

"To ask her to get in, to drive her about here for half an hour, so that the world may see she is not running absolutely wild, and then to take her safely home."

"I don't think it's a very happy thought," said Winterbourne; "but you can try."

Mrs. Walker tried. The young man went in pursuit of Miss Miller, who had simply nodded and smiled at his interlocutor in the carriage, and had gone her way with her companion. Daisy, on learning that Mrs. Walker wished to speak to her, retraced her steps with a perfect good grace and with Mr. Giovanelli at her side. She declared that she was delighted to have a chance to present this gentleman to Mrs. Walker. She immediately achieved the introduction, and declared that she had never in her life seen anything so lovely as Mrs. Walker's carriage-rug.

"I am glad you admire it," said this lady, smiling sweetly. "Will you get in and let me put it over you?"

"Oh, no, thank you," said Daisy. "I shall admire it much more as I see you driving round with it."

"Do get in and drive with me!" said Mrs. Walker.

"That would be charming, but it's so enchanting just as I am!" and Daisy gave a brilliant glance at the gentlemen on either side of her.

"It may be enchanting, dear child, but it is not the custom here," urged Mrs. Walker, leaning forward in her victoria, with her hands devoutly clasped.

"Well, it ought to be, then!" said Daisy. "If I didn't walk I should expire."

"You should walk with your mother, dear," cried the lady from Geneva, losing patience.

"With my mother dear!" exclaimed the young girl. Winterbourne saw that she scented interference. "My mother never walked ten steps in her life. And then, you know," she added, with a laugh, "I am more than five years old."

"You are old enough to be more reasonable. You are old enough, dear Miss Miller, to be talked about."

Daisy looked at Mrs. Walker, smiling intensely. "Talked about? What do you mean?"

"Come into my carriage, and I will tell you."

Daisy turned her quickened glance again from one of the gentlemen beside her to the other. Mr. Giovanelli was bowing to and fro, rubbing down his gloves and laughing very agreeably; Winterbourne thought it a most unpleasant scene. "I don't think I want to know what you mean," said Daisy, presently. "I don't think I should like it."

Winterbourne wished that Mrs. Walker would tuck in her carriage-rug and drive away; but this lady did not enjoy being defied, as she afterward told him. "Should you prefer being thought a very reckless girl?" she demanded.

"Gracious!" exclaimed Daisy. She looked again at Mr. Giovanelli, then she turned to Winterbourne. There was a little pink flush in her cheek; she was tremendously pretty. "Does Mr. Winterbourne think," she asked, slowly, smiling, throwing back her head and glancing at him from head to foot, "that, to save my reputation, I ought to get into the carriage?"

Winterbourne colored; for an instant he hesitated greatly. It seemed to strange to hear her speak that way of her "reputation." But he himself, in fact, must speak in accordance with gallantry. The finest gallantry, here, was simply to tell her the truth; and the truth, for Winterbourne, as the few indications I have been able to give have made him known to the reader, was that Daisy Miller should take Mrs. Walker's advice. He looked at her exquisite prettiness, and then he said, very gently, "I think you should get into the carriage."

Daisy gave a violent laugh. "I never heard anything so stiff! If this is improper, Mrs. Walker," she pursued, "then I am all improper, and you must give me up. "Good-bye; I hope you'll have a lovely ride!" and, with Mr. Giovanelli, who made a triumphantly obsequious salute, she turned away.

Mrs. Walker sat looking after her, and there were tears in Mrs. Walker's eyes. "Get in here, sir," she said to Winterbourne, indicating the place beside her. The young man answered that he felt bound to accompany Miss Miller; whereupon Mrs. Walker declared that if he refused her this favor she would never speak to him again. She was evidently in earnest. Winterbourne overtook Daisy and her companion, and, offering the young girl his hand, told her that Mrs. Walker had made an imperious claim upon his society. He expected that in answer she would say something rather free, something to commit herself still further to that "recklessness" from which Mrs. Walker had so charitably endeavored to dissuade her. But she only shook his hand, hardly looking at him; while Mr. Giovanelli bade him farewell with a too emphatic flourish of the hat.

Winterbourne was not in the best possible humor as he took his seat in Mrs. Walker's victoria. "That was not clever of you," he said, candidly, while the vehicle mingled again with the throng of carriages.

"In such a case," his companion answered, "I don't wish to be clever; I wish to be *earnest*!"

"Well, your earnestness has only offended her and put her off."

"It has happened very well," said Mrs. Walker. "If she is so perfectly determined to compromise herself, the sooner one knows it the better; one can act accordingly."

"I suspect she meant no harm," Winterbourne rejoined.

"So I thought a month ago. But she has been going too far."

"What has she been doing?"

"Everything that is not done here. Flirting with any man she could pick up; sitting in corners with mysterious Italians; dancing all the evening with the same partners; receiving visits at eleven o'clock at night. Her mother goes away when visitors come."

"But her brother," said Winterbourne, laughing, "sits up till midnight."

"He must be edified by what he sees. I'm told that at their hotel every one is talking about her, and that a smile goes round among all the servants when a gentleman comes and asks for Miss Miller."

"The servants be hanged!" said Winterbourne angrily. "The poor girl's only fault," he presently added, "is that she is very uncultivated."

"She is naturally indelicate," Mrs. Walker declared. "Take that example this morning. How long had you known her at Vevay?"

"A couple of days."

"Fancy, then, her making it a personal matter that you should have left the place!"

Winterbourne was silent for some moments, then he said, "I suspect, Mrs. Walker, that you and I have lived too long at Geneva!" And he added a request that she should inform him with what particular design she had made him enter her carriage.

"I wished to beg you to cease your relations with Miss Miller—not to flirt with her—to give her no further opportunity to expose herself— to let her alone, in short."

"I'm afraid I can't do that," said Winterbourne. "I like her extremely."

"All the more reason that you shouldn't help her to make a scandal."

"There shall be nothing scandalous in my attentions to her."

"There certainly will be in the way she takes them. But I have said what I had on my conscience," Mrs. Walker pursued. "If you wish to rejoin the young lady I will put you down. Here, by-the-way, you have a chance."

The carriage was traversing that part of the Pincian Garden that overhangs the wall of Rome and overlooks the beautiful Villa Borghese. It is bordered by a large parapet, near which there are several seats. One of the seats at a distance was occupied by a gentleman and a lady, toward whom Mrs. Walker gave a toss of her head. At the same moment these persons rose and walked toward the parapet. Winterbourne had asked the coachman to stop; he now descended from the carriage. His companion looked at him a moment in silence; then, while he raised his hat, she drove majestically away. Winterbourne stood there; he had turned his eyes toward Daisy and her cavalier. They evidently saw no one; they were too deeply occupied with each other. When they reached the low garden-wall, they stood a moment looking off at the great flat-topped pine-clusters of the Villa Borghese; then Giovanelli seated himself, familiarly, upon the broad ledge of the wall. The western sun in the opposite sky sent out a brilliant shaft through a couple of cloud-bars, whereupon Daisy's companion took her parasol out of her hands and opened it. She came a little nearer, and he held the parasol over her; then, still holding it, he let it rest upon her shoulder, so that both of their heads were hidden from Winterbourne. This young man lingered a moment, then he began to walk. But he walked—not toward the couple with the parasol; toward the residence of his aunt, Mrs. Costello.

He flattered himself on the following day that there was no smiling among the servants when he, at least, asked for Mrs. Miller at her hotel. This lady and her daughter, however, were not at home; and on the next day after, repeating his visit, Winterbourne again had the misfortune not to find them. Mrs. Walker's party took place on the evening of the third day, and, in spite of the frigidity of his last interview with the hostess, Winterbourne was among the guests. Mrs. Walker was one of those American ladies, who, while residing abroad, make a point, in their own phrase, of studying European society; and she had on this occasion collected several specimens of her diversely-born fellow-mortals to serve, as it were, as text-books. When Winterbourne arrived, Daisy Miller was not there, but in a few moments he saw her mother come in alone, very shyly and ruefully. Mrs. Miller's hair above her exposed-looking temples was more frizzled than ever. As she approached Mrs. Walker, Winterbourne also drew near.

"You see, I've come all alone," said poor Mrs. Miller. "I'm so frightened; I don't know what to do. It's the first time I've ever been to a party alone, especially in this country. I wanted to bring Randolph or Eugenio, or some one, but Daisy just pushed me off by myself. I ain't used to going round alone."

"And does not your daughter intend to favor us with her society?" demanded Mrs. Walker, impressively.

"Well, Daisy's all dressed," said Mrs. Miller, with that accent of the dispassionate, if not of the philosophic, historian with which she always recorded the current incidents of her daughter's career. "She got dressed on purpose before dinner. But she's got a friend of hers there; that gentleman—the Italian—that she wanted to bring. They've got going at the piano; it seems as if they couldn't leave off. Mr. Giovanelli sings splendidly. But I guess they'll come before very long," concluded Mrs. Miller, hopefully.

"I'm sorry she should come in that way," said Mrs. Walker.

"Well, I told her that there was no use in her getting dressed before dinner if she was going to wait three hours," responded Daisy's mamma. "I didn't see the use of her putting on such a dress as that to sit round with Mr. Giovanelli."

"This is most horrible!" said Mrs. Walker, turning away and addressing herself to Winterbourne. *"Elle s'affiche.* It's her revenge for my having ventured to remonstrate with her. When she comes, I shall not speak to her."

Daisy came after eleven o'clock; but she was not, on such an occasion, a young lady to wait to be spoken to. She rustled forward in radiant loveliness, smiling and chattering, carrying a large bouquet, and attended by Mr. Giovanelli. Every one stopped talking, and turned and looked at her. She came straight to Mrs. Walker. "I'm afraid you thought I never was coming, so I sent mother off to tell you. I wanted to make Mr. Giovanelli practise some things before he came; you know he sings beautifully, and I want you to ask him to sing. This is Mr. Giovanelli; you know I introduced him to you; he's got the most lovely voice, and he knows the most charming set of songs. I made him go over them this evening on purpose; we had the greatest time at the hotel." Of all this Daisy delivered herself with the sweetest, brightest audibleness, looking now at her hostess and now round the room, while she gave a series of little pats, round her shoulders, to the edges of her dress. "Is there any one I know?" she asked.

"I think every one knows you!" said Mrs. Walker, pregnantly, and she gave a very cursory greeting to Mr. Giovanelli. This gentleman bore himself gallantly. He smiled and bowed, and showed his white teeth; he curled his mustaches and rolled his eyes, and performed all the proper functions of a handsome Italian at an evening party. He sang very prettily half a dozen songs, though Mrs. Walker afterward declared that she had been quite unable to find out who asked him. It was apparently not Daisy who had given him his orders. Daisy sat at a distance from the piano; and though she had publicly, as it were, professed a high admiration for his singing, talked, not inaudibly, while it was going on.

"It's a pity these rooms are so small; we can't dance," she said to Winterbourne, as if she had seen him five minutes before.

"I am not sorry we can't dance," Winterbourne answered; "I don't dance."

"Of course you don't dance; you're too stiff," said Miss Daisy. "I hope you enjoyed your drive with Mrs. Walker!"

"No, I didn't enjoy it; I preferred walking with you."

"We paired off: that was much better," said Daisy. "But did you ever hear anything so cool as Mrs. Walker's wanting me to get into her carriage and drop poor Mr. Giovanelli, and under the pretext that it was proper? People have different ideas! It would have been most unkind; he had been talking about that walk for ten days."

"He should not have talked about it at all," said Winterbourne; "he would never have proposed to a young lady of this country to walk about the streets with him."

"About the streets?" cried Daisy, with her pretty stare. "Where, then, would he have proposed to her to walk? The Pincio is not the streets, either; and I, thank goodness, am not a young lady of this country. The young ladies of this country have a dreadfully poky time of it, so far as I can learn; I don't see why I should change my habits for *them*."

"I am afraid your habits are those of a flirt," said Winterbourne, gravely.

"Of course they are," she cried, giving him her little smiling stare again. "I'm a fearful, frightful flirt! Did you ever hear of a nice girl that was not? But I suppose you will tell me now that I am not a nice girl."

"You're a very nice girl; but I wish you would flirt with me, and me only," said Winterbourne.

"Ah! thank you—thank you very much; you are the last man I should think of flirting with. As I have had the pleasure of informing you, you are too stiff."

"You say that too often," said Winterbourne.

Daisy gave a delighted laugh. "If I could have the sweet hope of making you angry, I should say it again."

"Don't do that; when I am angry I'm stiffer than ever. But if you won't flirt with me, do cease, at least, to flirt with your friend at the piano; they don't understand that sort of thing here."

"I thought they understood nothing else!" exclaimed Daisy.

"Not in young unmarried women."

"It seems to me much more proper in young unmarried women than in old married ones," Daisy declared.

"Well," said Winterbourne, "when you deal with natives you must go by the custom of the place. Flirting is a purely American custom; it doesn't exist here. So when you show yourself in public with Mr. Giovanelli, and without your mother—"

"Gracious! poor mother!" interposed Daisy.

"Though you may be flirting, Mr. Giovanelli is not; he means something else."

"He isn't preaching, at any rate," said Daisy, with vivacity. "And if you want very much to know, we are neither of us flirting; we are too good friends for that: we are very intimate friends."

"Ah!" rejoined Winterbourne, "if you are in love with each other, it is another affair."

She had allowed him up to this point to talk so frankly that he had no expectation of shocking her by this ejaculation; but she immediately got up, blushing visibly, and leaving him to exclaim mentally that little American flirts were the queerest creatures in the world. "Mr. Giovanelli, at least," she said, giving her interlocutor a single glance, "never says such very disagreeable things to me."

Winterbourne was bewildered; he stood staring. Mr. Giovanelli had finished singing. He left the piano and came over to Daisy. "Won't you come into the other room and have some tea?" he asked, bending before her with his ornamental smile.

Daisy turned to Winterbourne, beginning to smile again. He was still more perplexed, for this inconsequent smile made nothing clear, though it seemed to prove, indeed, that she had a sweetness and softness that reverted instinctively to the pardon of offences. "It has never occured to Mr. Winterbourne to offer me any tea," she said, with her little tormenting manner.

"I have offered you advice," Winterbourne rejoined.

"I prefer weak tea!" cried Daisy, and she went off with the brilliant Giovanelli. She sat with him in the adjoining room, in the embrasure of the window, for the rest of the evening. There was an interesting performance at the piano, but neither of these young people gave heed to it. When Daisy came to take leave of Mrs. Walker, this lady conscientiously repaired the weakness of which she had been guilty at the moment of the young girl's arrival. She turned her back straight upon Miss Miller, and left her to depart with what grace she might. Winterbourne was standing near the door; he saw it all. Daisy turned very pale, and looked at her mother; but Mrs. Miller was humbly unconscious of any violation of the usual social forms. She appeared, indeed, to have felt an incongruous impulse to draw attention to her own striking observance of them. "Good-night, Mrs. Walker," she said; "we've had a beautiful evening. You see, if I let Daisy come to parties without me, I don't want her to go away without me." Daisy turned away, looking with a pale, grave face at the circle near the door; Winterbourne saw that, for the first moment, she was too much shocked and puzzled even for indignation. He on his side was greatly touched.

"That was very cruel," he said to Mrs. Walker.

"She never enters my drawing room again!" replied his hostess.

Since Winterbourne was not to meet her in Mrs. Walker's drawing-room, he went as often as possible to Mrs. Miller's hotel. The ladies were rarely at home; but when he found them, the devoted Giovanelli was always present. Very often the brilliant little Roman was in the drawing-room with Daisy alone, Mrs. Miller being apparently constantly of the opinion that discretion is the better part of surveillance. Winterbourne noted, at first with surprise, that Daisy on these occasions

was never embarrassed or annoyed by his own entrance; but he very
presently began to feel that she had no more surprises for him; the
unexpected in her behavior was the only thing to expect. She showed
no displeasure at her *tete-a-tete* with Giovanelli being interrupted; she
could chatter as freshly and freely with two gentlemen as with one;
there was always, in her conversation, the same odd mixture of audacity
and puerility. Winterbourne remarked to himself that if she was seriously interested in Giovanelli, it was very singular that she should not
take more trouble to preserve the sanctity of their interview; and he
liked her the more for her innocent-looking indifference and her apparently inexhaustible good-humor. He could hardly have said why, but
she seemed to him a girl who would never be jealous. At the risk of
exciting a somewhat derisive smile on the reader's part, I may affirm
that with regard to the women who had hitherto interested him, it very
often seemed to Winterbourne among the possibilities that, given certain contingencies, he should be afraid—literally afraid—of these ladies;
he had a pleasant sense that he should never be afraid of Daisy Miller.
It must be added that this sentiment was not altogether flattering to
Daisy; it was part of his conviction, or rather of his apprehension, that
she would prove a very light young person.

But she was evidently very much interested in Giovanelli. She looked
at him whenever he spoke; she was perpetually telling him to do this
and to do that; she was constantly "chaffing" and abusing him. She
appeared completely to have forgotten that Winterbourne had said
anything to displease her at Mrs. Walker's little party. One Sunday
afternoon, having gone to St. Peter's with his aunt, Winterbourne perceived Daisy strolling about the great church in company with the
inevitable Giovanelli. Presently he pointed out the young girl and her
cavalier to Mrs. Costello. This lady looked at them a moment through
her eye-glass, and then she said:

"That's what makes you so pensive in these days, eh?"

"I had not the least idea I was pensive," said the young man.

"You are very much preoccupied; you are thinking of something."

"And what is it," he asked, "that you accuse me of thinking of?"

"Of that young lady's—Miss Baker's, Miss Chandler's—what's her
name?—Miss Miller's intrigue with that little barber's block."

"Do you call it an intrigue," Winterbourne asked—"an affair that
goes on with such peculiar publicity?"

"That's their folly," said Mrs. Costello; "it's not their merit."

"No," rejoined Winterbourne, with something of that pensiveness to which his aunt had alluded. "I don't believe that there is anything to be called an intrigue."

"I have heard a dozen people speak of it; they say she is quite carried away by him."

"They are certainly very intimate," said Winterbourne.

Mrs. Costello inspected the young couple again with her optical instrument. "He is very handsome. One easily sees how it is. She thinks him the most elegant man in the world, the finest gentleman. She has never seen anything like him; he is better, even, than the courier. It was the courier probably who introduced him; and if he succeeds in marrying the young lady, the courier will come in for a magnificent commission."

"I don't believe she thinks of marrying him," said Winterbourne, "and I don't believe he hopes to marry her."

"You may be very sure she thinks of nothing. She goes on from day to day, from hour to hour, as they did in the Golden Age. I can imagine nothing more vulgar. And at the same time," added Mrs. Costello, "depend upon it that she may tell you any moment that she is 'engaged.'"

"I think that is more than Giovanelli expects," said Winterbourne.

"Who is Giovanelli?"

"The little Italian. I have asked questions about him, and learned something. He is apparently a perfectly respectable little man. I believe he is, in a small way, a *cavaliere avvocato*. But he doesn't move in what are called the first circles. I think it is really not absolutely impossible that the courier introduced him. He is evidently immensely charmed with Miss Miller. If she thinks him the finest gentleman in the world, he, on his side, has never found himself in personal contact with such splendor, such opulence, such expensiveness, as this young lady's. And then she must seem to him wonderfully pretty and interesting. I rather doubt that he dreams of marrying her. That must appear to him too impossible a piece of luck. He has nothing but his handsome face to offer, and there is a substantial Mr. Miller in that mysterious land of dollars. Giovanelli knows that he hasn't a title to offer. If he were only a count or a *marchese!* He must wonder at his luck, at the way they have taken him up."

"He accounts for it by his handsome face, and thinks Miss Miller a young lady *qui se passe ses fantaisies!*" said Mrs. Costello.

"It is very true," Winterbourne pursued, "that Daisy and her mamma have not yet risen to that stage of—what shall I call it? —of culture at which the idea of catching a count or a *marchese* begins. I believe that they are intellectually incapable of that conception."

"Ah! but the *avvocato* can't believe it," said Mrs. Costello.

Of the observation excited by Daisy's "intrigue," Winterbourne gathered that day at St. Peter's sufficient evidence. A dozen of the American colonists in Rome came to talk with Mrs. Costello, who sat on a little portable stool at the base of one of the great pilasters. The vesper service was going forward in splendid chants and organ-tones in the adjacent choir, and meanwhile, between Mrs. Costello and her friends, there was a great deal said about poor little Miss Miller's going really "too far." Winterbourne was not pleased with what he heard; but when, coming out upon the great steps of the church, he saw Daisy, who had emerged before him, get into an open cab with her accomplice and roll away through the cynical streets of Rome, he could not deny to himself that she was going very far indeed. He felt very sorry for her—not exactly that he believed that she had completely lost her head, but because it was painful to hear so much that was pretty, and un-defended, and natural, assigned to a vulgar place among the categories of disorder. He made an attempt after this to give a hint to Mrs. Miller. He met one day in the Corso a friend, a tourist like himself, who had just come out of the Doria Palace, where he had been walking through the beautiful gallery. His friend talked for a moment about the superb portrait of Innocent X by Velasquez which hangs in one of the cabinets of the palace, and then said, "And in the same cabinet, by-the-way, I had the pleasure of contemplating a picture of a different kind—that pretty American girl whom you pointed out to me last week." In answer to Winterbourne's inquiries, his friend narrated that the pretty American girl—prettier than ever—was seated with a companion in the secluded nook in which the great papal portrait was enshrined.

"Who was her companion?" asked Winterbourne.

"A little Italian with a bouquet in his button-hole. The girl is delightfully pretty, but I thought I understood from you the other day that she was a young lady *du meilleur monde.*"

"So she is!" answered Winterbourne; and having assured himself that his informant had seen Daisy and her companion but five minutes before, he jumped into a cab and went to call on Mrs. Miller. She was at home; but she apologized to him for receiving him in Daisy's absence.

"She's gone out somewhere with Mr. Giovanelli," said Mrs. Miller. "She's always going round with Mr. Giovanelli."

"I have noticed that they are very intimate," Winterbourne observed.

"Oh, it seems as if they couldn't live without each other!" said Mrs. Miller. "Well, he's a real gentleman, anyhow. I keep telling Daisy she's engaged!"

"And what does Daisy say?"

"Oh, she says she isn't engaged. But she might as well be!" this impartial parent resumed; "she goes on as if she was. But I've made Mr. Giovanelli promise to tell me, if *she* doesn't. I should want to write to Mr. Miller about it—shouldn't you?"

Winterbourne replied that he certainly should; and the state of mind of Daisy's mamma struck him as so unprecedented in the annals of parental vigilance that he gave up as utterly irrelevant the attempt to place her upon her guard.

After this Daisy was never at home, and Winterbourne ceased to meet her at the houses of their common acquaintance, because, as he perceived, these shrewd people had quite made up their minds that she was going too far. They ceased to invite her; and they intimated that they desired to express to observant Europeans the great truth that, though Miss Daisy Miller was a young American lady, her behavior was not representative—was regarded by her compatriots as abnormal. Winterbourne wondered how she felt about all the cold shoulders that were turned toward her and sometimes it annoyed him to suspect that she did not feel at all. He said to himself that she was too light and childish, too uncultivated and unreasoning, too provincial, to have reflected upon her ostracism, or even to have perceived it. Then at other moments he believed that she carried about in her elegant and irresponsible little organism, a defiant, passionate, perfectly observant consciousness of the impression she produced. He asked himself whether Daisy's defiance came from the consciousness of innocence, or from her being, essentially, a young person of the reckless class. It must be admitted that holding one's self to a belief in Daisy's "innocence" came to seem to Winterbourne more and more a matter of fine-spun gallantry.

As I have already had occasion to relate, he was angry at finding himself reduced to chopping logic about this young lady; he was vexed at his want of instinctive certitude as to how far her eccentricities were generic, national, and how far they were personal. From either view of them he had somehow missed her, and now it was too late. She was "carried away" by Mr. Giovanelli.

A few days after his brief interview with her mother, he encountered her in that beautiful abode of flowering desolation known as the Palace of the Caesars. The early Roman spring had filled the air with bloom and perfume, and the rugged surface of the Palatine was muffled with tender verdure. Daisy was strolling along the top of one of those great mounds of ruin that are embanked with mossy marble and paved with monumental inscriptions. It seemed to him that Rome had never been so lovely as just then. He stood looking off at the enchanting harmony of line and colour that remotely encircles the city, inhaling the softly humid odours and feeling the freshness of the year and the antiquity of the place reaffirm themselves in mysterious interfusion. It seemed to him also that Daisy had never looked so pretty; but this had been an observation of his whenever he met her. Giovanelli was at her side, and Giovanelli, too, wore an aspect of even unwonted brilliancy.

"Well," said Daisy, "I should think you would be lonesome!"

"Lonesome?" asked Winterbourne.

"You are always going round by yourself. Can't you get anyone to walk with you?"

"I am not so fortunate," said Winterbourne, "as your companion."

Giovanelli, from the first, had treated Winterbourne with distin-guishedpoliteness; he listened with a deferential air to his remarks; he laughed, punctiliously, at his pleasantries; he seemed disposed to testify to his belief that Winterbourne was a superior young man. He carried himself in no degree like a jealous wooer; he had obviously a great deal of tact; he had no objection to your expecting a little humility of him. It even seemed to Winterbourne at times that Giovanelli would find a certain mental relief in being able to have a private understanding with him—to say to him, as an intelligent man, that, bless you, *he* knew how extraordinary was this young lady, and didn't flatter himself with delusive—or at least *too* delusive—hopes of matrimony and dollars. On this occasion he strolled away from his companion to pluck a sprig of almond-blossom, which he carefully arranged in his button-hole.

"I know why you say that," said Daisy, watching Giovanelli. "Because you think I go round too much with *him!*" And she nodded at her attendant.

"Every one thinks so—if you care to know," said Winterbourne.

"Of course I care to know!" Daisy exclaimed seriously. "But I don't believe it. They are only pretending to be shocked. They don't really care a straw what I do. Besides, I don't go round so much."

"I think you will find they do care. They will show it—disagreeably."

Daisy looked at him a moment. "How—disagreeably?"

"Haven't you noticed anything?" Winterbourne asked.

"I have noticed you. But I noticed you were as stiff as an umbrella the first time I saw you."

"You will find I am not so stiff as several others," said Winterbourne, smiling.

"How shall I find it?"

"By going to see the others."

"What will they do to me?"

"They will give you the cold shoulder. Do you know what that means?"

Daisy was looking at him intently; she began to colour. "Do you mean as Mrs. Walker did the other night?"

"Exactly!" said Winterbourne.

She looked away at Giovanelli, who was decorating himself with his almond-blossom. Then looking back at Winterbourne—"I shouldn't think you would let people be so unkind!" she said.

"How can I help it?" he asked.

"I should think you would say something."

"I do say something;" and he paused a moment. "I say that your mother tells me that she believes you are engaged."

"Well, she does," said Daisy very simply.

Winterbourne began to laugh. "And does Randolph believe it?" he asked.

"I guess Randolph doesn't believe anything," said Daisy. Randolph's scepticism excited Winterbourne to further hilarity, and he observed that Giovanelli was coming back to them. Daisy, observing it too, addressed herself again to her countryman. "Since you have mentioned it," she said. "I *am* engaged." ... Winterbourne looked at her; he had stopped laughing. "You don't believe it!" she added.

He was silent a moment; and then, "Yes, I believe it!" he said.

"Oh, no, you don't," she answered. "Well, then—I am not!"

The young girl and her cicerone were on their way to the gate of the enclosure, so that Winterbourne, who had but lately entered, presently took leave of them. A week afterward he went to dine at a beautiful villa on the Caelian Hill, and, on arriving, dismissed his hired vehicle. The evening was charming, and he promised himself the satisfaction of walking home beneath the Arch of Constantine and past the vaguely-lighted monuments of the Forum. There was a waning moon in the sky, and her radiance was not brilliant, but she was veiled in a thin cloud-curtain which seemed to diffuse and equalize it. When, on his return from the villa (it was eleven o'clock), Winterbourne approached the dusky circle of the Colosseum, it recurred to him, as a lover of the picturesque, that the interior, in the pale moonshine, would be well worth a glance. He turned aside and walked to one of the empty arches, near which, as he observed, an open carriage—one of the little Roman street-cabs—was stationed. Then he passed in, among the cavernous shadows of the great structure, and emerged upon the clear and silent arena. The place had never seemed to him more impressive. One-half of the gigantic circus was in deep shade, the other was sleeping in the luminous dusk. As he stood there he began to murmur Byron's famous lines, out of "Manfred;" but before he had finished his quotation he remembered that if nocturnal meditations in the Colosseum are recommended by the poets, they are deprecated by the doctors. The historic atmosphere was there, certainly; but the historic atmosphere, scientifically considered, was no better than a villainous miasma. Winterbourne walked to the middle of the arena, to take a more general glance, intending thereafter to make a hasty retreat. The great cross in the centre was covered with shadow; it was only as he drew near it that he made it out distinctly. Then he saw that two persons were stationed upon the low steps which formed its base. One of these was a woman, seated; her companion was standing in front of her.

Presently the sound of the woman's voice came to him distinctly in the warm night air. "Well, he looks at us as one of the old lions or tigers may have looked at the Christian martyrs!" These were the words he heard, in the familiar accent of Miss Daisy Miller.

"Let us hope he is not very hungry," responded the ingenious Giovanelli. "He will have to take me first; you will serve for dessert!"

Winterbourne stopped, with a sort of horror, and, it must be added, with a sort of relief. It was as if a sudden illumination had been flashed upon the ambiguity of Daisy's behavior, and the riddle had become easy to read. She was a young lady whom a gentleman need no longer be at pains to respect. He stood looking at her—looking at her companion, and not reflecting that though he saw them vaguely, he himself must have been more brightly visible. He felt angry with himself that he had bothered so much about the right ways of regarding Miss Daisy Miller. Then, as he was going to advance again, he checked himself; not from the fear that he was doing her injustice, but from a sense of the danger of appearing unbecomingly exhilarated by this sudden revulsion from cautious criticism. He turned away toward the entrance of the place, but, as he did so, he heard Daisy speak again.

"Why, it was Mr. Winterbourne! He saw me, and he cuts me!"

What a clever little reprobate she was, and how smartly she played at injured innocence! But he wouldn't cut her. Winterbourne came forward again, and went toward the great cross. Daisy had got up; Giovanelli lifted his hat. Winterbourne had now begun to think simply of the craziness, from a sanitary point of view, of a delicate young girl lounging away the evening in this nest of malaria. What if she *were* a clever little reprobate? that was no reason for her dying of the *perniciosa*. "How long have you been here?" he asked, almost brutally.

Daisy, lovely in the flattering moonlight, looked at him a moment. Then—"All the evening," she answered, gently. * * * "I never saw anything so pretty."

"I am afraid," said Winterbourne, "that you will not think Roman fever very pretty. This is the way people catch it. I wonder," he added, turning to Giovanelli, "that you, a native Roman, should countenance such a terrible indiscretion."

"Ah," said the handsome native, "for myself I am not afraid."

"Neither am I—for you! I am speaking for this young lady."

Giovanelli lifted his well-shaped eyebrows and showed his brilliant teeth. But he took Winterbourne's rebuke with docility. "I told the Signorina it was a grave indiscretion; but when was the Signorina ever prudent?"

"I never was sick, and I don't mean to be!" the Signorina declared. "I don't look like much, but I'm healthy! I was bound to see the Colosseum by moonlight; I shouldn't have wanted to go home without

that; and we have had the most beautiful time, haven't we, Mr. Giovanelli? If there has been any danger, Eugenio can give me some pills.
He has got some splendid pills."

"I should advise you," said Winterbourne, "to drive home as fast
as possible and take one!"

"What you say is very wise," Giovanelli rejoined. "I will go and
make sure the carriage is at hand." And he went forward rapidly.

Daisy followed with Winterbourne. He kept looking at her; she
seemed not in the least embarrassed. Winterbourne said nothing; Daisy
chattered about the beauty of the place. "Well, I *have* seen the Colosseum by moonlight!" she exclaimed. "That's one good thing." Then,
noticing Winterbourne's silence, she asked him why he didn't speak.
He made no answer; he only began to laugh. They passed under one
of the dark archways; Giovanelli was in front with the carriage. Here
Daisy stopped a moment, looking at the young American. "*Did* you
believe I was engaged, the other day?" she asked.

"It doesn't matter what I believed the other day," said Winterbourne,
still laughing.

"Well, what do you believe now?"

"I believe that it makes very little difference whether you are engaged
or not!"

He felt the young girl's pretty eyes fixed upon him through the
thick gloom of the archway; she was apparently going to answer. But
Giovanelli hurried her forward. "Quick! quick!" he said; "if we get in
by midnight we are quite safe."

Daisy took her seat in the carriage, and the fortunate Italian placed
himself beside her. "Don't forget Eugenio's pills!" said Winterbourne,
as he lifted his hat.

"I don't care," said Daisy, in a little strange tone, "whether I have
Roman fever or not!" Upon this the cab-driver cracked his whip, and
they rolled away over the desultory patches of the antique pavement.

Winterbourne, to do him justice, as it were, mentioned to no one
that he had encountered Miss Miller, at midnight, in the Colosseum
with a gentleman; but nevertheless, a couple of days later, the fact of
her having been there under these circumstances was known to every
 member of the little American circle, and commented accordingly.
Winterbourne reflected that they had of course known it at the hotel,
and that, after Daisy's return, there had been an exchange of remarks

between the porter and the cab-driver. But the young man was conscious, at the same moment, that it had ceased to be a matter of serious regret to him that the little American flirt should be "talked about" by low-minded menials. These people, a day or two later, had serious information to give: the little American flirt was alarmingly ill. Winterbourne, when the rumor came to him, immediately went to the hotel for more news. He found that two or three charitable friends had preceded him, and that they were being entertained in Mrs. Miller's salon by Randolph.

"It's going round at night," said Randolph—"that's what made her sick. She's always going round at night. I shouldn't think she'd want to, it's so plaguy dark. You can't see anything here at night, except when there's a moon. In America there's always a moon!" Mrs. Miller was invisible; she was now, at least, giving her daughter the advantage of her society. It was evident that Daisy was dangerously ill.

Winterbourne went often to ask for news of her, and once he saw Mrs. Miller, who, though deeply alarmed, was, rather to his surprise, perfectly composed, and, as it appeared, a most efficient and judicious nurse. She talked a good deal about Dr. Davis, but Winterbourne paid her the compliment of saying to himself that she was not, after all, such a monstrous goose. "Daisy spoke of you the other day," she said to him. "Half the time she doesn't know what she's saying, but that time I think she did. She gave me a message, she told me to tell you. She told me to tell you that she never was engaged to that handsome Italian. I am sure I am very glad; Mr. Giovanelli hasn't been near us since she was taken ill. I thought he was so much of a gentleman; but I don't call that very polite! A lady told me that he was afraid I was angry with him for taking Daisy round at night. Well, so I am; but I suppose he knows I'm a lady. I would scorn to scold him. Anyway, she says she's not engaged. I don't know why she wanted you to know; but she said to me three times, 'Mind you tell Mr. Winterbourne.' And then she told me to ask if you remembered the time you went to that castle in Switzerland. But I said I wouldn't give any such messages as that. Only, if she is not engaged, I'm sure I'm glad to know it."

But, as Winterbourne had said, it mattered very little. A week after this the poor girl died; it had been a terrible case of the fever. Daisy's grave was in the little Protestant cemetery, in an angle of the wall of imperial Rome, beneath the cypresses and the thick spring-flowers.

Winterbourne stood there beside it, with a number of other mourners; a number larger than the scandal excited by the young lady's career would have led you to expect. Near him stood Giovanelli, who came nearer still before Winterbourne turned away. Giovanelli was very pale: on this occasion he had no flower in his button-hole; he seemed to wish to say something. At last he said, "She was the most beautiful young lady I ever saw, and the most amiable;" and then he added in a moment, "and she was the most innocent."

Winterbourne looked at him, and presently repeated his words, "And the most innocent?"

"The most innocent!"

Winterbourne felt sore and angry. "Why the devil," he asked, "did you take her to that fatal place?"

Mr. Giovanelli's urbanity was apparently imperturbable. He looked on the ground a moment, and then he said, "For myself I had no fear; and she wanted to go."

"That was no reason!" Winterbourne declared.

The subtle Roman again dropped his eyes. "If she had lived, I should have got nothing. She would never have married me, I am sure."

"She would never have married you?"

"For a moment I hoped so. But no. I am sure."

Winterbourne listened to him: he stood staring at the raw protuberance among the April daisies. When he turned away again, Mr. Giovanelli, with his light, slow step, had retired.

Winterbourne almost immediately left Rome; but the following summer he again met his aunt, Mrs. Costello, at Vevay. Mrs. Costello was fond of Vevay. In the interval Winterbourne had often thought of Daisy Miller and her mystifying manners. One day he spoke of her to his aunt—said it was on his conscience that he had done her injustice.

"I am sure I don't know," said Mrs. Costello. "How did your injustice affect her?"

"She sent me a message before her death which I didn't understand at the time; but I have understood it since. She would have appreciated one's esteem."

"Is that a modest way," asked Mrs. Costello, "of saying that she would have reciprocated one's affection?"

Winterbourne offered no answer to this question; but he presently said, "You were right in that remark that you made last summer. I was booked to make a mistake. I have lived too long in foreign parts."

Nevertheless, he went back to live at Geneva, whence there continue to come the most contradictory accounts of his motives of sojourn: a report that he is "studying" hard—an intimation that he is much interested in a very clever foreign lady.

THE LIAR

I

The train was half an hour late and the drive from the station longer than he had supposed, so that when he reached the house its inmates had dispersed to dress for dinner and he was conducted straight to his room. The curtains were drawn in this asylum, the candles were lighted, the fire was bright, and when the servant had quickly put out his clothes the comfortable place became suggestive—seemed to promise a pleasant house, a various party, talks, acquaintances, affinities, to say nothing of very good cheer. He was too occupied with his profession to pay many country visits, but he had heard people who had more time for them speak of establishments where "they do you very well." He foresaw that the proprietors of Stayes would do him very well. In his bedroom at a country house he always looked first at the books on the shelf and the prints on the walls; he considered that these things gave a sort of measure of the culture and even of the character of his hosts. Though he had but little time to devote to them on this occasion a cursory inspection assured him that if the literature, as usual, was mainly American and humorous the art consisted neither of the water-colour studies of the children nor of "goody" engravings. The walls were adorned with old-fashioned lithographs, principally portraits of country gentlemen with high collars and riding gloves: this suggested—and it was encouraging—that the tradition of portraiture was held in esteem. There was the customary novel of Mr. Le Fanu, for the bedside; the ideal reading in a country house for the hours after midnight. Oliver Lyon could scarcely forbear beginning it while he buttoned his shirt.

Perhaps that is why he not only found every one assembled in the hall when he went down, but perceived from the way the move to dinner was instantly made that they had been waiting for him. There was no delay, to introduce him to a lady, for he went out in a group of unmatched men, without this appendage. The men, straggling behind, sidled and edged as usual at the door of the dining-room, and the *dénouement* of this little comedy was that he came to his place last of all. This made him think that he was in a sufficiently distinguished company, for if he had been humiliated (which he was not), he could not have consoled himself with the reflection that such a fate was natural to an obscure, struggling young artist. He could no longer think of himself as very young, alas, and if his position was not so brilliant as it ought to be he could no longer justify it by calling it a struggle. He was something of a celebrity and he was apparently in a society of celebrities. This idea added to the curiosity with which he looked up and down the long table as he settled himself in his place.

It was a numerous party—five and twenty people; rather an odd occasion to have proposed to him, as he thought. He would not be surrounded by the quiet that ministers to good work; however, it had never interfered with his work to see the spectacle of human life before him in the intervals. And though he did not know it, it was never quiet at Stayes. When he was working well he found himself in that happy state—the happiest of all for an artist—in which things in general contribute to the particular idea and fall in with it, help it on and justify it, so that he feels for the hour as if nothing in the world can happen to him, even if it come in the guise of disaster or suffering, that will not be an enhancement of his subject. Moreover there was an exhilaration (he had felt it before) in the rapid change of scene—the jump, in the dusk of the afternoon, from foggy London and his familiar studio to a centre of festivity in the middle of Hertfordshire and a drama half acted, a drama of pretty women and noted men and wonderful orchids in silver jars. He observed as a not unimportant fact that one of the pretty women was beside him: a gentleman sat on his other hand. But he went into his neighbours little as yet: he was busy looking out for Sir David, whom he had never seen and about whom he naturally was curious. Evidently, however, Sir David was not at dinner, a circumstance sufficiently explained by the other circumstance which constituted our friend's principal knowledge of him—his being ninety years of age. Oliver Lyon had looked forward with great pleasure to the chance of painting a nonagenarian, and though the old man's absence from table was something of a disappointment (it was an opportunity the less to observe him before going to work), it seemed a sign that he was rather a sacred and perhaps therefore an impressive relic. Lyon looked at his son with the greater interest—wondered whether the glazed bloom of his cheek had been transmitted from Sir David. That would be jolly to paint, in the old man—the withered ruddiness of a winter apple, especially if the eye were still alive and the white hair carried out the frosty look. Arthur Ashmore's hair had a midsummer glow, but Lyon was glad his commission had been to delineate the father rather than the son, in spite of his never having seen the one and of the other being seated there before him now in the happy expansion of liberal hospitality.

Arthur Ashmore was a fresh-coloured, thick-necked English gentleman, but he was just not a subject; he might have been a farmer and he might have been a banker: you could scarcely paint him in characters. His wife did not make up the amount; she was a large, bright, negative woman, who had the same air as her husband of being somehow tremendously new; a sort of appearance of fresh varnish (Lyon could scarcely tell whether it came from her complexion or from her clothes), so that one felt she ought to sit in a gilt frame, suggesting reference to a catalogue or a price-list. It was as if she were already rather a bad though expensive portrait, knocked off by an eminent hand, and Lyon had no wish to copy that work. The pretty woman on his right was engaged with her neighbour and the gentleman on his other side looked shrinking and scared, so that he had time to lose himself in his favourite diversion of watching face after face. This amusement gave him the greatest pleasure he knew, and he often thought it a mercy that the human mask did interest him and that it was not less vivid than it was (sometimes it ran its success in this line very close), since he was to make his living by reproducing it. Even if Arthur Ashmore would not be inspiring to paint (a certain anxiety rose in him lest if he should make a hit with her father-in-law Mrs. Arthur should take it into her head that he had now proved himself worthy to *aborder* her husband); even if he had looked a little less like a page (fine as to print and margin) without punctuation, he would still be a refreshing, iridescent surface. But the gentleman four persons off—what was he? Would he be a subject, or was his face only the legible door-plate of his identity, burnished with punctual washing and shaving—the least thing that was decent that you would know him by?

This face arrested Oliver Lyon: it struck him at first as very handsome. The gentleman might still be called young, and his features were regular: he had a plentiful, fair moustache that curled up at the ends, a brilliant, gallant, almost adventurous air, and a big shining breastpin in the middle of his shirt. He appeared a fine satisfied soul, and Lyon perceived that wherever he rested his friendly eye there fell an influence as pleasant as the September sun—as if he could make grapes and pears or even human affection ripen by looking at them. What was odd in him was a certain mixture of the correct and the extravagant: as if he were an adventurer imitating a gentleman with rare perfection or a gentleman who had taken a fancy to go about with hidden arms. He might have been a dethroned prince or the war-correspondent of a newspaper: he represented both enterprise and tradition, good manners and bad taste. Lyon at length fell into conversation with the lady beside him—they dispensed, as he had had to dispense by dinner-parties before, with an introduction—by asking who this personage might be.

"Oh, he's Colonel Capadose, don't you know?" Lyon didn't know and he asked for further information. His neighbour had a sociable manner and evidently was accustomed to quick transitions; she turned from her other interlocutor with a methodical air, as a good cook lifts the cover of the next saucepan. "He has been a great deal in India— isn't he rather celebrated?" she inquired. Lyon confessed he had never heard of him, and she went on, "Well, perhaps he isn't; but he says he is, and if you think it, that's just the same, isn't it?"

"If *you* think it?"

"I mean if he thinks it—that's just as good, I suppose."

"Do you mean that he says that which is not?"

"Oh dear, no—because I never know. He is exceedingly clever and amusing—quite the cleverest person in the house, unless indeed you are more so. But that I can't tell yet, can I? I only know about the people I know; I think that's celebrity enough!"

"Enough for them?"

"Oh, I see you're clever. Enough for me! But I have heard of you," the lady went on. "I know your pictures; I admire them. But I don't think you look like them."

"They are mostly portraits," Lyon said; "and what I usually try for is not my own resemblance."

"I see what you mean. But they have much more colour. And now you are going to do some one here?"

"I have been invited to do Sir David. I'm rather disappointed at not seeing him this evening."

"Oh, he goes to bed at some unnatural hour—eight o'clock or something of that sort. You know he's rather an old mummy."

"An old mummy?" Oliver Lyon repeated.

"I mean he wears half a dozen waistcoats, and that sort of thing. He's always cold."

"I have never seen him and never seen any portrait or photograph of him," Lyon said. "I'm surprised at his never having had anything done—at their waiting all these years."

"Ah, that's because he was afraid, you know; it was a kind of superstition. He was sure that if anything were done he would die directly afterwards. He has only consented to-day."

"He's ready to die then?"

"Oh, now he's so old he doesn't care."

"Well, I hope I shan't kill him," said Lyon. "It was rather unnatural in his son to send for me."

"Oh, they have nothing to gain—everything is theirs already!" his companion rejoined, as if she took this speech quite literally. Her talkativeness was systematic—she fraternised as seriously as she might have played whist. "They do as they like—they fill the house with people—they have *carte blanche*."

"I see—but there's still the title."

"Yes, but what is it?"

Our artist broke into laughter at this, whereat his companion stared. Before he had recovered himself she was scouring the plain with her other neighbour. The gentleman on his left at last risked an observation, and they had some fragmentary talk. This personage played his part with difficulty: he uttered a remark as a lady fires a pistol, looking the other way. To catch the ball Lyon had to bend his ear, and this movement led to his observing a handsome creature who was seated on the same side, beyond his interlocutor. Her profile was presented to him and at first he was only struck with its beauty; then it produced an impression still more agreeable—a sense of undimmed remembrance and intimate association. He had not recognised her on the instant only because he had so little expected to see her there; he had not seen her anywhere for so long, and no news of her ever came to him. She was often in his thoughts, but she had passed out of his life. He thought of her twice a week; that may be called often in relation to a person one has not seen for twelve years. The moment after he recognised her he felt how true it was that it was only she who could look like that: of the most charming head in the world (and this lady had it) there could never be a replica. She was leaning forward a little; she remained in profile, apparently listening to some one on the other side of her. She was listening, but she was also looking, and after a moment Lyon followed the direction of her eyes. They rested upon the gentleman who had been described to him as Colonel Capadose—rested, as it appeared to him, with a kind of habitual, visible complacency. This was not strange, for the Colonel was unmistakably formed to attract the sympathetic gaze of woman; but Lyon was slightly disappointed that she could let him look at her so long without giving him a glance. There was nothing between them to-day and he had no rights, but she must have known he was coming (it was of course not such a tremendous event, but she could not have been staying in the house without hearing of it), and it was not natural that that should absolutely fail to affect her.

She was looking at Colonel Capadose as if she were in love with him—a queer accident for the proudest, most reserved of women. But doubtless it was all right, if her husband liked it or didn't notice it: he had heard indefinitely, years before, that she was married, and he took for granted (as he had not heard that she had become a widow) the presence of the happy man on whom she had conferred what she had refused to *him*, the poor art-student at Munich. Colonel Capadose appeared to be aware of nothing, and this circumstance, incongruously enough, rather irritated Lyon than gratified him. Suddenly the lady turned her head, showing her full face to our hero. He was so prepared with a greeting that he instantly smiled, as a shaken jug overflows; but she gave him no response, turned away again and sank back in her chair. All that her face said in that instant was, "You see I'm as handsome as ever." To which he mentally subjoined, "Yes, and as much good it does me!" He asked the young man beside him if he knew who that beautiful being was—the fifth person beyond him. The young man leaned forward, considered and then said, "I think she's Mrs. Capadose."

"Do you mean his wife—that fellow's?" And Lyon indicated the subject of the information given him by his other neighbour.

"Oh, is *he* Mr. Capadose?" said the young man, who appeared very vague. He admitted his vagueness and explained it by saying that there were so many people and he had come only the day before. What was definite to Lyon was that Mrs. Capadose was in love with her husband; so that he wished more than ever that he had married her.

"She's very faithful," he found himself saying three minutes later to the lady on his right. He added that he meant Mrs. Capadose.

"Ah, you know her then?"

"I knew her once upon a time—when I was living abroad."

"Why then were you asking me about her husband?"

"Precisely for that reason. She married after that—I didn't even know her present name."

"How then do you know it now?"

"This gentleman has just told me—he appears to know."

"I didn't know he knew anything," said the lady, glancing forward.

"I don't think he knows anything but that."

"Then you have found out for yourself that she is faithful. What do you mean by that?"

"Ah, you mustn't question me—I want to question you," Lyon said. "How do you all like her here?"

"You ask too much! I can only speak for myself. I think she's hard."

"That's only because she's honest and straightforward."

"Do you mean I like people in proportion as they deceive?"

"I think we all do, so long as we don't find them out," Lyon said. "And then there's something in her face—a sort of Roman type, in spite of her having such an English eye. In fact she's English down to the ground; but her complexion, her low forehead and that beautiful close little wave in her dark hair make her look like a glorified *contadina*."

"Yes, and she always sticks pins and daggers into her head, to increase that effect. I must say I like her husband better: he is so clever."

"Well, when I knew her there was no comparison that could injure her. She was altogether the most delightful thing in Munich."

"In Munich?"

"Her people lived there; they were not rich—in pursuit of economy in fact, and Munich was very cheap. Her father was the younger son of some noble house; he had married a second time and had a lot of little mouths to feed. She was the child of the first wife and she didn't like her stepmother, but she was charming to her little brothers and sisters. I once made a sketch of her as Werther's Charlotte, cutting bread and butter while they clustered all round her. All the artists in the place were in love with her but she wouldn't look at 'the likes' of us. She was too proud—I grant you that; but she wasn't stuck up nor young ladyish; she was simple and frank and kind about it. She used to remind me of Thackeray's Ethel Newcome. She told me she must marry well: it was the only thing she could do for her family. I suppose you would say that she *has* married well."

"She told *you?*" smiled Lyon's neighbour.

"Oh, of course I proposed to her too. But she evidently thinks so herself!" he added.

When the ladies left the table the host as usual bade the gentlemen draw together, so that Lyon found himself opposite to Colonel Capadose. The conversation was mainly about the "run," for it had apparently been a great day in the hunting-field. Most of the gentlemen communicated their adventures and opinions, but Colonel Capadose's pleasant voice was the most audible in the chorus. It was a bright and fresh but masculine organ, just such a voice as, to Lyon's sense, such a "fine man" ought to have had. It appeared from his remarks that he was a very straight rider, which was also very much what Lyon would have expected. Not that he swaggered, for his allusions were very quietly and casually made; but they were all too dangerous experiments and close shaves. Lyon perceived after a little that the attention paid by the company to the Colonel's remarks was not in direct relation to the interest they seemed to offer; the result of which was that the speaker, who noticed that *he* at least was listening, began to treat him as his particular auditor and to fix his eyes on him as he talked. Lyon had nothing to do but to look sympathetic and assent—Colonel Capadose appeared to take so much sympathy and assent for granted. A neighbouring squire had had an accident; he had come a cropper in an awkward place—just at the finish—with consequences that looked grave. He had struck his head; he remained insensible, up to the last accounts: there had evidently been concussion of the brain. There was some exchange of views as to his recovery—how soon it would take place or whether it would take place at all; which led the Colonel to confide to our artist across the table that *he* shouldn't despair of a fellow even if

he didn't come round for weeks—for weeks and weeks and weeks—
for months, almost for years. He leaned forward; Lyon leaned forward
to listen, and Colonel Capadose mentioned that he knew from personal
experience that there was really no limit to the time one might lie
unconscious without being any the worse for it. It had happened to
him in Ireland, years before; he had been pitched out of a dogcart, had
turned a sheer somersault and landed on his head. They thought he
was dead, but he wasn't; they carried him first to the nearest cabin,
where he lay for some days with the pigs, and then to an inn in a
neighbouring town—it was a near thing they didn't put him under
ground. He had been completely insensible—without a ray of recognition of any human thing—for three whole months; had not a glimmer
of consciousness of any blessed thing. It was touch and go to that degree
that they couldn't come near him, they couldn't feed him, they could
scarcely look at him. Then one day he had opened his eyes—as fit as
a flea!

"I give you my honour it had done me good—it rested my brain."
He appeared to intimate that with an intelligence so active as his these
periods of repose were providential. Lyon thought his story very striking,
but he wanted to ask him whether he had not shammed a little—not
in relating it, but in keeping so quiet. He hesitated however, in time,
to imply a doubt—he was so impressed with the tone in which Colonel
Capadose said that it was the turn of a hair that they hadn't buried
him alive. That had happened to a friend of his in India—a fellow who
was supposed to have died of jungle fever—they clapped him into a
coffin. He was going on to recite the further fate of this unfortunate
gentleman when Mr. Ashmore made a move and every one got up to
adjourn to the drawing-room. Lyon noticed that by this time no one
was heeding what his new friend said to him. They came round on
either side of the table and met while the gentleman dawdled before
going out.

"And do you mean that your friend was literally buried alive?" asked
Lyon, in some suspense.

Colonel Capadose looked at him a moment, as if he had already
lost the thread of the conversation. Then his face brightened—and
when it brightened it was doubly handsome. "Upon my soul he was
chucked into the ground!"

"And was he left there?"

"He was left there till I came and hauled him out."

"*You* came?"

"I dreamed about him—it's the most extraordinary story: I heard him calling to me in the night. I took upon myself to dig him up. You know there are people in India—a kind of beastly race, the ghouls—who violate graves. I had a sort of presentiment that they would get at him first. I rode straight, I can tell you; and, by Jove, a couple of them had just broken ground! Crack - crack, from a couple of barrels, and they showed me their heels, as you may believe. Would you credit that I took him out myself? The air brought him to and he was none the worse. He has got his pension—he came home the other day; he would do anything for me."

"He called to you in the night?" said Lyon, much startled.

"That's the interesting point. Now *what was it*? It wasn't his ghost, because he wasn't dead. It wasn't himself, because he couldn't. It was something or other! You see India's a strange country—there's an element of the mysterious: the air is full of things you can't explain."

They passed out of the dining-room, and Colonel Capadose, who went among the first, was separated from Lyon; but a minute later, before they reached the drawing-room, he joined him again. "Ashmore tells me who you are. Of course I have often heard of you—I'm very glad to make your acquaintance; my wife used to know you."

"I'm glad she remembers me. I recognised her at dinner and I was afraid she didn't."

"Ah, I daresay she was ashamed," said the Colonel, with indulgent humour.

"Ashamed of me?" Lyon replied, in the same key.

"Wasn't there something about a picture? Yes; you painted her portrait."

"Many times," said the artist; "and she may very well have been ashamed of what I made of her."

"Well, I wasn't, my dear sir; it was the sight of that picture, which you were so good as to present to her, that made me first fall in love with her."

"Do you mean that one with the children—cutting bread and butter?"

"Bread and butter? Bless me, no—vine leaves and a leopard skin—a kind of Bacchante."

"Ah, yes," said Lyon; "I remember. It was the first decent portrait I painted. I should be curious to see it to-day."

"Don't ask her to show it to you—she'll be mortified!" the Colonel exclaimed.

"Mortified?"

"We parted with it—in the most disinterested manner," he laughed. "An old friend of my wife's—her family had known him intimately when they arrived in Germany—took the most extraordinary fancy to it: the Grand Duke of Silberstadt-Schreckenstein, don't you know? He came out to Bombay while were were there and he spotted your picture (you know he's one of the greatest collectors in Europe), and made such eyes at it that, upon my word—it happened to be his birthday— she told him he might have it, to get rid of him. He was perfectly enchanged—but we miss the picture."

"It is very good of you," Lyon said. "If it's in a great collection— a work of my incompetent youth—I am infinitely honoured."

"Oh, he has got it in one of his castles; I don't know which—you know he has so many. He sent us, before he left India—to return the compliment—a magnificent old vase."

"That was more than the thing was worth," Lyon remarked.

Colonel Capadose gave no heed to this observation; he seemed to be thinking of something. After a moment he said, "If you'll come and see us in town she'll show you the vase." And as they passed into the drawing-room he gave the artist a friendly propulsion. "Go and speak to her; there she is—she'll be delighted."

Oliver Lyon took but a few steps into the wide saloon; he stood there a moment looking at the bright composition of the lamplit group of fair women, the single figures, the great setting of white and gold, the panels of old damask, in the centre of each of which was a single celebrated picture. There was a subdued lustre in the scene and an air as of the shining trains of dresses tumbled over the carpet. At the furthest end of the room sat Mrs. Capadose, rather isolated; she was on a small sofa, with an empty place beside her. Lyon could not flatter himself she had been keeping it for him; her failure to respond to his recognition at table contradicted that, but he felt an extreme desire to go and occupy it. Moreover he had her husband's sanction; so he crossed the room, stepping over the tails of gowns, and stood before his old friend.

"I hope you don't mean to repudiate me," he said.

She looked up at him with an expression of unalloyed pleasure. "I am so glad to see you. I was delighted when I heard you were coming."

"I tried to get a smile from you at dinner—but I couldn't".

"I didn't see—I didn't understand. Besides, I hate smirking and telegraphing. Also I'm very shy—you won't have forgotten that. Now we can communicate comfortably." And she made a better place for him on the little sofa. He sat down and they had a talk that he enjoyed, while the reason for which he used to like her so came back to him, as well as a good deal of the very same old liking. She was still the least spoiled beauty he had ever seen, with an absence of coquetry or any insinuating art that seemed almost like an omitted faculty; there were moments when she struck her interlocutor as some fine creature from an asylum—a surprising deaf-mute or one of the operative blind. Her noble pagan head gave her privileges that she neglected, and when people were admiring her brow she was wondering whether there were a good fire in her bedroom. She was simple, kind and good; inexpressive but not inhuman or stupid. Now and again she dropped something that had a sifted, selected air—the sound of an impression at first hand. She had no imagination, but she had added up her feelings, some of her reflections, about life. Lyon talked of the old days in Munich, reminded her of incidents, pleasures and pains, asked her about her father and the others; and she told him in return that she was so impressed with his own fame, his brilliant position in the world, that she had not felt very sure he would speak to her or that his little sign at table was meant for her. This was plainly a perfectly truthful speech— she was incapable of any other—and he was affected by such humility on the part of a woman whose grand line was unique. Her father was dead; one of her brothers was in the navy and the other on a ranch in America; two of her sisters were married and the youngest was just coming out and very pretty. She didn't mention her stepmother. She asked him about his own personal history and he said that the principal thing that had happened to him was that he had never married.

"Oh, you ought to," she answered. "It's the best thing."

"I like that—from you!" he returned.

"Why not from me? I am very happy."

"That's just why I can't be. It's cruel of you to praise your state. But I have had the pleasure of making the acquaintance of your husband. We had a good bit of talk in the other room."

"You must know him better—you must know him really well," said Mrs. Capadose.

"I am sure that the further you go the more you find. But he makes a fine show, too."

She rested her good gray eyes on Lyon. "Don't you think he's handsome?"

"Handsome and clever and entertaining. You see I'm generous."

"Yes; you must know him well," Mrs. Capadose repeated.

"He has seen a great deal of life," said her companion.

"Yes, we have been in so many places. You must see my little girl. She is nine years old—she's too beautiful."

"You must bring her to my studio some day—I should like to paint her."

"Ah, don't speak of that," said Mrs. Capadose. "It reminds me of something so distressing."

"I hope you don't mean when *you* used to sit to me—though that may well have bored you."

"It's not what you did—it's what we have done. It's a confession I must make—it's a weight on my mind! I mean about that beautiful picture you gave me—it used to be so much admired. When you come to see me in London (I count on your doing that very soon) I shall see you looking all round. I can't tell you I keep it in my own room because I love it so, for the simple reason—" And she paused a moment.

"Because you can't tell wicked lies," said Lyon.

"No, I can't. So before you ask for it—"

"Oh, I know you parted with it—the blow has already fallen," Lyon interrupted.

"Ah then, you have heard? I was sure you would! But do you know what we got for it? Two hundred pounds."

"You might have got much more," said Lyon, smiling.

"That seemed a great deal at the time. We were in want of the money—it was a good while ago, when we first married. Our means were very small then, but fortunately that has changed rather for the better. We had the chance; it really seemed a big sum, and I am afraid we jumped at it. My husband had expectations which have partly come into effect, so that now we do well enough. But meanwhile the picture went."

"Fortunately the original remained. But do you mean that two hundred was the value of the vase?" Lyon asked.

"Of the vase?"

"The beautiful old Indian vase—the Grand Duke's offering."

"The Grand Duke?"

"What's his name? —Silberstadt-Schreckenstein. Your husband mentioned the transaction."

"Oh, my husband," said Mrs. Capadose; and Lyon saw that she coloured a little.

Not to add to her embarrassment, but to clear up the ambiguity, which he perceived the next moment he had better have left alone, he went on: "He tells me it's now in his collection."

"In the Grand Duke's? Ah, you know its reputation? I believe it contains treasures." She was bewildered, but she recovered herself, and Lyon made the mental reflection that for some reason which would seem good when he knew it the husband and the wife had prepared different versions of the same incident. It was true that he did not exactly see Everina Brant preparing a version; that was not her line of old, and indeed it was not in her eyes to-day. At any rate they both had the matter too much on their conscience. He changed the subject, said Mrs. Capadose must really bring the little girl. He sat with her some time longer and thought—perhaps it was only a fancy—that she was rather absent, as if she were annoyed at their having been even for a moment at cross-purposes. This did not prevent him from saying to her at the last, just as the ladies began to gather themselves together to go to bed: "You seem much impressed, from what you say, with my renown and my prosperity, and you are so good as greatly to exaggerate them. Would you have married me if you had known that I was destined to success?"

"I did know it."

"Well, I didn't."

"You were too modest."

"You didn't think so when I proposed to you."

"Well, if I had married you I couldn't have married *him*—and he's so nice," Mrs. Capadose said. Lyon knew she thought it—he had learned that at dinner—but it vexed him a little to hear her say it. The gentleman designated by the pronoun came up, amid the prolonged handshaking for good-night, and Mrs. Capadose remarked to her husband as she turned away, "He wants to paint Amy."

"Ah, she's a charming child, a most interesting little creature," the Colonel said to Lyon. "She does the most remarkable things."

Mrs. Capadose stopped, in the rustling procession that followed the hostess out of the room. "Don't tell him, please don't," she said.

"Don't tell him what?"

"Why, what she does. Let him find out for himself." And she passed on.

"She thinks I swagger about the child—that I bore people," said the Colonel. "I hope you smoke." He appeared ten minutes later in the smoking-room, in a brilliant equipment, a suit of crimson foulard covered with little white spots. He gratified Lyon's eye, made him feel that the modern age has its splendour too and its opportunities for costume. If his wife was an antique he was a fine specimen of the period of colour: he might have passed for a Venetian of the sixteenth century. They were a remarkable couple, Lyon thought, and as he looked at the Colonel standing in bright erectness before the chimney-piece while he emitted great smoke-puffs he did not wonder that Everina could not regret she had not married *him*. All the gentlemen collected at Stayes were not smokers and some of them had gone to bed. Colonel Capadose remarked that there probably would be a smallish muster, they had had such a hard day's work. That was the worst of a hunting-house—the men were so sleepy after dinner; it was devilish stupid for the ladies, even for those who hunted themselves—for women were so extraordinary, they never showed it. But most fellows revived under the stimulating influences of the smoking-room, and some of them, in this confidence, would turn up yet. Some of the grounds of their confidence—not all of them—might have been seen in a cluster of glasses and bottles on a table near the fire, which made the great salver and its contents twinkle sociably. The others lurked as yet in various improper corners of the minds of the most loquacious. Lyon was alone with Colonel Capadose for some moments before their companions, in varied eccentricities of uniform, straggled in, and he perceived that this wonderful man had but little loss of vital tissue to repair.

They talked about the house, Lyon having noticed an oddity of construction in the smoking-room; and the Colonel explained that it consisted of two distinct parts, one of which was of very great antiquity.

They were two complete houses in short, the old one and the new, each of great extent and each very fine in its way. The two formed together an enormous structure—Lyon must make a point of going all over it. The modern portion had been erected by the old man when he bought the property; oh yes, he had bought it, forty years before— it hadn't been in the family: there hadn't been any particular family for it to be in. He had had the good taste not to spoil the original house— he had not touched it beyond what was just necessary for joining it on. It was very curious indeed—a most irregular, rambling, mysterious pile, where they every now and then discovered a walled-up room or a secret staircase. To his mind it was essentially gloomy, however; even the modern additions, splendid as they were, failed to make it cheerful. There was some story about a skeleton having been found years before, during some repairs, under a stone slab of the floor of one of the passages; but the family were rather shy of its being talked about. The place they were in was of course in the old part, which contained after all some of the best rooms: he had an idea it had been the primitive kitchen, half modernised at some intermediate period.

"My room is in the old part too then—I'm very glad," Lyon said. "It's very comfortable and contains all the latest conveniences, but I observed the depth of the recess of the door and the evident antiquity of the corridor and staircase—the first short one—after I came out. That panelled corridor is admirable; it looks as if it stretched away, in its brown dimness (the lamps didn't seem to me to make much impression on it), for half a mile."

"Oh, don't go to the end of it!" exclaimed the Colonel, smiling.

"Does it lead to the haunted room?" Lyon asked.

His companion looked at him a moment. "Ah, you know about that?"

"No, I don't speak from knowledge, only from hope. I have never had any luck—I have never stayed in a dangerous house. The places I go to are always as safe as Charing Cross. I want to see—whatever there is, the regular thing. *Is* there a ghost here?"

"Of course there is—a rattling good one."

"And have you seen him?"

"Oh, don't ask me what *I've* seen—I should tax your credulity. I don't like to talk of these things. But there are two or three as bad— that is, as good!—rooms as you'll find anywhere."

"Do you mean in my corridor?" Lyon asked.

"I believe the worst is at the far end. But you would be ill-advised to sleep there."

"Ill-advised?"

"Until you've finished your job. You'll get letters of importance the next morning, and you'll take the 10:20."

"Do you mean I will invent a pretext for running away?"

"Unless you are braver than almost any one has ever been. They don't often put people to sleep there, but sometimes the house is so crowded that they have to. The same thing always happens—ill-concealed agitation at the breakfast-table and letters of the greatest importance. Of course it's a bachelor's room, and my wife and I are at the other end of the house. But we saw the comedy three days ago—the day after we got here. A young fellow had been put there—I forget his name—the house was so full; and the usual consequence followed. Letters at breakfast—an awfully queer face—an urgent call to town—so very sorry his visit was cut short. Ashmore and his wife looked at each other, and off the poor devil went."

"Ah, that wouldn't suit me; I must paint my picture," said Lyon. "But do they mind your speaking of it? Some people who have a good ghost are very proud of it, you know."

What answer Colonel Capadose was on the point of making to this inquiry our hero was not to learn, for at that moment their host had walked into the room accompanied by three or four gentlemen. Lyon was conscious that he was partly answered by the Colonel's not going on with the subject. This however on the other hand was rendered natural by the fact that one of the gentlemen appealed to him for an opinion on a point under discussion, something to do with the ever-lasting history of the day's run. To Lyon himself Mr. Ashmore began to talk, expressing his regret at having had so little direct conversation with him as yet. The topic that suggested itself was naturally that most closely connected with the motive of the artist's visit. Lyon remarked that it was a great disadvantage to him not to have had some preliminary acquaintance with Sir David—in most cases he found that so important. But the present sitter was so far advanced in life that there was doubtless no time to lose. "Oh, I can tell you all about him," said Mr. Ashmore; and for half an hour he told him a good deal. It was very interesting as well as very eulogistic, and Lyon could see that he was a very nice old man, to have endeared himself so to a son who was evidently not a gusher. At last he got up—he said he must go to bed if he wished to be fresh for his work in the morning. To which his host replied, "Then you must take your candle; the lights are out; I don't keep my servants up."

In a moment Lyon had his glimmering taper in hand, and as he was leaving the room (he did not disturb the others with a good-night; they were absorbed in the lemon-squeezer and the soda-water cork) he remembered other occasions on which he had made his way to bed alone through a darkened country-house; such occasions had not been rare, for he was almost always the first to leave the smoking-room. If he had not stayed in houses conspicuously haunted he had, none the less (having the artistic temperament), sometimes found the great black halls and staircases rather "creepy": there had been often a sinister effect, to his imagination, in the sound of his tread in the long passages or the way the winter moon peeped into tall windows on landings. It occurred to him that if houses without supernatural pretensions could look so wicked at night, the old corridors of Stayes would certainly give him a sensation. He didn't know whether the proprietors were sensitive; very often, as he had said to Colonel Capadose, people enjoyed the impeachment. What determined him to speak, with a certain sense of the risk, was the impression that the Colonel told queer stories. As he had his hand on the door he said to Arthur Ashmore, "I hope I shan't meet any ghosts."

"Any ghosts?"

"You ought to have some—in this fine old part."

"We do our best, but *que voulez-vous?*" said Mr. Ashmore. "I don't think they like the hot-water pipes."

"They remind them too much of their own climate? But haven't you a haunted room—at the end of my passage?"

"Oh, there are stories—we try to keep them up."

"I should like very much to sleep there," Lyon said.

"Well, you can move there to-morrow if you like."

"Perhaps I had better wait till I have done my work."

"Very good; but you won't work there, you know. My father will sit to you in his own apartments."

"Oh, it isn't that; it's the fear of running away, like that gentleman three days ago."

"Three days ago? What gentleman?" Mr. Ashmore asked.

"The one who got urgent letters at breakfast and fled by the 10:20. Did he stand more than one night?"

"I don't know what you are talking about. There was no such gentleman—three days ago."

"Ah, so much the better," said Lyon, nodding good-night and departing. He took his course, as he remembered it, with his wavering candle, and, though he encountered a great many gruesome objects, safely reached the passage out of which his room opened. In the complete darkness it seemed to stretch away still further, but he followed it, for the curiosity of the thing, to the end. He passed several doors with the name of the room painted upon them, but he found nothing else. He was tempted to try the last door—to look into the room of evil fame; but he reflected that this would be indiscreet, since Colonel Capadose handled the brush—as a *raconteur*—with such freedom. There might be a ghost and there might not; but the Colonel himself, he inclined to think, was the most mystifying figure in the house.

II

Lyon found Sir David Ashmore a capital subject and a very comfortable sitter into the bargain. Moreover he was a very agreeable old man, tremendously puckered but not in the least dim; and he wore exactly the furred dressing-gown that Lyon would have chosen. He was proud of his age but ashamed of his infirmities, which however he greatly exaggerated and which did not prevent him from sitting there as submissive as if portraiture in oils had been a branch of surgery. He demolished the legend of his having feared the operation would be fatal, giving an explanation which pleased our friend much better. He held that a gentleman should be painted but once in his life—that it was eager and fatuous to be hung up all over the place. That was good for women, who made a pretty wall-pattern; but the male face didn't lend itself to decorative repetition. The proper time for the likeness was at the last, when the whole man was there—you got the totality of his experience. Lyon could not reply that that period was not a real compendium—you had to allow so for leakage; for there had been no crack in Sir David's crystallisation. He spoke of his portrait as a plain

map of the country, to be consulted by his children in a case of uncertainty. A proper map could be drawn up only when the country had
been travelled. He gave Lyon his mornings, till luncheon, and they
talked of many things, not neglecting, as a stimulus to gossip, the people
in the house. Now that he did not "go out," as he said, he saw much
less of the visitors at Stayes: people came and went whom he knew
nothing about, and he liked to hear Lyon describe them. The artist
sketched with a fine point and did not caricature, and it usually befell
that when Sir David did not know the sons and daughters he had known
the fathers and mothers. He was one of those terrible old gentlemen
who are a repository of antecedents. But in the case of the Capadose
family, at whom they arrived by an easy stage, his knowledge embraced
two, or even three, generations. General Capadose was an old crony,
and he remembered his father before him. The general was rather a
smart soldier, but in private life of too speculative a turn—always
sneaking into the City to put his money into some rotten thing. He
married a girl who brought him something and they had half a dozen
children. He scarcely knew what had become of the rest of them, except
that one was in the Church and had found preferment—wasn't he Dean
of Rockingham? Clement, the fellow who was at Stayes, had some
military talent; he had served in the East, he had married a pretty girl.
He had been at Eton with his son, and he used to come to Stayes in
his holidays. Lately, coming back to England, he had turned up with
his wife again; that was before he—the old man—had been put to
grass. He was a taking dog, but he had a monstrous foible.

"A monstrous foible?" said Lyon.

"He's a thumping liar."

Lyon's brush stopped short, while he repeated, for somehow the
formula startled him, "A thumping liar?"

"You are very lucky not to have found it out."

"Well, I confess I have noticed a romantic tinge—"

"Oh, it isn't always romantic. He'll lie about the time of day, about
the name of his hatter. It appears there are people like that."

"Well, they are precious scoundrels," Lyon declared, his voice trembling a little with the thought of what Everina Brant had done with
herself.

"Oh, not always," said the old man. "This fellow isn't in the least
a scoundrel. There is no harm in him and no bad intention; he doesn't

steal nor cheat nor gamble nor drink; he's very kind—he sticks to his wife, is fond of his children. He simply can't give you a straight answer."

"Then everything he told me last night, I suppose, was mendacious: he delivered himself of a series of the stiffest statements. They stuck, when I tried to swallow them, but I never thought of so simple an explanation."

"No doubt he was in the vein," Sir David went on. "It's a natural peculiarity—as you might limp or stutter or be left-handed. I believe it comes and goes, like intermittent fever. My son tells me that his friends usually understand it and don't haul him up—for the sake of his wife."

"Oh, his wife—his wife!" Lyon murmured, painting fast.

"I daresay she's used to it."

"Never in the world, Sir David. How can she be used to it?"

"Why, my dear sir, when a woman's fond! —And don't they mostly handle the long bow themselves? They are connoisseurs—they have a sympathy for a fellow-performer."

Lyon was silent a moment; he had no ground for denying that Mrs. Capadose was attached to her husband. But after a little he rejoined: "Oh, not this one! I knew her years ago—before her marriage; knew her well and admired her. She was as clear as a bell."

"I like her very much," Sir David said, "but I have seen her back him up."

Lyon considered Sir David for a moment, not in the light of a model. "Are you very sure?"

The old man hesitated; then he answered, smiling, "You're in love with her."

"Very likely. God knows I used to be!"

"She must help him out—she can't expose him."

"She can hold her tongue," Lyon remarked.

"Well, before you probably she will."

"That's what I am curious to see." And Lyon added, privately, "Mercy on us, what he must have made of her!" He kept this reflection to himself, for he considered that he had sufficiently betrayed his state of mind with regard to Mrs. Capadose. None the less it occupied him now immensely, the question of how such a woman would arrange herself in such a predicament. He watched her with an interest deeply quickened when he mingled with the company; he had had his own troubles in life, but he had rarely been so anxious about anything as he was now to see what the loyalty of a wife and the infection of an example would have made of an absolutely truthful mind. Oh, he held it as immutably established that whatever other women might be prone to do she, of old, had been perfectly incapable of a deviation. Even if she had not been too simple to deceive she would have been too proud; and if she had not had too much conscience she would have had too little eagerness. It was the last thing she would have endured or condoned—the particular thing she would not have forgiven. Did she sit in torment while her husband turned his somersaults, or was she now too so perverse that she thought it a fine thing to be striking at the expense of one's honour? It would have taken a wondrous alchemy—working backwards, as it were—to produce this latter result. Besides these two alternatives (that she suffered tortures in silence and that she was so much in love that her husband's humiliating idiosyncrasy seemed to her only an added richness—a proof of life and talent), there was still the possibility that she had not found him out, that she took his false pieces at his own valuation. A little reflection rendered this hypothesis untenable; it was too evident that the account he gave of things must repeatedly have contradicted her own knowledge. Within an hour or two of his meeting them Lyon had seen her confronted with that perfectly gratuitous invention about the profit they had made off his early picture. Even then indeed she had not, so far as he could see, smarted, and—but for the present he could only contemplate the case.

Even if it had not been interfused, through his uneradicated tenderness for Mrs. Capadose, with an element of suspense, the question would still have presented itself to him as a very curious problem, for he had not painted portraits during so many years without becoming something of a psychologist. His inquiry was limited for the moment to the opportunity that the following three days might yield, as the Colonel and his wife were going on to another house. It fixed itself largely of course upon the Colonel too—this gentleman was such a rare anomaly. Moreover it had to go on very quickly. Lyon was too scrupulous to ask other people what they thought of the business—he was too afraid of exposing the woman he once had loved. It was probable also that light would come to him from the talk of the rest of the company: the Colonel's queer habit, both as it affected his own situation and as it affected his wife, would be a familiar theme in any house in which he was in the habit of staying. Lyon had not observed in the circles in which he visited any marked abstention from comment on the singularities of their members. It interfered with his progress that the Colonel hunted all day, while he plied his brushes and chatted with Sir David; but a Sunday intervened and that partly made it up. Mrs. Capadose fortunately did not hunt, and when his work was over she was not inaccessible. He took a couple of longish walks with her (she was fond of that), and beguiled her at tea into a friendly nook in the hall. Regard her as he might he could not make out to himself that she was consumed by a hidden shame; the sense of being married to a man whose word had no worth was not, in her spirit, so far as he could guess, the canker within the rose. Her mind appeared to have nothing on it but its own placid frankness, and when he looked into her eyes (deeply, as he occasionally permitted himself to do), they had no uncomfortable consciousness. He talked to her again and still again of the dear old days—reminded her of things that he had not (before this reunion) the least idea that he remembered. Then he spoke to her of her husband, praised his appearance, his talent for conversation, professed to have felt a quick friendship for him and asked (with an inward audacity at which he trembled a little) what manner of man he was. "What manner?" said Mrs. Capadose. "Dear me, how can one describe one's husband? I like him very much."

"Ah, you have told me that already!" Lyon exclaimed, with exaggerated ruefulness.

"Then why do you ask me again?" She added in a moment, as if she were so happy that she could afford to take pity on him, "He is everything that's good and kind. He's a soldier—and a gentleman—and a dear! He hasn't a fault. And he has great ability."

"Yes; he strikes one as having great ability. But of course I can't think him a dear."

"I don't care what you think him!" said Mrs. Capadose, looking, it seemed to him, as she smiled, handsomer than he had ever seen her. She was either deeply cynical or still more deeply impenetrable, and he had little prospect of winning from her the intimation that he longed for—some hint that it had come over her that after all she had better have married a man who was not a by-word for the most contemptible, the least heroic, of vices. Had she not seen—had she not felt—the smile go round when her husband executed some especially characteristic conversational caper? How could a woman of her quality endure that day after day, year after year, except by her quality's altering? But he would believe in the alteration only when he should have heard *her* lie. He was fascinated by his problem and yet half exasperated, and he asked himself all kinds of questions. Did she not lie, after all, when she let his falsehoods pass without a protest? Was not her life a perpetual complicity, and did she not aid and abet him by the simple fact that she was not disgusted with him? Then again perhaps she *was* disgusted and it was the mere desperation of her pride that had given her an inscrutable mask. Perhaps she protested in private, passionately; perhaps every night, in their own apartments, after the day's hideous perform- ance, she made him the most scorching scene. But if such scenes were of no avail and he took no more trouble to cure himself, how could she regard him, and after so many years of marriage too, with the perfectly artless complacency that Lyon had surprised in her in the course of the first day's dinner? If our friend had not been in love with her he could have taken the diverting view of the Colonel's delinquen- cies; but as it was they turned to the tragical in his mind, even while he had a sense that his solicitude might also have been laughed at.

The observation of these three days showed him that if Capadose was an abundant he was not a malignant liar and that his fine faculty exercised itself mainly on subjects of small direct importance. "He is the liar platonic," he said to himself; "he is disinterested, he doesn't operate with a hope of gain or with a desire to injure. It is art for art and he is prompted by the love of beauty. He has an inner vision of what might have been, of what ought to be, and he helps on the good cause by the simple substitution of a *nuance*. He paints, as it were, and so do I!" His manifestations had a considerable variety, but a family likeness ran through them, which consisted mainly of their singular futility. It was this that made them offensive; they encumbered the field of conversation, took up valuable space, converted it into a sort of brilliant sun-shot fog. For a fib told under pressure a convenient place can usually be found, as for a person who presents himself with an author's order at the first night of a play. But the supererogatory lie is the gentleman without a voucher or a ticket who accommodates himself with a stool in the passage.

In one particular Lyon acquitted his successful rival; it had puzzled him that irrepressible as he was he had not got into a mess in the

service. But he perceived that he respected the service—that august
institution was sacred from his depredations. Moreover though there
was a great deal of swagger in his talk it was, oddly enough, rarely
swagger about his military exploits. He had a passion for the chase, he
had followed it in far countries and some of his finest flowers were
reminiscences of lonely danger and escape. The more solitary the scene
the bigger of course the flower. A new acquaintance, with the Colonel,
always received the tribute of a bouquet: that generalisation Lyon very
promptly made. And this extraordinary man had inconsistencies and
unexpected lapses—lapses into flat veracity. Lyon recognised what Sir
David had told him, that his aberrations came in fits or periods—that
he would sometimes keep the truce of God for a month at a time. The
muse breathed upon him at her pleasure; she often left him alone. He
would neglect the finest openings and then set sail in the teeth of the
breeze. As a general thing he affirmed the false rather than denied the
true; yet this proportion was sometimes strikingly reversed. Very often
he joined in the laugh against himself—he admitted that he was trying
it on and that a good many of his anecdotes had an experimental
character. Still he never completely retracted nor retreated—he dived
and came up in another place. Lyon divined that he was capable at
intervals of defending his position with violence, but only when it was
a very bad one. Then he might easily be dangerous—then he would
hit out and become calumnious. Such occasions would test his wife's
equanimity—Lyon would have liked to see her there. In the smoking-
room and elsewhere the company, so far as it was composed of his
familiars, had an hilarious protest always at hand; but among the men
who had known him long his rich tone was an old story, so old that
they had ceased to talk about it, and Lyon did not care, as I have said,
to elicit the judgment of those who might have shared his own surprise.

   The oddest thing of all was that neither surprise nor familiarity
prevented the Colonel's being liked; his largest drafts on a sceptical
attention passed for an overflow of life and gaiety—almost of good
looks. He was fond of portraying his bravery and used a very big brush,
and yet he was unmistakably brave. He was a capital rider and shot,
in spite of his fund of anecdote illustrating these accomplishments: in
short he was very nearly as clever and his career had been very nearly
as wonderful as he pretended. His best quality however remained that
indiscriminate sociability which took interest and credulity for granted

and about which he bragged least. It made him cheap, it made him even in a manner vulgar; but it was so contagious that his listener was more or less on his side as against the probabilities. It was a private reflection of Oliver Lyon's that he not only lied but made one feel one's self a bit of a liar, even (or especially) if one contradicted him. In the evening, at dinner and afterwards, our friend watched his wife's face to see if some faint shade or spasm never passed over it. But she showed nothing, and the wonder was that when he spoke she almost always listened. That was her pride: she wished not to be even suspected of not facing the music. Lyon had none the less an importunate vision of a veiled figure coming the next day in the dusk to certain places to repair the Colonel's ravages, as the relatives of kleptomaniacs punctually call at the shops that have suffered from their pilferings.

"I must apologise, of course it wasn't true, I hope no harm is done, it is only his incorrigible—" Oh, to hear that woman's voice in that deep abasement! Lyon had no nefarious plan, no conscious wish to practise upon her shame or her loyalty; but he did say to himself that he should like to bring her round to feel that there would have been more dignity in a union with a certain other person. He even dreamed of the hour when, with a burning face, she would ask *him* not to take it up. Then he should be almost consoled—he would be magnanimous.

Lyon finished his picture and took his departure, after having worked in a glow of interest which made him believe in his success, until he found he had pleased every one, especially Mr. and Mrs. Ashmore, when he began to be sceptical. The party at any rate changed: Colonel and Mrs. Capadose went their way. He was able to say to himself however that his separation from the lady was not so much an end as a beginning, and he called on her soon after his return to town. She had told him the hours she was at home —she seemed to like him. If she liked him why had she not married him or at any rate why was she not sorry she had not? If she was sorry she concealed it too well. Lyon's curiosity on this point may strike the reader as fatuous, but something must be allowed to a disappointed man. He did not ask much after all; not that she should love him to-day or that she should allow him to tell her that he loved her, but only that she should give him some sign she was sorry. Instead of this, for the present, she contented herself with exhibiting her little daughter to him. The child was beautiful and had the prettiest eyes of innocence he had ever seen:

which did not prevent him from wondering whether she told horrid fibs. This idea gave him much entertainment—the picture of the anxiety with which her mother would watch as she grew older for the symptoms of heredity. That was a nice occupation for Everina Brant! Did she lie to the child herself, about her father—was that necessary, when she pressed her daughter to her bosom, to cover up his tracks? Did he control himself before the little girl—so that she might not hear him say things she knew to be other than he said? Lyon doubted this: his genius would be too strong for him, and the only safety for the child would be in her being too stupid to analyse. One couldn't judge yet—she was too young. If she should grow up clever she would be sure to tread in his steps—a delightful improvement in her mother's situation! Her little face was not shifty, but neither was her father's big one: so that proved nothing.

Lyon reminded his friends more than once of their promise that Amy should sit to him, and it was only a question of his leisure. The desire grew in him to paint the Colonel also—an operation from which he promised himself a rich private satisfaction. He would draw him out, he would set him up in that totality about which he had talked with Sir David, and none but the initiated would know. They, however, would rank the picture high, and it would be indeed six rows deep—a masterpiece of subtle characterisation, of legitimate treachery. He had dreamed for years of producing something which should bear the stamp of the psychologist as well as of the painter, and here at last was his subject. It was a pity it was not better, but that was not *his* fault. It was his impression that already no one drew the Colonel out more than he, and he did it not only by instinct but on a plan. There were moments when he was almost frightened at the success of his plan—the poor gentleman went so terribly far. He would pull up some day, look at Lyon between the eyes—guess he was being played upon—which would lead to his wife's guessing it also. Not that Lyon cared much for that however, so long as she failed to suppose (as she must) that *she* was a part of his joke. He formed such a habit now of going to see her of a Sunday afternoon that he was angry when she went out of town. This occurred often, as the couple were great visitors and the Colonel was always looking for sport, which he liked best when it could be had at other people's expense. Lyon would have supposed that this sort of life was particularly little to her taste, for he had an idea that it was in country-houses that her husband came out strongest. To let him go off without her, not to see him expose himself—that ought properly to have been a relief and a luxury to her. She told Lyon in fact that she preferred staying at home; but she neglected to say it was because in other people's houses she was on the rack: the reason she gave was that she liked so to be with the child. It was not perhaps criminal to draw such a bow, but it was vulgar: poor Lyon was delighted when he arrived at that formula. Certainly some day too he would cross the line—he would become a noxious animal. Yes, in the meantime he was vulgar, in spite of his talents, his fine person, his impunity. Twice, by exception, toward the end of the winter, when he left town for a few days' hunting, his wife remained at home. Lyon had not yet reached the point of asking himself whether the desire not to miss two of his visits had something to do with her immobility. That inquiry would perhaps have been more in place later, when he began to paint the child and she always came with her. But it was not in her to give the wrong name, to pretend, and Lyon could see that she had the maternal passion, in spite of the bad blood in the little girl's veins.

She came inveterately, though Lyon multiplied the sittings: Amy was never entrusted to the governess or the maid. He had knocked off poor old sir David in ten days, but the portrait of the simple-faced child bade fair to stretch over into the following year. He asked for sitting after sitting, and it would have struck any one who might have witnessed the affair that he was wearing the little girl out. He knew better however and Mrs. Capadose also knew: they were present together at the long intermissions he gave her, when she left her pose and roamed about the great studio, amusing herself with its curiosities, playing with the old draperies and costumes, having unlimited leave to handle. Then her mother and Mr. Lyon sat and talked; he laid aside his brushes and leaned back in his chair; he always gave her tea. What Mrs. Capadose did not know was the way that during these weeks he neglected other orders: women have no faculty of imagination with regard to a man's work beyond a vague idea that it doesn't matter. In fact Lyon put off everything and made several celebrities wait. There were half-hours of silence, when he plied his brushes, during which he was mainly conscious that Everina was sitting there. She easily fell into that if he did not insist on talking, and she was not embarrassed nor bored by it. Sometimes she took up a book—there were plenty of them about; sometimes, a little way off, in her chair, she watched his progress (though without in the least advising or correcting), as if she cared for every stroke that represented her daughter. These strokes were occasionally a little wild; he was thinking so much more of his heart than of his hand. He was not more embarrassed than she was, but he was agitated: it was as if in the sittings (for the child, too, was beautifully quiet) something was growing between them or had already grown— a tacit confidence, an inexpressible secret. He felt it that way; but after all he could not be sure that she did. What he wanted her to do for him was very little; it was not even to confess that she was unhappy. He would be superabundantly gratified if she should simply let him know, even by a silent sign, that she recognised that with him her life would have been finer. Sometimes he guessed—his presumption went so far—that he might see this sign in her contentedly sitting there.

III

At last he broached the question of painting the Colonel: it was now very late in the season—there would be little time before the general dispersal. He said they must make the most of it; the great thing was to begin; then in the autumn, with the resumption of their London life, they could go forward. Mrs. Capadose objected to this that she really could not consent to accept another present of such value. Lyon had given her the portrait of herself of old, and he had seen what they had had the indelicacy to do with it. Now he had offered her this beautiful memorial of the child—beautiful it would evidently be when it was finished, if he could ever satisfy himself; a precious possession which they would cherish for ever. But his generosity must stop there—they couldn't be so tremendously "beholden" to him. They couldn't order the picture—of course he would understand that, without her explaining: it was a luxury beyond their reach, for they knew the great prices he received. Besides, what had they ever done—what above all had *she* ever done, that he should overload them with benefits? No, he was too dreadfully good; it was really impossible that Clement should sit. Lyon listened to her without protest, without interruption, while he bent forward at his work, and at last he said: "Well, if you won't take it why not let him sit for me for my own pleasure and profit? Let it be a favour, a service I ask of him. It will do me a lot of good to paint him and the picture will remain in my hands."

"How will it do you a lot of good?" Mrs. Capadose asked.

"Why, he's such a rare model—such an interesting subject. He has such an expressive face. It will teach me no end of things."

"Expressive of what?" said Mrs. Capadose.

"Why, of his nature."

"And do you want to paint his nature?"

"Of course I do. That's what a great portrait gives you, and I shall make the Colonel's a great one. It will put me up high. So you see my request is eminently interested."

"How can you be higher than you are?"

"Oh, I'm insatiable! Do consent," said Lyon.

"Well, his nature is very noble," Mrs. Capadose remarked.

"Ah, trust me, I shall bring it out!" Lyon exclaimed, feeling a little ashamed of himself.

Mrs. Capadose said before she went away that her husband would probably comply with his invitation, but she added, "Nothing would induce me to let you pry into *me* that way!"

"Oh, you," Lyon laughed—"I could do you in the dark!"

The Colonel shortly afterwards placed his leisure at the painter's disposal and by the end of July had paid him several visits. Lyon was disappointed neither in the quality of his sitter nor in the degree to which he himself rose to the occasion; he felt really confident that he should produce a fine thing. He was in the humour; he was charmed with his *motif* and deeply interested in his problem. The only point that troubled him was the idea that when he should send his picture to the Academy he should not be able to give the title, for the catalogue, simply as "The Liar." However, it little mattered, for he had now determined that this character should be perceptible even to the meanest intelligence—as overtopping as it had become to his own sense in the living man. As he saw nothing else in the Colonel to-day, so he gave himself up to the joy of painting nothing else. How he did it he could not have told you, but it seemed to him that the mystery of how to do it was revealed to him afresh every time he sat down to his work. It was in the eyes and it was in the mouth, it was in every line of the face and every fact of the attitude, in the indentation of the chin, in the way the hair was planted, the moustache was twisted, the smile

came and went, the breath rose and fell. It was in the way he looked
out at a bamboozled world in short—the way he would look out for
ever. There were half a dozen portraits in Europe that Lyon rated as
supreme; he regarded them as immortal, for they were as perfectly
preserved as they were consummately painted. It was to this small
exemplary group that he aspired to annex the canvas on which he was
now engaged. One of the productions that helped to compose it was
the magnificent Moroni of the National Gallery—the young tailor, in
the white jacket, at his board with his shears. The Colonel was not a
tailor, nor was Moroni's model, unlike many tailors, a liar; but as regards
the masterly clearness with which the individual should be rendered
his work would be on the same line as that. He had to a degree in
which he had rarely had it before the satisfaction of feeling life grow
and grow under his brush. The Colonel, as it turned out, liked to sit
and he liked to talk while he was sitting: which was very fortunate, as
his talk largely constituted Lyon's inspiration. Lyon put into practice
that idea of drawing him out which he had been nursing for so many
weeks: he could not possibly have been in a better relation to him for
that purpose. He encouraged, beguiled, excited him, manifested an
unfathomable credulity, and his only interruptions were when the Colonel did not respond to it. He had his intermissions, his hours of sterility,
and then Lyon felt that the picture also languished. The higher his
companion soared, the more gyrations he executed, in the blue, the
better he painted; he couldn't make his flights long enough. He lashed
him on when he flagged; his apprehension became great at moments
that the Colonel would discover his game. But he never did, apparently;
he basked and expanded in the fine steady light of the painter's attention.
In this way the picture grew very fast; it was astonishing what a short
business it was, compared with the little girl's. By the fifth of August
it was pretty well finished: that was the date of the last sitting the
Colonel was for the present able to give, as he was leaving town the
next day with his wife. Lyon was amply content—he saw his way so
clear: he should be able to do at his convenience what remained, with
or without his friend's attendance. At any rate, as there was no hurry,
he would let the thing stand over till his own return to London, in
November, when he would come back to it with a fresh eye. On the
Colonel's asking him if his wife might come and see it the next day,
if she should find a minute—this was so greatly her desire—Lyon

begged as a special favour that she would wait: he was so far from satisfied as yet. This was the repetition of a proposal Mrs. Capadose had made on the occasion of his last visit to her, and he had then asked for a delay—declared that he was by no means content. He was really delighted, and he was again a little ashamed of himself.

By the fifth of August the weather was very warm, and on that day, while the Colonel sat straight and gossiped, Lyon opened for the sake of ventilation a little subsidiary door which led directly from his studio into the garden and sometimes served as an entrance and an exit for models and for visitors of the humbler sort, and as a passage for canvases, frames, packing-boxes and other professional gear. The main entrance was through the house and his own apartments, and this approach had the charming effect of admitting you first to a high gallery, from which a crooked picturesque staircase enabled you to descend to the wide, decorated, encumbered room. The view of this room, beneath them, with all its artistic ingenuities and the objects of value that Lyon had collected, never failed to elicit exclamations of delight from persons stepping into the gallery. The way from the garden was plainer and at once more practicable and more private. Lyon's domain, in St. John's Wood, was not vast, but when the door stood open of a summer's day it offered a glimpse of flowers and trees, you smelt something sweet and you heard the birds. On this particular morning the side-door had been found convenient by an unannounced visitor, a youngish woman who stood in the room before the Colonel perceived her and whom he perceived before she was noticed by his friend. She was very quiet, and she looked from one of the men to the other. "Oh, dear, here's another!" Lyon exclaimed, as soon as his eyes rested on her. She belonged, in fact, to a somewhat importunate class—the model in search of employment, and she explained that she had ventured to come straight in, that way, because very often when she went to call upon gentlemen the servants played her tricks, turned her off and wouldn't take in her name.

"But how did you get into the garden?" Lyon asked.

"The gate was open, sir—the servants' gate. The butcher's cart was there."

"The butcher ought to have closed it," said Lyon.

"Then you don't require me, sir?" the lady continued.

Lyon went on with his painting; he had given her a sharp look at first, but now his eyes lighted on her no more. The Colonel, however, examined her with interest. She was a person of whom you could scarcely say whether being young she looked old or old she looked young; she had at any rate evidently rounded several of the corners of life and had a face that was rosy but that somehow failed to suggest freshness. Nevertheless she was pretty and even looked as if at one time she might have sat for the complexion. She wore a hat with many feathers, a dress with many bugles, long black gloves, encircled with silver bracelets, and very bad shoes. There was something about her that was not exactly of the governess out of place nor completely of the actress seeking an engagement, but that savoured of an interrupted profession or even of a blighted career. She was rather soiled and tarnished, and after she had been in the room a few moments the air, or any rate the nostril, became acquainted with a certain alcoholic waft. She was unpractised in the *h*, and when Lyon at last thanked her and said he didn't want her—he was doing nothing for which she could be useful—she replied with rather a wounded manner, "Well, you know you *'ave* 'ad me!"

"I don't remember you," Lyon answered.

"Well, I daresay the people that saw your pictures do! I haven't much time, but I thought I would look in."

"I am much obliged to you."

"If ever you should require me, if you just send a postcard—"

"I never send postcards," said Lyon.

"Oh, well, I should value a private letter! Anything to Miss Geraldine, Mortimer Terrace Mews, Notting 'ill—"

"Very good; I'll remember," said Lyon.

Miss Geraldine lingered. "I thought I'd just stop, on the chance."

"I'm afraid I can't hold out hopes, I'm so busy with portraits," Lyon continued.

"Yes; I see you are. I wish I was in the gentleman's place."

"I'm afraid in that case it wouldn't look like me," said the Colonel, laughing.

"Oh, of course it couldn't compare—it wouldn't be so 'andsome! But I do hate them portraits!" Miss Geraldine declared. "It's so much bread out of our mouths."

"Well, there are many who can't paint them," Lyon suggested, comfortingly.

"Oh, I've sat to the very first—and only to the first! There's many that couldn't do anything without me."

"I'm glad you're in such demand." Lyon was beginning to be bored and he added that he wouldn't detain her—he would send for her in case of need.

"Very well; remember it's the Mews—more's the pity! You don't sit so well as *us*!" Miss Geraldine pursued, looking at the Colonel. "If *you* should require me, sir—"

"You put him out; you embarrass him," said Lyon.

"Embarrass him, oh gracious!" the visitor cried, with a laugh which diffused a fragrance. "Perhaps *you* send postcards, eh?" she went on to the Colonel; and then she retreated with a wavering step. She passed out into the garden as she had come.

"How dreadful—she's drunk!" said Lyon. He was painting hard, but he looked up, checking himself: Miss Geraldine, in the open doorway, had thrust back her head.

"Yes, I do hate it—that sort of thing!" she cried with an explosion of mirth which confirmed Lyon's declaration. And then she disappeared.

"What sort of thing—what does she mean?" the Colonel asked.

"Oh, my painting you, when I might be painting her."

"And have you ever painted her?"

"Never in the world; I have never seen her. She is quite mistaken."

The Colonel was silent a moment; then he remarked, "She was very pretty—ten years ago."

"I daresay, but she's quite ruined. For me the least drop too much spoils them; I shouldn't care for her at all."

"My dear fellow, she's not a model," said the Colonel, laughing.

"To-day, no doubt, she's not worthy of the name; but she has been one."

"*Jamais de la vie!* That's all a pretext.

"A pretext?" Lyon pricked up his ears—he began to wonder what was coming now.

"She didn't want you—she wanted me."

"I noticed she paid you some attention. What does she want of you?"

"Oh, to do me an ill turn. She hates me—lots of women do. She's watching me—she follows me."

Lyon leaned back in his chair—he didn't believe a word of this. He was all the more delighted with it and with the Colonel's bright, candid manner. The story had bloomed, fragrant, on the spot. "My dear Colonel!" he murmured, with friendly interest and commiseration.

"I was annoyed when she came in—but I wasn't startled," his sitter continued.

"You concealed it very well, if you were."

"Ah, when one has been through what I have! To-day however I confess I was half prepared. I have seen her hanging about—she knows my movements. She was near my house this morning—she must have followed me."

"But who is she then—with such a *toupet?*"

"Yes, she has that," said the Colonel; "but as you observe she was primed. Still, there was a cheek, as they say, in her coming in. Oh, she's a a bad one! She isn't a model and she never was; no doubt she has known some of those women and picked up their form. She had hold of a friend of mine ten years ago—a stupid young gander who might have been left to be plucked but whom I was obliged to take an interest in for family reasons. It's a long story—I had really forgotten all about it. She's thirty-seven if she's a day. I cut in and made him get rid of her—I sent her about her business. She knew it was me she had to thank. She has never forgiven me—I think she's off her head. Her name isn't Geraldine at all and I doubt very much if that's her address."

"Ah, what is her name?" Lyon asked, most attentive. The details always began to multiply, to abound, when once his companion was well launched—they flowed forth in battalions.

"It's Pearson—Harriet Pearson; but she used to call herself Grenadine—wasn't that a rum appellation? Grenadine—Geraldine—the jump was easy." Lyon was charmed with the promptitude of this response, and his interlocutor went on: "I hadn't thought of her for years—I had quite lost sight of her. I don't know what her idea is, but practically she's harmless. As I came in I thought I saw her a little way up the road. She must have found out I come here and have arrived before me. I daresay—or rather I'm sure—she is waiting for me there now."

"Hadn't you better have protection?" Lyon asked, laughing.

"The best protection is five shillings—I'm willing to go that length. Unless indeed she has a bottle of vitriol. But they only throw vitriol on the men who have deceived them, and I never deceived her—I told her the first time I saw her that it wouldn't do. Oh, if she's there we'll walk a little way together and talk it over and, as I say, I'll go as far as five shillings."

"Well," said Lyon, "I'll contribute another five." He felt that this was little to pay for his entertainment.

That entertainment was interrupted however for the time by the Colonel's departure. Lyon hoped for a letter recounting the fictive sequel; but apparently his brilliant sitter did not operate with the pen. At any rate he left town without writing; they had taken a rendezvous for three months later. Oliver Lyon always passed the holidays in the same way; during the first weeks he paid a visit to his elder brother, the happy possessor, in the south of England, of a rambling old house with formal gardens, in which he delighted, and then he went abroad— usually to Italy or Spain. This year he carried out his custom after taking a last look at his all but finished work and feeling as nearly pleased with it as he ever felt with the translation of the idea by the hand—always, as it seemed to him, a pitiful compromise. One yellow afternoon, in the country, as he was smoking his pipe on one of the old terraces he was seized with the desire to see it again and do two or three things more to it: he had thought of it so often while he lounged there. The impulse was too strong to be dismissed, and though he expected to return to town in the course of another week he was unable to face the delay. To look at the picture for five minutes would be enough—it would clear up certain questions which hummed in his brain; so that the next morning, to give himself this luxury, he took the train for London. He sent no word in advance; he would lunch at his club and probably return into Sussex by the 5:45.

In St. John's Wood the tide of human life flows at no time very fast, and in the first days of September Lyon found unmitigated emptiness in the straight sunny roads where the little plastered garden-walls, with their incommunicative doors, looked slightly Oriental. There was definite stillness in his own house, to which he admitted himself by his pass-key, having a theory that it was well sometimes to take servants unprepared. The good woman who was mainly in charge and who cumulated the functions of cook and housekeeper was, however, quickly summoned by his step, and (he cultivated frankness of inter-course with his domestics) received him without the confusion of sur-prise. He told her that she needn't mind the place being not quite straight, he had only come up for a few hours—he should be busy in the studio. To this she replied that he was just in time to see a lady and a gentleman who were there at the moment—they had arrived five minutes before. She had told them he was away from home but they said it was all right; they only wanted to look at a picture and would be very careful of everything. "I hope it is all right, sir," the housekeeper concluded. "The gentleman says he's a sitter and he gave me his name— rather an odd name; I think it's military. The lady's a very fine lady, sir; at any rate there they are."

"Oh, it's all right," Lyon said, the identity of his visitors being clear. The good woman couldn't know, for she usually had little to do with the comings and goings; his man, who showed people in and out, had accompanied him to the country. He was a good deal surprised at Mrs. Capadose's having come to see her husband's portrait when she knew that the artist himself wished her to forbear; but it was a familiar truth to him that she was a woman of a high spirit. Besides, perhaps the lady was not Mrs. Capadose; the Colonel might have brought some inquisitive friend, a person who wanted a portrait of *her* husband. What were they doing in town, at any rate, at that moment? Lyon made his way to the studio with a certain curiosity; he wondered vaguely what his friends were "up to." He pushed aside the curtain that hung in the door of communication—the door opening upon the gallery which it had been found convenient to construct at the time the studio was added to the house. When I say he pushed it aside I should amend my phrase; he laid his hand upon it, but at that moment he was arrested by a very singular sound. It came from the floor of the room beneath him and it startled him extremely, consisting apparently as it did of a passionate wail—a sort of smothered shriek—accompanied by a violent burst of tears. Oliver Lyon listened intently a moment, and then he passed out upon the balcony, which was covered with an old thick Moorish rug. His step was noiseless, though he had not endeavoured to make it so, and after that first instant he found himself profiting irresistibly by the accident of his not having attracted the attention of the two persons in the studio, who were some twenty feet below him. In truth they were so deeply and so strangely engaged that their un- consciousness of observation was explained. The scene that took place before Lyon's eyes was one of the most extraordinary they had ever rested upon. Delicacy and the failure to comprehend kept him at first from interrupting it—for what he saw was a woman who had thrown herself in a flood of tears on her companion's bosom—and these influences were succeeded after a minute (the minutes were very few and very short) by a definite motive which presently had the force to make him step back behind the curtain. I may add that it also had the force to make him avail himself for further contemplation of a crevice formed by his gathering together the two halves of the *portière*. He was perfectly aware of what he was about—he was for the moment an eavesdropper, a spy; but he was also aware that a very odd business, in which his confidence had been trifled with, was going forward, and that if in a measure it didn't concern him, in a measure it very definitely did. His observation, his reflections, accomplished themselves in a flash.

His visitors were in the middle of the room; Mrs. Capadose clung to her husband, weeping, sobbing as if her heart would break. Her distress was horrible to Oliver Lyon but his astonishment was greater than his horror when he heard the Colonel respond to it by the words, vehemently uttered, "Damn him, damn him, damn him!" What in the world had happened? why was she sobbing and whom was he damning? What had happened, Lyon saw the next instant, was that the Colonel had finally rummaged out his unfinished portrait (he knew the corner where the artist usually placed it, out of the way, with its face to the wall) and had set it up before his wife on an empty easel. She had looked at it a few moments and then—apparently—what she saw in it had produced an explosion of dismay and resentment. She was too busy sobbing and the Colonel was too busy holding her and reiterating his objurgation, to look round or look up. The scene was so unexpected to Lyon that he could not take it, on the spot, as a proof of the triumph of his hand—of a tremendous hit: he could only wonder what on earth was the matter. The idea of the triumph came a little later. Yet he could see the portrait from where he stood; he was startled with its look of life—he had not thought it so masterly. Mrs. Capadose flung herself away from her husband—she dropped into the nearest chair, buried her face in her arms, leaning on a table. Her weeping suddenly ceased to be audible, but she shuddered there as if she were overwhelmed with anguish and shame. Her husband remained a moment staring at the picture; then he went to her, bent over her, took hold of her again, soothed her. "What is it, darling, what the devil is it?" he demanded.

"Lyon heard her answer. "It's cruel—oh, it's too cruel!"

"Damn him—damn him—damn him!" the Colonel repeated.

"It's all there—it's all there!" Mrs. Capadose went on.

"Hang it, what's all there?"

"Everything there oughtn't to be—everything he has seen—it's too dreadful!"

"Everything he has seen? Why, ain't I a good-looking fellow? He has made me rather handsome."

Mrs. Capadose had sprung up again; she had darted another glance at the painted betrayal. "Handsome? Hideous, hideous! Not that—never, never!"

"Not *what*, in heaven's name?" the Colonel almost shouted. Lyon could see his flushed, bewildered face.

"What he has made of you—what you know! *He* knows—he has seen. Every one will know—every one will see. Fancy that thing in the Academy!"

"You're going wild, darling; but if you hate it so it needn't go."

"Oh, he'll send it—it's so good! Come away—come away!" Mrs. Capadose wailed, seizing her husband.

"It's so good?" the poor man cried.

"Come away—come away," she only repeated; and she turned toward the staircase that ascended to the gallery.

"Not that way—not through the house, in the state you're in," Lyon heard the Colonel object. "This way—we can pass," he added; and he drew his wife to the small door that opened into the garden. It was bolted, but he pushed the bolt and opened the door. She passed out quickly, but he stood there looking back into the room. "Wait for me a moment!" he cried out to her; and with an excited stride he re-entered the studio. He came up the the picture again, and again he stood looking at it. "Damn him—damn him—damn him!" he broke out once more. It was not clear to Lyon whether this malediction had for its object the original or the painter of the portrait. The Colonel turned away, and moved rapidly about the room, as if he were looking for something; Lyon was unable for the instant to guess his intention. Then the artist said to himself, below his breath, "He's going to do it a harm!" His first impulse was to rush down and stop him; but he paused with the sound of Everina Brant's sobs still in his ears. The Colonel found what he was looking for—found it among some odds and ends on a small table and rushed back with it to the easel. At one and the same moment

Lyon perceived that the object he had seized was a small Eastern dagger and that he had plunged it into the canvas. He seemed animated by a sudden fury, for with extreme vigour of hand he dragged the instrument down (Lyon knew it to have no very fine edge) making a long, abominable gash. Then he plucked it out and dashed it again several times into the face of the likeness, exactly as if he were stabbing a human victim: it had the oddest effect—that of a sort of figurative suicide. In a few seconds more the Colonel had tossed the dagger away—he looked at it as he did so, as if he expected it to reek with blood—and hurried out of the place, closing the door after him.

The strangest part of all was—as will doubtless appear—that Oliver Lyon made no movement to save his picture. But he did not feel as if he were losing it or cared not if he were, so much more did he feel that he was gaining a certitude. His old friend *was* ashamed of her husband, and he had made her so, and he had scored a great success, even though the picture had been reduced to rags. The revelation excited him so—as indeed the whole scene did—that when he came down the steps after the Colonel had gone he trembled with his happy agitation; he was dizzy and had to sit down a moment. The portrait had a dozen jagged wounds—the Colonel literally had hacked it to death. Lyon left it where it was, never touched it, scarcely looked at it; he only walked up and down his studio, still excited, for an hour. At the end of this time his good woman came to recommend that he should have some luncheon; there was a passage under the staircase from the offices.

"Ah, the lady and gentleman have gone, sir? I didn't hear them."

"Yes; they went by the garden."

But she stopped, staring at the picture on the easel. "Gracious, how you 'ave served it, sir!"

Lyon imitated the Colonel. "Yes, I cut it up—in a fit of disgust."

"Mercy after all your trouble! Because they weren't pleased, sir?"

"Yes, they weren't pleased."

"Well, they must be very grand! Blessed if I would!"

"Have it chopped up; it will do to light fires," Lyon said.

He returned to the country by the 3:30 and a few days later passed over to France. During the two months that he was absent from England he expected something—he could hardly have said what; a manifestation of some sort on the Colonel's part. Wouldn't he write, wouldn't he explain, wouldn't he take for granted Lyon had discovered the way

he had, as the cook said, served him and deem it only decent to take
pity in some fashion or other on his mystification? Would he plead
guilty or would he repudiate suspicion? The latter course would be
difficult and make a considerable draft upon his genius, in view of the
certain testimony of Lyon's housekeeper, who had admitted the visitors
and would establish the connection between their presence and the
violence wrought. Would the Colonel proffer some apology or some
amends, or would any word from him be only a further expression of
that destructive petulance which our friend had seen his wife so suddenly
and so potently communicate to him? He would have either to declare
that he had not touched the picture or to admit that he had, and in
either case he would have to tell a fine story. Lyon was impatient for
the story and, as no letter came, disappointed that it was not produced.
His impatience however was much greater in respect to Mrs. Capadose's
version, if version there was to be; for certainly that would be the real
test, would show how far she would go for her husband, on the one
side, or for him, Oliver Lyon, on the other. He could scarcely wait to
see what line she would take; whether she would simply adopt the
Colonel's, whatever it might be. He wanted to draw her out without
waiting, to get an idea in advance. He wrote to her, to this end, from
Venice, in the tone of their established friendship, asking for news,
narrating his wanderings, hoping they should soon meet in town and
not saying a word about the picture. Day followed day, after the time,
and he received no answer; upon which he reflected that she couldn't
trust herself to write—was still too much under the influence of the
emotion produced by his "betrayal." Her husband had espoused that
emotion and she had espoused the action he had taken in consequence
of it, and it was a complete rupture and everything was at an end. Lyon
considered this prospect rather ruefully, at the same time that he thought
it deplorable that such charming people should have put themselves so
grossly in the wrong. He was at last cheered, though little further
enlightened, by the arrival of a letter, brief but breathing good-humour
and hinting neither at a grievance nor at a bad conscience. The most
interesting part of it to Lyon was the postscript, which consisted of
these words: "I have a confession to make to you. We were in town
for a couple of days, the 1st of September, and I took the occasion to
defy your authority—it was very bad of me but I couldn't help it. I
made Clement take me to your studio—I wanted so dreadfully to see

what you had done with him, your wishes to the contrary notwith-standing. We made your servants let us in and I took a good look at the picture. It is really wonderful!" "Wonderful" was non-committal, but at least with this letter there was no rupture.

The third day after Lyon's return to London was a Sunday, so that he could go and ask Mrs. Capadose for luncheon. She had given him in the spring a general invitation to do so and he had availed himself of it several times. These had been the occasions (before he sat to him) when he saw the Colonel most familiarly. Directly after his meal his host disappeared (he went out, as he said, to call on *his* women) and the second half-hour was the best, even when there were other people. Now, in the first days of December, Lyon had the luck to find the pair alone, without even Amy, who appeared but little in public. They were in the drawing-room, waiting for the repast to be announced, and as soon as he came in the Colonel broke out, "My dear fellow, I'm delighted to see you! I'm so keen to begin again."

"Oh, do go on, it's so beautiful." Mrs. Capadose said, as she gave him her hand.

Lyon looked from one to the other; he didn't know what he had expected, but he had not expected this. "Ah, then you think I've got something?"

"You've got everything," said Mrs. Capadose, smiling from her golden-brown eyes.

"She wrote you of our little crime?" her husband asked. "She dragged me there—I had to go." Lyon wondered for a moment whether he meant by their little crime the assault on the canvas; but the Colonel's next words didn't confirm this interpretation. "You know I like to sit—it gives such a chance to my *bavardise*. And just now I have time."

"You must remember I had almost finished," Lyon remarked. "So you had. More's the pity. I should like you to begin again."

"My dear fellow, I shall have to begin again!" said Oliver Lyon with a laugh, looking at Mrs. Capadose. She did not meet his eyes—she had got up to ring for luncheon. "The picture has been smashed," Lyon continued.

"Smashed? Ah, what did you do that for?" Mrs. Capadose asked, standing there before him in all her clear, rich beauty. Now that she looked at him she was impenetrable.

"I didn't—I found it so—with a dozen holes punched in it!"

"I say!" cried the Colonel.

Lyon turned his eyes to him, smiling. "I hope *you* didn't do it?"

"Is it ruined?" the Colonel inquired. He was as brightly true as his wife and he looked simply as if Lyon's question could not be serious. "For the love of sitting to you? My dear fellow, if I had thought of it I would!"

"Nor you either?" the painter demanded of Mrs. Capadose.

Before she had time to reply her husband had seized her arm, as if a highly suggestive idea had come to him. "I say, my dear, that woman—that woman!"

"That woman?" Mrs. Capadose repeated; and Lyon too wondered what woman he meant.

"Don't you remember when we came out, she was at the door—or a little way from it? I spoke to you of her—I told you about her. Geraldine—Grenadine—the one who burst in that day," he explained to Lyon. "We saw her hanging about—I called Everina's attention to her."

"Do you mean she got at my picture?"

"Ah yes, I remember," said Mrs. Capadose, with a sigh.

"She burst in again—she had learned the way—she was waiting for her chance," the Colonel continued. "Ah, the little brute!"

Lyon looked down; he felt himself colouring. This was what he had been waiting for—the day the Colonel should wantonly sacrifice some innocent person. And could his wife be a party to that final atrocity? Lyon had reminded himself repeatedly during the previous weeks that when the Colonel perpetrated his misdeed she had already quitted the room; but he had argued none the less—it was a virtual certainly—that he had on rejoining her immediately made his achievement plain to her. He was in the flush of performance; and even if he had not mentioned what he had done she would have guessed it. He did not for an instant believe that poor Miss Geraldine had been hovering about his door, nor had the account given by the Colonel the summer before of his relations with this lady deceived him in the slightest degree. Lyon had never seen her before the day she planted herself in his studio; but he knew her and classified her as if he had made her. He was acquainted with the London female model in all her varieties—in every phase of her development and every step of her decay. When he entered his house that September morning just after the arrival of his two friends there had been no symptoms whatever, up and down the road, of Miss Geraldine's reappearance. That fact had been fixed in his mind by his recollecting the vacancy of the prospect when his cook told him that a lady and a gentleman were in his studio: he had wondered there was not a carriage nor a cab at his door. Then he had reflected that they would have come by the underground railway; he was close to the Marlborough Road station and he knew the Colonel, coming to his sittings, more than once had availed himself of that convenience. "How in the world did she get in?" He addressed the question to his companions indifferently.

"Let us go down to luncheon," said Mrs. Capadose, passing out of the room.

"We went by the garden—without troubling your servant—I wanted to show my wife." Lyon followed his hostess with her husband and the Colonel stopped him at the top of the stairs. "My dear fellow, I *can't* have been guilty of the folly of not fastening the door?"

"I am sure I don't know, Colonel," Lyon said as they went down. "It was a very determined hand—a perfect wild-cat."

"Well, she *is* a wild-cat—confound her! That's why I wanted to get him away from her."

"But I don't understand her motive."

"She's off her head—and she hates me; that was her motive."

"But she doesn't hate me, my dear fellow!" Lyon said, laughing.

"She hated the picture—don't you remember she said so? The more portraits there are the less employment for such as her."

"Yes; but if she is not really the model she pretends to be, how can that hurt her?" Lyon asked.

The inquiry baffled the Colonel an instant—but only an instant. "Ah, she was in a vicious muddle! As I say, she's off her head."

They went into the dining-room, where Mrs. Capadose was taking her place. "It's too bad, it's too horrid!" she said. "You see the fates are against you. Providence won't let you be so disinterested—painting masterpieces for nothing."

"Did *you* see the woman?" Lyon demanded, with something like a sternness that he could not mitigate.

Mrs. Capadose appeared not to perceive it or not to heed it if she did. "There was a person, not far from your door, whom Clement called my attention to. He told me something about her but we were going the other way."

"And do you think she did it?"

"How can I tell? If she did she was mad, poor wretch."

"I should like very much to get hold of her," said Lyon. This was a false statement, for he had no desire for any further conversation with Miss Geraldine. He had exposed his friends to himself, but he had no desire to expose them to any one else, least of all to themselves.

"Oh, depend upon it she will never show again. You're safe!" the Colonel exclaimed.

"But I remember her address—Mortimer Terrace Mews, Notting Hill."

"Oh, that's pure humbug; there isn't any such place."

"Lord, what a deceiver!" said Lyon.

"Is there any one else you suspect?" the Colonel went on.

"Not a creature."

"And what do your servants say?"

"They say it wasn't *them*, and I reply that I never said it was. That's about the substance of our conferences."

"And when did they discover the havoc?"

"They never discovered it at all. I noticed it first—when I came back."

"Well, she could easily have stepped in," said the Colonel. "Don't you remember how she turned up that day, like the clown in the ring?"

"Yes, yes; she could have done the job, in three seconds, except that the picture wasn't out."

"My dear fellow, don't curse me! —but of course I dragged it out."

"You didn't put it back?" Lyon asked tragically.

"Ah, Clement, Clement, didn't I tell you to?" Mrs. Capadose exclaimed in a tone of exquisite reproach.

The Colonel groaned, dramatically; he covered his face with his hands. His wife's words were for Lyon the finishing touch; they made his whole vision crumble—his theory that she had secretly kept herself true. Even to her old lover she wouldn't be so! He was sick; he couldn't eat; he knew that he looked very strange. He murmered something about it being useless to cry over spilled milk—he tried to turn the conversation to other things. But it was a horrid effort and he wondered whether they felt it as much as he. He wondered all sorts of things:

whether they guessed he disbelieved them (that he had seen them of course they would never guess); whether they had arranged their story in advance or it was only an inspiration of the moment; whether she had resisted, protested, when the Colonel proposed it to her, and then had been borne down by him; whether in short she didn't loathe herself as she sat there. The cruelty, the cowardice of fastening their unholy act upon the wretched woman struck him as monstrous—no less monstrous indeed than the levity that could make them run the risk of her giving them, in her righteous indignation, the lie. Of course that risk could only exculpate her and not inculpate them—the probabilities protected them so perfectly; and what the Colonel counted on (what he would have counted upon the day he delivered himself, after first seeing her, at the studio, if he had thought about the matter then at all and not spoken from the pure spontaneity of his genius) was simply that Miss Geraldine had really vanished for ever into her native unknown. Lyon wanted so much to quit the subject that when after a little Mrs. Capadose said to him, "But can nothing be done, can't the picture be repaired? You know they do such wonders in that way now," he only replied, "I don't know, I don't care, it's all over, *n'en parlons plus!*" Her hypocrisy revolted him. And yet, by way of plucking off the last veil of her shame, he broke out to her again, shortly afterward, "And you *did* like it, really?" To which she returned, looking him straight in his face, without a blush, a pallor, an evasion, "Oh, I loved it!" Truly her husband had trained her well. After that Lyon said no more and his companions forbore temporarily to insist, like people of tact and sympathy aware that the odious accident had made him sore.

When they quitted the table the Colonel went away without coming upstairs; but Lyon returned to the drawing-room with his hostess, remarking to her however on the way that he could remain but a moment. He spent that moment—it prolonged itself a little—standing with her before the chimney-piece. She neither sat down nor asked him to; her manner denoted that she intended to go out. Yes, her husband had trained her well; yet Lyon dreamed for a moment that now he was alone with her she would perhaps break down, retract, apologise, confide, say to him, "My dear old friend, forgive this hideous comedy—you understand!" And then how he would have loved her and pitied her, guarded her, helped her always! If she were not ready to do something of that sort why had she treated him as if he were a dear

old friend; why had she let him for months suppose certain things—
or almost; why had she come to his studio day after day to sit near
him on the pretext of her child's protrait, as if she liked to think what
might have been? Why had she come so near a tacit confession, in a
word, if she was not willing to go an inch further? And she was not
willing—she was not; he could see that as he lingered there. She moved
about the room a little, rearranging two or three objects on the tables,
but she did nothing more. Suddenly he said to her: "Which way was
she going, when you came out?"

"She—the woman we saw?"

"Yes, your husband's strange friend. It's a clew worth following."
He had no desire to frighten her; he only wanted to communicate the
impulse which would make her say, "Ah, spare me—and spare *him*!
There was no such person."

Instead of this Mrs. Capadose replied, "She was going away from
us—she crossed the road. We were coming towards the station."

"And did she appear to recognise the Colonel —did she look round?"

"Yes; she looked round, but I didn't notice much. A hansom came
along and we got into it. It was not till then that Clement told me who
she was: I remember he said that she was there for no good. I suppose
we ought to have gone back."

"Yes; you would have saved the picture."

For a moment she said nothing; then she smiled. "For you, I am
very sorry. But you must remember that I possess the original!"

At this Lyon turned away. "Well, I must go," he said; and he left
her without any other farewell and made his way out of the house. As
he went slowly up the street the sense came back to him of that first
glimpse of her he had had at Stayes—the way he had seen her gaze
across the table at her husband. Lyon stopped at the corner, looking
vaguely up and down. He would never go back—he couldn't. She was
still in love with the Colonel—he had trained her too well.

THE REAL THING

I

When the porter's wife (she used to answer the house-bell), announced "A gentleman—with a lady, sir," I had, as I often had in those days, for the wish was father to the thought, an immediate vision of sitters. Sitters my visitors in this case proved to be; but not in the sense I should have preferred. However, there was nothing at first to indicate that they might not have come for a portrait. The gentleman, a man of fifty, very high and very straight, with a moustache slightly grizzled and a dark grey walking-coat admirably fitted, both of which I noted professionally—I don't mean as a barber or yet as a tailor—would have struck me as a celebrity if celebrities often were striking. It was a truth of which I had for some time been conscious that a figure with a good deal of frontage was, as one might say, almost never a public institution. A glance at the lady helped to remind me of this paradoxical law: she also looked too distinguished to be a "personality." Moreover one would scarcely come across two variations together.

Neither of the pair spoke immediately—they only prolonged the preliminary gaze which suggested that each wished to give the other a chance. They were visibly shy; they stood there letting me take them in—which, as I afterwards perceived, was the most practical thing they could have done. In this way their embarrassment served their cause. I had seen people painfully reluctant to mention that they desired anything so gross as to be represented on canvas; but the scruples of my new friends appeared almost insurmountable. Yet the gentleman might have said "I should like a portrait of my wife," and the lady might have said "I should like a portrait of my husband." Perhaps they were not husband and wife—this naturally would make the matter more delicate. Perhaps they wished to be done together—in which case they ought to have brought a third person to break the news.

"We come from Mr. Rivet," the lady said at last, with a dim smile which had the effect of a moist sponge passed over a "sunk" piece of painting, as well as of a vague allusion to vanished beauty. She was as tall and straight, in her degree, as her companion, and with ten years less to carry. She looked as sad as a woman could look whose face was not charged with expression; that is her tinted oval mask showed friction as an exposed surface shows it. The hand of time had played over her freely, but only to simplify. She was slim and stiff, and so well-dressed, in dark blue cloth, with lappets and pockets and buttons, that it was clear she employed the same tailor as her husband. The couple had an indefinable air of prosperous thrift—they evidently got a good deal of luxury for their money. If I was to be one of their luxuries it would behoove me to consider my terms.

"Ah, Claude Rivet recommended me?" I inquired; and I added that it was very kind of him, though I could reflect that, as he only painted landscape, this was not a sacrifice.

The lady looked very hard at the gentleman, and the gentleman looked round the room. Then staring at the floor a moment and stroking his moustache, he rested his pleasant eyes on me with the remark: "He said you were the right one."

"I try to be, when people want to sit."

"Yes, we should like to," said the lady anxiously.

"Do you mean together?"

My visitors exchanged a glance. "If you could do anything with *me*, I suppose it would be double," the gentleman stammered.

"Oh yes, there's naturally a higher charge for two figures than for one."

"We should like to make it pay," the husband confessed.

"That's very good of you," I returned, appreciating so unwonted a sympathy—for I supposed he meant pay the artist.

A sense of strangeness seemed to dawn on the lady. "We mean for the illustrations—Mr. Rivet said you might put one in."

"Put one in—an illustration?" I was equally confused.

"Sketch her off, you know," said the gentleman, colouring.

It was only then that I understood the service Claude Rivet had rendered me; he had told them that I worked in black and white, for magazines, for story-books, for sketches of contemporary life, and consequently had frequent employment for models. These things were true, but it was not less true (I may confess it now—whether because the aspiration was to lead to everything or to nothing I leave the reader to guess), that I couldn't get the honours, to say nothing of the emoluments, of a great painter of portraits out of my head. My "illustrations" were my pot-boilers; I looked to a different branch of art (far and away the most interesting it had always seemed to me), to perpetuate my fame. There was no shame in looking to it also to make my fortune; but that fortune was by so much further from being made from the moment my visitors wished to be "done" for nothing. I was disappointed; for in the pictorial sense I had immediately *seen* them. I had seized their type—I had already settled what I would do with it. Something that wouldn't absolutely have pleased them, I afterwards reflected.

"Ah, you're—you're—a—?" I began, as soon as I had mastered my surprise. I couldn't bring out the dingy word "models"; it seemed to fit the case so little.

"We haven't had much practice," said the lady.

"We've got to *do* something, and we've thought that an artist in your line might perhaps make something of us," her husband threw off. He further mentioned that they didn't know many artists and that they had gone first, on the off-chance (he painted views of course, but sometimes put in figures—perhaps I remembered), to Mr. Rivet, whom they had met a few years before at a place in Norfolk where he was sketching.

"We used to sketch a little ourselves," the lady hinted.

"It's very awkward, but we absolutely *must* do something," her husband went on.

"Of course, we're not so *very* young," she admitted, with a wan smile.

With the remark that I might as well know something more about them, the husband had handed me a card extracted from a neat new pocket-book (their appurtenances were all of the freshest) and inscribed with the words "Major Monarch." Impressive as these words were they didn't carry my knowledge much further; but my visitor presently added: "I've left the army, and we've had the misfortune to lose our money. In fact our means are dreadfully small."

"It's an awful bore," said Mrs. Monarch.

They evidently wished to be discreet—to take care not to swagger because they were gentlefolks. I perceived they would have been willing to recognise this as something of a drawback, at the same time that I guessed at an underlying sense—their consolation in adversity—that they *had* their points. They certainly had; but these advantages struck me as preponderantly social; such for instance as would help to make a drawing-room look well. However, a drawing-room was always, or ought to be, a picture.

In consequence of his wife's allusion to their age Major Monarch observed: "Naturally, it's more for the figure that we thought of going in. We can still hold ourselves up." On the instant I saw that the figure was indeed their strong point. His "naturally" didn't sound vain, but it lighted up the question. "*She* has got the best," he continued, nodding at his wife, with a pleasant after-dinner absence of circumlocution. I could only reply, as if we were in fact sitting over our wine, that this didn't prevent his own from being very good; which led him in turn to rejoin: "We thought that if you ever have to do people like us, we might be something like it. *She*, particularly—for a lady in a book, you know."

I was so amused by them that, to get more of it, I did my best to take their point of view; and though it was an embarrassment to find myself appraising physically, as if they were animals on hire or useful blacks, a pair whom I should have expected to meet only in one of the relations in which criticism is tacit, I looked at Mrs. Monarch judicially enough to be able to exclaim, after a moment, with conviction: "Oh yes, a lady in a book!" She was singularly like a bad illustration.

"We'll stand up, if you like," said the Major; and he raised himself before me with a really grand air.

I could take his measure at a glance—he was six feet two and a perfect gentleman. It would have paid any club in process of formation and in want of a stamp to engage him at a salary to stand in the principal window. What struck me immediately was that in coming to me they had rather missed their vocation; they could surely have been turned to better account for advertising purposes. I couldn't of course see the thing in detail, but I could see them make someone's fortune—I don't mean their own. There was something in them for a waistcoat-maker, an hotel-keeper or a soap-vendor. I could imagine "We always use it" pinned on their bosoms with the greatest effect; I had a vision of the promptitude with which they would launch a table d'hôte.

Mrs. Monarch sat still, not from pride but from shyness, and presently her husband said to her: "Get up my dear and show how smart you are." She obeyed, but she had no need to get up to show it. She walked to the end of the studio, and then she came back blushing, with her fluttered eyes on her husband. I was reminded of an incident I had accidentally had a glimpse of in Paris—being with a friend there, a dramatist about to produce a play—when an actress came to him to ask to be intrusted with a part. She went through her paces before him, walked up and down as Mrs. Monarch was doing. Mrs. Monarch did it quite as well, but I abstained from applauding. It was very odd to see such people apply for such poor pay. She looked as if she had ten thousand a year. Her husband had used the word that described her: she was, in the London current jargon, essentially and typically "smart." Her figure was, in the same order of ideas, conspicuously and irreproachably "good." For a woman of her age her waist was surprisingly small; her elbow moreover had the orthodox crook. She held her head at the conventional angle; but why did she come to *me*? She ought to have tried on jackets at a big shop. I feared my visitors were not only destitute, but "artistic"—which would be a great complication. When she sat down again I thanked her, observing that what a draughtsman most valued in his model was the faculty of keeping quiet.

"Oh, *she* can keep quiet," said Major Monarch. Then he added, jocosely: "I've always kept her quiet."

"I'm not a nasty fidget, am I?" Mrs. Monarch appealed to her husband.

He addressed his answer to me. "Perhaps it isn't out of place to mention—because we ought to be quite business-like, oughtn't we? — that when I married her she was known as the Beautiful Statue."

"Oh, dear!" said Mrs. Monarch, ruefully.

"Oh course I should want a certain amount of expression," I rejoined.

"*Of course!*" they both exclaimed.

"And then I suppose you know that you'll get awfully tired."

"Oh, we *never* get tired!" they eagerly cried.

"Have you had any kind of practice?"

They hesitated—they looked at each other. "We've been photographed, *immensely*," said Mrs. Monarch.

"She means the fellows have asked us," added the Major.

"I see—because you're so good-looking."

"I don't know what they thought, but they were always after us."

"We always got our photographs for nothing," smiled Mrs. Monarch.

"We might have brought some, my dear," her husband remarked.

"I'm not sure we have any left. We've given quantities away," she explained to me.

"With our autographs and that sort of thing," said the Major.

"Are they to be got in the shops?" I inquired, as a harmless pleasantry.

"Oh, yes; *hers*—they used to be."

"Not now," said Mrs. Monarch, with her eyes on the floor.

II

I could fancy the "sort of thing" they put on the presentation-copies of their photographs, and I was sure they wrote a beautiful hand. It was odd how quickly I was sure of everything that concerned them. If they were now so poor as to have to earn shillings and pence, they never had had much of a margin. Their good looks had been their capital, and they had good-humouredly made the most of the career that this resource marked out for them. It was in their faces, the blankness, the deep intellectual repose of the twenty years of country-house visiting which had given them pleasant intonations. I could see the sunny drawing-rooms, sprinkled with periodicals she didn't read, in which Mrs. Monarch had continuously sat; I could see the wet shrubberies in which she had walked, equipped to admiration for either exercise. I could see the rich covers the Major had helped to shoot and the wonderful garments in which, late at night, he repaired to the smoking-room to talk about them. I could imagine their leggings and waterproofs, their knowing tweeds and rugs, their rolls of sticks and cases of tackle and neat umbrellas; and I could evoke the exact appearance of their servants and the compact variety of their luggage on the platforms of country stations.

They gave small tips, but they were liked; they didn't do anything themselves, but they were welcome. They looked so well everywhere; they gratified the general relish for stature, complexion and "form." They knew it without fatuity or vulgarity, and they respected themselves in consequence. They were not superficial; they were thorough and kept themselves up—it had been their line. People with such a taste for activity had to have some line. I could feel how, even in a dull house, they could have been counted upon for cheerfulness. At present something had happened—it didn't matter what, their little income had grown less, it had grown least—and they had to do something for pocket-money. Their friends liked them, but didn't like to support them. There was something about them that represented credit—their clothes, their manners, their type; but if credit is a large empty pocket in which an occasional chink reverberates, the chink at least must be audible. What they wanted of me was to help to make it so. Fortunately they had no children—I soon divined that. They would also perhaps wish our relations to be kept secret: this was why it was "for the figure"— the reproduction of the face would betray them.

I liked them—they were so simple, and I had no objection to them if they would suit. But, somehow, with all their perfections I didn't easily believe in them. After all they were amateurs, and the ruling passion of my life was the detestation of the amateur. Combined with this was another perversity—an innate preference for the represented subject over the real one: the defect of the real one was so apt to be a lack of representation. I liked things that appeared; then one was sure. Whether they *were* or not was a subordinate and almost always a profitless question. There were other considerations, the first of which was that I already had two or three people in use, notably a young person with big feet, in alpaca, from Kilburn, who for a couple of years had come to me regularly for my illustrations and with whom I was still—perhaps ignobly—satisfied. I frankly explained to my visitors how the case stood; but they had taken more precautions than I supposed. They had reasoned out their opportunity, for Claude Rivet had told them of the projected *édition de luxe* of one of the writers of our day— the rarest of the novelists—who, long neglected by the multitudinous vulgar and dearly prized by the attentive (need I mention Philip Vincent?) had had the happy fortune of seeing, late in life, the dawn and then the full light of a higher criticism—an estimate in which, on the part of the public, there was something really of expiation. The edition in question, planned by a publisher of taste, was practically an act of high reparation; the wood-cuts with which it was to be enriched were the homage of English art to one of the most independent representatives of English letters. Major and Mrs. Monarch confessed to me that they had hoped I might be able to work *them* into my share of the enterprise. They knew I was to do the first of the books, "Rutland Ramsay," but I had to make clear to them that my participation in the rest of the affair—this first book was to be a test—was to depend on the satisfaction I should give. If this should be limited my employers would drop me without a scruple. It was therefore a crisis for me, and naturally I was making special preparations, looking about for new people, if they should be necessary, and securing the best types. I admitted however that I should like to settle down to two or three good models who would do for everything.

"Should we have often to—a—put on special clothes?" Mrs. Monarch timidly demanded.

"Dear, yes—that's half the business."

"And should we be expected to supply our own costumes?"

"Oh, no; I've got a lot of things. A painter's models put on—or put off—anything he likes."

"And do you mean—a—the same?"

"The same?"

Mrs. Monarch looked at her husband again.

"Oh, she was just wondering," he explained, "if the costumes are in *general* use." I had to confess that they were, and I mentioned further that some of them (I had a lot of genuine, greasy last-century things), had served their time, a hundred years ago, on living, world-stained men and women. "We'll put on anything that *fits*," said the Major.

"Oh, I arrange that—they fit in the pictures."

"I'm afraid I should do better for the modern books. I would come as you like," said Mrs. Monarch.

"She has got a lot of clothes at home: they might do for contemporary life," her husband continued.

"Oh, I can fancy scenes in which you'd be quite natural." And indeed I could see the slipshod rearrangements of stale properties—the stories I tried to produce pictures for without the exasperation of reading them—whose sandy tracts the good lady might help to people. But I had to return to the fact that for this sort of work—the daily mechanical grind—I was already equipped; the people I was working with were fully adequate.

"We only thought we might be more like *some* characters," said Mrs. Monarch mildly, getting up.

Her husband also rose; he stood looking at me with a dim wistfulness that was touching in so fine a man. "Wouldn't it be rather a pull sometimes to have—a—to have—?" He hung fire; he wanted me to help him by phrasing what he meant. But I couldn't—I didn't know. So he brought it out, awkwardly: "The *real* thing; a gentleman, you know, or a lady." I was quite ready to give a general assent—I admitted that there was a great deal in that. This encouraged Major Monarch to say, following up his appeal with an unacted gulp: "It's awfully hard—we've tried everything." The gulp was communicative; it proved too much for his wife. Before I knew it Mrs. Monarch had dropped again upon a divan and burst into tears. Her husband sat down beside her, holding one of her hands; whereupon she quickly dried her eyes with the other, while I felt embarrassed as she looked up at me. "There isn't a confounded job I haven't applied for—waited for—prayed for. You can fancy we'd be pretty bad first. Secretaryships and that sort of thing? You might as well ask for a peerage. I'd be *anything*—I'm strong; a messenger or a coalheaver. I'd put on a gold-laced cap and open carriage-doors in front of the haberdasher's; I'd hang about a station, to carry portmanteaus; I'd be a postman. But they won't *look* at you; there are thousands, as good as yourself, already on the ground. *Gentlemen*, poor beggars, who have drunk their wine, who have kept their hunters!"

I was as reassuring as I knew how to be, and my visitors were presently on their feet again while, for the experiment, we agreed on an hour. We were discussing it when the door opened and Miss Churm came in with a wet umbrella. Miss Churm had to take the omnibus to Maida Vale and then walk half-a-mile. She looked a trifle blowsy and slightly splashed. I scarcely ever saw her come in without thinking afresh how odd it was that, being so little in herself, she should yet be so much in others. She was a meagre little Miss Churm, but she was an ample heroine of romance. She was only a freckled cockney, but she could represent everything, from a fine lady to a shepherdess; she had the faculty, as she might have had a fine voice or long hair. She couldn't spell, and she loved beer, but she had two or three "points," and practice, and a knack, and mother-wit, and a kind of whimsical sensibility, and a love of the theatre, and seven sisters, and not an ounce of respect, especially for the *h*. The first thing my visitors saw was that her umbrella was wet and in their spotless perfection they visibly winced at it. The rain had come on since their arrival.

"I'm all in a soak; there *was* a mess of people in the 'bus. I wish you lived near a stytion," said Miss Churm. I requested her to get ready as quickly as possible, and she passed into the room in which she always changed her dress. But before going out she asked me what she was to get into this time.

"It's the Russian princess, don't you know?" I answered; "the one with the 'golden eyes,' in black velvet, for the long thing in the *Cheapside*."

"Golden eyes? I *say!*" cried Miss Churm, while my companions watched her with intensity as she withdrew. She always arranged herself, when she was late, before I could turn round; and I kept my visitors a little, on purpose, so that they might get an idea, from seeing her, what would be expected of themselves. I mentioned that she was quite my notion of an excellent model—she was really very clever.

"Do you think she looks like a Russian princess?" Major Monarch asked, with lurking alarm.

"When I make her, yes."

"Oh, if you have to *make* her—!" he reasoned, acutely.

"That's the most you can ask. There are so many that are not makeable."

"Well now, *here's* a lady"—and with a persuasive smile he passed his arm into his wife's—"who's already made!"

"Oh, I'm not a Russian princess," Mrs. Monarch protested, a little coldly. I could see that she had known some and didn't like them. There, immediately, was a complication of a kind that I never had to fear with Miss Churm.

This young lady came back in black velvet—the gown was rather rusty and very low on her lean shoulders—and with a Japanese fan in her red hands. I reminded her that in the scene I was doing she had to look over someone's head. "I forget whose it is; but it doesn't matter. Just look over a head."

"I'd rather look over a stove," said Miss Churm; and she took her station near the fire. She fell into position, settled herself into a tall attitude, gave a certain backward inclination to her head and a certain forward drop to her fan, and looked, at least to my prejudiced sense, distinguished and charming, foreign and dangerous. We left her looking so, while I went down-stairs with Major and Mrs. Monarch.

"I think I could come about as near it as that," said Mrs. Monarch.

"Oh, you think she's shabby, but you must allow for the alchemy of art."

However, they went off with an evident increase of comfort, founded on their demonstrable advantage in being the real thing. I could fancy them shuddering over Miss Churm. She was very droll about them when I went back, for I told her what they wanted.

"Well, if *she* can sit I'll tyke to bookkeeping," said my model.

"She's very lady-like," I replied, as an innocent form of aggravation.

"So much the worse for *you.* That means she can't turn round."

"She'll do for the fashionable novels."

"Oh yes, she'll *do* for them!" my model humorously declared. "Ain't they bad enough without her?" I had often sociably denounced them to Miss Churm.

III

It was for the elucidation of a mystery in one of these works that I first tried Mrs. Monarch. Her husband came with her, to be useful if necessary—it was sufficiently clear that as a general thing he would prefer to come with her. At first I wondered if this were for "propriety's" sake—if he were going to be jealous and meddling. The idea was too tiresome, and if it had been confirmed it would speedily have brought our acquaintance to a close. But I soon saw there was nothing in it and that if he accompanied Mrs. Monarch it was (in addition to the chance of being wanted), simply because he had nothing else to do. When she was away from him his occupation was gone—she never had been away from him. I judged, rightly, that in their awkward situation their close union was their main comfort and that this union had no weak spot. It was a real marriage, an encouragement to the hesitating, a nut for pessimists to crack. Their address was humble (I remember afterwards thinking it had been the only thing about them that was really professional), and I could fancy the lamentable lodgings in which the Major would have been left alone. He could bear them with his wife—he couldn't bear them without her.

He had too much tact to try and make himself agreeable when he couldn't be useful; so he simply sat and waited, when I was too absorbed in my work to talk. But I liked to make him talk—it made my work, when it didn't interrupt it, less sordid, less special. To listen to him was to combine the excitement of going out with the economy of staying at home. There was only one hindrance: that I seemed not to know any of the people he and his wife had known. I think he wondered extremely, during the term of our intercourse, whom the deuce I *did* know. He hadn't a stray sixpence of an idea to fumble for; so we didn't spin it very fine—we confined ourselves to questions of leather and even of liquor (saddlers and breeches-makers and how to get good claret cheap), and matters like "good trains" and the habits of small game. His lore on these last subjects was astonishing, he managed to interweave the station-master with the ornithologist. When he couldn't talk about greater things he could talk cheerfully about smaller, and since I couldn't accompany him into reminiscences of the fashionable world he could lower the conversation without a visible effort to my level.

So earnest a desire to please was touching in a man who could so easily have knocked one down. He looked after the fire and had an opinion on the draught of the stove, without my asking him, and I could see that he thought many of my arrangements not half clever enough. I remember telling him that if I were only rich I would offer him a salary to come and teach me how to live. Sometimes he gave a random sigh, of which the essence was: "Give me even such a bare old barrack as *this*, and I'd do something with it!" When I wanted to use him he came alone; which was an illustration of the superior courage of women. His wife could bear her solitary second floor, and she was in general more discreet; showing by various small reserves that she was alive to the propriety of keeping our relations markedly professional—not letting them slide into sociability. She wished it to remain clear that she and the Major were employed, not cultivated, and if she approved of me as a superior, who could be kept in his place, she never thought me quite good enough for an equal.

She sat with great intensity, giving the whole of her mind to it, and was capable of remaining for an hour almost as motionless as if she were before a photographer's lens. I could see she had been photographed often, but somehow the very habit that made her good for that purpose unfitted her for mine. At first I was extremely pleased with her lady-like air, and it was a satisfaction, on coming to follow her lines, to see how good they were and how far they could lead the pencil. But after a few times I began to find her too insurmountably stiff; do what I would with it my drawing looked like a photograph or a copy of a photograph. Her figure had no variety of expression—she herself had no sense of variety. You may say that this was my business, was only a question of placing her. I placed her in every conceivable position, but she managed to obliterate their differences. She was always a lady certainly, and into the bargain was always the same lady. She was the real thing but always the same thing. There were moments when I was oppressed by the serenity of her confidence that she *was* the real thing. All her dealings with me and all her husband's were an implication that this was lucky for *me*. Meanwhile I found myself trying to invent types that approached her own, instead of making her own transform itself—in the clever way that was not impossible, for instance, to poor Miss Churm. Arrange as I would and take the precautions I would, she always, in my pictures, came out too tall, landing me in the dilemma of having represented a fascinating woman as seven feet high, which, out of respect perhaps to my own very much scantier inches, was far from my idea of such a personage.

The case was worse with the Major—nothing I could do would keep *him* down, so that he became useful only for the representation of brawny giants. I adored variety and range, I cherished human accidents, the illustrative note; I wanted to characterise closely, and the thing in the world I most hated was the danger of being ridden by a type. I had quarrelled with some of my friends about it—I had parted company with them for maintaining that one *had* to be, and that if the type was beautiful (witness Raphael and Leonardo), the servitude was only a gain. I was neither Leonardo nor Raphael; I might only be a presumptuous young modern searcher, but I held that everything was to be sacrificed sooner than character. When they averred that the haunting type in question could easily be character, I retorted, perhaps superficially: "Whose?" It couldn't be everybody's—it might end in being nobody's.

After I had drawn Mrs. Monarch a dozen times I perceived more clearly than before that the value of such a model as Miss Churm resided precisely in the fact that she had no positive stamp, combined of course with the other fact that what she did have was a curious and inexplicable talent for imitation. Her usual appearance was like a curtain which she could draw up at request for a capital performance. This performance was simply suggestive; but it was a word to the wise—it was vivid and pretty. Sometimes, even, I thought it, though she was plain herself, too insipidly pretty; I made it a reproach to her that the figures drawn from her were monotonously (*bêtement*, as we used to say) graceful. Nothing made her more angry: it was so much her pride to feel that she could sit for characters that had nothing in common with each other. She would accuse me at such moments of taking away her "reputytion."

It suffered a certain shrinkage, this queer quantity, from the repeated visits of my new friends. Miss Churm was greatly in demand, never in want of employment, so I had no scruple in putting her off occasionally, to try them more at my ease. It was certainly amusing at first to do the real thing—it was amusing to do Major Monarch's trousers. They *were* the real thing, even if he did come out colossal. It was amusing to do his wife's back hair (it was so mathematically neat,) and the particular "smart" tension of her tight stays. She lent herself especially to positions in which the face was somewhat averted or blurred; she abounded in lady-like back views and *profils perdus*. When she stood erect she took naturally one of the attitudes in which court-painters represent queens and princesses; so that I found myself wondering whether, to draw out this accomplishment, I couldn't get the editor of the *Cheapside* to publish a really royal romance, "A Tale of Buckingham Palace." Sometimes, however, the real thing and the make-believe came into contact; by which I mean that Miss Churm, keeping an appointment or coming to make one on days when I had much work in hand, encountered her invidious rivals. The encounter was not on their part, for they noticed her no more than if she had been the housemaid; not from intentional loftiness, but simply because, as yet, professionally, they didn't know how to fraternise, as I could guess that they would have liked—or at least that the Major would. They couldn't talk about the omnibus—they always walked; and they didn't know what else to try—she wasn't interested in good trains or cheap claret. Besides, they must have felt—in the air—that she was amused at them, secretly derisive of their ever knowing how. She was not a person to conceal her scepticism if she had had a chance to show it. On the other hand Mrs. Monarch didn't think her tidy; for why else did she take pains to say to me (it was going out of the way, for Mrs. Monarch), that she didn't like dirty women?

One day when my young lady happened to be present with my other sitters (she even dropped in, when it was convenient, for a chat), I asked her to be so good as to lend a hand in getting tea—a service with which she was familiar and which was one of a class that, living as I did in a small way, with slender domestic resources, I often appealed to my models to render. They liked to lay hands on my property, to break the sitting, and sometimes the china—I made them feel Bohemian. The next time I saw Miss Churm after this incident she surprised me greatly by making a scene about it—she accused me of having wished to humiliate her. She had not resented the outrage at the time, but had seemed obliging and amused, enjoying the comedy of asking Mrs. Monarch, who sat vague and silent, whether she would have cream and sugar, and putting an exaggerated simper into the question. She had tried intonations—as if she too wished to pass for the real thing; till I was afraid my other visitors would take offence.

Oh, *they* were determined not to do this; and their touching patience was the measure of their great need. They would sit by the hour, uncomplaining, till I was ready to use them; they would come back on the chance of being wanted and would walk away cheerfully if they were not. I used to go to the door with them to see in what magnificent order they retreated. I tried to find other employment for them—I introduced them to several artists. But they didn't "take," for reasons I could appreciate, and I became conscious, rather anxiously, that after such disappointments they fell back upon me with a heavier weight. They did me the honour to think that it was I who was most *their* form. They were not picturesque enough for the painters, and in those days there were not so many serious workers in black and white. Besides, they had an eye to the great job I had mentioned to them—they had secretly set their hearts on supplying the right essence for my pictorial vindication of our fine novelist. They knew that for this undertaking I should want no costume-effects, none of the frippery of past ages— that it was a case in which everything would be contemporary and satirical and, presumably, genteel. If I could work them into it their future would be assured, for the labour would of course be long and the occupation steady.

One day Mrs. Monarch came without her husband—she explained his absence by his having to go to the City. While she sat there in her usual anxious stiffness there came, at the door, a knock which I immediately recognised as the subdued appeal of a model out of work. It was followed by the entrance of a young man whom I easily perceived to be a foreigner and who proved in fact an Italian acquainted with no English word but my name, which he uttered in a way that made it seem to include all others. I had not then visited his country, nor was I proficient in his tongue; but as he was not so meanly constituted— what Italian is?—as to depend only on that member for expression he conveyed to me, in familiar but graceful mimicry, that he was in search of exactly the employment in which the lady before me was engaged. I was not struck with him at first, and while I continued to draw I emitted rough sounds of discouragement and dismissal. He stood his ground, however, not importunately, but with a dumb, dog-like fidelity in his eyes which amounted to innocent impudence—the manner of a devoted servant (he might have been in the house for years), unjustly suspected. Suddenly I saw that this very attitude and expression made a picture, whereupon I told him to sit down and wait till I should be free. There was another picture in the way he obeyed me, and I observed as I worked that there were others still in the way he looked wonderingly, with his head thrown back, about the high studio. He might have been crossing himself in St. Peter's. Before I finished I said to myself: "The fellow's a bankrupt orange-monger, but he's a treasure!"

When Mrs. Monarch withdrew he passed across the room like a flash to open the door for her, standing there with the rapt, pure gaze of the young Dante spellbound by the young Beatrice. As I never insisted, in such situations, on the blankness of the British domestic, I reflected that he had the making of a servant (and I needed one, but couldn't pay him to be only that), as well as of a model; in short I made up my mind to adopt my bright adventurer if he would agree to officiate in the double capacity. He jumped at my offer, and in the event my rashness (for I had known nothing about him), was not brought home to me. He proved a sympathetic though a desultory ministrant, and had in a wonderful degree the *sentiment de la pose*. It was uncultivated, instinctive; a part of the happy instinct which had guided him to my door and helped him to spell out my name on the card nailed to it. He had had no other introduction to me than a guess, from the shape of my high north window, seen outside, that my place was a studio and that as a studio it would contain an artist. He had wandered to England in search of fortune, like other itinerants, and had embarked, with a partner and a small green handcart, on the sale of penny ices. The ices had melted away and the partner had dissolved in their train. My young man wore tight yellow trousers with reddish stripes and his name was Oronte. He was sallow but fair, and when I put him into some old clothes of my own he looked like an Englishman. He was as good as Miss Churm, who could look, when required, like an Italian.

IV

I thought Mrs. Monarch's face slightly convulsed when, on her coming back with her husband, she found Oronte installed. It was strange to have to recognise in a scrap of a lazzarone a competitor to her magnificent Major. It was she who scented danger first, for the Major was anecdotically unconscious. But Oronte gave us tea, with a hundred eager confusions (he had never seen such a queer process), and I think she thought better of me for having at last an "establishment." They saw a couple of drawings that I had made of the establishment, and Mrs. Monarch hinted that it never would have struck her that he had sat for them. "Now the drawings you make from *us*, they look exactly like us," she reminded me, smiling in triumph; and I recognised that this was indeed just their defect. When I drew the Monarchs I couldn't, somehow, get away from them—get into the character I wanted to represent; and I had not the least desire my model should be discoverable in my picture. Miss Churm never was, and Mrs. Monarch thought I hid her, very properly, because she was vulgar; whereas if she was lost it was only as the dead who go to heaven are lost—in the gain of an angel the more.

By this time I had got a certain start with "Rutland Ramsay," the first novel in the great projected series; that is I had produced a dozen drawings, several with the help of the Major and his wife, and I had sent them in for approval. My understanding with the publishers, as I have already hinted, had been that I was to be left to do my work, in this particular case, as I liked, with the whole book committed to me; but my connection with the rest of the series was only contingent. There were moments when, frankly, it *was* a comfort to have the real thing under one's hand; for there were characters in "Rutland Ramsay" that were very much like it. There were people presumably as straight as the Major and women of as good a fashion as Mrs. Monarch. There was a great deal of country-house life—treated, it is true, in a fine, fanciful, ironical, generalised way—and there was a considerable implication of knickerbockers and kilts. There were certain things I had to settle at the outset; such things for instance as the exact appearance of the hero, the particular bloom of the heroine. The author of course gave me a lead, but there was a margin for interpretation. I took the Monarchs into my confidence, I told them frankly what I was about, I mentioned my embarrassments and alternatives. "Oh, take *him!*" Mrs. Monarch murmured sweetly, looking at her husband; and "What could you want better than my wife?" the Major inquired, with the comfortable candour that now prevailed between us.

I was not obliged to answer these remarks—I was only obliged to place my sitters. I was not easy in mind, and I postponed, a little timidly perhaps, the solution of the question. The book was a large canvas, the other figures were numerous, and I worked off at first some of the episodes in which the hero and the heroine were not concerned. When once I had set *them* up I should have to stick to them—I couldn't make my young man seven feet high in one place and five feet nine in another. I inclined on the whole to the latter measurement, though the Major more than once reminded me that *he* looked about as young as anyone. It was indeed quite possible to arrange him, for the figure, so that it would have been difficult to detect his age. After the spontaneous Oronte had been with me a month, and after I had given him to understand several different times that his native exuberance would presently constitute an insurmountable barrier to our further intercourse, I waked to a sense of his heroic capacity. He was only five feet seven, but the remaining inches were latent. I tried him almost secretly at first, for I was really rather afraid of the judgment my other models would pass on such a choice. If they regarded Miss Churm as little better than a snare, what would they think of the representation by a person so little the real thing as an Italian street-vendor of a protagonist formed by a public school?

If I went a little in fear of them it was not because they bullied me, because they had got an oppressive foothold, but because in their really pathetic decorum and mysteriously permanent newness they counted on me so intensely. I was therefore very glad when Jack Hawley came home: he was always of such good counsel. He painted badly himself, but there was no one like him for putting his finger on the place. He had been absent from England for a year; he had been somewhere—I don't remember where—to get a fresh eye. I was in a good deal of dread of any such organ, but we were old friends; he had been away for months and a sense of emptiness was creeping into my life. I hadn't dodged a missile for a year.

He came back with a fresh eye, but with the same old black velvet blouse, and the first evening he spent in my studio we smoked cigarettes till the small hours. He had done no work himself, he had only got the eye; so the field was clear for the production of my little things. He wanted to see what I had done for the *Cheapside*, but he was disappointed in the exhibition. That at least seemed the meaning of two or three comprehensive groans which, as he lounged on my big divan, on a folded leg, looking at my latest drawings, issued from his lips with the smoke of the cigarette.

"What's the matter with you?" I asked.

"What's the matter with *you*?"

"Nothing save that I'm mystified."

"You are indeed. You're quite off the hinge. What's the meaning of this new fad?" And he tossed me, with visible irreverence, a drawing in which I happened to have depicted both my majestic models. I asked if he didn't think it good, and he replied that it struck him as execrable, given the sort of thing I had always represented myself to him as wishing to arrive at; but I let that pass, I was so anxious to see exactly what he meant. The two figures in the picture looked colossal, but I supposed this was *not* what he meant, inasmuch as, for aught he knew to the contrary, I might have been trying for that. I maintained that I was working exactly in the same way as when he last had done me the honour to commend me. "Well, there's a big hole somewhere," he answered; "wait a bit and I'll discover it." I depended upon him to do so: where else was the fresh eye? But he produced at last nothing more luminous than "I don't know—I don't like your types." This was lame, for a critic who had never consented to discuss with me anything but the question of execution, the direction of strokes and the mystery of values.

"In the drawings you've been looking at I think my types are very handsome."

"Oh, they won't do!"

"I've had a couple of new models."

"I see you have. *They* won't do."

"Are you very sure of that?"

"Absolutely—they're stupid."

"You mean I am—for I ought to get round that."

"You *can't*—with such people. Who are they?"

I told him, as far as was necessary, and he declared, heartlessly: "*Ce sont des gens qu'il faut mettre à la porte.*"

"You've never seen them; they're awfully good," I compassionately objected.

"Not seen them? Why, all this recent work of yours drops to pieces with them. It's all I want to see of them."

"No one else has said anything against it—the *Cheapside* people are pleased."

"Everyone else is an ass, and the *Cheapside* people the biggest asses of all. Come, don't pretend, at this time of day, to have pretty illusions about the public, especially about publishers and editors. It's not for *such* animals you work—it's for those who know, *coloro che sanno*; so keep straight for *me* if you can't keep straight for yourself. There's a certain sort of thing you tried for from the first—and a very good thing it is. But this twaddle isn't *in* it." When I talked with Hawley later about "Rutland Ramsay" and its possible successors he declared that I must get back into my boat again or I would go to the bottom. His voice in short was the voice of warning.

I noted the warning, but I didn't turn my friends out of doors. They bored me a good deal; but the very fact that they bored me admonished me not to sacrifice them—if there was anything to be done with them—simply to irritation. As I look back at this phase they seem to me to have pervaded my life not a little. I have a vision of them as most of the time in my studio, seated, against the wall, on an old velvet bench to be out of the way, and looking like a pair of patient courtiers in a royal ante-chamber. I am convinced that during the coldest weeks of the winter they held their ground because it saved them fire. Their newness was losing its gloss, and it was impossible not to feel that they were objects of charity. Whenever Miss Churm arrived they went away, and after I was fairly launched in "Rutland Ramsay" Miss Churm arrived pretty often. They managed to express to me tacitly that they supposed I wanted her for the low life of the book, and I let them suppose it, since they had attempted to study the work—it was lying about the studio—without discovering that it dealt only with the highest circles. They had dipped into the most brilliant of our novelists without deciphering many passages. I still took an hour from them, now and again, in spite of Jack Hawley's warning: it would be time enough to dismiss them, if dismissal should be necessary, when the rigour of the season was over. Hawley had made their acquaintance—he had met them at my fireside—and thought them a ridiculous pair. Learning that he was a painter they tried to approach him, to show him too that they were the real thing; but he looked at them, across the big room, as if they were miles away: they were a compendium of everything that he most objected to in the social system of his country. Such people as that, all convention and patent-leather, with ejaculations that stopped conversation, had no business in a studio. A studio was a place to learn to see, and how could you see through a pair of feather beds?

The main inconvenience I suffered at their hands was that, at first, I was shy of letting them discover how my artful little servant had begun to sit to me for "Rutland Ramsay." They knew that I had been odd enough (they were prepared by this time to allow oddity to artists,) to pick a foreign vagabond out of the streets, when I might have had a person with whiskers and credentials; but it was some time before they learned how high I rated his accomplishments. They found him in an attitude more than once, but they never doubted I was doing him as an organ-grinder. There were several things they never guessed, and one of them was that for a striking scene in the novel, in which a footman briefly figured, it occurred to me to make use of Major Monarch as the menial. I kept putting this off, I didn't like to ask him to don the livery—besides the difficulty of finding a livery to fit him. At last, one day late in the winter, when I was at work on the despised Oronte (he caught one's idea in an instant), and was in the glow of feeling that I was going very straight, they came in, the Major and his wife, with their society laugh about nothing (there was less and less to laugh at), like country-callers—they always reminded me of that—who have walked across the park after church and are presently persuaded to stay to luncheon. Luncheon was over, but they could stay to tea—I knew they wanted it. The fit was on me, however, and I couldn't let my ardour cool and my work wait, with the fading daylight, while my model prepared it. So I asked Mrs. Monarch if she would mind laying it out—

a request which, for an instant, brought all the blood to her face. Her eyes were on her husband's for a second, and some mute telegraphy passed between them. Their folly was over the next instant; his cheerful shrewdness put an end to it. So far from pitying their wounded pride, I must add, I was moved to give it as complete a lesson as I could. They bustled about together and got out the cups and saucers and made the kettle boil. I know they felt as if they were waiting on my servant, and when the tea was prepared I said: "He'll have a cup, please—he's tired." Mrs. Monarch brought him one where he stood, and he took it from her as if he had been a gentleman at a party, squeezing a crush-hat with an elbow.

Then it came over me that she had made a great effort for me— made it with a kind of nobleness—and that I owed her a compensation. Each time I saw her after this I wondered what the compensation could be. I couldn't go on doing the wrong thing to oblige them. Oh, it *was* the wrong thing, the stamp of the work for which they sat—Hawley was not the only person to say it now. I sent in a large number of the drawings I had made for "Rutland Ramsay," and I received a warning that was more to the point than Hawley's. The artistic adviser of the house for which I was working was of opinion that many of my illustrations were not what had been looked for. Most of these illustrations were the subjects in which the Monarchs had figured. Without going into the question of what *had* been looked for, I saw at this rate I shouldn't get the other boks to do. I hurled myself in despair upon Miss Churm, I put her through all her paces. I not only adopted Oronte publicly as my hero, but one morning when the Major looked in to see if I didn't require him to finish a figure for the *Cheapside*, for which he had begun to sit the week before, I told him that I had changed my mind—I would do the drawing from my man. At this my visitor turned pale and stood looking at me. "Is *he* your idea of an English gentleman?" he asked.

I was disappointed, I was nervous, I wanted to get on with my work; so I replied with irritation: "Oh, my dear Major—I can't be ruined for *you!*"

He stood another moment; then, without a word, he quitted the studio. I drew a long breath when he was gone, for I said to myself that I shouldn't see him again. I had not told him definitely that I was in danger of having my work rejected, but I was vexed at his not having felt the catastrophe in the air, read with me the moral of our fruitless collaboration, the lesson that, in the deceptive atmosphere of art, even the highest respectability may fail of being plastic.

I didn't owe my friends money, but I did see them again. They reappeared together, three days later, and under the circumstances there was something tragic in the fact. It was a proof to me that they could find nothing else in life to do. They had threshed the matter out in a dismal conference—they had digested the bad news that they were not in for the series. If they were not useful to me even for the *Cheapside* their function seemed difficult to determine, and I could only judge at first that they had come, forgivingly, decorously, to take a last leave. This made me rejoice in secret that I had little leisure for a scene; for I had placed both my other models in position together and I was pegging away at a drawing from which I hoped to derive glory. It had been suggested by the passage in which Rutland Ramsay, drawing up a chair to Artemisia's piano-stool, says extraordinary things to her while she ostensibly fingers out a difficult piece of music. I had done Miss Churm at the piano before—it was an attitude in which she knew how to take on an absolutely poetic grace. I wished the two figures to "compose" together, intensely, and my little Italian had entered perfectly into my conception. The pair were vividly before me, the piano had been pulled out; it was a charming picture of blended youth and murmured love, which I had only to catch and keep. My visitors stood and looked at it, and I was friendly to them over my shoulder.

They made no response, but I was used to silent company and went on with my work, only a little disconcerted (even though exhilarated by the sense that *this* was at least the ideal thing), at not having got rid of them after all. Presently I heard Mrs. Monarch's sweet voice beside, or rather above me: "I wish her hair was a little better done." I looked up and she was staring with a strange fixedness at Miss Churm, whose back was turned to her. "Do you mind my just touching it?" she went on—a question which made me spring up for an instant, as with the instinctive fear that she might do the young lady a harm. But she quieted me with a glance I shall never forget—I confess I should like to have been able to paint *that*—and went for a moment to my model. She spoke to her softly, laying a hand upon her shoulder and bending over her; and as the girl, understanding, gratefully assented, she disposed her rough curls, with a few quick passes, in such a way as to make Miss

Churm's head twice as charming. It was one of the most heroic personal services I have ever seen rendered. Then Mrs. Monarch turned away with a low sigh and, looking about her as if for something to do, stooped to the floor with a noble humility and picked up a dirty rag that had dropped out of my paint-box.

The Major meanwhile had also been looking for something to do and, wandering to the other end of the studio, saw before him my breakfast things, neglected, unremoved. "I say, can't I be useful *here?*" he called out to me with an irrepressible quaver. I assented with a laugh that I fear was awkward and for the next ten minutes, while I worked, I heard the light clatter of china and the tinkle of spoons and glass. Mrs. Monarch assisted her husband—they washed up my crockery, they put it away. They wandered off into my little scullery, and I afterwards found that they had cleaned my knives and that my slender stock of plate had an unprecedented surface. When it came over me, the latent eloquence of what they were doing, I confess that my drawing was blurred for a moment—the picture swam. They had accepted their failure, but they couldn't accept their fate. They had bowed their heads in bewilderment to the perverse and cruel law in virtue of which the real thing could be so much less precious than the unreal; but they didn't want to starve. If my servants were my models, my models might be my servants. They would reverse the parts—the others would sit for the ladies and gentlemen, and *they* would do the work. They would still be in the studio—it was an intense dumb appeal to me not to turn them out. "Take us on," they wanted to say—"we'll do *anything.*"

When all this hung before me the *afflatus* vanished—my pencil dropped from my hand. My sitting was spoiled and I got rid of my sitters, who were also evidently rather mystified and awestruck. Then, alone with the Major and his wife, I had a most uncomfortable moment. He put their prayer into a single sentence: "I say, you know—just let *us* do for you, can't you?" I couldn't—it was dreadful to see them emptying my slops; but I pretended I could, to oblige them, for about a week. Then I gave them a sum of money to go away; and I never saw them again. I obtained the remaining books, but my friend Hawley repeats that Major and Mrs. Monarch did me a permanent harm, got me into a second-rate trick. If it be true I am content to have paid the price—for the memory.

PASTE

"I've found a lot more things," her cousin said to her the day after the second funeral; "they're up in her room—but they're things I wish *you'd* look at."

The pair of mourners, sufficiently stricken, were in the garden of the vicarage together, before luncheon, waiting to be summoned to that meal, and Arthur Prime had still in his face the intention, she was moved to call it rather than the expression, of feeling something or other. Some such appearance was in itself of course natural within a week of his stepmother's death, within three of his father's; but what was most present to the girl, herself sensitive and shrewd, was that he seemed somehow to brood without sorrow, to suffer without what she in her own case would have called pain. He turned away from her after this last speech—it was a good deal his habit to drop an observation and leave her to pick it up without assistance. If the vicar's widow, now in her turn finally translated, had not really belonged to him it was not for want of her giving herself, so far as he ever would take her; and she had lain for three days all alone at the end of the passage, in the great cold chamber of hospitality, the dampish, greenish room where visitors slept and where several of the ladies of the parish had, without effect, offered, in pairs and successions, piously to watch with her. His personal connection with the parish was now slighter than ever, and he had really not waited for this opportunity to show the ladies what he thought of them. She felt that she herself had, during her doleful month's leave from Bleet, where she was governess, rather taken her place in the same snubbed order; but it was presently, none the less, with a better little hope of coming in for some remembrance, some relic, that she went up to look at the things he had spoken of, the identity of which, as a confused cluster of bright objects on a table in the darkened room, shimmered at her as soon as she had opened the door.

They met her eyes for the first time, but in a moment, before touching them, she knew them as things of the theatre, as very much too fine to have been, with any verisimilitude, things of the vicarage. They were too dreadfully good to be true, for her aunt had had no jewels to speak of, and these were coronets and girdles, diamonds, rubies and sapphires. Flagrant tinsel and glass, they looked strangely vulgar, but if, after the first queer shock of them, she found herself taking them up, it was for the very proof, never yet so distinct to her, of a far-off faded story. An honest widowed cleric with a small son and a large sense of Shakspeare had, on a brave latitude of habit as well as of taste—since it implied his having in very fact dropped deep into the "pit"—conceived for an obscure actress, several years older than himself, an admiration of which the prompt offer of his reverend name and hortatory hand was the sufficiently candid sign. The response had perhaps, in those dim years, in the way of eccentricity, even bettered the proposal, and Charlotte, turning the tale over, had long since drawn from it a measure of the career renounced by the undistinguished *comédienne*—doubtless also tragic, or perhaps pantomimic, at a pinch— of her late uncle's dreams. This career could not have been eminent and must much more probably have been comfortless.

"You see what it is—old stuff of the time she never liked to mention."

Our young woman gave a start; her companion had, after all, rejoined her and had apparently watched a moment her slightly scared recognition. "So I said to myself," she replied. Then, to show intelligence, yet keep clear of twaddle: "How peculiar they look!"

"They look awful," said Arthur Prime. "Cheap gilt, diamonds as big as potatoes. These are trappings of a ruder age than ours. Actors do themselves better now."

"Oh now," said Charlotte, not to be less knowing, "actresses have real diamonds."

"Some of them." Arthur spoke drily.

"I mean the bad ones—the nobodies too."

"Oh, some of the nobodies have the biggest. But mamma wasn't of that sort."

"A nobody?" Charlotte risked.

"Not a nobody to whom somebody—well, not a nobody with diamonds. It isn't all worth, this trash, five pounds."

There was something in the old gewgaws that spoke to her, and she continued to turn them over. "They're relics. I think they have their melancholy and even their dignity."

Arthur observed another pause. "Do you care for them?" he then asked. "I mean," he promptly added, "as a souvenir."

"Of you?" Charlotte threw off.

"Of me? What have I to do with it? Of your poor dead aunt who was so kind to you," he said with virtuous sternness.

"Well, I would rather have them than nothing."

"Then please take them," he returned in a tone of relief which expressed somehow more of the eager than of the gracious.

"Thank you." Charlotte lifted two or three objects up and set them down again. Though they were lighter than the materials they imitated they were so much more extravagant that they struck her in truth as rather an awkward heritage, to which she might have preferred even a matchbox or a penwiper. They were indeed shameless pinchbeck. "Had you any idea she had kept them?"

"I don't at all believe she *had* kept them or knew they were there, and I'm very sure my father didn't. They had quite equally worked off any tenderness for the connection. These odds and ends, which she thought had been given away or destroyed, had simply got thrust into a dark corner and been forgotten."

Charlotte wondered. "Where then did you find them?"

"In that old tin box"—and the young man pointed to the receptacle from which he had dislodged them and which stood on a neighbouring chair. "It's rather a good box still, but I'm afraid I can't give you *that*."

The girl gave the box no look; she continued only to look at the trinkets. "What corner had she found?"

"She hadn't 'found' it," her companion sharply insisted; "she had simply lost it. The whole thing had passed from her mind. The box was on the top shelf of the old schoolroom closet, which, until one put one's head into it from a step-ladder, looked, from below, quite cleared out. The door is narrow and the part of the closet to the left goes well into the wall. The box had stuck there for years."

Charlotte was conscious of a mind divided and a vision vaguely troubled, and once more she took up two or three of the subjects of this revelation; a big bracelet in the form of a gilt serpent with many twists and beady eyes, a brazen belt studded with emeralds and rubies, a chain, of flamboyant architecture, to which, at the Theatre Royal Little Peddlington, Hamlet's mother had probably been careful to attach the portrait of the successor to Hamlet's father. "Are you very sure they're not really worth something? Their mere weight alone—!" she vaguely observed, balancing a moment a royal diadem that might have crowned one of the creations of the famous Mrs. Jarley.

But Arthur Prime, it was clear, had already thought the question over and found the answer easy. "If they had been worth anything to speak of she would long ago have sold them. My father and she had unfortunately never been in a position to keep any considerable value locked up." And while his companion took in the obvious force of this he went on with a flourish just marked enough not to escape her: "If they're worth anything at all—why, you're only the more welcome to them."

Charlotte had now in her hand a small bag of faded, figured silk— one of those antique conveniences that speak to us, in the terms of evaporated camphor and lavender, of the part they have played in some personal history; but, though she had for the first time drawn the string, she looked much more at the young man than at the questionable treasure it appeared to contain. "I shall like them. They're all I have."

"All you have—?"

"That belonged to her."

He swelled a little, then looked about him as if to appeal—as against her avidity—to the whole poor place. "Well, what else do you want?"

"Nothing. Thank you very much." With which she bent her eyes on the article wrapped, and now only exposed, in her superannuated satchel—a necklace of large pearls, such as might once have graced the neck of a provincial Ophelia and borne company to a flaxen wig. "This perhaps *is* worth something. Feel it." And she passed him the necklace, the weight of which she had gathered for a moment into her hand.

He measured it in the same way with his own, but remained quite detached. "Worth at most thirty shillings."

"Not more?"

"Surely not if it's paste?"

"But *is* it paste?"

He gave a small sniff of impatience. "Pearls nearly as big as filberts?"

"But they're heavy," Charlotte declared.

"No heavier than anything else." And he gave them back with an allowance for her simplicity. "Do you imagine for a moment they're real?"

She studied them a little, feeling them, turning them round. "Mightn't they possibly be?"

"Of that size—stuck away with that trash?"

"I admit it isn't likely," Charlotte presently said. "And pearls are so easily imitated."

"That's just what—to a person who knows—they're not. These have no lustre, no play."

"No—they *are* dull. They're opaque."

"Besides," he lucidly inquired, "how could she ever have come by them?"

"Mightn't they have been a present?"

Arthur stared at the question as if it were almost improper. "Because actresses are exposed—?" He pulled up, however, not saying to what, and before she could supply the deficiency had, with the sharp ejaculation of "No, they mightn't!" turned his back on her and walked away. His manner made her feel that she had probably been wanting in tact, and before he returned to the subject, the last thing that evening, she had satisfied herself of the ground of his resentment. They had been talking of her departure the next morning, the hour of her train and the fly that would come for her, and it was precisely these things that gave him his effective chance. "I really can't allow you to leave the house under the impression that my stepmother was at *any* time of her life the sort of person to allow herself to be approached—"

"With pearl necklaces and that sort of thing?" Arthur had made for her somehow the difficulty that she couldn't show him she understood him without seeming pert.

It at any rate only added to his own gravity. "That sort of thing, exactly."

"I didn't think when I spoke this morning—but I see what you mean."

"I mean that she was beyond reproach," said Arthur Prime.

"A hundred times yes."

"Therefore if she couldn't, out of her slender gains, ever have paid for a row of pearls—"

"She couldn't, in that atmosphere, ever properly have had one? Of course she couldn't. I've seen perfectly since our talk," Charlotte went on, "that that string of beads isn't even, as an imitation, very good. The little clasp itself doesn't seem even gold. With false pearls, I suppose," the girl mused, "it naturally wouldn't be."

"The whole thing's rotten paste," her companion returned as if to have done with it. "If it were *not*, and she had kept it all these years hidden—"

"Yes?" Charlotte sounded as he paused.

"Why, I shouldn't know what to think!"

"Oh, I see." She had met him with a certain blankness, but adequately enough, it seemed, for him to regard the subject as dismissed; and there was no reversion to it between them before, on the morrow, when she had with difficulty made a place for them in her trunk, she carried off these florid survivals.

At Bleet she found small occasion to revert to them and, in an air charged with such quite other references, even felt, after she had laid them away, much enshrouded, beneath various piles of clothing, as if they formed a collection not wholly without its note of the ridiculous. Yet she was never, for the joke, tempted to show them to her pupils, though Gwendolen and Blanche, in particular, always wanted, on her return, to know what she had brought back; so that without an accident by which the case was quite changed they might have appeared to enter on a new phase of interment. The essence of the accident was the sudden illness, at the last moment, of Lady Bobby, whose advent had been so much counted on to spice the five days' feast laid out for the coming of age of the eldest son of the house; and its equally marked effect was the despatch of a pressing message, in quite another direction, to Mrs. Guy, who, could she by a miracle be secured—she was always engaged ten parties deep—might be trusted to supply, it was believed, an element of exuberance scarcely less active. Mrs. Guy was already known to several of the visitors already on the scene, but she was not yet known to our young lady, who found her, after many wires and counterwires had at last determined the triumph of her arrival, a strange, charming little red-haired, black-dressed woman, with the face of a baby and the authority of a commodore. She took on the spot the discreet, the exceptional young governess into the confidence of her designs and, still more, of her doubts; intimating that it was a policy she almost always promptly pursued.

"To-morrow and Thursday are all right," she said frankly to Charlotte on the second day, "but I'm not half satisfied with Friday."

"What improvement then do you suggest?"

"Well, my strong point, you know, is *tableaux vivants*."

"Charming. And what is your favourite character?"

"Boss!" said Mrs. Guy with decision; and it was very markedly under that ensign that she had, within a few hours, completely planned her campaign and recruited her troop. Every word she uttered was to the point, but none more so than, after a general survey of their equipment, her final inquiry of Charlotte. She had been looking about, but half appeased, at the muster of decoration and drapery. "We shall be dull. We shall want more colour. You've nothing else?"

Charlotte had a thought. "No—I've *some* things."

"Then why don't you bring them?"

The girl hesitated. "Would you come to my room?"

"No," said Mrs. Guy—"bring them to-night to mine."

So Charlotte, at the evening's end, after candlesticks had flickered through brown old passages bedward, arrived at her friend's door with the burden of her aunt's relics. But she promptly expressed a fear. "Are they too garish?"

When she had poured them out on the sofa Mrs. Guy was but a minute, before the glass, in clapping on the diadem. "Awfully jolly— we can do Ivanhoe!"

"But they're only glass and tin."

"Larger than life they are, *rather*! —which is exactly what, for tableaux, is wanted. *Our* jewels, for historic scenes, don't tell—the real thing falls short. Rowena must have rubies as big as eggs. Leave them with me," Mrs. Guy continued—"they'll inspire me. Goodnight."

The next morning she was in fact—yet very strangely—inspired. "Yes, *I'll* do Rowena. But I don't my dear, understand."

"Understand what?"

Mrs. Guy gave a very lighted stare. "How you come to have such things."

Poor Charlotte smiled. "By inheritance."

"Family jewels?"

"They belonged to my aunt, who died some months go. She was on the stage a few years in early life, and these are a part of her trappings."

"She left them to you?"

"No; my cousin, her stepson, who naturally has no use for them, gave them to me for remembrance of her. She was a dear kind thing, always so nice to me, and I was fond of her."

Mrs. Guy had listened with a visible interest. "But it's *he* who must be a dear kind thing!"

Charlotte wondered. "You think so?"

"Is he," her friend went on, "also 'always so nice' to you?"

The girl, at this, face to face there with the brilliant visitor in the deserted breakfast-room, took a deeper sounding. "What is it?"

"Don't you know?"

Something came over her. "The pearls—?" But the question fainted on her lips.

"Doesn't *he* know?"

Charlotte found herself flushing. "They're *not* paste?"

"Haven't you looked at them?"

She was conscious of two kinds of embarrassment. "*You* have?"

"Very carefully."

"And they're real?"

Mrs. Guy became slightly mystifying and returned for all answer: "Come again, when you've done with the children, to my room."

Our young woman found she had done with the children, that morning, with a promptitude that was a new joy to them, and when she reappeared before Mrs. Guy this lady had already encircled a plump white throat with the only ornament, surely, in all the late Mrs. Prime's— the effaced Miss Bradshaw's—collection, in the least qualified to raise a question. If Charlotte had never yet once, before the glass, tied the string of pearls about her own neck, this was because she had been capable of no such condescension to approved "imitation"; but she had now only to look at Mrs. Guy to see that, so disposed, the ambiguous objects might have passed for frank originals. "What in the world have you done to them?"

"Only handled them, understood them, admired them and put them on. That's what pearls want; they want to be worn—it wakes them up. They're alive, don't you see? How *have* these been treated? They must have been buried, ignored, despised. They were half dead. Don't you *know* about pearls?" Mrs. Guy threw off as she fondly fingered the necklace.

"How *should* I? Do *you*?"

"Everything. These were simply asleep, and from the moment I really touched them—well," said their wearer lovingly, "it only took one's eye!"

"It took more than mine—though I did just wonder; and than Arthur's," Charlotte brooded. She found herself almost panting. "Then their value—?"

"Oh, their value's excellent."

The girl, for a deep moment, took another plunge into the wonder, the beauty and mystery, of them. "Are you *sure*?"

Her companion wheeled round for impatience. "Sure? For what kind of an idiot, my dear, do you take me?"

It was beyond Charlotte Prime to say. "For the same kind as Arthur—and as myself," she could only suggest. "But my cousin didn't know. He thinks they're worthless."

"Because of the rest of the lot? Then your cousin's an ass. But what—if, as I understood you, he gave them to you—has he to do with it?"

"Why, if he gave them to me as worthless and they turn out precious—"

"You must give them back? I don't see that—if he was such a fool. He took the risk."

Charlotte fed, in fancy, on the pearls, which, decidedly, were exquisite, but which at the present moment somehow presented themselves much more as Mrs. Guy's than either as Arthur's or as her own. "Yes—he did take it; even after I had distinctly hinted to him that they looked to me different from the other pieces."

"Well, then!" said Mrs. Guy with something more than triumph—with a positive odd relief.

But it had the effect of making our young woman think with more intensity. "Ah, you see he thought they couldn't be different, because—so peculiarly—they shouldn't be."

"Shouldn't? I don't understand."

"Why, how would she have got them?"—so Charlotte candidly put it.

"She? Who?" There was a capacity in Mrs. Guy's tone for a sinking of persons—!

"Why, the person I told you of: his stepmother, my uncle's wife—among whose poor old things, extraordinarily thrust away and out of sight, he happened to find them."

Mrs. Guy came a step nearer to the effaced Miss Bradshaw. "Do you mean she may have stolen them?"

"No. But she had been an actress."

"Oh, well then," cried Mrs. Guy, "wouldn't that be just how?"

"Yes, except that she wasn't at all a brilliant one, nor in receipt of large pay." The girl even threw off a nervous joke. "I'm afraid she couldn't have been our Rowena."

Mrs. Guy took it up. "Was she very ugly?"

"No. She may very well, when young, have looked rather nice."

"Well, then!" was Mrs. Guy's sharp comment and fresh triumph.

"You mean it was a present? That's just what he so dislikes the idea of her having received—a present from an admirer capable of going such lengths."

"Because she wouldn't have taken it for nothing? *Speriamo*—that she wasn't a brute. The 'length' her admirer went was the length of a whole row. Let us hope she was just a little kind!"

"Well," Charlotte went on, "That she was 'kind' might seem to be shown by the fact that neither her husband, nor his son, nor I, his niece, knew or dreamed of her possessing anything so precious; by her having kept the gift all the rest of her life beyond discovery—out of sight and protected from suspicion."

"As if, you mean"—Mrs. Guy was quick—"she had been wedded to it and yet was ashamed of it? Fancy," she laughed while she manipulated the rare beads, "being ashamed of *these!*"

"But you see she had married a clergyman."

"Yes, she must have been 'rum.' But at any rate he had married *her*. What did he suppose?"

"Why, that she had never been of the sort by whom such offerings are encouraged."

"Ah, my dear, the sort by whom they are *not*—!" But Mrs. Guy caught herself up. "And her stepson thought the same?"

"Overwhelmingly."

"Was he, then if only her stepson—"

"So fond of her as that comes to? Yes; he had never known, consciously, his real mother, and, without children of her own, she was very patient and nice with him. And *I* liked her so," the girl pursued, "that at the end of ten years, in so strange a manner, to 'give her away'—"

"Is impossible to you? Then don't!" said Mrs. Guy with decision.

"Ah, but if they're real I can't keep them!" Charlotte, with her eyes on them, moaned in her impatience. "It's too difficult."

"Where's the difficulty, if he has such sentiments that he would rather sacrifice the necklace than admit it, with the presumption it carries with it, to be genuine? You've only to be silent."

"And keep it? How can *I* ever wear it?"

"You'd have to hide it, like your aunt?" Mrs. Guy was amused. "You can easily sell it."

Her companion walked round her for a look at the affair from behind. The clasp was certainly, doubtless intentionally, misleading, but everything else was indeed lovely. "Well, I must think. Why didn't *she* sell them?" Charlotte broke out in her trouble.

Mrs. Guy had an instant answer. "Doesn't that prove what they secretly recalled to her? You've only to be silent!" she ardently repeated.

"I must think—I must think!"

Mrs. Guy stood with her hands attached but motionless. "Then you want them back?"

As if with the dread of touching them Charlotte retreated to the door. "I'll tell you to-night."

"But may I wear them?"

"Meanwhile?"

"This evening—at dinner."

It was the sharp, selfish pressure of this that really, on the spot, determined the girl; but for the moment, before closing the door on the question, she only said: "As you like!"

They were busy much of the day with preparation and rehearsal, and at dinner, that evening, the concourse of guests was such that a place among them for Miss Prime failed to find itself marked. At the time the company rose she was therefore alone in the schoolroom, where, towards eleven o'clock, she received a visit from Mrs. Guy. This lady's white shoulders heaved, under the pearls, with an emotion that the very red lips which formed, as if for the full effect, the happiest opposition of colour, were not slow to translate. "My dear, you should have seen the sensation—they've had a success!"

Charlotte, dumb a moment, took it all in. "It is as if they knew it—they're more and more alive. But so much the worse for both of us! I can't," she brought out with an effort, "be silent."

"You mean to return them?"

"If I don't I'm a thief."

Mrs. Guy gave her a long, hard look: what was decidedly not of the baby in Mrs. Guy's face was a certain air of established habit in the eyes. Then, with a sharp little jerk of her head and a backward reach of her bare beautiful arms, she undid the clasp and, taking off the necklace, laid it on the table. "If you do, you're a goose."

"Well, of the two—!" said our young lady, gathering it up with a sigh. And as if to get it, for the pang it gave, out of sight as soon as possible, she shut it up, clicking the lock, in the drawer of her own little table; after which when she turned again, her companion, without it, looked naked and plain. "But what will you say?" it then occurred to her to demand.

"Downstairs—to explain?" Mrs. Guy was, after all, trying at least to keep her temper. "Oh, I'll put on something else and say that clasp is broken. And you won't of course name *me* to him," she added.

"As having undeceived me? No—I'll say that, looking at the thing more carefully, it's my own private idea."

"And does he know how little you really know?"

"As an expert—surely. And he has much, always, the conceit of his own opinion."

"Then he won't believe you—as he so hates to. He'll stick to his judgment and maintain his gift, and we shall have the darlings back!" With which reviving assurance Mrs. Guy kissed for good-night.

She was not, however, to be gratified or justified by any prompt event, for, whether or no paste entered into the composition of the ornament in question, Charlotte shrank from the temerity of despatching it to town by post. Mrs. Guy was thus disappointed of the hope of seeing the business settled—"by return," she had seemed to expect— before the end of the revels. The revels, moreover, rising to a frantic pitch, pressed for all her attention, and it was at last only in the general confusion of leave-taking that she made, parenthetically, a dash at her young friend.

"Come, what will you take for them?"

"The pearls? Ah, you'll have to treat with my cousin."

Mrs. Guy, with quick intensity, lent herself. "Where then does he live?"

"In chambers in the Temple. You can find him."

"But what's the use, if *you* do neither one thing nor the other?"

"Oh, I *shall* do the 'other,'" Charlotte said: "I'm only waiting till I go up. You want them so awfully?" She curiously, solemnly again, sounded her.

"I'm dying for them. There's a special charm in them—I don't know what it is: they tell so their history."

"But what do you know of that?"

"Just what they themsleves say. It's all *in* them—and it comes out. They breathe a tenderness—they have the white glow of it. My dear," hissed Mrs. Guy in supreme confidence and as she buttoned her glove— "they're things of love!"

"Oh!" our young woman vaguely exclaimed.

"They're things of passion!"

"Mercy!" she gasped, turning short off. But these words remained, though indeed their help was scarce needed, Charlotte being in private face to face with a new light, as she by this time felt she must call it, on the dear dead, kind, colourless lady whose career had turned so sharp a corner in the middle. The pearls had quite taken their place as a revelation. She might have received them for nothing—admit that; but she couldn't have kept them so long and so unprofitably hidden, couldn't have enjoyed them only in secret, for nothing; and she had mixed them, in her reliquary, with false things, in order to put curiosity and detection off the scent. Over this strange fact poor Charlotte in- terminably mused: it became more touching, more attaching for her than she could now confide to any ear. How bad, or how happy—in the sophisticated sense of Mrs. Guy and the young man at the Temple— the effaced Miss Bradshaw must have been to have had to be so mute! The little governess at Bleet put on the necklace now in secret sessions; she wore it sometimes under her dress; she came to feel, verily, a haunting passion for it. Yet in her penniless state she would have parted with it for money; she gave herself also to dreams of what in this direction it would do for her. The sophistry of her so often saying to herself that Arthur had after all definitely pronounced her welcome to any gain from his gift that might accrue—this trick remained innocent, as she perfectly knew it for what it was. Then there was always the possibility of his—as she could only picture it—rising to the occasion. Mightn't he have a grand magnanimous moment? —mightn't he just say: "Oh, of course I couldn't have afforded to let you have it if I had known; but since you *have* got it, and have made out the truth by your own wit, I really can't screw myself down to the shabbiness of taking it back"?

She had, as it proved, to wait a long time—to wait till, at the end of several months, the great house of Bleet had, with due deliberation, for the season, transferred itself to town; after which, however, she fairly snatched at her first freedom to knock, dressed in her best and armed with her disclosure, at the door of her doubting kinsman. It was still with doubt and not quite with the face she had hoped that he listened to her story. He had turned pale, she thought, as she produced the necklace, and he appeared, above all, disagreeably affected. Well, perhaps there was reason, she more than ever remembered; but what on earth was one, in close touch with the fact, to do? She had laid the pearls on his table, where, without his having at first put so much as a finger to them, they met his hard, cold stare.

"I don't believe in them," he simply said at last.

"That's exactly then," she returned with some spirit, "what I wanted to hear!"

She fancied that at this his colour changed; it was indeed vivid to her afterwards—for she was to have a long recall of the scene—that she had made him quite angrily flush. "It's a beastly unpleasant imputation, you know!" —and he walked away from her as he had always walked at the vicarage.

"It's none of *my* making, I'm sure," said Charlotte Prime. "If you're afraid to believe they're real—"

"Well?" —and he turned, across the room, sharp round at her.

"Why, it's not my fault."

He said nothing more, for a moment, on this; he only came back to the table. "They're what I originally said they were. They're rotten paste."

"Then I may keep them?"

"No. I want a better opinion."

"Than your own?"

"Than *your* own." He dropped on the pearls another queer stare, then, after a moment, bringing himself to touch them, did exactly what she had herself done in the presence of Mrs. Guy at Bleet—gathered them together, marched off with them to a drawer, put them in and clicked the key. "You say I'm afraid," he went on as he again met her; "but I shan't be afraid to take them to Bond Street."

"And if the people say they're real—?"

He hesitated—then had his strangest manner. "They won't say it! They shan't!"

There was something in the way he brought it out that deprived poor Charlotte, as she was perfectly aware, of any manner at all. "Oh!" she simply sounded, as she had sounded for her last word to Mrs. Guy; and, within a minute, without more conversation, she had taken her departure.

A fortnight later she received a communication from him, and towards the end of the season one of the entertainments in Eaton Square was graced by the presence of Mrs. Guy. Charlotte was not at dinner, but she came down afterwards, and this guest, on seeing her, abandoned a very beautiful young man on purpose to cross and speak to her. The guest had on a lovely necklace and had apparently not lost her habit of overflowing with the pride of such ornaments.

"Do you see?" She was in high joy.

They were indeed splendid pearls—so far as poor Charlotte could feel that she knew, after what had come and gone, about such mysteries. Charlotte had a sickly smile. "They're almost as fine as Arthur's."

"Almost? Where, my dear, are your eyes? They are 'Arthur's!'" After which, to meet the flood of crimson that accompanied her young friend's start: "I tracked them—after your folly, and, by miraculous luck, recognised them in the Bond Street window to which he had disposed of them."

"*Disposed* of them?" the girl gasped. "He wrote me that I had insulted his mother and that the people had shown him he was right—had pronounced them utter paste."

Mrs. Guy gave a stare. "Ah, I told you he wouldn't bear it! No. But I had, I assure you," she wound up, "to drive my bargain!"

Charlotte scarce heard or saw; she was full of her private wrong. "He wrote me," she panted, "that he had smashed them."

Mrs. Guy could only wonder and pity. "He's really morbid!" But it was not quite clear which of the pair she pitied; though Charlotte felt really morbid too after they had separated and she found herself full of thought. She even went the length of asking herself what sort of a bargain Mrs. Guy had driven and whether the marvel of the recognition in Bond Street had been a veracious account of the matter. Hadn't she perhaps in truth dealt with Arthur directly? It came back to Charlotte almost luridly that she had had his address.

THE GREAT GOOD PLACE

I

George Dane had waked up to a bright new day, the face of nature well washed by last night's downpour and shining as with high spirits, good resolutions, lively intentions—the great glare of recommencement, in short, fixed in his patch of sky. He had sat up late to finish work— arrears overwhelming; then at last had gone to bed with the pile but little reduced. He was now to return to it after the pause of the night; but he could only look at it, for the time, over the bristling hedge of letters planted by the early postman an hour before and already, on the customary table by the chimney-piece, formally rounded and squared by his systematic servant. It was something too merciless, the domestic perfection of Brown. There were newspapers on another table, ranged with the same rigour of custom, newspapers too many—what could any creature want of so much news? —and each with its hand on the neck of the other, so that the row of their bodiless heads was like a series of decapitations. Other journals, other periodicals of every sort, folded and in wrappers, made a huddled mound that had been growing for several days and of which he had been wearily, helplessly aware. There were new books, also in wrappers as well as disenveloped and dropped again—books from publishers, books from authors, books from friends, books from enemies, books from his own bookseller, who took, it sometimes struck him, inconceivable things for granted. He touched nothing, approached nothing, only turned a heavy eye over the work, as it were, of the night—the fact, in his high, wide-windowed room, where the hard light of duty could penetrate every corner, of the un- ashamed admonition of the day. It was the old rising tide, and it rose and rose even under a minute's watching. It had been up to his shoulders last night—it was up to his chin now.

Nothing had passed while he slept—everything had stayed; nothing, that he could yet feel, had died—many things had been born. To let them alone, these things, the new things, let them utterly alone and see if that, by chance, wouldn't somehow prove the best way to deal with them: this fancy brushed his face for a moment as a possible solution, just giving it, as many a time before, a cool wave of air. Then he knew again as well as ever that leaving was difficult, leaving impossible—that the only remedy, the true, soft, effacing sponge, would be to *be* left, to be forgotten. There was no footing on which a man who had ever liked life—liked it, at any rate, as *he* had—could now escape from it. He must reap as he had sown. It was a thing of meshes; he had simply gone to sleep under the net and had simply waked up there. The net was too fine; the cords crossed each other at spots so near together, making at each a little tight, hard knot that tired fingers, this morning, were too limp and too tender to touch. Our poor friend's touched nothing—only stole significantly into his pockets as he wandered over to the window and faintly gasped at the energy of nature. What was most overwhelming was that she herself was so ready. She had soothed him rather, the night before, in the small hours by the lamp. From behind the drawn curtain of his study the rain had been audible and in a manner merciful; washing the window in a steady flood, it had seemed the right thing, the retarding, interrupting thing, the thing that, if it would only last, might clear the ground by floating out to a boundless sea the innumerable objects among which his feet stumbled and strayed. He had positively laid down his pen as on a sense of friendly pressure from it. The kind, full swash had been on the glass when he turned out his lamp; he had left his phrase unfinished and his papers lying quite as if for the flood to bear them away on its bosom. But there still, on the table, were the bare bones of the sentence—and not all of those; the single thing borne away and that he could never recover was the missing half that might have paired with it and begotten a figure.

Yet he could at last only turn back from the window; the world was everywhere, without and within, and, with the great staring egotism of its health and strength, was not to be trusted for tact or delicacy. He faced about precisely to meet his servant and the absurd solemnity of two telegrams on a tray. Brown ought to have kicked them into the room—then he himself might have kicked them out.

"And you told me to remind you, sir—"

George Dane was at last angry. "Remind me of nothing!"

"But you insisted, sir, that I was to insist!"

He turned away in despair, speaking with a pathetic quaver at absurd variance with his words: "If you insist, Brown, I'll kill you!" He found himself anew at the window, whence, looking down from his fourth floor, he could see the vast neighbourhood, under the trumpet-blare of the sky, beginning to rush about. There was a silence, but he knew Brown had not left him—knew exactly how straight and serious and stupid and faithful he stood there. After a minute he heard him again.

"It's only because, sir, you know, sir, you can't remember—"

At this Dane did flash round; it was more than at such a moment he could bear. "Can't remember, Brown? I can't forget. That's what's the matter with me."

Brown looked at him with the advantage of eighteen years of consistency. "I'm afraid you're not well, sir."

Brown's master thought. "It's a shocking thing to say, but I wish to heaven I weren't! It would be perhaps an excuse."

Brown's blankness spread like the desert. "To put them off?"

"Ah!" The sound was a groan; the plural pronoun, *any* pronoun, so mistimed. "Who is it?"

"Those ladies you spoke of—to lunch."

"Oh!" The poor man dropped into the nearest chair and stared a while at the carpet. It was very complicated.

"How many will there be, sir?" Brown asked.

"Fifty!"

"Fifty, sir?"

Our friend, from his chair, looked vaguely about; under his hand were the telegrams, still unopened, one of which he now tore asunder. "'Do hope you sweetly won't mind, to-day, 1:30, my bringing poor dear Lady Mullet, who is so awfully bent,'" he read to his companion.

His companion weighed it. "How many does *she* make, sir?"

"Poor dear Lady Mullet? I haven't the least idea."

"Is she—a—deformed, sir?" Brown inquired, as if in this case she might make more.

His master wondered, then saw he figured some personal curvature. "No; she's only bent on coming!" Dane opened the other telegram and again read out: "'So sorry it's at eleventh hour impossible, and count on you here, as very greatest favour, at two sharp instead.'"

"How many does *that* make?" Brown imperturbably continued.

Dane crumped up the two missives and walked with them to the waste-paper basket, into which he thoughtfully dropped them. "I can't say. You must do it all yourself. I shan't be there."

It was only on this that Brown showed an expression. "You'll go instead—"

"I'll go instead!" Dane raved.

Brown, however, had had occasion to show before that *he* would never desert their post. "Isn't that rather sacrificing the three?" Between respect and reproach he paused.

"*Are* there three?"

"I lay for four in all."

His master had, at any rate, caught his thought. "Sacrificing the three to the one, you mean? Oh, I'm not going to *her!*"

Brown's famous "thoroughness"—his great virtue—had never been so dreadful. "Then where *are* you going?"

Dane sat down to his table and stared at his ragged phrase. "'There is a happy land—far, far away!'" He chanted it like a sick child and knew that for a minute Brown never moved. During this minute he felt between his shoulders the gimlet of criticism.

"Are you quite sure you'll be all right?"

"It's my certainty that overwhelms me, Brown. Look about you and judge. Could anything be more 'right,' in the view of the envious world, than everything that surrounds us here; that immense array of letters, notes, circulars; that pile of printers' proofs, magazines and books; these perpetual telegrams, these impending guests; this retarded, unfinished and interminable work? What could a man want more?"

"Do you mean there's too much, sir?" —Brown had sometimes these flashes.

"There's too much. There's too much. But you can't help it, Brown."

"No, sir," Brown assented. "Can't you?"

"I'm thinking—I must see. There are hours—!" Yes, there were hours, and this was one of them: he jerked himself up for another turn in his labyrinth, but still not touching, not even again meeting, his interlocutor's eye. If he was a genius for any one he was a genius for Brown; but it was terrible what that meant, being a genius for Brown.

There had been times when he had done full justice to the way it kept him up; now, however, it was almost the worst of the avalanche. "Don't trouble about me," he went on insincerely and looking askance through his window again at the bright and beautiful world. "Perhaps it will rain—that *may* not be over. I do love the rain," he weakly pursued. "Perhaps, better still, it will snow."

Brown now had indeed a perceptible expression, and the expression was fear. "Snow, sir—the end of May?" Without pressing this point he looked at his watch. "You'll feel better when you've had breakfast."

"I dare say," said Dane, whom breakfast struck in fact as a pleasant alternative to opening letters. "I'll come in immediately."

"But without waiting—?"

"Waiting for what?"

Brown had at last, under his apprehension, his first lapse from logic, which he betrayed by hesitating in the evident hope that his companion would, by a flash of remembrance, relieve him of an invidious duty. But the only flashes now were the good man's own. "You say you can't forget, sir; but you do forget—"

"Is it anything very horrible?" Dane broke in.

Brown hung fire. "Only the gentleman you told me you had asked—"

Dane again took him up; horrible or not, it came back—indeed its mere coming back classed it. "To breakfast to-day? It *was* to-day; I see." It came back, yes, came back; the appointment with the young man— he supposed him young—and whose letter, the letter about—what was it?—had struck him. "Yes, yes; wait, wait."

"Perhaps he'll do you good, sir," Brown suggested.

"Sure to—sure to. All right!" Whatever he might do, he would at least prevent some other doing: that was present to our friend as, on the vibration of the electric bell at the door of the flat, Brown moved away. Two things, in the short interval that followed, were present to Dane: his having utterly forgotten the connection, the whence, whither and why of his guest; and his continued disposition not to touch—no, not with the finger. Ah, if he might *never* again touch! All the unbroken seals and neglected appeals lay there while, for a pause that he couldn't measure, he stood before the chimney-piece with his hands still in his pockets. He heard a brief exchange of words in the hall, but never afterward recovered the time taken by Brown to reappear, to precede and announce another person—a person whose name, somehow, failed to reach Dane's ear. Brown went off again to serve breakfast, leaving host and guest confronted. The duration of this first stage also, later on, defied measurement; but that little mattered, for in the train of what happened came promptly the second, the third, the fourth, the rich succession of the others. Yet what happened was but that Dane took his hand from his pocket, held it straight out and felt it taken. Thus indeed, if he had wanted never again to touch, it was already done.

II

He might have been a week in the place—the scene of his new consciousness—before he spoke at all. The occasion of it then was that one of the quiet figures he had been idly watching drew at last nearer and showed him a face that was the highest expression—to his pleased but as yet slightly confused perception—of the general charm. What *was* the general charm? He couldn't, for that matter, easily have phrased it; it was such an abyss of negatives, such an absence of everything. The oddity was that, after a minute, he was struck as by the reflection of his own very image in this first interlocutor seated with him, on the easy bench, under the high, clear portico and above the wide, far-reaching garden, where the things that most showed in the greenness were the surface of still water and the white note of old statues. The absence of everything was, in the aspect of the Brother who had thus informally joined him—a man of his own age, tired, distinguished, modest, kind—really, as he could soon se, but the absence of what he didn't want. He didn't want, for the time, anything but just to *be* there, to stay in the bath. He was in the bath yet, the broad, deep bath of stillness. They sat in it together now with the water up to their chins. He had not had to talk, he had not had to think, he had scarce even had to feel. He had been sunk that way before, sunk—when and where? —in another flood; only a flood of rushing waters, in which bumping and gasping were all. This was a current so slow and so tepid that one floated practically without motion and without chill. The break of silence was not immediate, though Dane seemed indeed to feel it begin before a sound passed. It could pass quite sufficiently without words that he and his mate were Brothers, and what that meant.

Dane wondered, but with no want of ease—for want of ease was impossible—if his friend found in *him* the same likeness, the proof of peace, the gage of what the place could do. The long afternoon crept to its end; the shadows fell further and the sky glowed deeper; but nothing changed—nothing *could* change—in the element itself. It was a conscious security. It was wonderful! Dane had lived into it, but he was still immensely aware. He would have been sorry to lose that, for just this fact, as yet, the blessed fact of consciousness, seemed the greatest thing of all. Its only fault was that, being in itself such an occupation, so fine an unrest in the heart of gratitude, the life of the day all went to it. But what even then was the harm? He had come only to come, to take what he found. This was the part where the great cloister, inclosed externally on three sides and probably the largest, lightest, fairest effect, to his charmed sense, that human hands could ever have expressed in dimensions of length and breadth, opened to the south its splendid fourth quarter, turned to the great view an outer gallery that combined with the rest of the portico to form a high, dry loggia, such as he a little pretended to himself he had, in Italy, in old days, seen in old cities, old convents, old villas. This recall of the disposition of some great abode of an Order, some mild Monte Cassino, some Grande Chartreuse more accessible, was his main term of comparison; but he knew he had really never anywhere beheld anything at once so calculated and so generous.

Three impressions in particular had been with him all the week, and he could only recognise in silence their happy effect on his nerves. How it was all managed he couldn't have told—he had been content moreover till now with his ignorance of cause and pretext; but whenever he chose to listen with a certain intentness he made out, as from a distance, the sound of slow, sweet bells. How could they be so far and yet so audible? How could they be so near and yet so faint? How, above all, could they, in such an arrest of life, be, to *time* things, so frequent? The very essence of the bliss of Dane's whole change had been precisely that there was nothing now to time. It was the same with the slow footsteps that always, within earshot, to the vague attention, marked the space and the leisure, seemed, in long, cool arcades, lightly to fall and perpetually to recede. This was the second impression, and it melted into the third, as, for that matter, every form of softness, in the great good place, was but a further turn, without jerk or gap, of the endless roll of serenity. The quiet footsteps were quiet figures; the quiet figures that, to the eye, kept the picture human and brought its perfection within reach. This perfection, he felt on the bench by his friend, was now more in reach than ever. His friend at last turned to him a look different from the looks of friends in London clubs.

"The thing was to find it out!"

It was extraordinary how this remark fitted into his thought. "Ah, wasn't it? And when I think," said Dane, "of all the people who haven't and who never will!" He sighed over these unfortunates with a tenderness that, in its degree, was practically new to him, feeling, too, how well his companion would know the people he meant. He only meant some, but they were all who would want it; though of these, no doubt— well, for reasons, for things that, in the world, he had observed—there would never be too many. Not all perhaps who wanted would really find; but none at least would find who didn't really want. And then what the need would have to have been first! What it at first had to be for himself! He felt afresh, in the light of his companion's face, what it might still be even when deeply satisfied, as well as what communication was established by the mere mutual knowledge of it.

"Every man must arrive by himself and on his own feet—isn't that so? We're brothers here for the time, as in a great monastery, and we immediately think of each other and recognise each other as such; but we must have first got here as we can, and we meet after long journeys by complicated ways. Moreover we meet—don't we? —with closed eyes."

"Ah, don't speak as if we were dead!" Dane laughed.

"I shan't mind death if it's like this," his friend replied.

It was too obvious, as Dane gazed before him, that one wouldn't; but after a moment he asked, with the first articulation, as yet, of his most elementary wonder: "Where is it?"

"I shouldn't be surprised if it were much nearer than one ever suspected."

"Nearer town, do you mean?"

"Nearer everything—nearer every one."

George Dane thought. "Somewhere, for instance, down in Surrey?"

His Brother met him on this with a shade of reluctance. "Why should we call it names? It must have a climate, you see."

"Yes," Dane happily mused; "without that—!" All it so securely did have overwhelmed him again, and he couldn't help breaking out: "*What is it?*"

"Oh, it's positively a part of our ease and our rest and our change, I think, that we don't at all know and that we may really call it, for that matter, anything in the world we like—the thing, for instance, we love it most for being."

"I know what *I* call it," said Dane after a moment. Then as his friend listened with interest: "Just simply 'The Great Good Place.'"

"I see—what can you say more? I've put it to myself perhaps a little differently." They sat there as innocently as small boys confiding to each other the names of toy animals. "The Great Want Met."

"Ah, yes, that's it!"

"Isn't it enough for us that it's a place carried on, for our benefit, so admirably that we strain our ears in vain for a creak of the machinery? Isn't it enough for us that it's simply a thorough hit?"

"Ah, a hit!" Dane benignantly murmured.

"It does for us what it pretends to do," his companion went on; "the mystery isn't deeper than that. The thing is probably simple enough in fact, and on a thoroughly practical basis; only it has had its origin in a splendid thought, in a real stroke of genius."

"Yes," Dane exclaimed, "in a sense—on somebody or other's part— so exquisitely personal!"

"Precisely—it rests, like all good things, on experience. The 'great want' comes home—that's the great thing it does! On the day it came home to the right mind this dear place was constituted. It always, moreover, in the long run, *has* been met—it always must be. How can it not require to be, more and more, as pressure of every sort grows?"

Dane, with his hands folded in his lap, took in these words of wisdom. "Pressure of every sort *is* growing!" he placidly observed.

"I see well enough what that fact has done to *you*," his Brother returned.

Dane smiled. "I couldn't have borne it longer. I don't know what would have become of me."

"I know what would have become of *me*."

"Well, it's the same thing."

"Yes," said Dane's companion, "it's doubtless the same thing." On which they sat in silence a little, seeming pleasantly to follow, in the view of the green garden, the vague movements of the monster—madness, surrender, collapse—they had escaped. Their bench was like a box at the opera. "And I may perfectly, you know," the Brother pursued, "have seen you before. I may even have known you well. We don't know."

They looked at each other again serenely enough, and at last Dane said: "No, we don't know."

"That's what I meant by our coming with our eyes closed. Yes—there's something out. There's a gap—a link missing, the great hiatus!" the Brother laughed. "It's as simple a story as the old, old rupture—the break that lucky Catholics have always been able to make, that they are still, with their innumerable religious houses, able to make, by going into "retreat." I don't speak of the pious exercises; I speak only of the material simplification. I don't speak of the putting off of one's self; I speak only—if one has a self worth sixpence—of the getting it back. The place, the time, the way were, for those of the old persuasion, always there—are indeed practically there for them as much as ever. They can always get off—the blessed houses receive. So it was high time that we—we of the great Protestant peoples, still more, if possible, in the sensitive individual case, overscored and overwhelmed, still more congested with mere quantity and prostituted, through our 'enterprise,' to mere profanity—should learn how to get off, should find somewhere *our* retreat and remedy. There was such a huge chance for it!"

Dane laid his hand on his companion's arm. "It's charming, how, when we speak for ourselves, we speak for each other. That was exactly what I said!" He had fallen to recalling from over the gulf the last occasion.

The Brother, as if it would do them both good, only desired to draw him out. "What you said—?"

"To *him*—that morning." Dane caught a far bell again and heard a slow footstep. A quiet figure passed somewhere—neither of them turned to look. What was, little by little, more present to him was the perfect taste. It was supreme—it was everywhere. "I just dropped my burden—and he received it."

"And was it very great?"

"Oh, such a load!" Dane laughed.

"Trouble, sorrow, doubt?"

"Oh, no; worse than that!"

"Worse?"

"'Success'—the vulgarest kind!" And Dane laughed again.

"Ah, I know that, too! No one in future, as things are going, will be able to face success."

"Without something of this sort—never. The better it is the worse— the greater the deadlier. But my one pain here," Dane continued, "is in thinking of my poor friend."

"The person to whom you've already alluded?"

"My substitute in the world. Such an unutterable benefactor. He turned up that morning when everything had somehow got on my nerves, when the whole great globe indeed, nerves, or no nerves, seemed to have squeezed itself into my study. It wasn't a question of nerves, it was a mere question of the displacement of everything—of submersion by our eternal too much. I didn't know *où donner de la tête*—I couldn't have gone a step further."

The intelligence with which the Brother listened kept them as children feeding from the same bowl. "And then you got the tip."

"I got the tip!" Dane happily sighed.

"Well, we all get it. But I dare say differently."

"Then how did *you*—?"

The Brother hesitated, smiling. "You tell me first."

III

"Well," said George Dane, "it was a young man I had never seen— a man, at any rate, much younger than myself—who had written to me and sent me some article, some book. I read the stuff, was much struck with it, I told him so and thanked him—on which, of course, I heard from him again. He asked me things—his questions were interesting; but to save time and writing I said to him: "Come to see me— we can talk a little; but all I can give you is half an hour at breakfast." He turned up at the hour on a day when, more than ever in my life before, I seemed, as it happened, in the endless press and stress, to have lost possession of my soul and to be surrounded only with the affairs of other people and the irrelevant, destructive, brutalising sides of life. It made me literally ill—made me feel as I had never felt that if I should once really, for an hour, lose hold of the thing itself, the thing I was trying for, I should never recover it again. The wild waters would close over me, and I should drop straight to the bottom where the vanquished dead lie."

"I follow you every step of your way," said the friendly Brother. "The wild waters, you mean, of our horrible time."

"Of our horrible time—precisely. Not, of course—as we sometimes dream—of any other."

"Yes, any other is only a dream. We really know none but our own."

"No, thank God—that's enough," Dane said. "Well, my young man turned up, and I hadn't been a minute in his presence before making out that practically it would be in him somehow or other to help me. He came to me with envy, envy extravagant—really passionate. I was, heaven save us, the great 'success' for him; he himself was broken and beaten. How can I say what passed between us? —it was so strange, so swift, so much a matter, from one to the other, of instant perception and agreement. He was so clever and haggard and hungry!"

"Hungry?" the Brother asked.

"I don't mean for bread, though he had none too much, I think, even of that. I mean for—well, what I had and what I was a monument of to him as I stood there up to my neck in preposterous evidence. He, poor chap, had been for ten years serenading closed windows and had never yet caused a shutter to show that it stirred. My dim blind was the first to be raised an inch; my reading of his book, my impression of it, my note and my invitation, formed literally the only response ever dropped into his dark street. He saw in my littered room, my shattered day, my bored face and spoiled temper—it's embarrassing, but I must tell you—the very blaze of my glory. And he saw in the blaze of my glory—deluded innocent! —what he had yearned for in vain."

"What he had yearned for was to *be* you," said the Brother. Then he added: "I see where you're coming out."

"At my saying to him by the end of five minutes: 'My dear fellow, I wish you'd just try it—wish you'd, for a while, just *be* me!' You go straight to the mark, and that was exactly what occurred—extraordinary though it was that we should both have understood. I saw what he could give, and he did too. He saw moreover what I could take; in fact what he saw was wonderful."

"He must be very remarkable!" the Brother laughed.

"There's no doubt of it whatever—far more remarkable than I. That's just the reason why what I put to him in joke—with a fantastic, desperate irony—became, on his hands, with his vision of his change, the blessed guarantee of my sitting on this spot in your company. 'Oh, if I could just shift it all—make it straight over for an hour to other shoulders! If there only *were* a pair!' —that's the way I put it to him. And then at something in his face, 'Would *you*, by a miracle, undertake it?' I asked. I let him know all it meant—how it meant that he should at that very moment step in. It meant that he should finish my work and open my letters and keep my engagements and be subject, for better or worse, to my contacts and complications. It meant that he should live with my life, and think with my brain, and write with my hand, and speak with my voice. It meant, above all, that I should get off. He accepted with magnificence—rose to it like a hero. Only he said: 'What will become of *you*?'"

"There was the hitch!" the Brother admitted.

"Ah, but only for a minute. He came to my help again," Dane pursued, "when he saw I couldn't quite meet that, could at least only say that I wanted to think, wanted to cease, wanted to do the thing itself—the thing I was trying for, miserable me, and that thing only— and therefore wanted first of all really to *see* it again, planted out, crowded out, frozen out as it now so long had been. 'I know what you want,' he after a moment quietly remarked to me. 'Ah, what I want doesn't exist!' 'I know what you want,' he repeated. At that I began to believe him."

"Had you any idea yourself?" the Brother asked.

"Oh, yes," said Dane, "and it was just my idea that made me despair. There it was as sharp as possible in my imagination and my longing— there it was so utterly *not* in fact. We were sitting together on my sofa as we waited for breakfast. He presently laid his hand on my knee— showed me a face that the sudden great light in it had made, for me, indescribably beautiful. 'It exists—it exists,' he at last said. And so, I remember, we sat a while and looked at each other, with the final effect of my finding that I absolutely believed him. I remember we weren't at all solemn—we smiled with the joy of discoverers. He was as glad as I—he was tremendously glad. That came out in the whole manner of his reply to the appeal that broke from me: 'Where is it, then, in God's name? Tell me without delay where it is!'"

The Brother had attended with a sympathy! "He gave you the address?"

"He was thinking it out—feeling for it, catching it. He has a wonderful head of his own and must be making of the whole thing, while we sit here gossiping, something much better than ever *I* did. The mere sight of his face, the sense of his hand on my knee, made me, after a little, feel that he not only knew what I wanted, but was getting nearer to it than I could have got in ten years. He suddenly sprang up and went over to my study-table—sat straight down there as if to write me my passport. Then it was—at the mere sight of his back, which was turned to me—that I felt the spell work. I simply sat and watched him with the queerest, deepest, sweetest sense in the world—the sense of an ache that had stopped. All life was lifted; I myself at least was somehow off the ground. He was already where I had been."

"And where were you?" the Brother amusedly inquired.

"Just on the sofa always, leaning back on the cushion and feeling a delicious ease. He was already me."

"And who were you?" the Brother continued.

"Nobody. That was the fun."

"That *is* the fun," said the Brother, with a sigh like soft music.

Dane echoed the sigh, and, as nobody talking with nobody, they sat there together still and watched the sweet wide picture darken into tepid night.

IV

At the end of three weeks—so far as time was distinct—Dane began to feel there was something he had recovered. It was the thing they never named—partly for want of the need and partly for lack of the word; for what indeed was the description that would cover it all? The only real need was to know it, to see it, in silence. Dane had a private, practical sign for it, which, however, he had appropriated by theft—"the vision and the faculty divine." That, doubtless, was a flattering phrase for his idea of his genius; the genius, at all events, was what he had been in danger of losing and had at last held by a thread that might at any moment have broken. The change was that, little by little, his hold had grown firmer, so that he drew in the line—more and more each day—with a pull that he was delighted to find it would bear. The mere dream-sweetness of the place was superseded; it was more and more a world of reason and order, of sensible, visible arrangement. It ceased to be strange—it was high, triumphant clearness. He cultivated, however, but vaguely, the question of where he was, finding it near enough the mark to be almost sure that if he was not in Kent he was probably in Hampshire. He paid for everything but that—that wasn't one of the items. Payment, he had soon learned, was definite; it consisted of sovereigns and shillings—just like those of the world he had left, only parted with more ecstatically—that he put, in his room, in a designated place and that were taken away in his absence by one of the unobtrusive, effaced agents—shadows projected on the hours like the noiseless march of the sundial—that were always at work. The institution had sides that had their recalls, and a pleased, resigned perception of these things was at once the effect and the cause of its grace.

Dane picked out of his dim past a dozen halting similes. The sacred, silent convent was one; another was the bright country-house. He did the place no outrage to liken it to an hotel; he permitted himself on occasion to trace its resemblance to a club. Such images, however, but flickered and went out—they lasted only long enough to light up the difference. An hotel without noise, a club without newspapers—when he turned his face to what it was "without" the view opened wide. The only approach to a real analogy was in himself and his companions. They were brothers, guests, members; they were even, if one liked— and they didn't in the least mind what they were called—"regular boarders." It was not they who made the conditions, it was the conditions that made them. These conditions found themselves accepted, clearly, with an appreciation, with a rapture, it was rather to be called, that had to do—as the very air that pervaded them and the force that sustained—with their quiet and noble assurance. They combined to form the large, simple idea of a general refuge—an image of embracing arms, of liberal accommodation. What was the effect, really, but the poetisation by perfect taste of a type common enough? There was no daily miracle; the perfect taste, with the aid of space, did the trick.

200   *Tales of Art and Life*

What underlay and overhung it all, better yet, Dane mused, was some original inspiration, but confirmed, unquenched, some happy thought of an individual breast. It had been born somehow and somewhere— it had had to insist on being—the blessed conception. The author might remain in the obscure, for that was part of the perfection: personal service so hushed and regulated that you scarce caught it in the act and only knew it by its results. Yet the wise mind was everywhere—the whole thing, infallibly, centred, at the core, in a consciousness. And what a consciousness it had been, Dane thought, a consciousness how like his own! The wise mind had felt, the wise mind had seen a chance. Of the creation thus arrived at you could none the less never have said if it were the last echo of the old or the sharpest note of the modern.

Dane again and again, among the far bells and the soft footfalls, in cool cloister and warm garden, found himself wanting not to know more and yet liking not to know less. It was part of the general beauty that there was no personal publicity, much less any personal success. Those things were in the world—in what he had left; there was no vulgarity here of credit or claim or fame. The real exquisite was to be without the complication of an identity, and the greatest boon of all, doubtless, the solid security, the clear confidence one could feel in the keeping of the contract. That was what had been most in the wise mind—the importance of the absolute sense, on the part of its bene-ficiaries, that what was offered was guaranteed. They had no concern but to pay—the wise mind knew what they paid for. It was present to Dane each hour that he could never be overcharged. Oh, the deep, deep bath, the soft, cool plash in the stillness! —this, time after time, as if under regular treatment, a sublimated German "cure," was the vivid name for his luxury. The inner life woke up again, and it was the inner life, for people of his generation, victims of the modern madness, mere maniacal extension and motion, that was returning health. He had talked of independence and written of it, but what a cold, flat word it had been! This was the wordless fact itself—the uncontested pos-session of the long, sweet, stupid day. The fragrance of flowers just wandered through the void, and the quiet recurrence of delicate, plain fare in a high, clean refectory where the soundless, simple service was the triumph of art. That, as he analysed, remained the constant expla-nation: all the sweetness and serenity were created, calculated things. He analysed, however, but in a desultory way and with a positive delight in the residuum of mystery that made for the great artist in the background the innermost shrine of the idol of a temple; there were odd moments for it, mild meditations when, in the broad cloister of peace or some garden-nook where the air was light, a special glimpse of beauty or reminder of felicity seemed, in passing, to hover and linger. In the mere ecstasy of change that had at first possessed him he had not discriminated—had only let himself sink, as I have mentioned, down to hushed depths. Then had come the slow, soft stages of intelligence and notation, more marked and more fruitful perhaps after that long talk with his mild mate in the twilight, and seeming to wind up the process by putting the key into his hand. This key, pure gold, was simply the cancelled list. Slowly and blissfully he read into the general wealth of his comfort all the particular absences of which it was composed. One by one he touched, as it were, all the things it was such rapture to be without.

It was the paradise of his own room that was most indebted to them—a great square, fair chamber, all beautified with omissions, from which, high up, he looked over a long valley to a far horizon, and in which he was vaguely and pleasantly reminded of some old Italian picture, some Carpaccio or some early Tuscan, the representation of a world without newspapers and letters, without telegrams and photographs, without the dreadful, fatal too much. There, for a blessing, he *could* read and write; there, above all, he could do nothing—he could live. And there were all sorts of freedoms—always, for the occasion, the particular right one. He could bring a book from the library—he could bring two, he could bring three. An effect produced by the charming place was that, for some reason, he never wanted to bring more. The library was a benediction—high and clear and plain, like everything else, but with something, in all its arched amplitude, unconfused and brave and gay. He should never forget, he knew, the throb of immediate perception with which he first stood there, a single glance round sufficing so to show him that it would give him what for years he had desired. He had not had detachment, but there was detachment here—the sense of a great silver bowl from which he could ladle up the melted hours. He strolled about from wall to wall, too pleasantly in tune on that occasion to sit down punctually or to choose; only recognising from shelf to shelf every dear old book that he had had to put off or never returned to; every deep, distinct voice of another time that, in the hubbub of the world, he had had to take for lost and unheard. He came back, of course, soon, came back every day; enjoyed there, of all the rare, strange moments, those that were at once most quickened and most caught—moments in which every apprehension counted double and every act of the mind was a lover's embrace. It was the quarter he perhaps, as the days went on, liked best; though indeed it only shared with the rest of the place, with every aspect to which his face happened to be turned, the power to remind him of the masterly general control.

There were times when he looked up from his book to lose himself in the mere tone of the picture that never failed at any moment or at any angle. The picture was always there, yet was made up of things common enough. It was in the way an open window in a broad recess let in the pleasant morning; in the way the dry air pricked into faint freshness the gilt of old bindings; in the way an empty chair beside a table unlittered showed a volume just laid down; in the way a happy Brother—as detached as oneself and with his innocent back presented—lingered before a shelf with the slow sound of turned pages. It was a part of the whole impression that, by some extraordinary law, one's vision seemed less from the facts than the facts from one's vision; that the elements were determined at the moment by the moment's need or the moment's sympathy. What most prompted this reflection was the degree in which, after a while, Dane had a consciousness of company. After that talk with the good Brother on the bench there were other good Brothers in other places—always in cloister or garden some figure that stopped if he himself stopped and with which a greeting became, in the easiest way in the world, a sign of the diffused amenity. Always, always, however, in all contacts, was the balm of a happy ignorance. What he had felt the first time recurred: the friend was always new and yet at the same time—it was amusing, not disturbing—suggested the possibility that he might be but an old one altered. That was only delightful—as positively delightful in the particular, the actual conditions as it might have been the reverse in the conditions abolished. These others, the abolished, came back to Dane at last so easily that he could exactly measure each difference, but with what he had finally been hustled on to hate in them robbed of its terror in consequence of something that had happened. What had happened was that in tranquil walks and talks the deep spell had worked and he had got his soul again. He had drawn in by this time, with his lightened hand, the whole of the long line, and that fact just dangled at the end. He could put his other hand on it, he could unhook it, he was once more in possession. This, as it befell, was exactly what he supposed he must have said to a comrade beside whom, one afternoon in the cloister, he found himself measuring steps.

"Oh, it comes—comes of itself, doesn't it, thank goodness? —just by the simple fact of finding room and time!"

The comrade was possibly a novice or in a different stage from his own; there was at any rate a vague envy in the recognition that shone out of the fatigued, yet freshened face. "It has come to you then? — you've got what you wanted?" That was the gossip and interchange that could pass to and fro. Dane, years before, had gone in for three months of hydropathy, and there was a droll echo, in this scene, of the old questions of the water-cure, the questions asked in the periodical pursuit of the "reaction"—the ailment, the progress of each, the action of the skin and the state of the appetite. Such memories worked in now—all familiar reference, all easy play of mind; and among them our friends, round and round, fraternised ever so softly, until, suddenly stopping short, Dane, with a hand on his companion's arm, broke into the happiest laugh he had yet sounded.

V

"Why, it's raining!" And he stood and looked at the splash of the shower and the shine of the wet leaves. It was one of the summer sprinkles that bring out sweet smells.

"Yes—but why not?" his mate demanded.

"Well—because it's so charming. It's so exactly right."

"But everything *is*. Isn't that just why we're here?"

"Just exactly," Dane said; "only I've been living in the beguiled supposition that we've somehow or other a climate."

"So have I; so, I dare say, has every one. Isn't that the blessed moral? —that we live in beguiled suppositions. They come so easily here, and nothing contradicts them." The good Brother looked placidly forth—Dane could identify his phase. "A climate doesn't consist in its never raining, does it?"

"No, I dare say not. But somehow the good I've got has been half the great, easy, absence of all that friction of which the question of weather mostly forms a part—has been indeed largely the great, easy, perpetual air-bath."

"Ah, yes—that's not a delusion; but perhaps the sense comes a little from our breathing an emptier medium. There are fewer things *in* it! Leave people alone, at all events, and the air is what they take to. Into the closed and the stuffy they have to be driven. I've had, too—I think we must all have—a fond sense of the south."

"But imagine it," said Dane, laughing, "in the beloved British islands and so near as we are to Bradford!"

His friend was ready enough to imagine. "To Bradford?" he asked, quite unperturbed. "How near?"

Dane's gaiety grew. "Oh, it doesn't matter!"

His friend, quite unmystified, accepted it. "There are things to puzzle out—otherwise it would be dull. It seems to me one can puzzle them."

"It's because we're so well disposed," Dane said.

"Precisely—we find good in everything."

"In everything," Dane went on. "The conditions settle that—they determine us."

They resumed their stroll, which evidently represented on the good Brother's part infinite agreement. "Aren't they probably in fact very simple?" he presently inquired. "Isn't simplification the secret?"

"Yes, but applied with a tact!"

"There it is. The thing's so perfect that it's open to as many interpretations as any other great work—a poem of Goethe, a dialogue of Plato, a symphony of Beethoven."

"It simply stands quiet, you mean," said Dane, "and lets us call it names?"

"Yes, but all such loving ones. We're 'staying' with some one—some delicious host or hostess who never shows."

"It's liberty-hall—absolutely," Dane assented.

"Yes—or a convalescent home."

To this, however, Dane demurred. "Ah, that, it seems to me, scarcely puts it. You weren't *ill*—were you? I'm very sure *I* really wasn't. I was only, as the world goes, too 'beastly well'!"

The good Brother wondered. "But if we couldn't keep it up—?"

"We couldn't keep it *down*—that was all the matter!"

"I see—I see." The good Brother sighed contentedly; after which he brought out again with kindly humour: "It's a sort of kindergarten!"

"The next thing you'll be saying that we're babes at the breast!"

"Of some great mild, invisible mother who stretches away into space and whose lap is the whole valley—?"

"And her bosom"—Dane completed the figure—"the noble eminence of our hill? That will do; anything will do that covers the essential fact."

"And what do you call the essential fact?"

"Why, that—as in old days on Swiss lake-sides—we're *en pension*."

The good Brother took this gently up. "I remember—I remember: seven francs a day without wine! But, alas, it's more than seven francs here."

"Yes, it's considerably more," Dane had to confess. "Perhaps it isn't particularly cheap."

"Yet, should you call it particularly dear?" his friend after a moment inquired.

George Dane had to think. "How do I know, after all? What practice has one ever had in estimating the inestimable? Particular cheapness certainly isn't the note that we feel struck all round; but don't we fall naturally into the view that there *must* be a price to anything so awfully sane?"

The good Brother in his turn reflected. "We fall into the view that it must pay—that it does pay."

"Oh, yes; it does pay!" Dane eagerly echoed. "If it didn't it wouldn't last. It has *got* to last, of course!" he declared.

"So that we can come back?"

"Yes—think of knowing that we shall be able to!"

They pulled up again at this and, facing each other, thought of it, or at any rate pretended to; for what was really in their eyes was the dread of a loss of the clue. "Oh, when we want it again we shall find it," said the good Brother. "If the place really pays, it will keep on."

"Yes, that's the beauty; that it isn't, thank heaven, carried on only for love."

"No doubt, no doubt; and yet, thank heaven, there's love in it too." They had lingered as if, in the mild, moist air, they were charmed with the patter of the rain and the way the garden drank it. After a little, however, it did look rather as if they were trying to talk each other out of a faint, small fear. They saw the increasing rage of life and the recurrent need, and they wondered proportionately whether to return to the front when their hour should sharply strike would be the end of the dream. Was this a threshold perhaps, after all, that could only be crossed one way? They must return to the front sooner or later—that was certain: for each his hour would strike. The flower would have been gathered and the trick played—the sands, in short, would have run.

There, in its place *was* life—with all its rage; the vague unrest of the need for action knew it again, the stir of the faculty that had been refreshed and reconsecrated. They seemed each, thus confronted, to close their eyes a moment for dizziness; then they were again at peace, and the Brother's confidence rang out. "Oh, we shall meet!"

"Here, do you mean?"

"Yes—and I dare say in the world too."

"But we shan't recognise or know," said Dane.

"In the world, do you mean?"

"Neither in the world nor here."

"Not a bit—not the least little bit, you think?"

Dane turned it over. "Well, so it is that it seems to me all best to hang together. But we shall see."

His friend happily concurred. "We shall see." And at this, for farewell, the Brother held out his hand.

"You're going?" Dane asked.

"No, but I thought *you* were."

It was odd, but at this Dane's hour seemed to strike—his consciousness to crystallise. "Well, I am. I've got it. You stay?" he went on.

"A little longer."

Dane hesitated. "You haven't yet got it?"

"Not altogether—but I think it's coming."

"Good!" Dane kept his hand, giving it a final shake, and at that moment the sun glimmered again through the shower, but with the rain still falling on the hither side of it and seeming to patter even more in the brightness. "Hallo—how charming!"

The brother looked a moment from under the high arch—then again turned his face to our friend. He gave this time his longest, happiest sigh. "Oh, it's all right!"

But why was it, Dane after a moment found himself wondering, that in the act of separation his own hand was so long retained? Why but through a queer phenomenon of change, on the spot, in his companion's face—change that gave it another, but an increasing and above all a much more familiar identity, an identity with that of his servant, with the most conspicuous, the physiognomic seat of the public propriety of Brown? To this anomaly his eyes slowly opened; it was not his good Brother, it was verily Brown who possessed his hand. If his eyes had to open, it was because they had been closed and because Brown appeared to think he had better wake up. So much as this Dane took in, but the effect of his taking it was a relapse into darkness, a recontraction of the lids just prolonged enough to give Brown time, on a second thought, to withdraw his touch and move softly away. Dane's next consciousness was that of the desire to make sure he *was* away, and this desire had somehow the result of dissipating the obscurity. The obscurity was completely gone by the time he had made out that the back of a person writing at his study-table was presented to him. He recognised a portion of a figure that he had somewhere described to somebody—the intent shoulders of the unsuccessful young man who had come that bad morning to breakfast. It was strange, he at last reflected, but the young man was still there. How long had he stayed—days, weeks, months? He was exactly in the position in which Dane had last seen him. Everything—stranger still—was exactly in that position; everything, at least, but the light of the window, which came in from another quarter and showed a different hour. It wasn't after breakfast now; it was after—well, what? He suppressed a gasp—it was after everything. And yet—quite literally—there were but two other differences. One of these was that if he was still on the sofa he was now lying down; the other was the patter on the glass that showed him how the rain—the great rain of the night—had come back. It was the rain of the night, yet when had he last heard it? But two minutes before? Then how many were there before the young man at the table, who seemed intensely occupied, found a moment to look round at him and, on meeting his open eyes, get up and draw near?

"You've slept all day," said the young man.

"All day?"

The young man looked at his watch. "From ten to six. You were extraordinarily tired. I just, after a bit, let you alone, and you were soon off." Yes, that was it; he had been "off"—off, off, off. He began to fit it together; while he had been off the young man had been on. But there were still some few confusions; Dane lay looking up. "Everything's done," the young man continued.

"Everything?"

"Everything."

Dane tried to take it all in, but was embarrassed and could only say weakly and quite apart from the matter: "I've been so happy!"

"So have I," said the young man. He positively looked so; seeing which George Dane wondered afresh, and then, in his wonder, read it indeed quite as another face, quite, in a puzzling way, as another person's. Every one was a little some one else. While he asked himself who else then the young man was, this benefactor, struck by his appealing stare, broke again into perfect cheer. "It's all right!" That answered Dane's question; the face was the face turned to him by the good Brother there in the portico while they listened together to the rustle of the shower. It was all queer, but all pleasant and all distinct, so distinct that the last words in his ear—the same from both quarters—appeared the effect of a single voice. Dane rose and looked about his room, which seemed disencumbered, different, twice as large. It *was* all right.

THE BEAST IN THE JUNGLE

I

What determined the speech that startled him in the course of their encounter scarcely matters, being probably but some words spoken by himself quite without intention—spoken as they lingered and slowly moved together after their renewal of acquaintance. He had been conveyed by friends, an hour or two before, to the house at which she was staying; the party of visitors at the other house, of whom he was one, and thanks to whom it was his theory, as always, that he was lost in the crowd, had been invited over to luncheon. There had been after luncheon much dispersal, all in the interest of the original motive, a view of Weatherend itself and the fine things, intrinsic features, pictures, heirlooms, treasures of all the arts that made the place almost famous; and the great rooms were so numerous that guests could wander at their will, hang back from the principal group, and, in cases where they took such matters with the least seriousness, give themselves up to mysterious appreciations and measurements. There were persons to be observed, singly or in couples, bending toward objects in out-of-the-way corners with their hands on their knees and their heads nodding quite as with the emphasis of an excited sense of smell. When they were two they either mingled their sounds of ecstasy or melted into silences of even deeper import, so that there were aspects of the occasion that gave it for Marcher much the air of the "look round," previous to a sale highly advertised, that excites or quenches, as may be, the dream of acquisition. The dream of acquisition at Weatherend would have had to be wild indeed, and John Marcher found himself, among such suggestions, disconcerted almost equally by the presence of those who knew too much and by that of those who knew nothing. The great rooms caused so much poetry and history to press upon him that he needed to wander apart to feel in a proper relation with them, though his doing so was not, as happened, like the gloating of some of his companions, to be compared to the movements of a dog sniffing a cupboard. It had an issue promptly enough in a direction that was not to have been calculated.

It led, in short, in the course of the October afternoon, to his closer meeting with May Bartram, whose face, a reminder, yet not quite a remembrance, as they sat, much separated, at a very long table, had begun merely by troubling him rather pleasantly. It affected him as the sequel of something of which he had lost the beginning. He knew it, and for the time quite welcomed it, as a continuation, but didn't know what it continued, which was an interest, or an amusement, the greater as he was also somehow aware—yet without a direct sign from her— that the young woman herself had not lost the thread. She had not lost it, but she wouldn't give it back to him, he saw, without some putting forth of his hand for it; and he not only saw that, but saw several things more, things odd enough in the light of the fact that at the moment some accident of grouping brought them face to face he was still merely fumbling with the idea that any contact between them in the past would have had no importance. If it had had no importance he scarcely knew why his actual impression of her should so seem to have so much; the answer to which, however, was that in such a life as they all appeared to be leading for the moment one could but take things as they came. He was satisfied, without in the least being able to say why, that this young lady might roughly have ranked in the house as a poor relation; satisfied also that she was not there on a brief visit, but was more or less a part of the establishment—almost a working, a remunerated part. Didn't she enjoy at periods a protection that she paid for by helping, among other services, to show the place and explain it, deal with the tiresome people, answer questions about the dates of the buildings, the styles of the furniture, the authorship of the pictures, the favourite haunts of the ghost? It wasn't that she looked as if you could have given her shillings—it was impossible to look less so. Yet when she finally drifted toward him, distinctly handsome, though ever so much older— older than when he had seen her before—it might have been as an effect of her guessing that he had, within the couple of hours, devoted more imagination to her than to all the others put together, and had thereby penetrated to a kind of truth that the others were too stupid for. She *was* there on harder terms than anyone; she was there as a consequence of things suffered, in one way and another, in the interval of years; and she remembered him very much as she was remembered—only a good deal better.

By the time they at last thus came to speech they were alone in one of the rooms—remarkable for a fine portrait over the chimney-place—out of which their friends had passed, and the charm of it was that even before they had spoken they had practically arranged with each other to stay behind for talk. The charm, happily, was in other things too; it was partly in there being scarce a spot at Weatherend without something to stay behind for. It was in the way the autumn day looked into the high windows as it waned; in the way the red light, breaking at the close from under a low, sombre sky, reached out in a long shaft and played over old wainscots, old tapestry, old gold, old colour. It was most of all perhaps in the way she came to him as if, since she had been turned on to deal with the simpler sort, he might, should he choose to keep the whole thing down, just take her mild attention for a part of her general business. As soon as he heard her voice, however, the gap was filled up and the missing link supplied; the slight irony he divined in her attitude lost its advantage. He almost jumped at it to get there before her. "I met you years and years ago in Rome. I remember all about it." She confessed to disappointment—she had been so sure he didn't; and to prove how well he did he began to pour forth the particular recollections that popped up as he called for them. Her face and her voice, all at his service now, worked the miracle—the impression operating like the torch of a lamplighter who touches into flame, one by one, a long row of gas jets. Marcher flattered himself that the illumination was brilliant, yet he was really still more pleased on her showing him, with amusement, that in his haste to make everything right he had got most things rather wrong. It hadn't been at Rome—it had been at Naples; and it hadn't been seven years before—it had been more nearly ten. She hadn't been either with her uncle and aunt, but with her mother and her brother; in addition to which it was not with the Pembles that *he* had been, but with the Boyers, coming down in their company from Rome—a point on which she insisted, a little to his confusion, and as to which she had her evidence in hand. The Boyers she had known, but she didn't know the Pembles, though she had heard of them, and it was the people he was with who had

made them acquainted. The incident of the thunderstorm that had
raged round them with such violence as to drive them for refuge into
an excavation—this incident had not occurred at the Palace of the
Caesars, but at Pompeii, on an occasion when they had been present
there at an important find.

He accepted her amendments, he enjoyed her corrections, though
the moral of them was, she pointed out, that he *really* didn't remember
the least thing about her; and he only felt it as a drawback that when
all was made conformable to the truth there didn't appear much of
anything left. They lingered together still, she neglecting her office—
for from the moment he was so clever she had no proper right to
him—and both neglecting the house, just waiting to see if a memory
or two more wouldn't again breathe upon them. It had not taken them
many minutes, after all, to put down on the table, like the cards of a
pack, those that constituted their respective hands; only what came out
was that the pack was unfortunately not perfect—that the past, invoked,
invited, encouraged, could give them, naturally, no more than it had.
It had made them meet—her at twenty, him at twenty-five; but nothing
was so strange, they seemed to say to each other, as that, while so
occupied, it hadn't done a little more for them. They looked at each
other as with the feeling of an occasion missed; the present one would
have been so much better if the other, in the far distance, in the foreign
land, hadn't been so stupidly meagre. There weren't, apparently, all
counted, more than a dozen little old things that had succeeded in
coming to pass between them; trivialities of youth, simplicities of freshness, stupidities of ignorance, small possible germs, but too deeply
buried—too deeply (didn't it seem?) to sprout after so many years.
Marcher said to himself that he ought to have rendered her some
service—saved her from a capsized boat in the Bay, or at least recovered
her dressing-bag, filched from her cab, in the streets of Naples, by a
lazzarone with a stiletto. Or it would have been nice if he could have
been taken with fever, alone, at his hotel, and she could have come to
look after him, to write to his people, to drive him out in convalescence.
Then they would be in possession of the something or other that their
actual show seemed to lack. It yet somehow presented itself, this show,
as too good to be spoiled; so that they were reduced for a few minutes
more to wondering a little helplessly why—since they seemed to know
a certain number of the same people—their reunion had been so long

averted. They didn't use that name for it, but their delay from minute to minute to join the others was a kind of confession that they didn't quite want it to be a failure. Their attempted supposition of reasons for their not having met but showed how little they knew of each other. There came in fact a moment when Marcher felt a positive pang. It was vain to pretend she was an old friend, for all the communities were wanting, in spite of which it was as an old friend that he saw she would have suited him. He had new ones enough—was surrounded with them, for instance, at that hour at the other house; as a new one he probably wouldn't have so much as noticed her. He would have liked to invent something, get her to make-believe with him that some passage of a romantic or critical kind *had* originally occurred. He was really almost reaching out in imagination—as against time—for something that would do, and saying to himself that if it didn't come this new incident would simply and rather awkwardly close. They would separate, and now for no second or for no third chance. They would have tried and not succeeded. Then it was, just at the turn, as he afterwards made it out to himself, that, everything else failing, she herself decided to take up the case and, as it were, save the situation. He felt as soon as she spoke that she had been consciously keeping back what she said and hoping to get on without it; a scruple in her that immensely touched him when, by the end of three or four minutes more, he was able to measure it. What she brought out, at any rate, quite cleared the air and supplied the link—the link it was such a mystery he should frivolously have managed to lose.

"You know you told me something that I've never forgotten and that again and again has made me think of you since; it was that tremendously hot day when we went to Sorrento, across the bay, for the breeze. What I allude to was what you said to me, on the way back, as we sat, under the awning of the boat, enjoying the cool. Have you forgotten?"

He had forgotten, and he was even more surprised than ashamed. But the great thing was that he saw it was no vulgar reminder of any "sweet" speech. The vanity of women had long memories, but she was making no claim on him of a compliment or a mistake. With another woman, a totally different one, he might have feared the recall possibly even some imbecile "offer." So, in having to say that he had indeed forgotten, he was conscious rather of a loss than of a gain; he already saw an interest in the matter of her reference. "I try to think—but I give it up. Yet I remember the Sorrento day."

"I'm not very sure you do," May Bartram after a moment said; "and I'm not very sure I ought to want you to. It's dreadful to bring a person back, at any time, to what he was ten years before. If you've lived away from it," she smiled, "so much the better."

"Ah, if *you* haven't why should I?" he asked.

"Lived away, you mean from what I myself was?"

"From what *I* was. I was of course an ass," Marcher went on; "but I would rather know from you just the sort of ass I was than—from the moment you have something in your mind—not know anything."

Still, however, she hesitated. "But if you've completely ceased to be that sort—?"

"Why, I can then just so all the more bear to know. Besides, perhaps I haven't."

"Perhaps. Yet if you haven't," she added, "I should suppose you would remember. Not indeed that *I* in the least connect with my impression the invidious name you use. If I had only thought you foolish," she explained, "the thing I speak of wouldn't so have remained with me. It was about yourself." She waited, as if it might come to him; but as, only meeting her eyes in wonder, he gave no sign, she burnt her ships. "Has it ever happened?"

Then it was that, while he continued to stare, a light broke for him and the blood slowly came to his face, which began to burn with recognition. "Do you mean I told you—?" But he faltered, lest what came to him shouldn't be right, lest he should only give himself away.

"It was something about yourself that it was natural one shouldn't forget—that is if one remembered you at all. That's why I ask you," she smiled, "if the thing you then spoke of has ever come to pass?"

Oh, then he saw, but he was lost in wonder and found himself embarrassed. This, he also saw, made her sorry for him, as if her allusion had been a mistake. It took him but a moment, however, to feel it had not been, much as it had been a surprise. After the first little shock of it her knowledge on the contrary began, even if rather strangely, to taste sweet to him. She was the only other person in the world then who would have it, and she had had it all these years, while the fact of his having so breathed his secret had unaccountably faded from him. No wonder they couldn't have met as if nothing had happened. "I judge," he finally said, "that I know what you mean. Only I had strangely enough lost the consciousness of having taken you so far into my confidence."

"Is it because you've taken so many others as well?"

"I've taken nobody. Not a creature since then."

"So that I'm the only person who knows?"

"The only person in the world."

"Well," she quickly replied, "I myself have never spoken. I've never, never repeated of you what you told me." She looked at him so that he perfectly believed her. Their eyes met over it in such a way that he was without a doubt. "And I never will."

She spoke with an earnestness that, as if almost excessive, put him at ease about her possible derision. Somehow the whole question was a new luxury to him—that is, from the moment she was in possession. If she didn't take the ironic view she clearly took the sympathetic, and that was what he had had, in all the long time, from no one whomsoever. What he felt was that he couldn't at present have begun to tell her and yet could profit perhaps exquisitely by the accident of having done so of old. "Please don't then. We're just right as it is."

"Oh, I am," she laughed, "if you are!" To which she added: "Then you do still feel in the same way?"

It was impossible to him not to take to himself that she was really interested, and it all kept coming as a sort of revelation. He had thought of himself so long as abominably alone, and, lo, he wasn't alone a bit. He hadn't been, it appeared, for an hour—since those moments on the Sorrento boat. It was *she* who had been, he seemed to see as he looked at her—she who had been made so by the graceless fact of his lapse of fidelity. To tell her what he had told her—what had it been but to ask something of her? Something that she had given, in her charity, without his having, by a remembrance, by a return of the spirit, failing another encounter, so much as thanked her. What he had asked of her had been simply at first not to laugh at him. She had beautifully not done so for ten years, and she was not doing so now. So he had endless gratitude to make up. Only for that he must see just how he had figured to her. "What, exactly, was the account I gave—?"

"Of the way you did feel? Well, it was very simple. You said you had had from your earliest time, as the deepest thing within you, the sense of being kept for something rare and strange, possibly prodigious and terrible, that was sooner or later to happen to you, that you had in your bones the foreboding and the conviction of, and that would perhaps overwhelm you."

"Do you call that very simple?" John Marcher asked.

She thought a moment. "It was perhaps because I seemed, as you spoke, to understand it."

"You do understand it?" he eagerly asked.

Again she kept her kind eyes on him. "You still have the belief?"

"Oh!" he exclaimed helplessly. There was too much to say.

"Whatever it is to be," she clearly made out, "it hasn't yet come."

He shook his head in complete surrender now. "It hasn't yet come. Only, you know, it isn't anything I'm to *do*, to achieve in the world, to be distinguished or admired for. I'm not such an ass as *that*. It would be much better, no doubt, if I were."

"It's to be something you're merely to suffer?"

"Well, say to wait for—to have to meet, to face, to see suddenly break out in my life; possibly destroying all further consciousness, possibly annihilating me; possibly, on the other hand, only altering everything, striking at the root of all my world and leaving me to the consequences, however they shape themselves."

She took this in, but the light in her eyes continued for him not to be that of mockery. "Isn't what you describe perhaps but the expectation—or, at any rate, the sense of danger, familiar to so many people—of falling in love?"

John Marcher thought. "Did you ask me that before?"

"No—I wasn't so free-and-easy then. But it's what strikes me now."

"Of course," he said after a moment, "it strikes you. Of course it strikes *me*. Of course what's in store for me may be no more than that. The only thing is," he went on, "that I think that if it had been that, I should by this time know."

"Do you mean because you've *been* in love?" And then as he but looked at her in silence: "You've been in love, and it hasn't meant such a cataclysm, hasn't proved the great affair?"

"Here I am, you see. It hasn't been overwhelming."

"Then it hasn't been love," said May Bartram.

"Well, I at least thought it was. I took it for that—I've taken it till now. It was agreeable, it was delightful, it was miserable," he explained. "But it wasn't strange. It wasn't what *my* affair's to be."

"You want something all to yourself—something that nobody else knows or *has* known?"

"It isn't a question of what I 'want'—God knows I don't want anything. It's only a question of the apprehension that haunts me—that I live with day by day."

He said this so lucidly and consistently that, visibly, it further imposed itself. If she had not been interested before she would have been interested now. "Is it a sense of coming violence?"

Evidently now too, again, he liked to talk of it. "I don't think of it as—when it does come—necessarily violent. I only think of it as natural and as of course, above all, unmistakable. I think of it simply as *the* thing. *The* thing will of itself appear natural."

"Then how will it appear strange?"

Marcher bethought himself. "It won't—to *me*."

"To whom then?"

"Well," he replied, smiling at last, "say to you."

"Oh then, I'm to be present?"

"Why, you *are* present—since you know."

"I see." She turned it over. "But I mean at the catastrophe."

At this, for a minute, their lightness gave way to gravity; it was as if the long look they exchanged held them together. "It will only depend on yourself—if you'll watch with me."

"Are you afraid?" she asked.

"Don't leave me *now*," he went on.

"Are you afraid?" she repeated.

"Do you think me simply out of my mind?" he pursued instead of answering. "Do I merely strike you as a harmless lunatic?"

"No," said May Bartram. "I understand you. I believe you."

"You mean you feel how my obsession—poor old thing! —may correspond to some possible reality?"

"To some possible reality."

"Then you *will* watch with me?"

She hesitated, then for the third time put her question. "Are you afraid?"

"Did I tell you I was—at Naples?"

"No, you said nothing about it."

"Then I don't know. And I should *like* to know," said John Marcher. "You'll tell me yourself whether you think so. If you'll watch with me you'll see."

"Very good then." They had been moving by this time across the room, and at the door, before passing out, they paused as if for the full wind-up of their understanding. "I'll watch with you," said May Bartram.

II

The fact that she "knew"—knew and yet neither chaffed him nor betrayed him—had in a short time begun to constitute between them a sensible bond, which became more marked when, within the year that followed their afternoon at Weatherend, the opportunities for meeting multiplied. The event that thus promoted these occasions was the death of the ancient lady, her great-aunt, under whose wing, since losing her mother, she had to such an extent found shelter, and who, though but the widowed mother of the new successor to the property, had succeeded—thanks to a high tone and a high temper—in not forfeiting the supreme position at the great house. The deposition of this personage arrived but with her death, which, followed by many changes, made in particular a difference for the young woman in whom Marcher's expert attention had recognised from the first a dependent with a pride that might ache though it didn't bristle. Nothing for a long time had made him easier than the thought that the aching must have been much soothed by Miss Bartram's now finding herself able to set up a small home in London. She had acquired property, to an amount that made luxury just possible, under her aunt's extremely complicated will, and when the whole matter began to be straightened out, which indeed took time, she let him know that the happy issue was at last in view. He had seen her again before that day, both because she had more than once accompanied the ancient lady to town and because he had paid another visit to the friends who so conveniently made of Weatherend one of the charms of their own hospitality. These friends had taken him back there; he had achieved there again with Miss Bartram some quiet detachment; and he had in London succeeded in persuading her to more than one brief absence from her aunt. They went together, on these latter occasions, to the National Gallery and the South Kensington Museum, where, among vivid reminders, they talked of Italy at large— not now attempting to recover, as at first, the taste of their youth and their ignorance. That recovery, the first day at Weatherend, had served its purpose well, had given them quite enough; so that they were, to Marcher's sense, no longer hovering about the head-waters of their stream, but had felt their boat pushed sharply off and down the current.

They were literally afloat together; for our gentleman this was marked, quite as marked as that the fortunate cause of it was just the buried treasure of her knowledge. He had with his own hands dug up this little hoard, brought to light—that is to within reach of the dim day constituted by their discretions and privacies—the object of value the hiding-place of which he had, after putting it into the ground himself, so strangely, so long forgotten. The exquisite luck of having again just stumbled on the spot made him indifferent to any other question; he would doubtless have devoted more time to the odd accident of his lapse of memory if he had not been moved to devote so much to the sweetness, the comfort, as he felt, for the future, that this accident itself had helped to keep fresh. It had never entered into his plan that anyone should "know," and mainly for the reason that it was not in him to tell anyone. That would have been impossible, since nothing but the amuse- ment of a cold world would have waited on it. Since, however, a mysterious fate had opened his mouth in youth, in spite of him, he would count that a compensation and profit by it to the utmost. That the right person *should* know tempered the asperity of his secret more even than his shyness had permitted him to imagine; and May Bartram was clearly right, because—well, because there she was. Her knowledge simply settled it; he would have been sure enough by this time had she been wrong. There was that in his situation, no doubt, that disposed him too much to see her as a mere confidant, taking all her light for him from the fact—the fact only—of her interest in his predicament, from her mercy, sympathy, seriousness, her consent not to regard him as the funniest of the funny. Aware, in fine, that her price for him was just in her giving him this constant sense of his being admirably spared, he was careful to remember that she had, after all, also a life of her own, with things that might happen to *her*, things that in friendship one should likewise take account of. Something fairly remarkable came to pass with him, for that matter, in this connection—something represented by a certain passage of his consciousness, in the suddenest way, from one extreme to the other.

He had thought himself, so long as nobody knew, the most dis-interested person in the world, carrying his concentrated burden, his perpetual suspense, ever so quietly, holding his tongue about it, giving others no glimpse of it nor of its effect upon his life, asking of them no allowance and only making on his side all those that were asked. He had disturbed nobody with the queerness of having to know a haunted man, though he had had moments of rather special temptation on hearing people say that they were "unsettled." If they were as un-settled as he was—he who had never been settled for an hour in his life—they would know what it meant. Yet it wasn't, all the same, for him to make them, and he listened to them civilly enough. This was why he had such good—though possibly such rather colourless—man-ners; this was why, above all, he could regard himself, in a greedy world, as decently—as, in fact, perhaps even a little sublimely—un-selfish. Our point is accordingly that he valued this character quite sufficiently to measure his present danger of letting it lapse, against which he promised himself to be much on his guard. He was quite ready, none the less, to be selfish just a little, since, surely, no more charming occasion for it had come to him. "Just a little," in a word, was just as much as Miss Bartram, taking one day with another, would let him. He never would be in the least coercive, and he would keep well before him the lines on which consideration for her—the very highest—ought to proceed. He would thoroughly establish the heads under which her affairs, her requirements, her peculiarities—he went so far as to give them the latitude of that name—would come into their intercourse. All this naturally was a sign of how much he took the intercourse itself for granted. There was nothing more to be done about *that*. It simply existed; had sprung into being with her first penetrating question to him in the autumn light there at Weatherend. The real form it should have taken on the basis that stood out large was the form of their marrying. But the devil in this was that the very basis itself put marrying out of the question. His conviction, his apprehension, his obsession, in short, was not a condition he could invite a woman to share; and that consequence of it was precisely what was the matter with him. Something or other lay in wait for him, amid the twists and the turns of the months and the years, like a crouching beast in the jungle. It signified little whether the crouching beast were destined to slay him or to be slain. The definite point was the inevitable spring of the creature; and the definite lesson from that was that a man of feeling didn't cause himself to be accompanied by a lady on a tiger-hunt. Such was the image under which he had ended by figuring his life.

They had at first, none the less, in the scattered hours spent together, made no allusion to that view of it; which was a sign he was handsomely ready to give that he didn't expect, that he in fact didn't care always to be talking about it. Such a feature in one's outlook was really like a hump on one's back. The difference it made every minute of the day existed quite independently of discussion. One discussed, of course, *like* a hunchback, for there was always, if nothing else, the hunchback face. That remained, and she was watching him; but people watched best, as a general thing, in silence, so that such would be predominantly the manner of their vigil. Yet he didn't want, at the same time, to be solemn; solemn was what he imagined he too much tended to be with other people. The thing to be, with the one person who knew, was easy and natural—to make the reference rather than be seeming to avoid it, to avoid it rather than be seeming to make it, and to keep it, in any case, familiar, facetious even, rather than pedantic and portentous. Some such consideration as the latter was doubtless in his mind, for instance, when he wrote pleasantly to Miss Bartram that perhaps the great thing he had so long felt as in the lap of the gods was no more than this circumstance, which touched him so nearly, of her acquiring a house in London. It was the first allusion they had yet again made, needing any other hitherto so little; but when she replied, after having given him the news, that she was by no means satisfied with such a trifle, as the climax to so special a suspense, she almost set him wondering if she hadn't even a larger conception of singularity for him than he had for himself. He was at all events destined to become aware little by little, as time went by, that she was all the while looking at his life, judging it, measuring it, in the light of the thing she knew, which grew to be at last, with the consecration of the years, never mentioned between them save as "the real truth" about him. That had always been his own form of reference to it, but she adopted the form so quietly that, looking back at the end of a period, he knew there was no moment at which it was traceable that she had, as he might say, got inside his condition, or exchanged the attitude of beautifully indulging for that of still more beautifully believing him.

It was always open to him to accuse her of seeing him but as the most harmless of maniacs, and this, in the long run—since it covered so much ground—was his easiest description of their friendship. He had a screw loose for her, but she liked him in spite of it, and was practically, against the rest of the world, his kind, wise keeper, unre-munerated, but fairly amused and, in the absence of other near ties, not disreputably occupied. The rest of the world of course thought him queer, but she, she only, knew how, and above all why, queer; which was precisely what enabled her to dispose the concealing veil in the right folds. She took his gaiety from him—since it had to pass with them for gaiety—as she took everything else; but she certainly so far justified by her unerring touch his finer sense of the degree to which he had ended by convincing her. *She* at least never spoke of the secret of his life except as "the real truth about you," and she had in fact a wonderful way of making it seem, as such, the secret of her own life too. That was in fine how he so constantly felt her as allowing for him; he couldn't on the whole call it anything else. He allowed for himself, but she, exactly, allowed still more; partly because, better placed for a sight of the matter, she traced his unhappy perversion through portions of its course into which he could scarce follow it. He knew how he felt, but, besides knowing that, she knew how he *looked* as well: he knew each of the things of importance he was insidiously kept from doing, but she could add up the amount they made, understand how much, with a lighter weight on his spirit, he might have done, and thereby establish how, clever as he was, he fell short. Above all she was in the secret of the difference between the forms he went through—those of his little office under Government, those of caring for his modest patrimony, for his library, for his garden in the country, for the people in London whose invitations he accepted and repaid—and the detach-ment that reigned beneath them and that made of all behaviour, all that could in the least be called behaviour, a long act of dissimulation. What it had come to was that he wore a mask painted with the social simper, out of the eye-holes of which there looked eyes of an expression not in the least matching the other features. This the stupid world, even after years, had never more than half discovered. It was only May Bartram who had, and she achieved, by an art indescribable, the feat of at once—or perhaps it was only alternately—meeting the eyes from in front and mingling her own vision, as from over his shoulder, with their peep through the apertures.

So, while they grew older together, she did watch with him, and so she let this association give shape and colour to her own existence. Beneath *her* forms as well detachment had learned to sit, and behaviour had become for her, in the social sense, a false account of herself. There was but one account of her that would have been true all the while, and that she could give, directly, to nobody, least of all to John Marcher. Her whole attitude was a virtual statement, but the perception of that only seemed destined to take its place for him as one of the many things necessarily crowded out of his consciousness. If she had, more-over, like himself, to make sacrifices to their real truth, it was to be granted that her compensation might have affected her as more prompt and more natural. They had long periods, in this London time, during which, when they were together, a stranger might have listened to them without in the least pricking up his ears; on the other hand, the real truth was equally liable at any moment to rise to the surface, and the auditor would then have wondered indeed what they were talking about. They had from an early time made up their mind that society was, luckily, unintelligent, and the margin that this gave them had fairly become one of their commonplaces. Yet there were still moments when the situation turned almost fresh—usually under the effect of some expression drawn from herself. Her expressions doubtless repeated themselves, but her intervals were generous. "What saves us, you know, is that we answer so completely to so usual an appearance: that of the man and woman whose friendship has become such a daily habit, or almost, as to be at last indispensable." That, for instance, was a remark she had frequently enough had occasion to make, though she had given it at different times different developments. What we are especially concerned with is the turn it happened to take from her one afternoon when he had come to see her in honour of her birthday. This anniversary had fallen on a Sunday, at a season of thick fog and general outward gloom; but he had brought her his customary offering, having known her now long enough to have established a hundred little customs. It was one of his proofs to himself, the present he made her on her birthday, that he had not sunk into real selfishness. It was mostly nothing more than a small trinket, but it was always fine of its kind, and he was regularly careful to pay for it more than he thought he could afford. "Our habit saves you, at least, don't you see? because it makes you, after all, for the vulgar, indistinguishable from other men. What's the most inveterate mark of men in general? Why, the capacity to spend endless time with dull women—to spend it I won't say without being bored, but without minding that they are, without being driven off at a tangent by it; which comes to the same thing. I'm your dull woman, a part of the daily bread for which you pray at church. That covers your tracks more than anything."

"And what covers yours?" asked Marcher, whom his dull woman could mostly to this extent amuse. "I see of course what you mean by your saving me, in one way or another, so far as other people are concerned—I've seen it all along. Only, what is it that saves *you*? I often think, you know, of that."

She looked as if she sometimes thought of that too, but in rather a different way. "Where other people, you mean, are concerned?"

"Well, you're really so in with me, you know—as a sort of result of my being so in with yourself. I mean of my having such an immense regard for you, being so tremendously grateful for all you've done for me. I sometimes ask myself if it's quite fair. Fair I mean to have so involved and—since one may say it—interested you. I almost feel as if you hadn't really had time to do anything else."

"Anything else but be interested?" she asked. "Ah, what else does one ever want to be? If I've been 'watching' with you, as we long ago agreed that I was to do, watching is always in itself an absorption."

"Oh, certainly," John Marcher said, "if you hadn't had your curiosity—! Only, doesn't it sometimes come to you, as time goes on, that your curiosity is not being particularly repaid?"

May Bartram had a pause. "Do you ask that, by any chance, because you feel at all that yours isn't? I mean because you have to wait so long."

Oh, he understood what she meant. "For the thing to happen that never does happen? For the beast to jump out? No, I'm just where I was about it. It isn't a matter as to which I can *choose*, I can decide for a change. It isn't one as to which there *can* be a change. It's in the lap of the gods. One's in the hands of one's law—there one is. As to the form the law will take, the way it will operate, that's its own affair."

"Yes," Miss Bartram replied; "of course one's fate is coming, of course it *has* come, in its own form and its own way, all the while. Only, you know, the form and the way in your case were to have been— well, something so exceptional and, as one may say, so particularly *your* own."

Something in this made him look at her with suspicion. "You say 'were to *have* been,' as if in your heart you had begun to doubt."

"Oh!" she vaguely protested.

"As if you believed," he went on, "that nothing will now take place."

She shook her head slowly, but rather inscrutably. "You're far from my thought."

He continued to look at her. "What then is the matter with you?"

"Well," she said after another wait, "the matter with me is simply that I'm more sure than ever my curiosity, as you call it, will be but too well repaid."

They were frankly grave now; he had got up from his seat, had turned once more about the little drawing-room to which, year after year, he brought his inevitable topic; in which he had, as he might have said, tasted their intimate community with every sauce, where every object was as familiar to him as the things of his own house and the very carpets were worn with his fitful walk very much as the desks in old counting-houses are worn by the elbows of generations of clerks. The generations of his nervous moods had been at work there, and the place was the written history of his whole middle life. Under the impression of what his friend had just said he knew himself, for some reason, more aware of these things, which made him, after a moment, stop again before her. "Is it, possibly, that you've grown afraid?"

"Afraid?" He thought, as she repeated the word, that his question had made her, a little, change colour; so that, lest he should have touched on a truth, he explained very kindly. "You remember that that was what you asked *me* long ago—that first day at Weatherend."

"Oh yes, and you told me you didn't know—that I was to see for myself. We've said little about it since, even in so long a time."

"Precisely," Marcher interposed—"quite as if it were too delicate a matter for us to make free with. Quite as if we might find, on pressure, that I *am* afraid. For then," he said, "we shouldn't, should we? quite know what to do."

She had for the time no answer to this question. "There have been days when I thought you were. Only, of course," she added, "there have been days when we have thought almost anything."

"Everything. Oh!" Marcher softly groaned as with a gasp, half spent, at the face, more uncovered just then than it had been for a long while, of the imagination always with them. It had always had its incalculable moments of glaring out, quite as with the very eyes of the very Beast, and, used as he was to them, they could still draw from him the tribute of a sigh that rose from the depths of his being. All that they had thought, first and last, rolled over him; the past seemed to have been reduced to mere barren speculation. This in fact was what the place had just struck him as so full of—the simplification of everything but the state of suspense. That remained only by seeming to hang in the void surrounding it. Even his original fear, if fear it had been, had lost itself in the desert. "I judge, however," he continued, "that you see I'm not afraid now."

"What I see is, as I make it out, that you've achieved something almost unprecedented in the way of getting used to danger. Living with it so long and so closely, you've lost your sense of it; you know it's there, but you're indifferent, and you cease even, as of old, to have to whistle in the dark. Considering what the danger is," May Bartram wound up, "I'm bound to say that I don't think your attitude could well be surpassed."

John Marcher faintly smiled. "It's heroic?"

"Certainly—call it that."

He considered. "I *am*, then, a man of courage?"

"That's what you were to show me."

He still, however, wondered. "But doesn't the man of courage know what he's afraid of—or *not* afraid of? I don't know *that*, you see. I don't focus it. I can't name it. I only know I'm exposed."

"Yes, but exposed—how shall I say? —so directly. So intimately. That's surely enough."

"Enough to make you feel, then—as what we may call the end of our watch—that I'm not afraid?"

"You're not afraid. But it isn't," she said, "the end of our watch. That is it isn't the end of yours. You've everything still to see."

"Then why haven't *you*?" he asked. He had had, all along, to-day, the sense of her keeping something back, and he still had it. As this was his first impression of that, it made a kind of date. The case was the more marked as she didn't at first answer; which in turn made him go on. "You know something I don't." Then his voice, for that of a man of courage, trembled a little. "You know what's to happen." Her silence, with the face she showed, was almost a confession—it made him sure. "You know, and you're afraid to tell me. It's so bad that you're afraid I'll find out."

All this might be true, for she did look as if, unexpectedly to her, he had crossed some mystic line that she had secretly drawn round her. Yet she might, after all, not have worried; and the real upshot was that he himself, at all events, needn't. "You'll never find out."

III

It was all to have made, none the less, as I have said, a date; as came out in the fact that again and again, even after long intervals, other things that passed between them wore, in relation to this hour, but the character of recalls and results. Its immediate effect had been indeed rather to lighten insistence—almost to provoke a reaction; as if their topic had dropped by its own weight and as if moreover, for that matter, Marcher had been visited by one of his occasional warnings against egotism. He had kept up, he felt, and very decently on the whole, his consciousness of the importance of not being selfish, and it was true that he had never sinned in that direction without promptly enough trying to press the scales the other way. He often repaired his fault, the season permitting, by inviting his friend to accompany him to the opera; and it not infrequently thus happened that, to show he didn't wish her to have but one sort of food for her mind, he was the cause of her appearing there with him a dozen nights in the month. It even happened that, seeing her home at such times, he occasionally went in with her to finish, as he called it, the evening, and, the better to make his point, sat down to the frugal but always careful little supper that awaited his pleasure. His point was made, he thought, by his not eternally insisting with her on himself; made for instance, at such hours, when it befell that, her piano at hand and each of them familiar with it, they went over passages of the opera together. It chanced to be on one of these occasions, however, that he reminded her of her not having

answered a certain question he had put to her during the talk that had
taken place between them on her last birthday. "What is it that saves
you?" —saved her, he meant, from that appearance of variation from
the usual human type. If he had practically escaped remark, as she
pretended, by doing, in the most important particular, what most men
do—find the answer to life in patching up an alliance of a sort with a
woman no better than himself—how had she escaped it, and how could
the alliance, such as it was, since they must suppose it had been more
or less noticed, have failed to make her rather positively talked about?

"I never said," May Bartram replied, "that it hadn't made me talked
about."

"Ah well then, you're not 'saved.'"

"It has not been a question for me. If you've had your woman, I've
had," she said, "my man."

"And you mean that makes you all right?"

She hesitated. "I don't know why it shouldn't make me—humanly,
which is what we're speaking of—as right as it makes you."

"I see," Marcher returned. "'Humanly,' no doubt, as showing that
you're living for something. Not, that is, just for me and my secret."

May Bartram smiled. "I don't pretend it exactly shows that I'm not
living for you. It's my intimacy with you that's in question."

He laughed as he saw what she meant. "Yes, but since, as you say,
I'm only, so far as people make out, ordinary, you're—aren't you? —
no more than ordinary either. You help me to pass for a man like
another. So if I *am*, as I understand you, you're not compromised. Is
that it?"

She had another hesitation, but she spoke clearly enough. "That's
it. It's all that concerns me—to help you to pass for a man like another."

He was careful to acknowledge the remark handsomely. "How kind,
how beautiful, you are to me! How shall I ever repay you?"

She had her last grave pause, as if there might be a choice of ways.
But she chose. "By going on as you are."

It was into this going on as he was that they relapsed, and really
for so long a time that the day inevitably came for a further sounding
of their depths. It was as if these depths, constantly bridged over by a
structure that was firm enough in spite of its lightness and of its
occasional oscillation in the somewhat vertiginous air, invited on occasion, in the interest of their nerves, a dropping of the plummet and

a measurement of the abyss. A difference had been made moreover, once for all, by the fact that she had, all the while, not appeared to feel the need of rebutting his charge of an idea within her that she didn't dare to express, uttered just before one of the fullest of their later discussions ended. It had come up for him then that she "knew" something and that what she knew was bad—too bad to tell him. When he had spoken of it as visibly so bad that she was afraid he might find it out, her reply had left the matter too equivocal to be let alone and yet, for Marcher's special sensibility, almost too formidable again to touch. He circled about it at a distance that alternately narrowed and widened and that yet was not much affected by the consciousness in him that there was nothing she could "know," after all, any better than he did. She had no source of knowledge that he hadn't equally—except of course that she might have finer nerves. That was what women had where they were interested; they made out things, where people were concerned, that the people often couldn't have made out for themselves. Their nerves, their sensibility, their imagination, were conductors and revealers, and the beauty of May Bartram was in particular that she had given herself so to his case. He felt in these days what, oddly enough, he had never felt before, the growth of a dread of losing her by some catastrophe—some catastrophe that yet wouldn't at all be *the* catastrophe: partly because she had, almost of a sudden, begun to strike him as useful to him as never yet, and partly by reason of an appearance of uncertainty in her health, coincident and equally new. It was characteristic of the inner detachment he had hitherto so successfully cultivated and to which our whole account of him is a reference, it was characteristic that his complications, such as they were, had never yet seemed so as at this crisis to thicken about him, even to the point of making him ask himself if he were, by any chance, of a truth, within sight or sound, within touch or reach, within the immediate jurisdiction of the thing that waited.

When the day came, as come it had to, that his friend confessed to him her fear of a deep disorder in her blood, he felt somehow the shadow of a change and the chill of a shock. He immediately began to imagine aggravations and disasters, and above all to think of her peril as the direct menace for himself of personal privation. This indeed gave him one of those partial recoveries of equanimity that were aggreable to him—it showed him that what was still first in his mind was the loss she herself might suffer. "What if she should have to die before knowing, before seeing—?" It would have been brutal, in the early stages of her trouble, to put that question to her; but it had immediately sounded for him to his own concern, and the possibility was what most made him sorry for her. If she did "know," moreover, in the sense of her having had some—what should he think? —mystical, irresistible light, this would make the matter not better, but worse, inasmuch as her original adoption of his own curiosity had quite become the basis of her life. She had been living to see what would *be* to be seen, and it would be cruel to her to have to give up before the accomplishment of the vision. These reflections, as I say, refreshed his generosity; yet, make them as he might, he saw himself, with the lapse of the period, more and more disconcerted. It lapsed for him with a strange, steady sweep, and the oddest oddity was that it gave him, independently of the threat of much inconvenience, almost the only positive surprise his career, if career it could be called, had yet offered him. She kept the house as she had never done; he had to go to her to see her—she could meet him nowhere now, though there was scarce a corner of their loved old London in which she had not in the past, at one time or another, done so; and he found her always seated by her fire in the deep, old-fashioned chair she was less and less able to leave. He had been struck one day, after an absence exceeding his usual measure, with her suddenly looking much older to him than he had ever thought of her being; then he recognised that the suddenness was all on his side—he had just been suddenly struck. She looked older because inevitably, after so many years, she *was* old, or almost; which was of course true in still greater measure of her companion. If she was old, or almost, John Marcher assuredly was, and yet it was her showing of the lesson, not his own, that brought the truth home to him. His surprises began here; when once they had begun they multiplied; they came rather with a rush: it was as if, in the oddest way in the world, they had all been kept back, sown in a thick cluster, for the late afternoon of life, the time at which, for people in general, the unexpected has died out.

One of them was that he should have caught himself—for he *had* so done—*really* wondering if the great accident would take form now as nothing more than his being condemned to see this charming woman, this admirable friend, pass away from him. He had never so unreservedly qualified her as while confronted in thought with such a possibility; in spite of which there was small doubt for him that as an answer to his long riddle the mere effacement of even so fine a feature of his situation would be an abject anticlimax. It would represent, as connected with his past attitude, a drop of dignity under the shadow of which his existence could only become the most grotesque of failures. He had been far from holding it a failure—long as he had waited for the appearance that was to make it a success. He had waited for a quite other thing, not for such a one as that. The breath of his good faith came short, however, as he recognised how long he had waited, or how long, at least, his companion had. That she, at all events, might be recorded as having waited in vain—this affected him sharply, and all the more because of his at first having done little more than amuse himself with the idea. It grew more grave as the gravity of her condition grew, and the state of mind it produced in him, which he ended by watching, himself, as if it had been some definite disfigurement of his outer person, may pass for another of his surprises. This conjoined itself still with another, the really stupefying consciousness of a question that he would have allowed to shape itself had he dared. What did everything mean—what, that is, did *she* mean, she and her vain waiting and her probable death and the soundless admonition of it all—unless that, at this time of day, it was simply, it was overwhelmingly too late? He had never, at any stage of his queer consciousness, admitted the whisper of such a correction; he had never, till within these last few months, been so false to his conviction as not to hold that what was to come to him had time, whether *he* struck himself as having it or not. That at last, at last, he certainly hadn't it, to speak of, or had it but in the scantiest measure—such, soon enough, as things went with him, became the inference with which his old obsession had to reckon: and this it was not helped to do by the more and more confirmed appearance that the great vagueness casting the long shadow in which he had lived had, to attest itself, almost no margin left. Since it was in Time that he was to have met his fate, so it was in Time that his fate was to have acted; and as he waked up to the sense of no longer being young, which was exactly the sense of being stale, just as that, in turn, was the sense of being weak, he waked up to another matter beside. It all hung together; they were subject, he and the great vagueness, to an equal and indivisible law. When the possibilities themselves had, accordingly, turned stale, when the secret of the gods had grown faint, had perhaps even quite evaporated, that, and that only, was failure. It wouldn't have been failure to be bankrupt, dishonoured, pilloried, hanged; it was failure not to be anything. And so, in the dark valley into which his path had taken its unlooked-for twist, he wondered not a little as he groped. He didn't care what awful crash might overtake him, with what ignominy or what monstrosity he might yet be associated—since he wasn't, after all, too utterly old to suffer—if it would only be decently proportionate to the posture he had kept, all his life, in the promised presence of it. He had but one desire left—that he shouldn't have been "sold."

IV

Then it was that one afternoon, while the spring of the year was young and new, she met, all in her own way, his frankest betrayal of these alarms. He had gone in late to see her, but evening had not settled, and she was presented to him in that long, fresh light of waning April days which affects us often with a sadness sharper than the greyest hours of autumn. The week had been warm, the spring was supposed to have begun early, and May Bartram sat, for the first time in the year, without a fire, a fact that, to Marcher's sense, gave the scene of which she formed part a smooth and ultimate look, an air of knowing, in its immaculate order and its cold, meaningless cheer, that it would never see a fire again. Her own aspect—he could scarce have said why—intensified this note. Almost as white as wax, with the marks and signs in her face as numerous and as fine as if they had been etched by a needle, with soft white draperies relieved by a faded green scarf, the delicate tone of which had been consecrated by the years, she was the picture of a serene, exquisite, but impenetrable sphinx, whose head, or indeed all whose person, might have been *powdered* with silver. She was a sphinx, yet with her white petals and green fronds she might have been a lily too—only an artificial lily, wonderfully imitated and constantly kept, without dust or stain, though not exempt from a slight droop and a complexity of faint creases, under some clear glass bell. The perfection of household care, of high polish and finish, always reigned in her rooms, but they especially looked to Marcher at present as if everything had been wound up, tucked in, put away, so that she might sit with folded hands and with nothing more to do. She was "out of it," to his vision; her work was over; she communicated with him as across some gulf, or from some island of rest that she had already reached, and it made him feel strangely abandoned. Was it—or, rather, wasn't it—that if for so long she had been watching with him the answer to their question had swum into her ken and taken on its name, so that her occupation was verily gone? He had as much as charged her with this in saying to her, many months before, that she even then knew something she was keeping from him. It was a point he had never since ventured to press, vaguely fearing, as he did, that it might become a difference, perhaps a disagreement, between them. He had in short, in this later time, turned nervous, which was what, in all the other years, he had never been; and the oddity was that his nervousness should have waited till he had begun to doubt, should have held off so long as he was sure. There was something, it seemed to him, that the wrong word would bring down on his head, something that would so at least put an end to his suspense. But he wanted not to speak the wrong word; that would make everything ugly. He wanted the knowledge he lacked to drop on him, if drop it could, by its own august weight. If she was to forsake him it was surely for her to take leave. This was why he didn't ask her again, directly, what she knew; but it was also why, approaching the matter from another side, he said to her in the course of his visit: "What do you regard as the very worst that, at this time of day, *can* happen to me?"

He had asked her that in the past often enough; they had, with the odd, irregular rhythm of their intensities and avoidances, exchanged ideas about it and then had seen the ideas washed away by cool intervals, washed like figures traced in sea-sand. It had ever been the mark of their talk that the oldest allusions in it required but a little dismissal and reaction to come out again, sounding for the hour as new. She could thus at present meet his inquiry quite freshly and patiently. "Oh yes, I've repeatedly thought, only it always seemed to me of old that I couldn't quite make up my mind. I thought of dreadful things, between which it was difficult to choose; and so must you have done."

"Rather! I feel now as if I had scarce done anything else. I appear to myself to have spent my life in thinking of nothing *but* dreadful things. A great many of them I've at different times named to you, but there were others I couldn't name."

"They were too dreadful?"

"Too, too dreadful—some of them."

She looked at him a minute, and there came to him as he met it an inconsequent sense that her eyes, when one got their full clearness, were still as beautiful as they had been in youth, only beautiful with a strange, cold light—a light that somehow was a part of the effect, if it wasn't rather a part of the cause, of the pale, hard sweetness of the season and the hour. "And yet," she said at last, "there are horrors we have mentioned."

It deepened the strangeness to see her, as such a figure in such a picture, talk of "horrors," but she was to do, in a few minutes, something stranger yet—though even of this he was to take the full measure but afterwards—and the note of it was already in the air. It was, for the matter of that, one of the signs that her eyes were having again such a high flicker of their prime. He had to admit, however, what she said. "Oh yes, there were times when we did go far." He caught himself in the act, speaking as if it all were over. Well, he wished it were; and the consummation depended, for him, clearly, more and more on his companion.

But she had now a soft smile. "Oh, far—!"

It was oddly ironic. "Do you mean you're prepared to go further?"

She was frail and ancient and charming as she continued to look at him, yet it was rather as if she had lost the thread. "Do you consider that we went so far?"

"Why, I thought it the point you were just making—that we *had* looked most things in the face."

"Including each other?" She still smiled. "But you're quite right. We've had together great imaginations, often great fears; but some of them have been unspoken."

"Then the worst—we haven't faced that. I *could* face it, I believe, if I knew what you think it. I feel," he explained, "as if I had lost my power to conceive such things." And he wondered if he looked as blank as he sounded. "It's spent."

"Then why do you assume," she asked, "that mine isn't?"

"Because you've given me signs to the contrary. It isn't a question for you of conceiving, imagining, comparing. It isn't a question now of choosing." At last he came out with it. "You know something that I don't. You've showed me that before."

These last words affected her, he could see in a moment, remarkably, and she spoke with firmness. "I've shown you, my dear, nothing."

He shook his head. "You can't hide it."

"Oh, oh!" May Bartram murmured over what she couldn't hide. It was almost a smothered groan.

"You admitted it months ago, when I spoke of it to you as of something you were afraid I would find out. Your answer was that I couldn't, that I wouldn't, and I don't pretend I have. But you had something therefore in mind, and I see now that it must have been, that it still is, the possibility that, of all possibilities, has settled itself for you as the worst. This," he went on, "is why I appeal to you. I'm only afraid of ignorance now—I'm not afraid of knowledge." And then as for a while she said nothing: "What makes me sure is that I see in your face and feel here, in this air and amid these appearances, that you're out of it. You've done. You've had your experience. You leave me to my fate."

Well, she listened, motionless and white in her chair, as if she had in fact a decision to make, so that her whole manner was a virtual confession, though still with a small, fine, inner stiffness, an imperfect surrender. "It *would* be the worst," she finally let herself say. "I mean the thing that I've never said."

It hushed him a moment. "More monstrous than all the monstrosities we've named?"

"More monstrous. Isn't that what you sufficiently express," she asked, "in calling it the worst?"

Marcher thought. "Assuredly—if you mean, as I do, something that includes all the loss and all the shame that are thinkable."

"It would if it *should* happen," said May Bartram. "What we're speaking of, remember, is only my idea."

"It's your belief," Marcher returned. "That's enough for me. I feel your beliefs are right. Therefore if, having this one, you give me no more light on it, you abandon me."

"No, no!" she repeated. "I'm with you—don't you see? —still." And as if to make it more vivid to him she rose from her chair—a movement she seldom made in these days—and showed herself, all draped and all soft, in her fairness and slimness. "I haven't forsaken you."

It was really, in its effort against weakness, a generous assurance, and had the success of the impulse not, happily, been great, it would

have touched him to pain more than to pleasure. But the cold charm
in her eyes had spread, as she hovered before him, to all the rest of
her person, so that it was, for the minute, almost like a recovery of
youth. He couldn't pity her for that; he could only take her as she
showed—as capable still of helping him. It was as if, at the same time,
her light might at any instant go out; wherefore he must make the
most of it. There passed before him with intensity the three or four
things he wanted most to know; but the question that came of itself to
his lips really covered the others. "Then tell me if I shall consciously
suffer."

She promptly shook her head. "Never!"

It confirmed the authority he imputed to her, and it produced on
him an extraordinary effect. "Well, what's better than that? Do you call
that the worst?

"You think nothing is better?" she asked.

She seemed to mean something so special that he again sharply
wondered, though still with the dawn of a prospect of relief. "Why not,
if one doesn't *know*?" After which, as their eyes, over his question, met
in a silence, the dawn deepened and something to his purpose came,
prodigiously, out of her very face. His own, as he took it in, suddenly
flushed to the forehead, and he gasped with the force of a perception
to which, in the instant, everything fitted. The sound of his gasp filled
the air; then he became articulate. "I see—if I don't suffer!"

In her own look, however, was doubt. "You see what?"

"Why, what you mean—what you've always meant."

She again shook her head. "What I mean isn't what I've always
meant. It's different."

"It's something new?"

She hesitated. "Something new. It's not what you think. I see what
you think."

His divination drew breath then; only her correction might be
wrong. "It isn't that I *am* a donkey?" he asked between faintness and
grimness. "It isn't that it's all a mistake?"

"A mistake?" she pityingly echoed. *That* possibility, for her, he saw,
would be monstrous; and if she guaranteed him the immunity from
pain it would accordingly not be what she had in mind. "Oh, no," she
declared; "it's nothing of that sort. You've been right."

Yet he couldn't help asking himself if she weren't, thus pressed, speaking but to save him. It seemed to him he should be most lost if his history should prove all a platitude. "Are you telling me the truth, so that I shan't have been a bigger idiot than I can bear to know? I *haven't* lived with a vain imagination, in the most besotted illusion? I haven't waited but to see the door shut in my face?"

She shook her head again. "However the case stands *that* isn't the truth. Whatever the reality, it *is* a reality. The door isn't shut. The door's open," said May Bartram.

"Then something's to come?"

She waited once again, always with her cold, sweet eyes on him. "It's never too late." She had, with her gliding step, diminished the distance between them, and she stood nearer to him, close to him, a minute, as if still full of the unspoken. Her movement might have been for some finer emphasis of what she was at once hesitating and deciding to say. He had been standing by the chimney-piece, fireless and sparely adorned, a small, perfect old French clock and two morsels of rosy Dresden constituting all its furniture: and her hand grasped the shelf while she kept him waiting, grasped it a little as for support and encouragement. She only kept him waiting, however; that is he only waited. It had become suddenly, from her movement and attitude, beautiful and vivid to him that she had something more to give him; her wasted face delicately shone with it, and it glittered, almost as with the white lustre of silver, in her expression. She was right, incontestably, for what he saw in her face was the truth, and strangely, without consequence, while their talk of it as dreadful was still in the air, she appeared to present it as inordinately soft. This, prompting bewilderment, made him but gape the more gratefully for her revelation, so that they continued for some minutes silent, her face shining at him, her contact imponderably pressing, and his stare all kind, but all expectant. The end, none the less, was that what he had expected failed to sound. Something else took place instead, which seemed to consist at first in the mere closing of her eyes. She gave way at the same instant to a slow, fine shudder, and though he remained staring—though he stared, in fact, but the harder—she turned off and regained her chair. It was the end of what she had been intending, but it left him thinking only of that.

"Well, you don't say—?"

She had touched in her passage a bell near the chimney and had sunk back, strangely pale. "I'm afraid I'm too ill."

"Too ill to tell me?" It sprang up sharp to him, and almost to his lips, the fear that she would die without giving him light. He checked himself in time from so expressing his question, but she answered as if she had heard the words.

"Don't you know—now?"

"'Now'—?" She had spoken as if something that had made a difference had come up within the moment. But her maid, quickly obedient to her bell, was already with them. "I know nothing." And he was afterwards to say to himself that he must have spoken with odious impatience, such an impatience as to show that, supremely disconcerted, he washed his hands of the whole question.

"Oh!" said May Bartram.

"Are you in pain?" he asked, as the woman went to her.

"No," said May Bartram.

Her maid, who had put an arm round her as if to take her to her room, fixed on him eyes that appealingly contradicted her; in spite of which, however, he showed once more his mystification. "What then has happened?"

She was once more, with her companion's help, on her feet, and, feeling withdrawal imposed on him, he had found, blankly, his hat and gloves and had reached the door. Yet he waited for her answer. "What *was* to," she said.

V

He came back the next day, but she was then unable to see him, and as it was literally the first time this had occurred in the long stretch of their acquaintance he turned away, defeated and sore, almost angry— or feeling at least that such a break in their custom was really the beginning of the end—and wandered alone with his thoughts, especially with one of them that he was unable to keep down. She was dying, and he would lose her; she was dying, and his life would end. He stopped in the park, into which he had passed, and stared before him at his recurrent doubt. Away from her the doubt pressed again; in her presence he had believed her, but as he felt his forlornness he threw himself into the explanation that, nearest at hand, had most of a miserable warmth for him and least of a cold torment. She had deceived him to save him—to put him off with something in which he should be able to rest. What could the thing that was to happen to him be, after all, but just this thing that had begun to happen? Her dying, her death, his consequent solitude—*that* was what he had figured as the beast in the jungle, that was what had been in the lap of the gods. He had had her word for it as he left her; for what else, on earth, could she have meant? It wasn't a thing of a monstrous order; not a fate rare and distinguished; not a stroke of fortune that overwhelmed and immortalised; it had only the stamp of the common doom. But poor Marcher, at this hour, judged the common doom sufficient. It would serve his turn, and even as the consummation of infinite waiting he would bend his pride to accept it. He sat down on a bench in the twilight. He hadn't been a fool. Something had *been*, as she had said, to come. Before he rose indeed it had quite struck him that the final fact really matched with the long avenue through which he had had to reach it. As sharing his suspense, and as giving herself all, giving her life, to bring it to an end, she had come with him every step of the way. He had lived by her aid, and to leave her behind would be cruelly, damnably to miss her. What could be more overwhelming than that?

Well, he was to know within the week, for though she kept him a while at bay, left him restless and wretched during a series of days on each of which he asked about her only again to have to turn away, she ended his trial by receiving him where she had always received him. Yet she had been brought out at some hazard into the presence of so many of the things that were, consciously, vainly, half their past, and there was scant service left in the gentleness of her mere desire, all too visible, to check his obsession and wind up his long trouble. That was clearly what she wanted; the one thing more, for her own peace, while she could still put out her hand. He was so affected by her state that, once seated by her chair, he was moved to let everything go; it was she herself therefore who brought him back, took up again, before she dismissed him, her last word of the other time. She showed how she wished to leave their affair in order. "I'm not sure you understood. You've nothing to wait for more. It *has* come."

Oh, how he looked at her! "Really?"

"Really."

"The thing that, as you said, *was* to?"

"The thing that we began in our youth to watch for."

Face to face with her once more he believed her; it was a claim to which he had so abjectly little to oppose. "You mean that it has come as a positive, definite occurrence, with a name and a date?"

"Positive. Definite. I don't know about the 'name,' but, oh, with a date!"

He found himself again too helplessly at sea. "But come in the night—come and passed me by?"

May Bartram had her strange, faint smile. "Oh no, it hasn't passed you by!"

"But if I haven't been aware of it, and it hasn't touched me—?"

"Ah, your not being aware of it," and she seemed to hesitate an instant to deal with this—"your not being aware of it is the strangeness *in* the strangeness. It's the wonder *of* the wonder." She spoke as with the softness almost of a sick child, yet now at last, at the end of all, with the perfect straightness of a sybil. She visibly knew that she knew, and the effect on him was of something co-ordinate, in its high character, with the law that had ruled him. It was the true voice of the law; so on her lips would the law itself have sounded. "It *has* touched you," she went on. "It has done its office. It has made you all its own."

"So utterly without my knowing it?"

"So utterly without your knowing it." His hand, as he leaned to her, was on the arm of her chair, and, dimly smiling always now, she placed her own on it. "It's enough if *I* know it."

"Oh!" he confusedly sounded, as she herself of late so often had done.

"What I long ago said is true. You'll never know now, and I think you ought to be content. You've *had* it," said May Bartram.

"But had what?"

"Why, what was to have marked you out. The proof of your law. It has acted. I'm too glad," she then bravely added, "to have been able to see what it's *not*."

He continued to attach his eyes to her, and with the sense that it was all beyond him, and that *she* was too, he would still have sharply challenged her, had he not felt it an abuse of her weakness to do more than take devoutly what she gave him, take it as hushed as to a revelation.

If he did speak, it was out of the foreknowledge of his loneliness to come. "If you're glad of what it's 'not,' it might then have been worse?"

She turned her eyes away, she looked straight before her with which, after a moment: "Well, you know our fears."

He wondered. "It's something then we never feared?"

On this, slowly, she turned to him. "Did we ever dream, with all our dreams, that we should sit and talk of it thus?"

He tried for a little to make out if they had; but it was as if their dreams, numberless enough, were in solution in some thick, cold mist, in which thought lost itself. "It might have been that we couldn't talk?"

"Well"—she did her best for him—"not from this side. This, you see," she said, "is the *other* side."

"I think," poor Marcher returned, "that all sides are the same to me." Then, however, as she softly shook her head in correction: "We mightn't, as it were, have got across—?"

"To where we are—no. We're *here*"—she made her weak emphasis.

"And much good does it do us!" was her friend's frank comment.

"It does us the good it can. It does us the good that *it* isn't here. It's past. It's behind," said May Bartram. "Before—" but her voice dropped.

He had got up, not to tire her, but it was hard to combat his yearning. She after all told him nothing but that his light had failed—which he knew well enough without her. "Before—?" he blankly echoed.

"Before, you see, it was always to *come*. That kept it present."

"Oh, I don't care what comes now! Besides," Marcher added, "it seems to me that I liked it better present, as you say, than I can like it absent with *your* absence."

"Oh, mine!" —and her pale hands made light of it.

"With the absence of everything." He had a dreadful sense of standing there before her for—so far as anything but this proved, this bottomless drop was concerned—the last time of their life. It rested on him with a weight he felt he could scarce bear, and this weight it apparently was that still pressed out what remained in him of speakable protest. "I believe you; but I can't begin to pretend I understand. *Nothing*, for me, is past; nothing *will* pass until I pass myself, which I pray my stars may be as soon as possible. Say, however," he added, "that I've eaten my cake, as you contend, to the last crumb—how can the thing I've never felt at all be the thing I was marked out to feel?"

She met him, perhaps, less directly, but she met him unperturbed. "You take your 'feelings' for granted. You were to suffer your fate. That was not necessarily to know it."

"How in the world—when what is such knowledge but suffering?"

She looked up at him a while, in silence. "No—you don't understand."

"I suffer," said John Marcher.

"Don't, don't!"

"How can I help at least *that*?"

"*Don't!*" May Bartram repeated.

She spoke it in a tone so special, in spite of her weakness, that he stared an instant—stared as if some light, hitherto hidden, had shimmered across his vision. Darkness again closed over it, but the gleam had already become for him an idea. "Because I haven't the right—?"

"Don't *know*—when you needn't," she mercifully urged. "You needn't—for we shouldn't."

"Shouldn't?" If he could but know what she meant!

"No—it's too much."

"Too much?" he still asked—but with a mystification that was the next moment, of a sudden, to give way. Her words, if they meant something, affected him in this light—the light also of her wasted face—as meaning *all*, and the sense of what knowledge had been for herself came over him with a rush which broke through into a question. "Is it of that, then, you're dying?"

She but watched him, gravely at first, as if to see, with this, where he was, and she might have seen something, or feared something, that moved her sympathy. "I would live for you still—if I could." Her eyes closed for a little, as if, withdrawn into herself, she were, for a last time, trying. "But I can't!" she said as she raised them again to take leave of him.

She couldn't indeed, as but too promptly and sharply appeared, and he had no vision of her after this that was anything but darkness and doom. They had parted forever in that strange talk; access to her chamber of pain, rigidly guarded, was almost wholly forbidden him; he was feeling now moreover, in the face of doctors, nurses, the two or three relatives attracted doubtless by the presumption of what she had to "leave," how few were the rights, as they were called in such cases, that he had to put forward, and how odd it might even seem that their intimacy shouldn't have given him more of them. The stupidest fourth cousin had more, even though she had been nothing in such a person's life. She had been a feature of features in *his*, for what else was it to have been so indispensable? Strange beyond saying were the ways of existence, baffling for him the anomaly of his lack, as he felt it to be, of producible claim. A woman might have been, as it were, everything to him, and it might yet present him in no connection that anyone appeared obliged to recognise. If this was the case in these closing weeks it was the case more sharply on the occasion of the last offices rendered, in the great grey London cemetery, to what had been mortal, to what had been precious, in his friend. The concourse at her grave was not numerous, but he saw himself treated as scarce more nearly concerned with it than if there had been a thousand others. He was in short from this moment face to face with the fact that he was to profit extraordinarily little by the interest May Bartram had taken in him. He couldn't quite have said what he expected, but he had somehow not expected this approach to a double privation. Not only had her interest failed him, but he seemed to feel himself unattended— and for a reason he couldn't sound—by the distinction, the dignity, the propriety, if nothing else, of the man markedly bereaved. It was as if, in the view of society, he had not *been* markedly bereaved, as if there still failed some sign or proof of it, and as if, none the less, his character could never be affirmed, nor the deficiency ever made up. There were moments, as the weeks went by, when he would have liked, by some almost aggressive act, to take his stand on the intimacy of his loss, in order that it *might* be questioned and his retort, to the relief of his spirit, so recorded; but the moments of an irritation more helpless followed fast on these, the moments during which, turning things over with a good conscience but with a bare horizon, he found himself wondering if he oughtn't to have begun, so to speak, further back.

He found himself wondering indeed at many things, and this last speculation had others to keep it company. What could he have done, after all, in her lifetime, without giving them both, as it were, away? He couldn't have made it known she was watching him, for that would have published the superstition of the Beast. This was what closed his mouth now—now that the Jungle had been threshed to vacancy and that the Beast had stolen away. It sounded too foolish and too flat; the difference for him in this particular, the extinction in his life of the element of suspense, was such in fact as to surprise him. He could scarce have said what the effect resembled; the abrupt cessation, the positive prohibition, of music perhaps, more than anything else, in some place all adjusted and all accustomed to sonoreity and to attention. If he could at any rate have conceived lifting the veil from his image at some moment of the past (what had he done, after all, if not lift it to *her*?) so to do this to-day, to talk to people at large of the jungle cleared and confide to them that he now felt it as safe, would have been not only to see them listen as to a goodwife's tale, but really to hear himself tell one. What it presently came to in truth was that poor Marcher waded through his beaten grass, where no life stirred, where no breath sounded, where no evil eye seemed to gleam from a Beast, and still more as if missing it. He walked about in an existence that had grown strangely more spacious, and, stopping fitfully in places where the undergrowth of life struck him as closer, asked himself yearningly, wondered secretly and sorely, if it would have lurked here or there. It would have at all events *sprung*; what was at least complete was his belief in the truth itself of the assurance given him. The change from his old sense to his new was absolute and final: what was to happen *had* so absolutely and finally happened that he was as little able to know a fear for his future as to know a hope; so absent in short was any question of anything still to come. He was to live entirely with the other question, that of his unidentified past, that of his having to see his fortune impenetrably muffled and masked.

The torment of this vision became then his occupation; he couldn't perhaps have consented to live but for the possibility of guessing. She had told him, his friend, not to guess; she had forbidden him, so far as he might, to know, and she had even in a sort denied the power in him to learn: which were so many things, precisely, to deprive him of rest. It wasn't that he wanted, he argued for fairness, that anything that had happened to him should happen over again; it was only that he shouldn't, as an anticlimax, have been taken sleeping so sound as not to be able to win back by an effort of thought the lost stuff of consciousness. He declared to himself at moments that he would either win it back or have done with consciousness for ever; he made this idea his one motive, in fine, made it so much his passion that none other, to compare with it, seemed ever to have touched him. The lost stuff of consciousness became thus for him as a strayed or stolen child to an unappeasable father; he hunted it up and down very much as if he were knocking at doors and inquiring of the police. This was the spirit in which, inevitably, he set himself to travel; he started on a journey that was to be as long as he could make it; it danced before him that, as the other side of the globe couldn't possibly have less to say to him, it might, by a possibility of suggestion, have more. Before he quitted London, however, he made a pilgrimage to May Bartram's grave, took his way to it through the endless avenues of the grim suburban necropolis, sought it out in the wilderness of tombs, and, though he had come but for the renewal of the act of farewell, found himself, when he had at last stood by it, beguiled into long intensities. He stood for an hour, powerless to turn away and yet powerless to penetrate the darkness of death; fixing with his eyes her inscribed name and date, beating his forehead against the fact of the secret they kept, drawing his breath, while he waited as if, in pity of him, some sense would rise from the stones. He kneeled on the stones, however, in vain; they kept what they concealed; and if the face of the tomb did become a face for him it was because her two names were like a pair of eyes that didn't know him. He gave them a last long look, but no palest light broke.

VI

He stayed away, after this, for a year; he visited the depths of Asia, spending himself on scenes of romantic interest, of superlative sanctity; but what was present to him everywhere was that for a man who had known what *he* had known the world was vulgar and vain. The state of mind in which he had lived for so many years shone out to him, in reflection, as a light that coloured and refined, a light beside which the glow of the East was garish, cheap and thin. The terrible truth was that he had lost—with everything else—a distinction as well; the things he saw couldn't help being common when he had become common to look at them. He was simply now one of them himself—he was in the dust, without a peg for the sense of difference; and there were hours when, before the temples of gods and the sepulchres of kings, his spirit turned, for nobleness of association, to the barely discriminated slab in the London suburb. That had become for him, and more intensely with time and distance, his one witness of a past glory. It was all that was left to him for proof or pride, yet the past glories of Pharaohs were nothing to him as he thought of it. Small wonder then that he came back to it on the morrow of his return. He was drawn there this time as irresistibly as the other, yet with a confidence, almost, that was doubtless the effect of the many months that had elapsed. He had lived, in spite of himself, into his change of feeling, and in wandering over the earth had wandered, as might be said, from the circumference to the centre of his desert. He had settled to his safety and accepted perforce his extinction; figuring to himself, with some colour, in the likeness of certain little old men he remembered to have seen, of whom, all meagre and wizened as they might look, it was related that they had in their time fought twenty duels or been loved by ten princesses. They indeed had been wondrous for others, while he was but wondrous for himself; which, however, was exactly the cause of his haste to renew the wonder by getting back, as he might put it, into his own presence. That had quickened his steps and checked his delay. If his visit was prompt it was because he had been separated so long from the part of himself that alone he now valued.

It is accordingly not false to say that he reached his goal with a certain elation, and stood there again with a certain assurance. The creature beneath the sod *knew* of his rare experience, so that, strangely now, the place had lost for him its mere blankness of expression. It met him in mildness—not, as before, in mockery; it wore for him the air of conscious greeting that we find, after absence, in things that have closely belonged to us and which seem to confess of themselves to the connection. The plot of ground, the graven tablet, the tended flowers affected him so as belonging to him that he quite felt for the hour like a contented landlord reviewing a piece of property. Whatever had happened—well, had happened. He had not come back this time with the vanity of that question, his former worrying, "What, *what?*" now practically so spent. Yet he would, none the less, never again so cut himself off from the spot; he would come back to it every month, for if he did nothing else by its aid he at least held up his head. It thus grew for him, in the oddest way, a positive resource; he carried out his idea of periodical returns, which took their place at last among the most inveterate of his habits. What it all amounted to, oddly enough, was that, in his now so simplified world, this garden of death gave him the few square feet of earth on which he could still most live. It was as if, being nothing anywhere else for anyone, nothing even for himself, he were just everything here, and if not for a crowd of witnesses, or indeed for any witness but John Marcher, then by clear right of the register that he could scan like an open page. The open page was the tomb of his friend, and *there* were the facts of the past, there the truth of his life, there the backward reaches in which he could lose himself. He did this, from time to time, with such effect that he seemed to wander through the old years with his hand in the arm of a companion who was, in the most extraordinary manner, his other, his younger self; and to wander, which was more extraordinary yet, round and round a third presence—not wandering she, but stationary, still, whose eyes, turning with his revolution, never ceased to follow him, and whose seat was his point, so to speak, of orientation. Thus in short he settled to live— feeding only on the sense that he once *had* lived, and dependent on it not only for a support but for an identity.

It sufficed him, in its way, for months, and the year elapsed; it would doubtless even have carried him further but for an accident, superficially slight, which moved him, in a quite other direction, with a force beyond any of his impressions of Egypt or of India. It was a thing of the merest chance—the turn, as he afterwards felt, of a hair, though he was indeed to live to believe that if light hadn't come to him in this particular fashion it would still have come in another. He was to live to believe this, I say, though he was not to live, I may not less definitely mention, to do much else. We allow him at any rate the benefit of the conviction, struggling up for him at the end, that, whatever might have happened or not happened, he would have come round of himself to the light. The incident of an autumn day had put the match to the train laid from of old by his misery. With the light before him he knew that even of late his ache had only been smothered. It was strangely drugged, but it throbbed; at the touch it began to bleed. And the touch, in the event, was the face of a fellow-mortal. This face, one grey afternoon when the leaves were thick in the alleys, looked into Marcher's own, at the cemetery, with an expression like the cut of a blade. He felt it, that is, so deep down that he winced at the steady thrust. The person who so mutely assaulted him was a figure he had noticed, on reaching his own goal, absorbed by a grave a short distance away, a grave apparently fresh, so that the emotion of the visitor would probably match it for frankness. This fact alone forbade further atten- tion, though during the time he stayed he remained vaguely conscious of his neighbour, a middle-aged man apparently, in mourning, whose bowed back, among the clustered monuments and mortuary yews, was constantly presented. Marcher's theory that these were elements in contact with which he himself revived, had suffered, on this occasion, it may be granted, a sensible though inscrutable check. The autumn day was dire for him as none had recently been, and he rested with a heaviness he had not yet known on the low stone table that bore May Bartram's name. He rested without power to move, as if some spring in him, some spell vouchsafed, had suddenly been broken forever. If he could have done that moment as he wanted he would simply have stretched himself on the slab that was ready to take him, treating it as a place prepared to receive his last sleep. What in all the wide world had he now to keep awake for? He stared before him with the question, and it was then that, as one of the cemetery walks passed near him, he caught the shock of the face.

His neighbour at the other grave had withdrawn, as he himself, with force in him to move, would have done by now, and was advancing along the path on his way to one of the gates. This brought him near, and his pace was slow, so that—and all the more as there was a kind of hunger in his look—the two men were for a minute directly confronted. Marcher felt him on the spot as one of the deeply stricken— a perception so sharp that nothing else in the picture lived for it, neither his dress, his age, nor his presumable character and class; nothing lived but the deep ravage of the features that he showed. He *showed* them— that was the point; he was moved, as he passed, by some impulse that was either a signal for sympathy or, more possibly, a challenge to another sorrow. He might already have been aware of our friend, might, at some previous hour, have noticed in him the smooth habit of the scene, with which the state of his own senses so scantly consorted, and might thereby have been stirred as by a kind of overt discord. What Marcher was at all events conscious of was, in the first place, that the image of scarred passion presented to him was conscious too—of something that profaned the air; and, in the second, that, roused, startled, shocked, he was yet the next moment looking after it, as it went, with envy. The most extraordinary thing that had happened to him—though he had given that name to other matters as well—took place, after his immediate vague stare, as a consequence of this impression. The stranger passed, but the raw glare of his grief remained, making our friend wonder in pity what wrong, what wound it expressed, what injury not to be healed. What had the man *had* to make him, by the loss of it, so bleed and yet live?

Something—and this reached him with a pang—that *he*, John Marcher, hadn't; the proof of which was precisely John Marcher's arid end. No passion had ever touched him, for this was what passion meant; he had survived and maundered and pined, but where had been *his* deep ravage? The extraordinary thing we speak of was the sudden rush of the result of this question. The sight that had just met his eyes named to him, as in letters of quick flame, something he had utterly, insanely missed, and what he had missed; made these things a train of fire, made them mark themselves in an anguish of inward throbs. He had seen *outside* of his life, not learned it within, the way a woman was mourned when she had been loved for herself; such was the force of his conviction of the meaning of the stranger's face, which still flared for him like a smoky torch. It had not come to him, the knowledge, on the wings of experience; it had brushed him, jostled him, upset him, with the disrespect of chance, the insolence of an accident. Now that the illumination had begun, however, it blazed to the zenith, and what he presently stood there gazing at was the sounded void of his life. He gazed, he drew breath, in pain; he turned in his dismay, and, turning, he had before him in sharper incision than ever the open page of his story. The name on the table smote him as the passage of his neighbour had done, and what it said to him, full in the face, was that *she* was what he had missed. This was the awful thought, the answer to all the past, the vision at the dread clearness of which he turned as cold as the stone beneath him. Everything fell together, confessed, explained, overwhelmed; leaving him most of all stupefied at the blindness he had cherished. The fate he had been marked for he had met with a vengeance—he had emptied the cup to the lees; he had been the man of his time, *the* man, to whom nothing on earth was to have happened. That was the rare stroke—that was his visitation. So he saw it, as we say, in pale horror, while the pieces fitted and fitted. So *she* had seen it, while he didn't, and so she served at this hour to drive the truth home. It was the truth, vivid and monstrous, that all the while he had waited the wait was itself his portion. This the companion of his vigil had at a given moment perceived, and she had then offered him the chance to baffle his doom. One's doom, however, was never baffled, and on the day she had told him that his own had come down she had seen him but stupidly stare at the escape she offered him.

The escape would have been to love her; then, *then* he would have lived. *She* had lived—who could say now with what passion? —since she had loved him for himself; whereas he had never thought of her (ah, how it hugely glared at him!) but in the chill of his egotism and the light of her use. Her spoken words came back to him, and the chain stretched and stretched. The beast had lurked indeed, and the beast, at its hour, had sprung; it had sprung in that twilight of the cold April when, pale, ill, wasted, but all beautiful, and perhaps even then recoverable, she had risen from her chair to stand before him and let him imaginably guess. It had sprung as he didn't guess; it had sprung as she hopelessly turned from him, and the mark, by the time he left her, had fallen where it *was* to fall. He had justified his fear and achieved his fate; he had failed, with the last exactitude, of all he was to fail of; and a moan now rose to his lips as he remembered she had prayed he mightn't know. This horror of waking—*this* was knowledge, knowledge under the breath of which the very tears in his eyes seemed to freeze. Through them, none the less, he tried to fix it and hold it; he kept it there before him so that he might feel the pain. That at least, belated and bitter, had something of the taste of life. But the bitterness suddenly sickened him, and it was as if, horribly, he saw, in the truth, in the cruelty of his image, what had been appointed and done. He saw the Jungle of his life and saw the lurking Beast; then, while he looked, perceived it, as by a stir of the air, rise, huge and hideous, for the leap that was to settle him. His eyes darkened—it was close; and, instinctively turning, in his hallucination, to avoid it, he flung himself, on his face, on the tomb.

THE JOLLY CORNER

I

"Every one asks me what I 'think' of everything," said Spencer
Brydon; "and I make answer as I can—begging or dodging the question,
putting them off with any nonsense. It wouldn't matter to any of them
really," he went on, "for, even were it possible to meet in that stand-
and-deliver way so silly a demand on so big a subject, my 'thoughts'
would still be almost altogether about something that concerns only
myself." He was talking to Miss Staverton, with whom for a couple of
months now he had availed himself of every possible occasion to talk;
this disposition and this resource, this comfort and support, as the
situation in fact presented itself, having promptly enough taken the first
place in the considerable array of rather unattenuated surprises attending
his so strangely belated return to America. Everything was somehow
a surprise; and that might be natural when one had so long and so
consistently neglected everything, taken pains to give surprises so much
margin for play. He had given them more than thirty years—thirty-
three, to be exact; and they now seemed to him to have organised their
performance quite on the scale of that licence. He had been twenty-
three on leaving New York—he was fifty-six to-day: unless indeed he
were to reckon as he had sometimes, since his repatriation, found himself
feeling; in which case he would have lived longer than is often allotted
to man. It would have taken a century, he repeatedly said to himself,
and said also to Alice Staverton, it would have taken a longer absence
and a more averted mind than those even of which he had been guilty,
to pile up the differences, the newnesses, the queernesses, above all the
bignesses, for the better or the worse, that at present assaulted his vision
wherever he looked.

The great fact all the while however had been the incalculability; since he *had* supposed himself, from decade to decade, to be allowing, and in the most liberal and intelligent manner, for brilliancy of change. He actually saw that he had allowed for nothing; he missed what he would have been sure of finding, he found what he would never have imagined. Proportions and values were upside-down; the ugly things he had expected, the ugly things of his far-away youth, when he had too promptly waked up to a sense of the ugly—these uncanny phenomena placed him rather, as it happened, under the charm; whereas the "swagger" things, the modern, the monstrous, the famous things, those he had more particularly, like thousands of ingenuous enquirers every year, come over to see, were exactly his sources of dismay. They were as so many set traps for displeasure, above all for reaction, of which his restless tread was constantly pressing the spring. It was interesting, doubtless, the whole show, but it would have been too disconcerting hadn't a certain finer truth saved the situation. He had distinctly not, in this steadier light, come over *all* the monstrosities; he had come, not only in the last analysis but quite on the face of the act, under an impulse with which they had nothing to do. He had come— putting the thing pompously—to look at his "property," which he had thus for a third of a century not been within four thousand miles of; or, expressing it less sordidly, he had yielded to the humour of seeing again his house on the jolly corner, as he usually, and quite fondly, described it—the one in which he had first seen the light, in which various members of his family had lived and had died, in which the holidays of his overschooled boyhood had been passed and the few social flowers of his chilled adolescence gathered, and which, alienated then for so long a period, had, through the successive deaths of his two brothers and the termination of old arrangements, come wholly into his hands. He was the owner of another, not quite so "good"— the jolly corner having been, from far back, superlatively extended and consecrated; and the value of the pair represented his main capital, with an income consisting, in these later years, of their respective rents which (thanks precisely to their original excellent type) had never been depressingly low. He could live in "Europe," as he had been in the habit of living, on the product of these flourishing New York leases, and all the better since, that of the second structure, the mere number in its long row, having within a twelvemonth fallen in, renovation at a high advance had proved beautifully possible.

These were items of property indeed, but he had found himself since his arrival distinguishing more than ever between them. The house within the street, two bristling blocks westward, was already in course of reconstruction as a tall mass of flats; he had acceded, some time before, to overtures for this conversion—in which, now that it was going forward, it had been not the least of his astonishments to find himself able, on the spot, and though without a previous ounce of such experience, to participate with a certain intelligence, almost with a certain authority. He had lived his life with his back so turned to such concerns and his face addressed to those of so different an order that he scarce knew what to make of this lively stir, in a compartment of his mind never yet penetrated, of a capacity for business and a sense for construction. These virtues, so common all round him now, had been dormant in his own organism—where it might be said of them perhaps that they had slept the sleep of the just. At present, in the splendid autumn weather—the autumn at least was a pure boon in the terrible place—he loafed about his "work" undeterred, secretly agitated; not in the least "minding" that the whole proposition, as they said, was vulgar and sordid, and ready to climb ladders, to walk the plank, to handle materials and look wise about them, to ask questions, in fine, and challenge explanations and really "go into" figures.

It amused, it verily quite charmed him; and, by the same stroke, it amused, and even more, Alice Staverton, though perhaps charming her perceptibly less. She wasn't however going to be better-off for it, as *he* was—and so astonishingly much: nothing was now likely, he knew, ever to make her better-off than she found herself, in the afternoon of life, as the delicately frugal possessor and tenant of the small house in Irving Place to which she had subtly managed to cling through her almost unbroken New York career. If he knew the way to it now better than to any other address among the dreadful multiplied numberings which seemed to him to reduce the whole place to some vast ledger-page, overgrown, fantastic, of ruled and criss-crossed lines and figures— if he had formed, for his consolation, that habit, it was really not a little because of the charm of his having encountered and recognised, in the vast wilderness of the wholesale, breaking through the mere gross generalisation of wealth and force and success, a small still scene where items and shades, all delicate things, kept the sharpness of the notes of a high voice perfectly trained, and where economy hung about like the scent of a garden. His old friend lived with one maid and herself dusted her relics and trimmed her lamps and polished her silver; she stood off, in the awful modern crush, when she could, but she sallied forth and did battle when the challenge was really to "spirit," the spirit she after all confessed to, proudly and a little shyly, as to that of the better time, that of *their* common, their quite far-away and antediluvian social period and order. She made use of the street-cars when need be, the terrible things that people scrambled for as the panic-stricken at sea scramble for the boats; she affronted, inscrutably, under stress, all the public concussions and ordeals; and yet, with that slim mystifying grace of her appearance, which defied you to say if she were a fair young woman who looked older through trouble, or a fine smooth older one who looked young through successful indifference; with her precious reference, above all, to memories and histories into which he could enter, she was as exquisite for him as some pale pressed flower (a rarity to begin with), and, failing other sweetnesses, she was a sufficient reward of his effort. They had communities of knowledge, "their" knowledge (this discriminating possessive was always on her lips) of presences of the other age, presences all overlaid, in his case, by the experience of a man and the freedom of a wanderer, overlaid by pleasure, by infidelity, by passages of life that were strange and dim to her, just by "Europe" in short, but still unobscured, still exposed and cherished, under that pious visitation of the spirit from which she had never been diverted.

She had come with him one day to see how his "apartment-house" was rising; he had helped her over gaps and explained to her plans, and while they were there had happened to have, before her, a brief but lively discussion with the man in charge, the representative of the building-firm that had undertaken his work. He had found himself quite "standing-up" to this personage over a failure on the latter's part to observe some detail of one of their noted conditions, and had so lucidly argued his case that, besides ever so prettily flushing, at the time, for sympathy in his triumph, she had afterwards said to him (though to a slightly greater effect of irony) that he had clearly for too many years neglected a real gift. If he had but stayed at home he would have anticipated the inventor of the sky-scraper. If he had but stayed at home he would have discovered his genius in time really to start some new variety of awful architectural hare and run it till it burrowed in a gold-mine. He was to remember these words, while the weeks elapsed, for the small silver ring they sounded over the queerest and deepest of his own lately most disguised and most muffled vibrations.

It had begun to be present to him after the first fortnight, it had broken out with the oddest abruptness, this particular wanton wonderment: it met him there—and this was the image under which he himself judged the matter, or at least, not a little, thrilled and flushed with it—very much as he might have been met by some strange figure, some unexpected occupant, at a turn of one of the dim passages of an empty house. The quaint analogy quite hauntingly remained with him, when he didn't indeed rather improve it by a still intenser form: that of his opening a door behind which he would have made sure of finding nothing, a door into a room shuttered and void, and yet so coming, with a great suppressed start, on some quite erect confronting presence, something planted in the middle of the place and facing him through the dusk. After that visit to the house in construction he walked with his companion to see the other and always so much the better one, which in the eastward direction formed one of the corners, the "jolly" one precisely, of the street now so generally dishonoured and disfigured in its westward reaches, and of the comparatively conservative Avenue. The Avenue still had pretensions, as Miss Staverton said, to decency; the old people had mostly gone, the old names were unknown, and here and there an old association seemed to stray, all vaguely, like some very aged person, out too late, whom you might meet and feel the impulse to watch or follow, in kindness, for safe restoration to shelter.

They went in together, our friends; he admitted himself with his key, as he kept no one there, he explained, preferring, for his reasons, to leave the place empty, under a simple arrangement with a good woman living in the neighbourhood and who came for a daily hour to open windows and dust and sweep. Spencer Brydon had his reasons and was growingly aware of them; they seemed to him better each time he was there, though he didn't name them all to his companion, any more than he told her as yet how often, how quite absurdly often, he himself came. He only let her see for the present, while they walked through the great blank rooms, that absolute vacancy reigned and that, from top to bottom, there was nothing but Mrs. Muldoon's broomstick, in a corner, to tempt the burglar. Mrs. Muldoon was then on the premises, and she loquaciously attended the visitors, preceding them from room to room and pushing back shutters and throwing up sashes—all to show them, as she remarked, how little there was to see. There was little indeed to see in the great gaunt shell where the main dispositions and the general apportionment of space, the style of an age of ampler allowances, had nevertheless for its master their honest pleading message, affecting him as some good old servant's, some lifelong retainer's appeal for a character, or even for a retiring-pension; yet it was also a remark of Mrs. Muldoon's that, glad as she was to oblige him by her noonday round, there was a request she greatly hoped he would never make of her. If he should wish her for any reason to come in after dark she would just tell him, if he "plased," that he must ask it of somebody else.

The fact that there was nothing to see didn't militate for the worthy woman against what one *might* see, and she put it frankly to Miss Staverton that no lady could be expected to like, could she? "craping up to thim top storeys in the ayvil hours." The gas and the electric light were off in the house, and she fairly evoked a gruesome vision of her march through the great grey rooms—so many of them as there were too! —with her glimmering taper. Miss Staverton met her honest glare with a smile and the profession that she herself certainly would recoil from such an adventure. Spencer Brydon meanwhile held his peace—for the moment; the question of the "evil" hours in his old home had already become too grave for him. He had begun some time since to "crape," and he knew just why a packet of candles addressed to that pursuit had been stowed by his own hand, three weeks before, at the back of a drawer of the fine old sideboard that occupied, as a "fixture," the deep recess in the dining-room. Just now he laughed at his companions—quickly however changing the subject; for the reason that, in the first place, his laugh struck him even at that moment as starting the odd echo, the conscious human resonance (he scarce knew how to qualify it) that sounds made while he was there alone sent back to his ear or his fancy; and that, in the second, he imagined Alice Staverton for the instant on the point of asking him, with a divination, if he ever so prowled. There were divinations he was unprepared for, and he had at all events averted enquiry by the time Mrs. Muldoon had left them, passing on to other parts.

There was happily enough to say, on so consecrated a spot, that could be said freely and fairly; so that a whole train of declarations was precipitated by his friend's having herself broken out, after a yearning look round: "But I hope you don't mean they want you to pull *this* to pieces!" His answer came, promptly, with his re-awakened wrath: it was of course exactly what they wanted, and what they were "at" him for, daily, with the iteration of people who couldn't for their life understand a man's liability to decent feelings. He had found the place, just as it stood and beyond what he could express, an interest and a joy. There were values other than the beastly rent-values, and in short, in short—! But it was thus Miss Staverton took him up. "In short you're to make so good a thing of your sky-scraper that, living in luxury on *those* ill-gotten gains, you can afford for a while to be sentimental here!" Her smile had for him, with the words, the particular mild irony with which he found half her talk suffused; an irony without bitterness and that came, exactly, from her having so much imagination—not, like the cheap sarcasms with which one heard most people, about the world of "society," bid for the reputation of cleverness, from nobody's really having any. It was agreeable to him at this very moment to be sure that when he had answered, after a brief demur, "Well yes: so, precisely, you may put it!" her imagination would still do him justice. He explained that even if never a dollar were to come to him from the other house he would nevertheless cherish this one; and he dwelt, further, while they lingered and wandered, on the fact of the stupefaction he was already exciting, the positive mystification he felt himself create.

He spoke of the value of all he read into it, into the mere sight of the walls, mere shapes of the rooms, mere sound of the floors, mere feel, in his hand, of the old silver-plated knobs of the several mahogany doors, which suggested the pressure of the palms of the dead; the seventy years of the past in fine that these things represented, the annals of nearly three generations, counting his grandfather's, the one that had ended there, and the impalpable ashes of his long-extinct youth, afloat in the very air like microscopic motes. She listened to everything; she was a woman who answered intimately but who didn't chatter. She scattered abroad therefore no cloud of words; she could assent, she could agree, above all she could encourage, without doing that. Only at the last she went a little further than he had done himself. "And then how do you know? You may still, after all, want to live here." It rather indeed pulled him up, for it wasn't what he had been thinking, at least in her sense of the words. "You mean I may decide to stay on for the sake of it?"

"Well, *with* such a home—!" But, quite beautifully, she had too much tact to dot so monstrous an *i*, and it was precisely an illustration of the way she didn't rattle. How could any one—of any wit—insist on any one else's "wanting" to live in New York?

"Oh," he said, "I *might* have lived here (since I had my opportunity early in life); I might have put in here all these years. Then everything would have been different enough—and, I dare say, 'funny' enough. But that's another matter. And then the beauty of it—I mean of my perversity, of my refusal to agree to a 'deal'—is just in the total absence of a reason. Don't you see that if I had a reason about the matter at all it would *have* to be the other way, and would then be inevitably a reason of dollars? There are no reasons here *but* dollars. Let us therefore have none whatever—not the ghost of one."

"They were back in the hall then for departure, but from where they stood the vista was large, through an open door, into the great square main saloon, with its almost antique felicity of brave spaces between windows. Her eyes came back from that reach and met his own a moment. "Are you very sure the 'ghost' of one doesn't, much rather, serve—?"

He had a positive sense of turning pale. But it was as near as they were then to come. For he made answer, he believed, between a glare and a grin: "Oh ghosts—of course the place must swarm with them! I should be ashamed of it if it didn't. Poor Mrs. Muldoon's right, and it's why I haven't asked her to do more than look in."

Miss Staverton's gaze again lost itself, and things she didn't utter, it was clear, came and went in her mind. She might even for the minute, off there in the fine room, have imagined some element dimly gathering. Simplified like the death-mask of a handsome face, it perhaps produced for her just then an effect akin to the stir of an expression in the "set" commemorative plaster. Yet whatever her impression may have been she produced instead a vague platitude. "Well, if it were only furnished and lived in—!"

She appeared to imply that in case of its being still furnished he might have been a little less opposed to the idea of a return. But she passed straight into the vestibule, as if to leave her words behind her, and the next moment he had opened the house-door and was standing with her on the steps. He closed the door and, while he re-pocketed his key, looking up and down, they took in the comparatively harsh actuality of the Avenue, which reminded him of the assault of the outer light of the Desert on the traveller emerging from an Egyptian tomb. But he risked before they stepped into the street his gathered answer to her speech. "For me it *is* lived in. For me it *is* furnished." At which it was easy for her to sigh "Ah yes—!" all vaguely and discreetly; since his parents and his favourite sister, to say nothing of other kin, in numbers, had run their course and met their end there. That represented, within the walls, ineffaceable life.

It was a few days after this that, during an hour passed with her again, he had expressed his impatience of the too flattering curiosity— among the people he met—about his appreciation of New York. He had arrived at none at all that was socially producible, and as for that matter of his "thinking" (thinking the better or the worse of anything there) he was wholly taken up with one subject of thought. It was mere vain egoism, and it was moreover, if she liked, a morbid obsession. He found all things come back to the question of what he personally might have been, how he might have led his life and "turned out," if he had not so, at the outset, given it up. And confessing for the first time to the intensity within him of this absurd speculation—which but proved also, no doubt, the habit of too selfishly thinking—he affirmed the impotence there of any other source of interest, any other native appeal. "What would it have made of me, what would it have made of me? I keep for ever wondering, all idiotically; as if I could possibly know! I see what it has made of dozens of others, those I meet, and it positively aches within me, to the point of exasperation, that it would have made something of me as well. Only I can't make out *what*, and the worry of it, the small rage of curiosity never to be satisfied, brings back what I remember to have felt, once or twice, after judging best, for reasons, to burn some important letter unopened. I've been sorry, I've hated it—I've never known what was in the letter. You may of course say it's a trifle—!"

"I don't say it's a trifle," Miss Staverton gravely interrupted.

She was seated by her fire, and before her, on his feet and restless, he turned to and fro between this intensity of his idea and a fitful and unseeing inspection, through his single eye-glass, of the dear little old objects on her chimney-piece. Her interruption made him for an instant look at her harder. "I shouldn't care if you did!" he laughed, however; "and it's only a figure, at any rate, for the way I now feel. *Not* to have followed my perverse young course—and almost in the teeth of my father's curse, as I may say; not to have kept it up, so, 'over there,' from that day to this, without a doubt or a pang; not, above all, to have liked it, to have loved it, so much, loved it, no doubt, with such an abysmal conceit of my own preference: some variation from *that*, I say, must have produced some different effect for my life and for my 'form.' I should have stuck here—if it had been possible; and I was too young, at twenty-three, to judge, *pour deux sous*, whether it *were* possible. If I had waited I might have seen it was, and then I might have been, by staying here, something nearer to one of these types who have been hammered so hard and made so keen by their conditions. It isn't that I admire them so much—the question of any charm in them, or of any charm, beyond that of the rank money-passion, exerted by their conditions *for* them, has nothing to do with the matter: it's only a question of what fantastic, yet perfectly possible, development of my own nature I mayn't have missed. It comes over me that I had then a strange *alter ego* deep down somewhere within me, as the full-blown flower is in the small tight bud, and that I just took the course, I just transferred him to the climate, that blighted him for once and for ever."

"And you wonder about the flower," Miss Staverton said. "So do I, if you want to know; and so I've been wondering these several weeks. I believe in the flower," she continued, "I feel it would have been quite splendid, quite huge and monstrous."

"Monstrous above all!" her visitor echoed; "and I imagine, by the same stroke, quite hideous and offensive."

"You don't believe that," she returned; "if you did you wouldn't wonder. You'd know, and that would be enough for you. What you feel—and what I feel *for* you—is that you'd have had power."

"You'd have liked me that way?" he asked.

She barely hung fire. "How should I·not have liked you?"

"I see. You'd have liked me, have preferred me, a billionaire!"

"How should I not have liked you?" she simply again asked.

He stood before her still—her question kept him motionless. He took it in, so much there was of it; and indeed his not otherwise meeting it testified to that. "I know at least what I am," he simply went on;

"the other side of the medal's clear enough. I've not been edifying—I believe I'm thought in a hundred quarters to have been barely decent. I've followed strange paths and worshipped strange gods; it must have come to you again and again—in fact you've admitted to me as much— that I was leading, at any time these thirty years, a selfish frivolous scandalous life. And you see what it has made of me."

She just waited, smiling at him. "You see what it has made of *me*."

"Oh you're a person whom nothing can have altered. You were born to be what you are, anywhere, anyway: you've the perfection nothing else could have blighted. And don't you see how, without my exile, I shouldn't have been waiting till now—?" But he pulled up for the strange pang.

"The great thing to see," she presently said, "seems to me to be that it has spoiled nothing. It hasn't spoiled your being here at last. It hasn't spoiled this. It hasn't spoiled your speaking—" She also however faltered.

He wondered at everything her controlled emotion might mean. "Do you believe then—too dreadfully! —that I *am* as good as I might ever have been?"

"Oh no! Far from it!" With which she got up from her chair and was nearer to him. "But I don't care," she smiled.

"You mean I'm good enough?"

She considered a little. "Will you believe it if I say so? I mean will you let that settle your question for you?" And then as if making out in his face that he drew back from this, that he had some idea which, however absurd, he couldn't yet bargain away: "Oh you don't care either—but very differently: you don't care for anything but yourself."

Spencer Brydon recognised it—it was in fact what he had absolutely professed. Yet he importantly qualified. "*He* isn't myself. He's the just so totally other person. But I do want to see him," he added. "And I can. And I shall."

Their eyes met for a minute while he guessed from something in hers that she divined his strange sense. But neither of them otherwise expressed it, and her apparent understanding, with no protesting shock, no easy derision, touched him more deeply than anything yet, consti- tuting for his stifled perversity, on the spot, an element that was like breatheable air. What she said however was unexpected. "Well, *I've* seen him."

"You—?"

"I've seen him in a dream."

"Oh a 'dream'—!" It let him down.

"But twice over," she continued. "I saw him as I see you now."

"You've dreamed the same dream—?"

"Twice over," she repeated. "The very same."

This did somehow a little speak to him, as it also gratified him. "You dream about me at that rate?"

"Ah about *him!*" she smiled.

His eyes again sounded her. "Then you know all about him." And as she said nothing more: "What's the wretch like?"

She hesitated, and it was as if he were pressing her so hard that, resisting for reasons of her own, she had to turn away. "I'll tell you some other time!"

II

It was after this that there was most of a virtue for him, most of a cultivated charm, most of a preposterous secret thrill, in the particular form of surrender to his obsession and of address to what he more and more believed to be his privilege. It was what in these weeks he was living for—since he really felt life to begin but after Mrs. Muldoon had retired from the scene and, visiting the ample house from attic to cellar, making sure he was alone, he knew himself in safe possession and, as he tacitly expressed it, let himself go. He sometimes came twice in the twenty-four hours; the moments he liked best were those of gathering dusk, of the short autumn twilight; this was the time of which, again and again, he found himself hoping most. Then he could, as seemed to him, most intimately wander and wait, linger and listen, feel his fine attention, never in his life before so fine, on the pulse of the great vague place: he preferred the lampless hour and only wished he might have prolonged each day the deep crepuscular spell. Later—rarely much before midnight, but then for a considerable vigil—he watched with his glimmering light; moving slowly, holding it high, playing it far, rejoicing above all, as much as he might, in open vistas, reaches of communication between rooms and by passages; the long straight chance or show, as he would have called it, for the revelation he pretended to invite. It was a practice he found he could perfectly "work" without exciting remark; no one was in the least the wiser for it; even Alice Staverton, who was moreover a well of discretion, didn't quite fully imagine.

He let himself in and let himself out with the assurance of calm proprietorship; and accident so far favoured him that, if a fat Avenue "officer" had happened on occasion to see him entering at eleven-thirty, he had never yet, to the best of his belief, been noticed as emerging at two. He walked there on the crisp November nights, arrived regularly at the evening's end; it was as easy to do this after dining as to take his way to a club or to his hotel. When he left his club, if he hadn't been dining out, it was ostensibly to go to his hotel; and when he left his hotel, if he had spent a part of the evening there, it was ostensibly to go to his club. Everything was easy in fine; everything conspired and promoted: there was truly even in the strain of his experience something that glossed over, something that salved and simplified, all the rest of consciousness. He circulated, talked, renewed, loosely and pleasantly, old relations—met indeed, so far as he could, new expectations and seemed to make out on the whole that in spite of the career, of such different contacts, which he had spoken of to Miss Staverton as ministering so little, for those who might have watched it, to edification, he was positively rather liked than not. He was a dim secondary social success—and all with people who had truly not an idea of him. It was all mere surface sound, this murmur of their welcome, this popping of their corks—just as his gestures of response were the extravagant shadows, emphatic in proportion as they meant little, of some game of *ombres chinoises.* He projected himself all day, in thought, straight over the bristling line of hard unconscious heads and into the other, the real, the waiting life; the life that, as soon as he had heard behind him the click of his great house-door, began for him, on the jolly corner, as beguilingly as the slow opening bars of some rich music follows the tap of the conductor's wand.

He always caught the first effect of the steel point of his stick on the old marble of the hall pavement, large black-and-white squares that he remembered as the admiration of his childhood and that had then made in him, as he now saw, for the growth of an early conception of style. This effect was the dim reverberating tinkle as of some far-off bell hung who should say where? —in the depths of the house, of the past, of that mystical other world that might have flourished for him had he not, for weal or woe, abandoned it. On this impression he did ever the same thing; he put his stick noiselessly away in a corner—feeling the place once more in the likeness of some great glass bowl, all precious concave crystal, set delicately humming by the play of a moist finger round its edge. The concave crystal held, as it were, this mystical other world, and the indescribably fine murmur of its rim was the sigh there, the scarce audible pathetic wail to his strained ear, of all the old baffled forsworn possibilities. What he did therefore by this appeal of his hushed presence was to wake them into such measure of ghostly life as they might still enjoy. They were shy, all but unappeasably shy, but they weren't really sinister; at least they weren't as he had hitherto felt them—before they had taken the Form he so yearned to make them take, the Form he at moments saw himself in the light of fairly hunting on tiptoe, the points of his evening-shoes, from room to room and from storey to storey.

That was the essence of his vision—which was all rank folly, if one would, while he was out of the house and otherwise occupied, but which took on the last verisimilitude as soon as he was placed and posted. He knew what he meant and what he wanted; it was as clear as the figure on a cheque presented in demand for cash. His *alter ego* "walked"—that was the note of his image of him, while his image of his motive for his own odd pastime was the desire to waylay him and meet him. He roamed, slowly, warily, but all restlessly, he himself did—Mrs. Muldoon had been right, absolutely, with her figure of their "craping"; and the presence he watched for would roam restlessly too. But it would be as cautious and as shifty; the conviction of its probable, in fact its already quite sensible, quite audible evasion of pursuit grew for him from night to night, laying on him finally a rigour to which nothing in his life had been comparable. It had been the theory of many super-ficially-judging persons, he knew, that he was wasting that life in a surrender to sensations, but he had tasted of no pleasure so fine as his actual tension, had been introduced to no sport that demanded at once the patience and the nerve of this stalking of a creature more subtle, yet at bay perhaps more formidable, than any beast of the forest. The terms, the comparisons, the very practices of the chase positively came again into play; there were even moments when passages of his occa-sional experience as a sportsman, stirred memories, from his younger time, of moor and mountain and desert, revived for him—and to the increase of his keenness—by the tremendous force of analogy. He found himself at moments—once he had placed his single light on some mantel-shelf or in some recess—stepping back into shelter or shade, effacing himself behind a door or in an embrasure, as he had sought of old the vantage of rock and tree; he found himself holding his breath and living in the joy of the instant, the supreme suspense created by big game alone.

He wasn't afraid (though putting himself the question as he believed gentlemen on Bengal tiger-shoots or in close quarters with the great bear of the Rockies had been known to confess to having put it); and this indeed—since here at least he might be frank! —because of the impression, so intimate and so strange, that he himself produced as yet a dread, produced certainly a strain, beyond the liveliest he was likely to feel. They fell for him into categories, they fairly became familiar, the signs, for his own perception, of the alarm his presence and his vigilance created; though leaving him always to remark, portentously, on his probably having formed a relation, his probably enjoying a consciousness, unique in the experience of man. People enough, first and last, had been in terror of apparitions, but who had ever before so turned the tables and become himself, in the apparitional world, an incalculable terror? He might have found this sublime had he quite dared to think of it; but he didn't too much insist, truly, on that side of his privilege. With habit and repetition he gained to an extraordinary degree the power to penetrate the dusk of distances and the darkness of corners, to resolve back into their innocence the treacheries of uncertain light, the evil-looking forms taken in the gloom by mere shadows, by accidents of the air, by shifting effects of perspective; putting down his dim luminary he could still wander on without it, pass into other rooms and, only knowing it was there behind him in case of need, see his way about, visually project for his purpose a comparative clearness. It made him feel, this acquired faculty, like some monstrous stealthy cat; he wondered if he would have glared at these moments with large shining yellow eyes, and what it mightn't verily be, for the poor hard-pressed *alter ego*, to be confronted with such a type.

He liked however the open shutters; he opened everywhere those Mrs. Muldoon had closed, closing them as carefully afterwards, so that she shouldn't notice: he liked—oh this he did like, and above all in the upper rooms! —the sense of the hard silver of the autumn stars through the window-panes, and scarcely less the flare of the street-lamps below, the white electric lustre which it would have taken curtains to keep out. This was human actual social; this was of the world he had lived in, and he was more at his ease certainly for the countenance, coldly general and impersonal, that all the while and in spite of his detachment it seemed to give him. He had support of course mostly in the rooms at the wide front and the prolonged side; it failed him considerably in the central shades and the parts at the back. But if he sometimes, on his rounds, was glad of his optical reach, so none the less often the rear of the house affected him as the very jungle of his prey. The place was there more subdivided; a large "extension" in particular, where small rooms for servants had been multiplied, abounded in nooks and corners, in closets and passages, in the ramifications especially of an ample back staircase over which he leaned, many a time, to look far down—not deterred from his gravity even while aware that he might, for a spectator, have figured some solemn simpleton playing at hide-and-seek. Outside in fact he might himself make that ironic *rapprochement*; but within the walls, and in spite of the clear windows, his consistency was proof against the cynical light of New York.

It had belonged to that idea of the exasperated consciousness of his victim to become a real test for him; since he had quite put it to himself from the first that, oh distinctly! he could "cultivate" his whole perception. He had felt it as above all open to cultivation—which indeed was but another name for his manner of spending his time. He was bringing it on, bringing it to perfection, by practice; in consequence of which it had grown so fine that he was now aware of impressions, attestations of his general postulate, that couldn't have broken upon him at once. This was the case more specifically with a phenomenon at last quite frequent for him in the upper rooms, the recognition— absolutely unmistakeable, and by a turn dating from a particular hour, his resumption of his campaign after a diplomatic drop, a calculated absence of three nights—of his being definitely followed, tracked at a distance carefully taken and to the express end that he should the less confidently, less arrogantly, appear to himself merely to pursue. It worried, it finally quite broke him up, for it proved, of all the conceivable impressions, the one least suited to his book. He was kept in sight while remaining himself—as regards the essence of his position—sightless, and his only recourse then was in abrupt turns, rapid recoveries of ground. He wheeled about, retracing his steps, as if he might so catch in his face at least the stirred air of some other quick revolution. It was indeed true that his fully dislocalised thought of these manoeuvres recalled to him Pantaloon, at the Christmas farce, buffeted and tricked from behind by ubiquitous Harlequin; but it left intact the influence of the conditions themselves each time he was re-exposed to them, so that in fact this association, had he suffered it to become constant, would on a certain side have but ministered to his intenser gravity. He had made, as I have said, to create on the premises the baseless sense of a reprieve, his three absences; and the result of the third was to confirm the after-effect of the second.

On his return, that night—the night succeeding his last intermission—he stood in the hall and looked up the staircase with a certainty more intimate than any he had yet known. "He's *there*, at the top, and waiting—not, as in general, falling back for disappearance. He's holding his ground, and it's the first time—which is a proof, isn't it? that something has happened for him." So Brydon argued with his hand on the banister and his foot on the lowest stair; in which position he felt as never before the air chilled by his logic. He himself turned cold in it, for he seemed of a sudden to know what now was involved. "Harder pressed? —yes, he takes it in, with its thus making clear to him that I've come, as they say, 'to stay.' He finally doesn't like and can't bear it, in the sense, I mean, that his wrath, his menaced interest, now balances with his dread. I've hunted him till he has 'turned': that, up there, is what has happened—he's the fanged or the antlered animal brought at last to bay." There came to him, as I say—but determined by an influence beyond my notation! —the acuteness of this certainty; under which however the next moment he had broken into a sweat that he would as little have consented to attribute to fear as he would have dared immediately to act upon it for enterprise. It marked none the less a prodigious thrill, a thrill that represented sudden dismay, no doubt, but also represented, and with the selfsame throb, the strangest, the most joyous, possibly the next minute almost the proudest, duplication of consciousness.

"He has been dodging, retreating, hiding, but now, worked up to anger, he'll fight!" —this intense impression made a single mouthful, as it were, of terror and applause. But what was wondrous was that the

applause, for the felt fact, was so eager, since, if it was his other self
he was running to earth, this ineffable identity was thus in the last
resort not unworthy of him. It bristled there—somewhere near at hand,
however unseen still—as the hunted thing, even as the trodden worm
of the adage *must* at last bristle; and Brydon at this instant tasted
probably of a sensation more complex than had ever before found itself
consistent with sanity. It was as if it would have shamed him that a
character so associated with his own should triumphantly succeed in
just skulking, should to the end not risk the open, so that the drop of
this danger was, on the spot, a great lift of the whole situation. Yet
with another rare shift of the same subtlety he was already trying to
measure by how much more he himself might now be in peril of fear;
so rejoicing that he could, in another form, actively inspire that fear,
and simultaneously quaking for the form in which he might passively
know it.

The apprehension of knowing it must after a little have grown in
him, and the strangest moment of his adventure perhaps, the most
memorable or really most interesting, afterwards, of his crisis, was the
lapse of certain instants of concentrated conscious *combat*, the sense of
a need to hold on to something, even after the manner of a man slipping
and slipping on some awful incline; the vivid impulse, above all, to
move, to act, to charge, somehow and upon something—to show himself, in a word, that he wasn't afraid. The state of "holding-on" was
thus the state to which he was momentarily reduced; if there had been
anything, in the great vacancy, to seize, he would presently have been
aware of having clutched it as he might under a shock at home have
clutched the nearest chair-back. He had been surprised at any rate—
of this he *was* aware—into something unprecedented since his original
appropriation of the place; he had closed his eyes, held them tight, for
a long minute, as with that instinct of dismay and that terror of vision.
When he opened them the room, the other contiguous rooms, extraordinarily, seemed lighter—so light, almost, that at first, he took the
change for day. He stood firm, however that might be, just where he
had paused; his resistance had helped him—it was as if there were
something he had tided over. He knew after a little what this was—it
had been in the imminent danger of flight. He had stiffened his will
against going; without this he would have made for the stairs, and it

seemed to him that, still with his eyes closed, he would have descended them, would have known how, straight and swiftly, to the bottom.

Well, as he had held out, here he was—still at the top, among the more intricate upper rooms and with the gauntlet of the others, of all the rest of the house, still to run when it should be his time to go. He would go at his time—only at his time: didn't he go every night very much at the same hour? He took out his watch—there was light for that: it was scarcely a quarter past one, and he had never withdrawn so soon. He reached his lodgings for the most part at two—with his walk of a quarter of an hour. He would wait for the last quarter—he wouldn't stir till then; and he kept his watch there with his eyes on it, reflecting while he held it that his deliberate wait, a wait with an effort, which he recognised, would serve perfectly for the attestation he desired to make. It would prove his courage—unless indeed the latter might most be proved by his budging at last from his place. What he mainly felt now was that, since he hadn't originally scuttled, he had his dignities— which had never in his life seemed so many—all to preserve and to carry aloft. This was before him in truth as a physical image, an image almost worthy of an age of greater romance. That remark indeed glim- mered for him only to glow the next instant with a finer light; since what age of romance, after all, could have matched either the state of his mind or, "objectively," as they said, the wonder of his situation? The only difference would have been that, brandishing his dignities over his head as in a parchment scroll, he might then—that is in the heroic time—have proceeded downstairs with a drawn sword in his other grasp.

At present, really, the light he had set down on the mantel of the next room would have to figure his sword; which utensil, in the course of a minute, he had taken the requisite number of steps to possess himself of. The door between the rooms was open, and from the second another door opened to a third. These rooms, as he remembered, gave all three upon a common corridor as well, but there was a fourth, beyond them, without issue save through the preceding. To have moved, to have heard his step again, was appreciably a help; though even in recognising this he lingered once more a little by the chimney-piece on which his light had rested. When he next moved, just hesitating where to turn, he found himself considering a circumstance that, after his first and comparatively vague apprehension of it, produced in him the start that often attends some pang of recollection, the violent shock of having ceased happily to forget. He had come into sight of the door in which the brief chain of communication ended and which he now surveyed from the nearer threshold, the one not directly facing it. Placed at some distance to the left of this point, it would have admitted him to the last room of the four, the room without other approach or egress, had it not, to his intimate conviction, been closed *since* his former visitation, the matter probably of a quarter of an hour before. He stared with all his eyes at the wonder of the fact, arrested again where he stood and again holding his breath while he sounded its sense. Surely it had been *subsequently* closed—that is it had been on his previous passage indubitably open!

He took it full in the face that something had happened between— that he couldn't not have noticed before (by which he meant on his original tour of all the rooms that evening) that such a barrier had exceptionally presented itself. He had indeed since that moment under- gone an agitation so extraordinary that it might have muddled for him any earlier view; and he tried to convince himself that he might perhaps then have gone into the room and, inadvertently, automatically, on coming out, have drawn the door after him. The difficulty was that this exactly was what he never did; it was against his whole policy, as he might have said, the essence of which was to keep vistas clear. He had them from the first, as he was well aware, quite on the brain: the strange apparition, at the far end of one of them, of his baffled "prey" (which had become by so sharp an irony so little the term now to apply!) was the form of success his imagination had most cherished, projecting into it always a refinement of beauty. He had known fifty times the start of perception that had afterwards dropped; had fifty times gasped to himself "There!" under some fond brief hallucination. The house, as the case stood, admirably lent itself; he might wonder at the taste, the native architecture of the particular time, which could rejoice so in the multiplication of doors—the opposite extreme to the modern, the actual almost complete proscription of them; but it had fairly contributed to provoke this obsession of the presence encountered telescopically, as he might say, focussed and studied in diminishing perspective and as by a rest for the elbow.

It was with these considerations that his present attention was charged—they perfectly availed to make what he saw portentous. He *couldn't*, by any lapse, have blocked that aperture; and if he hadn't, if it was unthinkable, why what else was clear but that there had been another agent? Another agent? —he had been catching, as he felt, a moment back, the very breath of him; but when had he been so close as in this simple, this logical, this completely personal act? It was so logical, that is, that one might have *taken* it for personal; yet for what did Brydon take it, he asked himself, while, softly panting, he felt his eyes almost leave their sockets. At this time at last they *were*, the two, the opposed projections of him, in presence; and this time, as much as one would, the question of danger loomed. With it rose, as not before, the question of courage—for what he knew the blank face of the door to say to him was "Show us how much you have!" It stared, it glared back at him with that challenge; it put to him the two alternatives: should he just push it open or not? Oh to have this consciousness was to *think*—and to think, Brydon knew, as he stood there, was, with the lapsing moments, not to have acted! Not to have acted—that was the misery and the pang—was even still not to act; was in fact *all* to feel the thing in another, in a new and terrible way. How long did he pause and how long did he debate? There was presently nothing to measure it; for his vibration had already changed—as just by the effect of its intensity. Shut up there, at bay, defiant, and with the prodigy of the thing palpably proveably *done*, thus giving notice like some stark sign-board—under that accession of accent the situation itself had turned; and Brydon at last remarkably made up his mind on what it had turned to.

It had turned altogether to a different admonition; to a supreme hint, for him, of the value of Discretion! This slowly dawned, no doubt—for it could take its time; so perfectly, on his threshold, had he been stayed, so little as yet had he either advanced or retreated. It was the strangest of all things that now when, by his taking ten steps and applying his hand to a latch, or even his shoulder and his knee, if necessary, to a panel, all the hunger of his prime need might have been met, his high curiosity crowned, his unrest assuaged—it was amazing, but it was also exquisite and rare, that insistence should have, at a touch, quite dropped from him. Discretion—he jumped at that; and yet not, verily, at such a pitch, because it saved his nerves or his skin, but because, much more valuably, it saved the situation. When I say he "jumped" at it I feel the consonance of this term with the fact that—

at the end indeed of I know not how long—he did move again, he crossed straight to the door. He wouldn't touch it—it seemed now that he might *if* he would: he would only just wait there a little, to show, to prove, that he wouldn't. He had thus another station, close to the thin partition by which revelation was denied him; but with his eyes bent and his hands held off in a mere intensity of stillness. He listened as if there had been something to hear, but this attitude, while it lasted, was his own communication. "If you won't then—good: I spare you and I give up. You affect me as by the appeal positively for pity: you convince me that for reasons rigid and sublime—what do I know? — we both of us should have suffered. I respect them then, and, though moved and privileged as, I believe, it has never been given to man, I retire, I renounce—never, on my honour, to try again. So rest for ever— and let *me!*"

That, for Brydon was the deep sense of this last demonstration— solemn, measured, directed, as he felt it to be. He brought it to a close, he turned away; and now verily he knew how deeply he had been stirred. He retraced his steps, taking up his candle, burnt, he observed, well-nigh to the socket, and marking again, lighten it as he would, the dintinctness of his footfall; after which, in a moment, he knew himself at the other side of the house. He did here what he had not yet done at these hours—he opened half a casement, one of those in the front, and let in the air of the night; a thing he would have taken at any time previous for a sharp rupture of his spell. His spell was broken now, and it didn't matter—broken by his concession and his surrender, which made it idle henceforth that he should ever come back. The empty street—its other life so marked even by the great lamplit vacancy— was within call, within touch; he stayed there as to be in it again, high above it though he was still perched; he watched as for some comforting common fact, some vulgar human note, the passage of a scavenger or a thief, some night-bird however base. He would have blessed that sign of life; he would have welcomed positively the slow approach of his friend the policeman, whom he had hitherto only sought to avoid, and was not sure that if the patrol had come into sight he mightn't have felt the impulse to get into relation with it, to hail it, on some pretext, from his fourth floor.

The pretext that wouldn't have been too silly or too compromising, the explanation that would have saved his dignity and kept his name, in such a case, out of the papers, was not definite to him: he was so occupied with the thought of recording his Discretion—as an effect of the vow he had just uttered to his intimate adversary—that the importance of this loomed large and something had overtaken all ironically his sense of proportion. If there had been a ladder applied to the front of the house, even one of the vertiginous perpendiculars employed by painters and roofers and sometimes left standing overnight, he would have managed somehow, astride of the window-sill, to compass by outstretched leg and arm that mode of descent. If there had been some such uncanny thing as he had found in his room at hotels, a workable fire-escape in the form of notched cable or a canvas shoot, he would have availed himself of it as a proof—well, of his present delicacy. He nursed that sentiment, as the question stood, a little in vain, and even— at the end of he scarce knew, once more, how long—found it, as by the action on his mind of the failure of response of the outer world, sinking back to vague anguish. It seemed to him he had waited an age for some stir of the great grim hush; the life of the town was itself under a spell—so unnaturally, up and down the whole prospect of known and rather ugly objects, the blankness and the silence lasted. Had they ever, he asked himself, the hard-faced houses, which had begun to look livid in the dim dawn, had they ever spoken so little to any need of his spirit? Great builded voids, great crowded stillnesses put on, often, in the heart of cities, for the small hours, a sort of sinister mask, and it was of this large collective negation that Brydon presently became conscious—all the more that the break of day was, almost incredibly, now at hand, proving to him what a night he had made of it.

He looked again at his watch, saw what had become of his time-values (he had taken hours for minutes—not, as in other tense situations, minutes for hours) and the strange air of the streets was but the weak, the sullen flush of a dawn in which everything was still locked up. His choked appeal from his own open window had been the sole note of life, and he could but break off at last as for a worse despair. Yet while so deeply demoralised he was capable again of an impulse denoting— at least by his present measure—extraordinary resolution; of retracing his steps to the spot where he had turned cold with the extinction of his last pulse of doubt as to there being in the place another presence than his own. This required an effort strong enough to sicken him; but he had his reason, which overmastered for the moment everything else. There was the whole of the rest of the house to traverse, and how should he screw himself to that if the door he had seen closed were at present open? He could hold to the idea that the closing had practically been for him an act of mercy, a chance offered him to descend, depart, get off the ground and never again profane it. This conception held together, it worked; but what it meant for him depended now clearly on the amount of forbearance his recent action, or rather his recent inaction, had engendered. The image of the "presence," whatever it was, waiting there for him to go—this image had not yet been so concrete for his nerves as when he stopped short of the point at which certainty would have come to him. For, with all his resolution, or more exactly with all his dread, he did stop short—he hung back from really seeing. The risk was too great and his fear too definite: it took at this moment an awful specific form.

He knew—yes, as he had never known anything—that, *should* he see the door open, it would all too abjectly be the end of him. It would mean that the agent of his shame—for his shame was the deep abjection—was once more at large and in general possession; and what glared him thus in the face was the act that this would determine for him. It would send him straight about to the window he had left open, and by that window, be long ladder and dangling rope as absent as they would, he saw himself uncontrollably insanely fatally take his way to the street. The hideous chance of this he at least could avert; but he could only avert it by recoiling in time from assurance. He had the whole house to deal with, this fact was still there; only he now knew that uncertainty alone could start him. He stole back from where he had checked himself—merely to do so was suddenly like safety—and, making blindly for the greater staircase, left gaping rooms and sounding passages behind. Here was the top of the stairs, with a fine large dim descent and three spacious landings to mark off. His instinct was all for mildness, but his feet were harsh on the floors, and, strangely, when he had in a couple of minutes become aware of this, it counted somehow for help. He couldn't have spoken, the tone of his voice would have scared him, and the common conceit or resource of "whistling in the dark" (whether literally or figuratively) have appeared basely vulgar; yet he liked none the less to hear himself go, and when he had reached his first landing—taking it all with no rush, but quite steadily—that stage of success drew from him a gasp of relief.

The house, withal, seemed immense, the scale of space again inordinate; the open rooms, to no one of which his eyes deflected, gloomed in their shuttered state like mouths of caverns; only the high skylight that formed the crown of the deep well created for him a medium in which he could advance, but which might have been, for queerness of colour, some watery under-world. He tried to think of something noble, as that his property was really grand, a splendid possession; but this nobleness took the form too of the clear delight with which he was finally to sacrifice it. They might come in now, the builders, the destroyers—they might come as soon as they would. At the end of two flights he had dropped to another zone, and from the middle of the third, with only one more left, he recognised the influence of the lower windows, of half-drawn blinds, of the occasional gleam of street-lamps, of the glazed spaces of the vestibule. This was the bottom of the sea, which showed an illumination of its own and which he even saw paved—when at a given moment he drew up to sink a long look over the banisters—with the marble squares of his childhood. By that time indubitably he felt, as he might have said in a commoner cause, better; it had allowed him to stop and draw breath, and the ease increased with the sight of the old black-and-white slabs. But what he most felt was that now surely, with the element of impunity pulling him as by hard firm hands, the case was settled for what he might have seen above had he dared that last look. The closed door, blessedly remote now, was still closed—and he had only in short to reach that of the house.

He came down further, he crossed the passage forming the access to the last flight; and if here again he stopped an instant it was almost for the sharpness of the thrill of assured escape. It made him shut his eyes—which opened again to the straight slope of the remainder of the stairs. Here was impunity still, but impunity almost excessive; inasmuch as the sidelights and the high fan-tracery of the entrance were glimmering straight into the hall; an appearance produced, he the next instant saw, by the fact that the vestibule gaped wide, that the hinged halves of the inner door had been thrown far back. Out of that again the *question* sprang at him, making his eyes, as he felt, half-start from his head, as they had done, at the top of the house, before the sign of the other door. If he had left that one open, hadn't he left this one closed, and wasn't he now in *most* immediate presence of some inconceivable occult activity? It was as sharp, the question, as a knife in his side, but the answer hung fire still and seemed to lose itself in the vague darkness to which the thin admitted dawn, glimmering archwise over the whole outer door, make a semicircular margin, a cold silvery nimbus that seemed to play a little as he looked—to shift and expand and contract.

It was as if there had been something within it, protected by indistinctness and corresponding in extent with the opaque surface behind, the painted panels of the last barrier to his escape, of which the key was in his pocket. The indistinctness mocked him even while he stared, affected him as somehow shrouding or challenging certitude, so that after faltering an instant on his step he let himself go with the sense that here *was* at last something to meet, to touch, to take, to know—something all unnatural and dreadful, but to advance upon which was the condition for him either of liberation or of supreme defeat. The penumbra, dense and dark, was the virtual screen of a figure which stood in it as still as some image erect in a niche or as some black-vizored sentinel guarding a treasure. Brydon was to know afterwards, was to recall and make out, the particular thing he had believed during the rest of his descent. He saw, in its great grey glimmering margin, the central vagueness diminish, and he felt it to be taking the very form toward which, for so many days, the passion of his curiosity had yearned. It gloomed, it loomed, it was something, it was somebody, the prodigy of a personal presence.

Rigid and conscious, spectral yet human, a man of his own substance and stature waited there to measure himself with his power to dismay. This only could it be—this only till he recognised, with his advance, that what made the face dim was the pair of raised hands that covered it and in which, so far from being offered in defiance, it was buried as for dark deprecation. So Brydon, before him, took him in; with every fact of him now, in the higher light, hard and acute—his planted stillness, his vivid truth, his grizzled bent head and white masking hands, his queer actuality of evening-dress, of dangling double eye-glass, of gleaming silk lappet and white linen, of pearl button and gold watch-guard and polished shoe. No portrait by a great modern master could have presented him with more intensity, thrust him out of his frame with more art, as if there had been "treatment," of the consummate sort, in his every shade and salience. The revulsion, for our friend, had become, before he knew it, immense—this drop, in the act of apprehension, to the sense of his adversary's inscrutable manoeuvre. That meaning at least, while he gaped, it offered him; for he could but gape at his other self in this other anguish, gape as a proof that *he*, standing there for the achieved, the enjoyed, the triumphant life, couldn't be faced in his triumph. Wasn't the proof in the splendid covering hands, strong and completely spread? —so spread and so intentional that, in spite of a special verity that surpassed every other, the fact that one of these hands had lost two fingers, which were reduced to stumps, as if accidentally shot away, the face was effectually guarded and saved.

"Saved," though, *would* it be? —Brydon breathed his wonder till the very impunity of his attitude and the very insistence of his eyes produced, as he felt a sudden stir which showed the next instant as a deeper portent, while the head raised itself, the betrayal of a braver purpose. The hands, as he looked, began to move, to open; then, as if deciding in a flash, dropped from the face and left it uncovered and presented. Horror, with the sight, had leaped into Brydon's throat, gasping there in a sound he couldn't utter; for the bared identity was too hideous as *his*, and his glare was the passion of his protest. The face, *that* face, Spencer Brydon's? —he searched it still, but looking away from it in dismay and denial, falling straight from his height of sublimity. It was unknown, inconceivable, awful, disconnected from any possibility—! He had been "sold," he inwardly moaned, stalking such game as this: the presence before him was a presence, the horror within him a horror, but the waste of his nights had been only grotesque and the success of his adventure an irony. Such an identity fitted his at *no* point, made its alternative monstrous. A thousand times yes, as it came upon him nearer now—the face was the face of a stranger. It came upon him nearer now, quite as one of those expanding fantastic images projected by the magic lantern of childhood; for the stranger, whoever he might be, evil, odious, blatant, vulgar, had advanced as for aggression, and he knew himself give ground. Then harder pressed still, sick with the force of his shock, and falling back as under the hot breath and the roused passion of a life larger than his own, a rage of personality before which his own collapsed, he felt the whole vision turn to darkness and

his very feet give way. His head went round; he was going; he had
gone.

III

What had next brought him back, clearly—though after how long?
—was Mrs. Muldoon's voice, coming to him from quite near, from so
near that he seemed presently to see her as kneeling on the ground
before him while he lay looking up at her; himself not wholly on the
ground, but half-raised and upheld—conscious, yes, of tenderness of
support and, more particularly, of a head pillowed in extraordinary
softness and fainly refreshing fragrance. He considered, he wondered,
his wit but half at his service; then another face intervened, bending
more directly over him, and he finally knew that Alice Staverton had
made her lap an ample and perfect cushion to him, and that she had
to this end seated herself on the lowest degree of the staircase, the rest
of his long person remaining stretched on his old black-and-white slabs.
They were cold, these marble squares of his youth; but *he* somehow
was not, in this rich return of consciousness—the most wonderful hour,
little by little, that he had ever known, leaving him, as it did, so
gratefully, so abysmally passive, and yet as with a treasure of intelligence
waiting all round him for quiet appropriation; dissolved, he might call
it, in the air of the place and producing the golden glow of a late autumn
afternoon. He had come back, yes—come back from further away than
any man but himself had ever travelled; but it was strange how with
this sense what he had come back *to* seemed really the great thing, and
as if his prodigious journey had been all for the sake of it. Slowly but
surely his consciousness grew, his vision of his state thus completing
itself: he had been miraculously *carried* back—lifted and carefully borne
as from where he had been picked up, the uttermost end of an interminable grey passage. Even with this he was suffered to rest, and what
had now brought him to knowledge was the break in the long mild
motion.

It had brought him to knowledge, to knowledge—yes, this was the
beauty of his state; which came to resemble more and more that of a
man who has gone to sleep on some news of a great inheritance, and
then, after dreaming it away, after profaning it with matters strange to

it, has waked up again to serenity of certitude and has only to lie and watch it grow. This was the drift of his patience—that he had only to let it shine on him. He must moreover, with intermissions, still have been lifted and borne; since why and how else should he have known himself, later on, with the afternoon glow intenser, no longer at the foot of his stairs—situated as these now seemed at that dark other end of his tunnel—but on a deep window-bench of his high saloon, over which had been spread, couch-fashion, a mantle of soft stuff lined with grey fur that was familiar to his eyes and that one of his hands kept fondly feeling as for its pledge of truth. Mrs. Muldoon's face had gone, but the other, the second he had recognised, hung over him in a way that showed how he was still propped and pillowed. He took it all in, and the more he took it the more it seemed to suffice: he was as much at peace as if he had had food and drink. It was the two women who had found him, on Mrs. Muldoon's having plied, at her usual hour, her latch-key—and on her having above all arrived while Miss Staverton still lingered near the house. She had been turning away, all anxiety, from worrying the vain bell-handle—her calculation having been of the hour of the good woman's visit; but the latter, blessedly, had come up while she was still there, and they had entered together. He had then lain, beyond the vestibule, very much as he was lying now—quite, that is, as he appeared to have fallen, but all so wondrously without bruise or gash; only in a depth of stupor. What he most took in, however, at present, with the steadier clearance, was that Alice Staverton had for a long unspeakable moment not doubted he was dead.

"It must have been that I *was*." He made it out as she held him. "Yes—I can only have died. You brought me literally to life. Only," he wondered, his eyes rising to her, "only, in the name of all the benedictions, how?"

It took her but an instant to bend her face and kiss him, and something in the manner of it, and in the way her hands clasped and locked his head while he felt the cool charity and virtue of her lips, something in all this beatitude somehow answered everything. "And now I keep you," she said.

"Oh keep me, keep me!" he pleaded while her face still hung over him: in response to which it dropped again and stayed close, clingingly close. It was the seal of their situation—of which he tasted the impress for a long blissful moment in silence. But he came back. "Yet how did you know—?"

"I was uneasy. You were to have come, you remember—and you had sent no word."

"Yes, I remember—I was to have gone to you at one to-day." It caught on to their "old" life and relation—which were so near and so far. "I was still out there in my strange darkness—where was it, what was it? I must have stayed there so long." He could but wonder at the depth and the duration of his swoon.

"Since last night?" she asked with a shade of fear for her possible indiscretion.

"Since this morning—it must have been: the cold dim dawn of to-day. Where have I been," he vaguely wailed, "where have I been?" He felt her hold him close, and it was as if this helped him now to make in all security his mild moan. "What a long dark day!"

All in her tenderness she had waited a moment. "In the cold dim dawn?" she quavered.

But he had already gone on piecing together the parts of the whole prodigy. "As I didn't turn up you came straight—?"

She barely cast about. "I went first to your hotel—where they told me of your absence. You had dined out last evening and hadn't been back since. But they appeared to know you had been at your club."

"So you had the idea of *this*—?"

"Of what?" she asked in a moment.

"Well—of what has happened."

"I believed at least you'd have been here. I've known, all along," she said, "that you've been coming."

"'Known' it—?"

"Well, I've believed it. I said nothing to you after that talk we had a month ago—but I felt sure. I knew you *would*," she declared.

"That I'd persist, you mean?"

"That you'd see him."

"Ah, but I didn't!" cried Brydon with his long wail. "There's somebody—an awful beast; whom I brought too horribly, to bay. But it's not me."

At this she bent over him again, and her eyes were in his eyes. "No—it's not you." And it was as if, while her face hovered, he might have made out in it, hadn't it been so near, some particular meaning blurred by a smile. "No, thank heaven," she repeated—"it's not you! Of course it wasn't to have been."

"Ah but it *was*," he gently insisted. And he stared before him now as he had been staring for so many weeks. "I was to have known myself."

"You couldn't!" she returned consolingly. And then reverting, and as if to account further for what she had herself done, "But it wasn't only *that*, that you hadn't been at home," she went on. "I waited till the hour at which we had found Mrs. Muldoon that day of my going with you; and she arrived, as I've told you, while, failing to bring any one to the door, I lingered in my despair on the steps. After a little, if she hadn't come, by such a mercy, I should have found means to hunt her up. But it wasn't," said Alice Staverton, as if once more with her fine intention—"it wasn't only that."

His eyes, as he lay, turned back to her. "What more than?"

She met it, the wonder she had stirred. "In the cold dim dawn, you say? Well, in the cold dim dawn of this morning I too saw you."

"Saw *me*—?"

"Saw *him*," said Alice Staverton. "It must have been at the same moment."

He lay an instant taking it in—as if he wished to be quite reasonable. "At the same moment?"

"Yes—in my dream again, the same one I've named to you. He came back to me. Then I knew it for a sign. He had come to you."

At this Brydon raised himself; he had to see her better. She helped him when she understood his movement, and he sat up, steadying himself beside her there on the window-bench and with his right hand grasping her left. "*He* didn't come to me."

"You came to yourself," she beautifully smiled.

"Ah I've come to myself now—thanks to you, dearest. But this brute, with his awful face—this brute's a black stranger. He's none of *me*, even as I *might* have been," Brydon sturdily declared.

But she kept the clearness that was like the breath of infallibility. "Isn't the whole point that you'd have been different?"

He almost scowled for it. "As different as *that*—?"

Her look was more beautiful to him than the things of this world. "Haven't you exactly wanted to know *how* different? So this morning," she said, "you appeared to me."

"Like *him*?"

"A black stranger!"

"Then how did you know it was I?"

"Because, as I told you weeks ago, my mind, my imagination, had worked so over what you might, what you mightn't have been—to show you, you see, how I've thought of you. In the midst of that you came to me—that my wonder might be answered. So I knew," she went on; "and I believed that, since the question held you too so fast, as you told me that day, you too would see for yourself. And when this morning I again saw I knew it would be because you had—and also then, from the first moment, because you somehow wanted me. *He* seemed to tell me of that. So why," she strangely smiled, "shouldn't I like him?"

It brought Spencer Brydon to his feet. "You 'like' that horror—?"

"I *could* have liked him. And to me," she said, "he was no horror. I had accepted him."

"'Accepted'—?" Brydon oddly sounded.

"Before, for the interest of his difference—yes. And as *I* didn't disown him, as *I* knew him—which you at last, confronted with him in his difference, so cruelly didn't, my dear—well, he must have been, you see, less dreadful to me. And it may have pleased him that I pitied him."

She was beside him on her feet, but still holding his hand—still with her arm supporting him. But though it all brought for him thus a dim light, "You 'pitied' him?" he grudgingly, resentfully asked.

"He has been unhappy, he has been ravaged," she said.

"And haven't I been unhappy? Am not I—you've only to look at me! —ravaged?"

"Ah I don't say I like him *better*," she granted after a thought. "But he's grim, he's worn—and things have happened to him. He doesn't make shift, for sight, with your charming monocle."

"No"—it struck Brydon: "I couldn't have sported mine 'downtown.' They'd have guyed me there."

"His great convex pince-nez—I saw it, I recognised the kind—is for his poor ruined sight. And his poor right hand—!"

"Ah!" Brydon winced—whether for his proved identity or for his lost fingers. Then, "He has a million a year," he lucidly added. "But he hasn't you."

"And he isn't—no, he isn't—*you!*" she murmured as he drew her to his breast.

THE NECKLACE

Guy de Maupassant

She was one of those pretty, charming girls, born, as if through an error of destiny, into a family of clerks. She had no dowry, no hopes, no means of meeting a wealthy, distinguished man and being understood, loved, and married by him; therefore, she let herself be wed to a little bureaucrat in the Ministry of Public Education.

Not able to be fashionable, she was plain, yet unhappy as though she had been exiled from her proper class; since women have neither caste nor lineage, their beauty, grace, and charm take the place of high birth and family. Their inborn finesse, their instinct for elegance, their supple spirit constitute their only hierarchy and raise plebian women to equality with the grandest ladies.

Feeling herself born for all the refinements and luxuries, she suffered constantly. She suffered from the poverty of her lodgings, from the mean walls, from the worn chairs, from the unsightliness of the drapes. Everything that would have escaped notice by another woman of her class was to her a torture and a cause of indignation. The sight of the little Breton woman who did her humble housework roused despairing regrets and wild fantasies in her. She dreamt of silent antechambers festooned with Oriental tapestries and lit by tall bronze candelabra, of valets in knee breeches who, made drowsy by the stove's heavy heat, slept in large armchairs. She dreamt of great salons dressed in ancient silk, of fine furniture exhibiting priceless trinkets, and of smart, perfumed little parlors meant for five-o'clock gossip with one's most intimate friends, and with famous, sought-after men, coveted by all women who long for their attention.

When she sat down to supper, and her husband, from across the round table covered with the same tablecloth it had had for three days, would remove the lid from the soup tureen and enchantedly declare, "Ah! A good stew! I know of nothing better than that!" she would dream of fine dinners, of sparkling silverware, of a wall decorated with a population of ancient personages and of strange birds in fairy forest surroundings; she would dream of exquisite dishes served on marvelous china, of whispered galantries to which one listened with a Sphinx's smile while eating the pink flesh of a trout or a quail wing.

She had no dresses, no jewels, nothing. And that was all she loved, all that she felt she was made for. She would so have liked to please, to be envied, to be fascinating and in demand.

She had a rich friend, a convent schoolmate whom she no longer wished to visit because it would pain her so when she had to return. She would weep for days at a time from chagrin, from regret, from despair and from distress.

But one evening, her husband came home with an air of triumph. He held a large envelope in his hand. "Take it," he said, "Here is something for you."

She hurriedly tore the paper and withdrew a printed card bearing these words:

"The Minister of Public Education and Mme. Georges Ramponeau request that M. and Mme. Loisel grant them the honor of their company at the palace of the Ministry on Monday evening, January eighteenth."

Instead of being delighted, as her husband had expected, she disdainfully threw the invitation on the table, muttering, "What would you have me do with that?"

"But my dear, I thought you would be glad. You never go out, and this is an occasion, a fine one! I went to an infinite amount of trouble to get it. Everyone wants one; they are much sought after, and they scarcely give many of them to clerks. You'll see the whole official world there."

She looked irritably at him, and impatiently declared, "And what would you have me put on my back?"

He hadn't imagined that; he stammered, "Why, the gown you go to the theater in. It looks fine to me...."

He stopped talking. Stupefied, distracted, he saw that his wife was crying. Two fat tears descended slowly from the corners of her eyes toward the corners of her mouth. He stuttered, "What is it? What is it?"

By violent effort, she vanquished her pain and replied in a calm voice while drying her wet cheeks, "Nothing. It's just that I have no dress, and therefore I can't go to this ball. Give the invitation to some colleague with a wife who may be better prepared than I."

He was desolate. He began again: "Let's see, Mathilde. How much would it cost, an appropriate dress, which you could use again on some other occasion, something very simple?"

She reflected several seconds, doing her calculations and wondering, too, what sum she could ask without eliciting an immediate refusal and an exclamation of fright from the penny-pinching clerk. At last, she responded, hesitantly, "I don't know exactly, but it would seem to me that I could make do with four hundred francs."

He grew a bit pale, because he had been saving just that amount to buy a gun and to join a hunting party to the plains of Nanterre the next summer with some friends who shot larks there on Sundays.

Nevertheless, he said: "Done. I'll give you four hundred francs. But try to get a pretty gown."

The day of the ball drew near, and Mme. Loisel seemed sad, uneasy, anxious. Her dress was ready, however. One evening, her husband said to her, "What is it? Come now, you've been acting oddly for the past three days."

And she answered: "I'm annoyed that I haven't a single jewel, not one gem, nothing to put on. I'll have an air of poverty about me. I'd almost rather not go at all to this party."

He came back with: "Wear fresh flowers. It's very chic in this season. For ten francs, you can get two or three magnificent roses."

She was not convinced. "No...there's nothing more humiliating than to look poor when one is surrounded by rich women."

But her husband cried: "What a dumb creature you are! Call on your friend Mme. Forestier and ask her to lend you some jewels. You're close enough with her to do that."

She let out a cry of joy. "That's true. I hadn't thought of it."

The next day, she went to her friend's house and told her her problem.

Mme. Forestier went to her mirrored wardrobe, removed a large jewel box, brought it back, opened it, and said to Mme. Loisel: "Choose, my dear."

She immediately saw some bracelets, then a pearl necklace, then a Venetian cross wonderfully wrought of gold and gems. She tried on the jewelry before a mirror, then hesitated; she could not bring herself to part with them, to return them. She kept asking: "Have you any more?"

"But of course. Just look. I don't know what your taste is."

All of a sudden, in a black satin box she discovered a superb diamond necklace, and her heart began beating with unmoderated desire. Her hands trembled as she took it. She fastened it around her throat, against her high-necked gown; she stood transfixed in ecstasy before her reflection.

Then she asked, hesitantly, filled with anguish, "Can you lend me that one, just that one?"

"Why, yes, certainly."

She jumped for her friend's neck, embracing it with a wild exuberance, then fled with her treasure.

The day of the ball arrived. Mme. Loisel was a success. She was prettier than all of them—elegant, gracious, smiling, and mad with joy. All the men looked at her, asked her name, tried to get introductions. All the attachés with the Cabinet wanted to waltz with her. The Minister remarked on her.

She danced with inebriation—passionately, drunk with pleasure, no longer thinking of anything in the triumph of her beauty, in the glory of her success, in a sort of cloud of happiness made up of all this tribute, all this admiration, of all these aroused desires, of this victory so complete and so sweet to a woman's heart.

She left around four in the morning. Her husband, since midnight, had been sleeping in a small, empty room with three other gentlemen whose wives were having such a very good time.

He threw over her shoulders the apparel he had brought for their exit, modest garments of ordinary life, the poverty of which clashed with the elegance of the ball gown. She felt it and wanted to flee before she could be talked about by the other women who were wrapping themselves in rich furs.

Loisel held her back: "Wait, now. You'll catch cold outside. I shall call a cab."

But she would not listen, and she quickly went down the stairs. When they were in the street, they could find no carriage; trying to get one, they shouted at the drivers who passed them by.

They went down towards the Seine, despairing, shivering. At last, on the quay, they found one of those fly-by-night coupés which, as if they were ashamed of their misery, one doesn't see in Paris except after the sun goes down.

It dropped them off right at their door in the Rue des Martyrs. Once more, sadly, they climbed to their home. It was all over for her. And as for him, he was thinking that he would have to be at the Ministry by ten o'clock.

She took off the garments in which she had wrapped her shoulders while standing in front of the mirror so that she could once more see herself in her glory. But suddenly, she screamed. She no longer had the necklace around her neck!

Her husband, already half-undressed, asked, "What's the matter with you?"

In a panic, she turned to him: "I have... I have... I don't have Mme. Forestier's necklace."

He stood up; he was beside himself. "What! ... how! ... It's impossible!"

And they searched in the folds of her gown, in the folds of the cloak, in the pockets, everywhere. They did not find it.

He asked, "You're sure you still had it when you left the ball?"

"Yes, I touched it in the Ministry's vestibule."

"But if you had lost it in the street, we would have heard it fall. It must be in the cab."

"Yes. Probably. Did you take his number?"

"No. And, didn't you notice it?"

"No."

Thunderstruck, they looked at each other. At last, Loisel put his clothes back on. "I'm going to retrace the whole way that we walked," he said, "to see if I can find it."

And he left. In her party dress, she was paralyzed, slumped in a chair, without fire, with a thought.

Her husband returned about seven o'clock. He had found nothing.

He went to the police station; to the newspapers, offering a reward; to the carriage companies—everywhere he could imagine there might be the slightest hope.

She waited all day, in the same state of mad fear before this frightful disaster.

Loisel returned that night with a pale, sunken face; he had turned up nothing.

"You must write to your friend," he said, "and say that you have broken the necklace's clasp, and that you are having it fixed. That should give us a chance to get hold of ourselves."

She wrote as he dictated.

At the end of a week, they had lost all hope.

And Loisel, having aged five years, stated: "We must think of a way to replace that jewel."

The next day, he took the box it had come in and went to the jewelry shop which had its name printed inside. He consulted his records. "It wasn't I, Madame, who sold that necklace; I only furnished the case."

Then they went from jeweler to jeweler, searching for a necklace like the other one, consulting their memories, both of them sick with chagrin and anguish.

In a boutique at the Palais Royal, they found a strand of diamonds that seemed exactly like the one they were looking for. It was worth forty thousand francs. He would let them have it for thirty-six.

Thus they pleaded with the jeweler not to sell it for three days. And they made a deal that, if the first were found by the end of February, he would buy this one back for thirty-four thousand francs.

Loisel had eighteen thousand francs his father had left him. He borrowed the rest.

He borrowed, asking a thousand francs from one, five hundred from another, five louis here, three louis there. He signed notes, accepted ruinous obligations, dealt with usurers and with the whole breed of lenders. He compromised the whole rest of his life, risked his signature without himself knowing whether he would be able to honor it, and, in fear because of the anguish yet to come, because of the prospect of physical privation and all manners of moral tortures, he went to get the new necklace, laying down thirty-six thousand francs on the merchant's counter.

When Mme. Loisel returned the necklace to Mme. Forestier, she was told, in a chilly tone, "You should have brought it to me sooner, as I might have needed it."

She did not open the case, as her friend dreaded she might. If she had spotted the substitution, what would she have thought? What would she have said? Wouldn't she have taken Mme. Loisel for a thief?

Mme. Loisel came to know the horrible life of those in need. She accepted her part, it must be added, heroically. That terrible debt had to be paid. She would pay it. They dismissed their servant; they changed their lodgings, renting a garret under a mansard roof.

She came to know what heavy housework was, the odious duties of the kitchen. She did the dishes, using her pink nails on the greasy pots and the bottoms of the pans. She washed the dirty linen, the shirts, and the dishcloths, which she hung to dry on the line; every morning, she carried the chamber pots to the street and brought up water, stopping for breath at each landing. And, dressed like a plebian woman, she made her rounds of the fruiterer, the grocer, the butcher, with her basket on her arm, haggling, being insulted, defending her miserable money sou by sou.

Each month, they had to pay some notes, renew others, gain time.

The husband worked evenings cleanly recording a merchant's accounts, and at night, making copies at five sous a page.

This life lasted ten years.

At the end of the ten years, they had paid back everything, everything, including the usurous rates and the accumulated compound interest.

Mme. Loisel looked old now. She had become a strong woman, and hard, and rough—a woman of a poverty-stricken household. Her hair badly combed, her skirts askew, her hands red, she talked in a loud voice while splashing water on the floors she washed. But at times, when her husband was at the office, she would sit at the window and dream of that evening from another time, of that ball where she had been so beautiful and so celebrated.

What would have happened had she not lost that necklace? Who knows? Who knows? How peculiar life is, how changeable! How so minor a thing can damn you or save you!

Now, one Sunday, as she was walking on the Champs Elysées to relax from the burdensome weekly duties, she suddenly spied a woman leading a child. It was Mme. Forestier, still young, still beautiful, still fascinating.

Mme. Loisel felt moved. Was she going to speak to her? Yes, for certain. And now that she had paid, she was going to tell her all about it. Why not?

She approached. "Good day, Jeanne."

The other, not recognizing her at all, was astonished at being so familiarly called by her first name by this quite ordinary woman. She stammered: "But...Madame!...I do not know...You must be mistaken."

"No. I am Mathilde Loisel."

Her friend gave a screech: "Oh!...my poor Mathilde, how you have changed!..."

"Yes, I have had some very hard days since I last saw you; and plenty of misery—and all because of you!..."

"Of me! How so?"

"Do you remember very well that diamond necklace that you lent me to wear to the ball at the Ministry?"

"Yes. Well, so what?"

"Well, I lost it."

"How so? You brought it back to me."

"I brought you another exactly its equal. And so, we have spent ten years paying for it. Understand, it was not easy for us, we who had nothing.... At last its over, and I am damned glad."

"You say that you bought a diamond necklace to replace mine?"

"Yes. You never realized it, then! They were very similar." And she smiled with a joy that was at once proud and naïve.

Mme. Forestier, strongly moved, took her two hands. "Oh, my poor Mathilde! But mine was false. It was worth at most five hundred francs."

(Translated by Frank Gado)

THE JEWELS

Guy de Maupassant

M. Lantin had met the young lady one evening at a party given by the assistant to the head of his department. It was love at first sight.

A few months before, her father, a country doctor, had died, and she and her mother had moved to Paris where, it was hoped, the daughter might find an advantageous match by making the rounds of the mother's acquaintances. Although poor, they were respectable, demure, and unpretentious.

A girl was a paragon of virtue, the sort every sensible young man dreams of one day making his own. Her simple beauty charmed with its seraphic modesty. A faint, barely detectable smile that always seemed to dance over her lips appeared to radiate from a pure and lovely soul. Her praises were sung everywhere. "How fortunate the man who wins her love! She would be the best of wives." It was an unending chorus.

This M. Lantin enjoyed a comfortable little income that, he reasoned, could support the financial responsibilities of wedded life. And so he proposed to this exemplary girl. She accepted.

She brought him ineffable bliss. She managed his household so shrewdly and with such an eye for the penny that they enjoyed the comforts of luxury. She spoiled her husband with intimate attention, flirted with him and covered him with caresses. After six years of first honeymoon days.

She had but two faults: her love of theater and an addiction to costume jewelry. Her friends, among whom were officers' wives, often got her a box at the theater, at times for premieres. Her husband, though too tired by his work to be anything but bored by these entertainments, was forced to escort her.

As time passed, Mr. Lantin urged his wife to seek the company of some girlfriends at these amusements. At first, she opposed the suggestion, but after much argument, she finally agreed—to her husband's utter delight.

Now, along with her love for the stage went a concern for her personal adornment. To be sure, her dress, as before, remained simple and in impeccable taste; soon, however, she began to wear big rhinestone earrings that dazzled like real diamonds. About her neck, she wore paste pearl necklaces, and on her arms, bracelets of imitation gold.

Her husband frequently upbraided her: "My dear, if you cannot afford real gems, you should let your beauty and modesty be your only adornments. They are the rarest ornaments for your sex."

And she would smile dearly, and say, "But what can I do? I love jewelry. It's my one weakness. We can't alter our nature."

Then she would turn the strings of pearls around her fingers and raise the bright jewels to her husband's eyes for his admiration, sweetly soliciting his praise. "Look, aren't they pretty? You could swear they are real."

Smiling, M. Lantin answered, "You have Bohemian tastes, my darling."

Often, chatting evenings by the fireplace, she would set the leather case containing what M. Lantin referred to as "the trash" on the tea table. She would pore over the imitation jewels passionately, as though they were linked to some clandestine joy. She frequently would insist on draping a necklace over her husband's neck and, roaring with laughter, would tease, "How funny you look!" Then she would fling herself into his embrace and kiss him lovingly.

One wintry night, on returning from the opera, she caught cold. By the next morning, she was coughing. Eight days later, she died of a lung inflammation.

M. Lantin's grief was so profound, his hair turned white within a month. He cried as though he could never stop, and he was haunted by memories of her smile, her voice, of every charm of his lovely deceased wife.

Time did not heal the pain of his longing. At the office, while his co-workers were discussing current events, tears often would fill his eyes, and overcome with grief, he would succumb to heartbroken sobbing. All the objects in his wife's room were left untouched, exactly as they were before her death. Here he would repair daily, and in the isolation imagine his treasured darling who had been the joy of his life.

Soon life grew hard. The income which, when managed by his wife, had met the household expenses, was now insufficient for his necessities. How, he wondered, had she been able to purchase the fine wines and exotic delicacies now beyond his modest means?

He went into debt and presently sank into indigence. One morning on discovering his pockets were empty, he decided to sell something. The first thing that came to his mind was to dispose of his wife's costume jewels. In his heart, he had long nursed a bitterness against them. They had constantly rankled him in the past, and now the very sight of them curdled his precious memories.

Up to the very end of her life, she had made purchases; almost every evening she bright home new jewels. It was the heavy necklace he chose to sell. She had seemed to favor it especially. It should bring six or seven francs, he thought, for even though it was paste, the quality of workmanship was unmistakable.

Pocketing it, he set out for a jewelry store. On entering the first one he encountered, he felt a twinge of shame in so exposing his low state by offering such a trifle for sale.

"Monsieur," he said to the merchant, "I am curious as to its worth."

The man took the necklace, inspected it, summoned his clerk, and muttered something; then, after placing the bauble back on the counter, he examined it from a distance to gauge the effect.

M. Lantin, perturbed by all this fussing, was on the verge of saying, "Oh, I'm well aware that it's worthless" when the jeweler spoke. "Monsieur, the value of that necklace is from twelve to fifteen thousand francs. But unless you tell me how you came by it, I couldn't buy it."

The widower's mouth fell open and his eyes stared. He could not comprehend the merchant's meaning. At last, he stammered: "What?—Are you certain?" The other answered crisply, "Inquire anywhere. See whether anyone will offer you a better price. It's worth, at most, fifteen thousand. If you can't get a better price, you may return."

A dumbfounded M. Lantin picked up the necklace and walked out of the store. He wanted time to think.

Outside, he felt like laughing. "The idiot," he said to himself, "I should have taken him up on it. He can't tell real jewels from paste."

Several moments later, he went into another store on the Rue de la Paix. No sooner than the owner saw the necklace, he exclaimed, "My word! How well I know it. It was purchased here."

Mr. Lantin was exercised. "How much is it worth?" he asked.

"Well, I sold it for twenty thousand francs. I'll buy it back for eighteen thousand if you can satisfy the legal requirements of explaining how you obtained it."

Now M. Lantin was flabbergasted. He replied: "But. . . but do examine it carefully. Up to this moment I was under the impression it was paste."

"Your name, Monsieur?" the jeweler inquired.

"Lantin. I'm employed at the Ministry of the Interior. I live at 16 Rue des Martyrs."

The merchant searched his books, found the entry, and said, "That particular necklace was sent to Mme. Lantin's address at 16 Rue des Martyrs on July 20, 1876."

The two men stared at each other—the widower dumb with astonishment, the jeweler sensing a thief. It was the latter who broke the silence. "Are you willing to deposit the necklace with me for twenty-four hours? I will give you a receipt."

"Of course," M. Lantin quickly replied. Then, placing the receipt into his pocket, he made his exit from the store.

He walked the streets aimlessly, terribly confused. He groped for answers, tried to understand. Obviously such an expensive gem was beyond his wife's means. That was certain. Well, then, it must have been a gift! A gift! But from whom? And why would he give it to her?

He stood in the middle of the street. A horrifying doubt came to his mind—she? Then all the other jewels must also have been gifts! The ground under him seemed to shake. A tree was falling before him. Flinging up his arms, he fell unconscious. He came to in a pharmacy to which some passers-by had taken him and was taken home. On arriving, he closeted himself in his room and cried until sundown. Eventually, drained from fatigue, he cast himself onto the bed where he spent an uneasy, restless night.

The next morning, he got up and readied himself for work. The shock made it difficult to think of going to the office, so he requested to be excused in a letter to his boss. Then, he remembered that he had to return to the jewelry store. He did not relish the idea, but he could not leave the necklace with that man. He dressed and went out.

It was a perfect day. A cerulean sky smiled down on the bustling city below. Men of leisure strolled with their hands in their pockets.

Watching them, M. Lantin said to himself, "They are indeed fortunate. Money makes it possible to forget even the deepest hurt. One can go anywhere and in traveling find distraction, the best cure for grief. If only I were rich!"

He felt hungry, but his pockets were empty. Then, he again thought of the necklace. Eighteen thousand francs! Eighteen thousand francs! What a princely sum!

He soon came to the Rue de la Paix, across from the jeweler's. Eighteen thousand francs! Twenty times, he was set to enter, but shame restrained him. But he *was* hungry—very hungry, and he was penniless. He made up his mind, sprang across the street before he could think better of his resolution, and went into the store.

The merchant stepped forward at once and politely asked him to sit down. The clerks looked knowingly at him.

"I've investigated the matter, M. Lantin, the proprietor said, "and if you are still of a mind to sell the gems, I am prepared to pay the sum I offered."

"Certainly, Monsieur," M. Lantin stammered.

With this, the jeweler withdrew eighteen large bills from a drawer, counted them out and handed them to M. Lantin, who then signed a receipt. His hand shaking, he stuffed the money into his pocket.

Just before he left the shop, he turned toward the jeweler, who continued to smile in his knowing way. "I. . . I have other gems, gems which I obtained in the same way," he said from under lowered eyes. "Would you purchase them, too?"

The storekeeper bowed. "But of course, Monsieur."

"I shall bring them to you," M. Lantin said solemnly. Within the hour, he returned with the jewels.

The big diamond earrings brought twenty thousand francs; the bracelets, thirty-five thousand; the rings, sixteen; emeralds and sapphires, fourteen; a gold chain with a solitaire pendant, forty—in all, a total of one hundred forty-three thousand francs.

The merchant treated the matter lightly. "She evidently invested everything in precious stones."

"It's a way of investing," M. Lantin answered gravely.

He dined at Voisin's that day and sipped wine that cost twenty francs a bottle. Renting a coach, he then toured the Bourse. As he looked out over the strollers, he found it hard to resist yelling to them, "I'm rich, too! I'm worth two hundred thousand francs!"

Suddenly, he remembered his boss. He drove to his office and, walking in jauntily, he proclaimed, "Monsieur, I am here to resign. I have come into an inheritance of three hundred thousand francs!"

In shaking hands with his former co-workers, he intimated grand plans for the future; then he left to sup at the Cafe Anglais.

He took a chair next to a man who exuded a patrician air; in the middle of the repast, he confided to the gentleman that he had just inherited a four hundred thousand franc fortune.

Remarkably, when he went to the theater, he was not bored for the first time in his life. The rest of the evening was a lark.

Six months later, he wed for the second time. His new wife was a woman of unimpeachable virtue with a tempestuous disposition. She brought him much sadness.

(Translated by Frank Gado)

THE VENUS OF ILLE

Prosper Mérimée

The sun had already set as I descended the last slope of the Canigou, but on the plain below I could make out the houses of Ille, the little town towards which I was heading.

"No doubt you know where Monsieur de Peyrehorade lives," I said to the Catalonian who had been my guide since the previous day.

"Do I!" he exclaimed. "Why, I know his house as well as my own. If it wasn't so dark, I'd point it out to you. It's the finest in Ille. M. de Peyrehorade has money, I tell you. And he's marrying his son to an even richer lady."

"Is the marriage to take place soon?" I asked.

"Soon! Why, the fiddlers may already have been booked for the wedding. Tonight, maybe, or tomorrow, or the day after, for all I know. It'll be at Puygarrig. Because the young man is marrying Mademoiselle de Puygarrig. It will be very grand."

I had an introduction to M. de Peyrehorade from my friend M. de P., who had told me he was a very learned antiquarian and a most obliging, good-natured man who would be delighted to show me all the ruins within ten leagues. Consequently, I had been looking forward to his company in the district around Ille, which I knew to have a wealth of ancient and medieval monuments. But this wedding, of which I had now been apprised for the first time, could upset all my plans. I would be an intruder, I told myself. Yet, since M. de P. had written to say I was coming, I was expected, and I would have to present myself.

"I'll wager, Monsieur," my guide said when we reached level ground, "I'll wager you a cigar I can guess why you're going to M. de Peyrehorade's."

"But that's not difficult to guess," I replied in offering him a cigar. "At this hour, after a six-league walk on the Canigou, the main object is supper."

"Yes, but tomorrow?... I'll wager you've come to Ille to see the idol! I guessed that when I saw you drawing pictures of the saints at Serrabona."

"The idol! What idol?" The word had stirred my curiosity.

"What! Didn't anyone in Perpignan tell you M. de Peyrehorade had found an idol in the ground?"

"A terracotta, you mean? A clay statue?"

"No, I do not. It's copper, and big enough to make a heap of sous. It weighs as much as a church bell. We found it at the foot of an olive tree, buried deep in the earth."

"So you were there when it was discovered?"

"Yes, sir. M. de Peyrehorade told Jean Coll and me, two weeks ago, to dig out an old olive tree the frost had killed last year—it was a very hard winter, if you recall. Well, while we were working, Jean Coll, who was really putting his back into it, struck his pick into the dirt, and I heard a *ding*, just as though he'd hit a bell. 'What's that?' says I. We kept on picking away, and then we saw a black hand, like the hand of a dead man coming out of the ground. I was scared, I tell you. Up to Monsieur I go and I say to him: "Dead men, master, under the olive tree. You'd best send for the priest."

"'What dead men?'" he asked.

"He followed me, and no sooner did he see the hand than he cried out: 'An antique! An antique!' You'd think he'd found a treasure. With a frantic desperation, he went for it with the pick and with his hands. Why, he did almost as much work as the two of us combined."

"And what did you find after all this?"

"A big black woman, more than half naked—pardon, Monsieur—copper through and through. M. de Peyrehorade told us it was an idol from the pagan time...from the time of Charlemagne."

"I see what it is...a bronze Holy Virgin from some convent in ruin."

"A Holy Virgin? Impossible! I would have recognized a Virgin. It's an idol, I tell you. You can tell from her look. She rivets her great white eyes on you. You'd think she was trying to stare you down. It forces you to look away.

"White eyes, eh? No doubt inlaid in the bronze. Probably some Roman statue."

"Roman! That's it! M. de Peyrehorade says it's Roman. Ah! I see you're a scholar, just like him."

"Is it complete, in good condition?"

"Oh, it's all there, Monsieur. Even more beautiful and slicker than the plaster bust of Louis-Philippe in the town hall. Yet the look on the idol's face disturbs me. It's wicked...and *she* is wicked, too."

"Wicked! What harm has she done you?"

"None to me exactly. But you be the judge. We'd gone down on hands and knees to lift her up—even M. de Peyrehorade was pulling the rope, though the dear man's got the strength of a chicken! With a lot of trouble, we got her to stand. Then, just as I was picking up a flat stone to wedge under her, *plop!* she crashed down again. 'Get away!' I shout, but I wasn't in time. Jean Coll couldn't jerk his leg out from under."

"And was he hurt?"

"His poor leg, broken to a stump. Damn, when I saw that, I was in a rage. I wanted to smash that idol with my pick, but M. de Peyrehorade stopped me. He gave Jean Coll money, but what's the good? He's been in bed the whole two weeks since it happened, and the doctor says he'll never again walk as well with that leg as with the other. It's a shame. He was our best runner and, next to Monsieur's son, our best tennis player. I swear, it really bothered M. Alphonse de Peyrehorade, 'cause he always played against Coll. It was a joy to see them volley. *Pow! Pow!* The balls never touched the ground."

Chatting in this manner, we entered Ille, and I soon found myself in M. de Peyrehorade's presence. He was a little old man, still spry and active, with powdered hair, a red nose, and a jovial, bantering way about him. Before even opening M. de P.'s letter, he placed me at a grandly-prepared table and introduced me to his wife and son as the renowned archaeologist destiny had chosen to lift Roussillon from the obscurity to which scholarly neglect had consigned it.

While eating heartily—for mountain air stimulates the appetite as nothing else can—I looked my hosts over. To the few words I have said about M. de Peyrehorade I should add that he was vivacity incarnate. He talked, ate, stood, ran to his library, fetched books, showed me engravings, filled my glass; he was never still for two minutes. His wife, a bit fat (as most Catalonian women over forty get to be), seemed typically provincial in her thorough immersion in household duties. Although the supper sufficed for at least six persons, she sprang to the kitchen, commanded the slaughtering of pigeons, gave orders as to the frying, and opened heaven knows how many pots of preserves. Just like that, the table was loaded down with dishes and bottles, and I would surely have died of indigestion had I just sampled from the entire proffered array. But with each new dish that I declined came another apology. They were afraid I would suffer in Ille...resources were so scarce in the provinces...Parisians were so difficult to please!

In the middle of his parents' comings and goings, M. Alphonse de Peyrehorade remained as still as a statue of Terminus. A tall young man of twenty-six, he had a handsome, well-struck face which, however, showed no expression. His figure and his athletic build fully warranted his reputation throughout the province as a tireless tennis player. This evening, his clothes were the latest fashion, the very image of the pictures in the most recent issue of the *Journal des Modes*. Even so, he seemed uncomfortable: stiff as a post in his velvet collar, he would turn as though he hadn't a joint in his whole body. His coarse sunburned hands and short fingernails presented a strange contrast to his costume: a ploughboy's hands jutting from the sleeves of a fop. Furthermore, despite his studying me from head to toe as a specimen Parisian, he only spoke once to me during the course of the evening, and that was to ask where I had bought my watchfob.

"See here, my esteemed guest," M. de Peyrehorade said to me as supper was drawing to a close, "you belong to me. You are in my house and I shall not release you until you have seen all the interesting sights in our mountains. You must learn to know our Roussillon and do it justice. You can't imagine all that we have to show you—Phoenician, Celtic, Roman, Arab, Byzantine monuments. You shall see them, one and all. I shall take you everywhere, and not a single stone will escape you."

A fit of coughing forced him to stop. I took the opportunity to interject that it would distress me if I were to inconvenience him at a time of such importance to his family. If he would be so kind as to give me the benefit of his excellent counsel as to the excursions I should make, I could, without burdening him further....

"Ah," he exclaimed, interrupting me, "you are referring to the boy's marriage! But that's of little concern—it will take place the day after tomorrow. You must attend the wedding with us, *en famille.* Since the bride is in mourning for an aunt, whose property she will inherit, the celebration will be modest, and there won't be a ball. It's a pity. Otherwise, you would have seen our Catalonian girls dance. As they are very pretty, you might have been tempted to follow Alphonse's example. One marriage, they say, leads to others.... But Saturday, after the young people are married, I'll be free and we'll sally forth. I must apologize for boring you with a provincial wedding. For a Parisian who has had his fill of all kinds of parties.... And, to top it all, a wedding without dancing! However, you will see a bride—a bride...but I must leave you to find the words. Ah, but you are a man with serious concerns, immune to distraction by women. I have something better to show you. Something worth your attention! I have a wonderful surprise in store for you tomorrow."

"Oh, dear," I replied, "it's hard to have a treasure in your house and keep it secret from the public. I believe I can surmise what you have in store for me. If I have guessed correctly and it's your statue, my guide's description of it has only fed my curiosity and predisposed me to marvel at it.

"Ah, so he told you about the idol, for that is what they call my beautiful Venus Tur—but I shall say nothing more for now. You will see her tomorrow, by daylight, and you tell me if I'm not right in calling her a masterwork. Upon my word, you could not have arrived at a better moment! It bears some inscriptions that, sorry scholar that I am, I can decipher only crudely. But a scholar from Paris! ... Perhaps you will ridicule my interpretation—for I have written an article about it. I, this old provincial antiquary who speaks to you, I have dared make a start; I propose to set the presses groaning. If you would be so kind as to read and correct me, I might hope. For example, I am curious as to how you would translate this inscription on the pedestal: CAVE.... But no, this is not the time to ask. Not yet! Tomorrow! tomorrow! Not a word about the Venus today."

"You are quite right, Peyrehorade," said his wife, "to give your old idol a rest. You should realize that you're interfering with Monsieur's dinner. I'm sure he has seen much finer statues than yours in Paris. There must be dozens of them in the Tuileries, and bronze, too."

"There," M. de Peyrehorade interrupted, "is ignorance—the sainted ignorance of the provinces! Imagine comparing a remarkable antique statue to the vapid figures of Coustou!

> *'With what irreverance*
> *Does my good wife talk of the gods!'*

Would you believe that my wife wanted me to melt my statue to make a bell for our church? She would have played the benefactor. A masterpiece of Myron, Monsieur!"

"Masterpiece! Masterpiece! A fine masterpiece she made, breaking a man's leg!"

"Look, wife," said M. de Peyrehorade in a calculated tone while extending his right leg, clad in a silk stocking, in her direction, "had my Venus broken this leg, I would not rue it."

"Good heavens! Peyrehorade, how can you say that? Luckily, the man is healing. Even so, I can't bring myself to look upon a statue that caused such a misfortune. Poor Jean Coll!"

"Wounded by Venus, Monsieur," said M. de Peyrehorade with a chortle, "wounded by Venus, the fool complains:

> *Veneris nec praemia noris.*

"Who has not been wounded by Venus?"

M. Alphonse, who understood French better than Latin, shot a glance at me and winked knowingly, as if to ask: "And you, my fine Parisian gentleman, do you understand?"

The supper ended. For the last hour, I had eaten nothing. I was so fatigued I could not hide the yawns that frequently slipped from me. Madame de Peyrehorade, the first to observe my difficulty, mentioned that it was time to retire. This loosed a new string of apologies for the miserable provision they could make. It would not be as comfortable as what I was used to in Paris. One has to do without in the provinces! I must make allowances for the Roussillonnais. Without effect, I protested that, after a tour of the mountains, a pile of straw would make a luxurious bed—but she kept pleading that I excuse poor country people for not treating me as well as they would have liked. Finally, escorted by M. de Peyrehorade, I climbed the stairs to the room I was assigned. The last flight of stairs, made of wood, ended in the middle of a hallway connecting several rooms.

"To the right," said my host, "is the apartment I'll give the future Madame Alphonse. Your room is at the other end of the hall. Then, with a sly, humorously-intended expression, he added, "You know, we must let a newly married couple have their privacy. You are at one end of the house; they, at the other."

As we entered a beautifully furnished room, my eye immediately fell on a bed seven foot long, six foot wide, and so high one needed a stool to reach the top. Then, after indicating where I would find the bell, checking to see that the sugar bowl was full and that the dresser had been set with bottles of Cologne, and asking repeatedly whether I required anything more, my host bade me good night and left me.

As the windows were shut, I opened one before undressing to get the fresh night air, always a delight after a big meal. I faced the Canigou, which, though always a lovely view, seemed by the moon's bright light this evening to be the most beautiful mountain in the world. After staring for a while at its marvelous profile, I was about to shut the window when, dropping my eyes, I saw the statue on a pedestal some forty yards from the house. It had been set at the corner of a quickset hedge separating a small garden from a large, perfectly even grass square (which, I later discovered, was the town's tennis court). Once M. de Peyrehorade's property, this land had been deeded to the community by him at his son's insistent request.

From my distance, I could not determine which way the statue faced, and I could only estimate its height at around six feet. Just then, two young town rogues strode along the hedge the width of the tennis court, whistling the pretty Roussillon tune, *Montagnes Régalades*. They stopped to look at the statue, and one of them apostrophized it in a loud voice. He spoke Catalan, but I had been in Roussillon long enough to understand almost all he said.

"So there you are, you bawd!" (The Catalonian word was much more forceful.) "So there you are!" he said. "So it was you who broke Jean Coll's leg! If you were mine, I'd break your neck!"

"Bah! With what?" said the other. "She's made of copper, and it's so hard that Etienne broke his file on it. It's ancient pagan copper, and harder than anything."

"If I had my cold chisel"—obviously he was a locksmith's apprentice— "I'd quickly dig out her big white eyes, just as easily as I'd shell an almond. There's over a hundred sous in silver in 'em."

They took a few steps away.

"I must say good night to the idol," the taller one said as he suddenly stopped again.

He stooped, apparently to pick up a stone. I saw him cock his arm and throw; instantly, the bronze rang. In the same moment, the apprentice held his head with his hand and cried in pain. "She threw it back at me!" he exclaimed.

With that, the pair of rogues took to their heels at top speed. Obviously, the stone had bounced off the metal and punished the chap for his offense against the goddess.

Enjoying a good laugh, I shut my window.

"One more vandal punished by Venus!" I thought. "All the destroyers of our ancient monuments should have their heads broken that way!"

And with that charitable prayer, I fell asleep.

It was broad daylight when I awoke. On one side of my bed stood M. de Peyrehorade in his robe; on the other, a servant, sent by his wife, holding a cup of chocolate in his hand.

"Get up now, Parisian! How like you slug-a-beds from the capital!" my host said as I dressed hurriedly. "Eight o'clock, and still in bed! I've been up since six. This is the third time I've been upstairs. I came on tiptoe to your door, but there wasn't a sound, not a sign of life. At your age too much sleep is harmful. And you've yet to see my Venus! Come, come, drink this cup of Barcelona chocolate quickly. It's genuine contraband. You can't get chocolate like this in Paris. Build up your strength so that, when you stand before my Venus, I won't be able to pry you away."

In five minutes I was ready—so to say, for I was half shaved, my clothes were half buttoned, and in swallowing the boiling hot chocolate, I had scalded my throat. Proceeding to the garden, I soon found myself before a truly beautiful statue.

It was, in fact, a Venus, and a marvelously lovely one. The upper part of the body was naked, as the ancients customarily presented their major deities; the right hand, held at the level of her breast, had the palm turned inward, with the thumb and first two fingers extended and the others slightly bent. The left hand, at the hip, clutched the drapery covering her lower body. The statue's pose brought to mind the *Morra Player* (for some reason usually called Germanicus). Perhaps the sculptor intended to show the goddess playing morra.

Be that as it may, one cannot imagine anything more perfect than the body of that Venus or anything more graceful and more dignified than her drapery. I had expected to see some Late Empire work; instead, I saw a masterpiece from scupture's golden age. I was especially struck by the exquisite formal fidelity, as if molded from nature—if nature ever produced such perfect artifacts.

The hair, brushed back from the forehead, seemed once to have been gilded. The head, small as were those of almost all Greek statues, bent forward slightly. As for the face, I could never hope to describe its peculiar character, for it was of a type quite unlike that of any ancient statue in my memory. It hadn't the tranquil, stark beauty of the Greeks, who systematically conveyed a regal immobility in every feature. To the contrary, here I noted with astonishment the artist's manifest intent to express a mischief almost tantamount to devilishness. Each feature was slightly contracted: the eyes, at a slight slant; the corners of the mouth, raised; the nostrils, a bit dilated. Disdain, irony, cruelty were printed on that face, yet, nevertheless, it was unfathomably lovely. Indeed, the more one gazed upon this wondrous statue, the more distressing was the thought that such surpassing beauty could merge with thorough insensibility.

"If the model ever lived," I said to M. de Peyrehorade—"and I doubt Heaven ever produced such a woman—how I pity her lovers! She must have delighted in killing them with despair. There is something utterly ferocious in her expression, and yet I have seen nothing ever so beautiful!"

"'Tis Venus, fixed upon her prey!" quoted M. de Peyrehorade in his joy over my enthusiasm.

Perhaps that expression of hellish irony was augmented by the contrast of the luminous silver eyes with the blackish-green coating time had applied to the entire statue. Those sparkling eyes created a certain illusion suggesting the reality of life itself. I remembered what my guide had said: that she forced those looking at her to lower their eyes. It was almost a fact, and I could not restrain my anger at myself as I became aware of my discomfort before that brazen face.

"Now that you have admired her every detail, my dear colleague in antiquarian research," said my host, "please let us begin a scholarly colloquy. What's your opinion as to this inscription, which you have not as yet noticed?"

He pointed to the statue's base, where I read: CAVE AMANTEM

"*Quid dicis, doctissime?*" he asked while rubbing his hands. "Let's see whether we shall concur on the meaning of this *cave amantem*."

"Two meanings are possible," I replied. "It may be translated: 'Beware of him who loves you—distrust lovers.' But I am not sure that, in that sense, *cave amantem* would be good Latin. Considering the lady's diabolical expression, I am almost persuaded that the artist meant to put the spectator on guard against that terrible beauty. Thus, I would translate it: 'Beware should *she* love you.'"

"Uhuh!" ejaculated M. de Peyrehorade. "Yes, it's possible, but, with all due respect, I prefer the first, and I'll explain a bit why. You know who Venus's lover was?"

"She had several."

"Yes, but the first was Vulcan. Couldn't the artist have meant: 'Despite all your beauty and your arrogance, you shall have a blacksmith, a wretched cripple, for a lover'? A grave moral for coquettes, Monsieur!"

I could not suppress a smile, so far-fetched was this interpretation.

"Latin is a taxing language, given its extraordinary conciseness," I stated in order to avoid openly contradicting my antiquarian companion. To have a better view of the statue, I took a few steps backward.

"One moment, colleague!" said M. de Peyrehorade, seizing my arm, "you have not seen everything. There is yet another inscription. Stand on the pedestal and look at the right arm." While he spoke, he assisted my ascent.

Rather unceremoniously, I embraced Venus's neck. I was beginning to feel myself on familiar terms with her. I even looked her in the eye for an second, and I found her still more fiendish, still lovelier at close range. Then I saw some letters engraved on the right arm in what I took to be ancient handwriting. With the aid of a powerful lens, I spelled out the following, M. de Peyrehorade repeating each word as I pronounced it, his voice and gestures registering his approval. I read:

VENERI TVRBVL—
EVTYCHES MYRO
IMPERIO FECIT

After TVRBVL in the first line, several letters seemed effaced, but TVRBVL was perfectly legible.

"Which means?" My host's face beamed and he winked maliciously as he posed the question, for he had shrewdly calculated that I could not easily deal with the TVRBVL.

"There is a word here I do not yet comprehend," I said; "the rest is simple. 'Eutyches Myron made this offering to Venus by her order.'"

"Excellent. But what do you make of TVRBVL? What is TVRBVL?"

"TVRBVL puzzles me very much. I have tried without success to think of some epithet of Venus to guide me. What would you say to Turbulenta? Venus, who disturbs, who excites—as you see, I am still captivated by her wicked expression. *Turbulenta* is not a very unapt epithet for Venus," I added modestly, for my explanation did not much convince me.

"Turbulent Venus! Venus the carouser! Ah! so you think my Venus a wine-shop Venus, do you? By no means, Monsieur. She is a Venus of good social standing. But I shall explain this TVRBVL for you. Of course, you must promise not to speak of my discovery before my article is in print. You see, I'm quite proud of this find of mine. You must leave us poor provincial devils a few grains in the field. You Parisian scholars have such rich harvests!"

From atop the pedestal, where I still perched, I solemnly promised never to be so base as to steal his discovery.

"TVRBVL—Monsieur," he said, approaching me and lowering his voice out of fear that someone else might overhear—"read TVRBVLNERAE."

"I now understand no better than I did before."

"Listen. About a league from here, at the foot of the mountain, lies the village of Boulternere—the name, a corruption of the Latin word *Turbulnera*. Such inversions are most common. Boulternere, Monsieur, was a Roman town. I have always suspected it, but I could never prove it. Herein is the proof. This Venus was the local deity of Boulternere; and the word Boulternere, whose ancient origin I just showed, proves something even more interesting—namely, that Boulternere, before it became Roman, was a Phoenician town!"

He paused a moment to draw breath and relish my astonishment. I successfully suppressed a powerful impulse to laugh.

"It's a fact," he went on, "*Turbulnera* is pure Phoenician; *Tur*, pronounced *Tour*— and *Tour* and *Sour* are the same word, are they not? *Sour* is the Phoenician name of *Tyre*; I need not remind you of its meaning. *Bul* is *Baal*; Bal, Bel, Bul—but slight alterations in pronunciation. As for *nera*—that's a bit sticky. Absent a Phoenician word, I lean toward the theory that it derives from the Greek *neros*, damp, swampy. If so, the word would be a hybrid. To support *neros*, I'll show you that, at Boulternere, the mountain streams form miasmatic pools. On the other hand, the suffix *nera* may have been added much later, in honor of Nera Pivesuvia, wife of Tetricus, who may have had a proprietary interest in Turbul. Given the pools, however, I prefer the *neros* etymology."

With great self-satisfaction, he took a pinch of snuff.

"But let us leave the Phoenicians and return to the inscription. I translate, then: 'To Venus of Boulternere, Myron, at her command, dedicates this statue, his work.'"

I had no intention of criticizing his etymology, but I did wish to show off a bit of my own perspicuity, so I said:

"Hold it there a moment, Monsieur. Myron dedicated something, but I see nothing pointing to this statue."

"What!" he cried, "wasn't Myron a famous Greek sculptor? The talent probably passed down through the family; one of his descendents executed this statue. Nothing can be more certain."

"But," I replied, "I see a tiny hole in the arm. I believe it was made for fastening something—a bracelet, perhaps, which this Myron presented to Venus as an propitiatory offering. Myron was unlucky in love; Venus was upset with him, and he appeased her by consecrating a gold bracelet to her. Note that *fecit* is very often used for *consecravit*; they are synonymous. Had I Gruter or Orellius on hand, I could show you more than one example. It would be quite natural for a lover to see Venus in a dream and to imagine her ordering him to present a gold bracelet to her statue. So Myron consecrated a bracelet to her; then the barbarians, or some sacrilegious thief—"

"Ah! It's obvious you've written some novels!" cried my host, extending me his hand for my descent. "No, Monsieur, it came from the Myronic school. Just examine the craftsmanship and you'll agree."

Since I've made a principle of never gainsaying a headstrong antiquarian, I bowed my head as though convinced and said, "It's admirable."

"Oh, good God!" cried M. de Peyrehorade, "more vandalism! Someone has evidently hit my statue with a stone!"

He had spotted a white mark just above Venus's breast. I noticed a similar mark across the right hand's fingers, which I then assumed had either been glanced by the stone itself or hit on the rebound by a fragment broken off in the impact. I reported the assault and the swift retaliation I had witnessed to my host. Enjoying a good laugh, he compared the apprentice to Diomedes and expressed a hope that, like the Greek hero, he might see all his companions turned into birds.

The breakfast bell interrupted this classical conversation, and, as on the previous evening, I was again prevailed upon to eat for four. Then M. de Peyrehorade's tenants arrived for an audience. While the father was thus occupied, his son took me to see a coach he had bought in Toulouse for his fiancée—which I, of course, admired. Then I went with him to the stables, where he boasted for half an hour about his horses, listing their pedigrees and reciting the prizes they had garnered at various races in the province. At last, through association with a gray mare he meant to give her, he reached the subject of his future wife.

"We'll see her today," he said. "I don't know whether you will think her pretty, but everyone here and at Perpignan considers her charming. Her chief merit is that she's very rich. Her aunt at Prades left her everything. Oh! I am going to be quite happy."

It revolted me to see a young man more moved by the dowry than by the beautiful eyes of his bride-to-be.

"You're knowledgeable about jewels," continued M. Alphonse, "what's your opinion of this ring I'll give her tomorrow?"

As he spoke, he removed a huge ring from the first joint of his pinky. It had a cluster of diamonds in the shape of two clasped hands—a surpassingly poetic concept, I thought. The workmanship was quite ancient, but I judged that it had been somewhat altered for the sake of mounting the diamonds. Engraved in Gothic script inside the ring were the words: *Sempr' ab ti*—"Always with thee."

"It's a handsome ring," I said, "but these diamonds have compromised its character."

"Oh! it's much handsomer this way," he answered smiling. "With twelve hundred francs' worth of diamonds. My mother gave it to my grandmother, who in turn got it from hers. God knows when it was made."

"The custom in Paris," I said, "is to give a very simple ring, usually made of two different metals, such as gold and platinum. For example, that other ring, the one you have on this finger, would be most appropriate. This one, with its diamonds and its hands in relief, is too large for a glove to slip over it."

"Oh! Madame Alphonse may work that out as she pleases. I imagine that, all the same, she'll be very happy to have it. Twelve hundred francs on one's finger is very pleasant. This little ring," he added, glancing smugly at the simple one he wore, "I received from a woman in Paris one Mardi Gras. Ah! how I carried on when I was in Paris two years ago! That's the place to have a good time!" He heaved a sigh of regret.

We were to dine that day with the bride's parents at Puygarrig; we drove in the coach to the château, about a league and a half from Ille. I was introduced and welcomed as a friend of the family. I will say nothing of the dinner, or of the conversation afterward, in which I took little part. M. Alphonse, seated beside his fiancée, whispered in her ear every quarter hour. As for her, she hardly raised her eyes, but whenever her future husband addressed her, she blushed modestly, replying, however, without embarrassment.

Mademoiselle de Puygarrig was eighteen years of age; her lithe, frail figure contrasted markedly with her athletic fiancé's bony build. More than lovely, she was fascinating. I admired how completely natural were her responses; her good-humor, tinged ever so slightly with malice, reminded me, despite myself, of my host's Venus. As I mentally made the comparison, I asked myself, regarding beauty, whether the superiority I was forced to recognize in the statue did not owe in large part to her tigress-like expression; for energy, even in the form of an evil passion, always arouses in us a certain astonishment and involuntary admiration.

"What a pity," I said to myself as we left Puygarrig, "that such an attractive person should be rich, and that her dowry should attract a marriage with a man so unworthy of her!"

On the return to Ille, experiencing some difficulty in making conversation with Madame de Peyrehorade—whom courtesy compelled me to address every now and then—I exclaimed: "You are confident of yourselves here in Roussillon! To dare have a wedding on a Friday, Madame! We are more superstitious in Paris; no one would risk taking a wife on that day."

"Good Lord, don't mention it!" said she. "Had it been my decision, they certainly would have chosen another day. But that's how Peyrehorade wanted it, and I had to give in. It worries me, however. What if something should happen? There must surely be some basis to the superstition. Otherwise, why should everyone be afraid of Friday?"

"Friday!" her husband declared, "Friday is Venus's day! A superb day for a wedding! You see, my dear colleague, I think of nothing but my Venus. On my honor, it was because of her I chose a Friday. Tomorrow, if you are willing, we will offer a small sacrifice to her before the wedding—two doves, and with incense, if I can find some."

"For shame, Peyrehorade!" his utterly scandalized wife interjected. "To burn incense for an idol! That would be blasphemy! What would the neighbors say?"

"At least," said M. de Peyrehorade, "let me lay a wreath of roses and lilies on her head:

Manibus date lilia plenis.

As you see, Monsieur, the Constitution is a hollow document. We enjoy no religious freedom!"

The schedule for the next day provided that everyone be fully dressed and ready at precisely ten o'clock. After a cup of chocolate, we were to drive to Puygarrig. The civil ceremony would take place at the town hall, and the religious ceremony in the château's chapel. Then we would have breakfast. Subsequently, we were to amuse ourselves until seven o'clock, when we were to return to M. de Peyrehorade's in Ille, where the two families would dine together. The rest followed as a matter of course. Given the proscription of dancing, the scheme called for eating as much as possible.

At eight o'clock, pencil in hand, I was already seated in front of the Venus, for the twentieth time beginning to draw the statue's head, with that expression that still completely eluded my efforts to capture it. M. de Peyrehorade hovered over me, dispensing advice while repeating his Phoenician etymologies; then he arranged some Bengal roses on the statue's base and tragi-comically intoned prayers to it for the welfare of the couple who were to live under his roof. About nine o'clock, when he returned to the house to dress, M. Alphonse arrived, encased in a tight-fitting new coat, white gloves, patent-leather shoes, and carved buttons. In his buttonhole, he wore a rose.

"Will you paint my wife's portrait?" he asked, leaning over my sketch. "She's pretty, too."

Just then, a tennis game began on the court I mentioned earlier. It instantly caught Alphonse's attention. And being rather tired out and despairing of reproducing that fiendish face, I, too, soon abandoned my drawing to watch the players. Among them, I saw several Spanish mule drivers who had come to town the night before—Aragonese and Navarrese, almost all of whom are exceptionally proficient players. The result was that the men of Ille, despite encouragement by the presence and advice of M. Alphonse, quickly fell to these new champions. The native spectators were aghast. M. Alphonse glanced at his watch. It was only 9:30. His mother's hair was still to be coiffed. Without further hesitation, he removed his coat, called for a jacket, and challenged the Spaniards. Smiling at his eagerness, and slightly surprised, I watched him. "I must defend the honor of the province," he said to me.

In that instant, I saw him as truly handsome. He was so sincere. His attire, in which he had been so absorbed a moment before, suddenly no longer mattered. Whereas, a few minutes earlier, he wouldn't risk turning his head for fear of disarranging his tie, he was now completely indifferent to his carefully curled locks, or to his beautifully laundered ruff. And as for his fiancée, I believe that, had it been necessary, he would have postponed the wedding. He hastily donned sandals, rolled his sleeves, and, exuding confidence, assumed his place at the head of the defeated team, like Caesar rallying his legions at Dryrrhachium. I jumped the hedge and found a good place under a shady plum tree from which I could see both sides.

Contrary to general expectation, M. Alphonse missed the first ball, a drive which, it must be said, his opponent had rocketed just above ground level. An Aragonese, and apparently the Spaniards' leader, he was a man of about forty, slim and wiry, approximately six feet tall, and his olive skin was almost as dark as the bronze of the Venus.

M. Alphonse threw his racquet down in an angry fit.

"It's this damned ring," he cried. "It trapped my finger and made me miss an easy shot!"

With some difficulty, he removed the diamond ring. I stepped forward to take it, but instead he ran to the Venus, slipped it onto her middle finger, and resumed his place at the head of his townsmen.

Though pale, he was calm and determined. Thereafter, not making a single mistake, he overwhelmed the Spaniards. The enthusiasm of the crowd was something to behold: some shouted salvos of joy and threw their caps in the air; others shook his hand and called him a credit to the province. Had he repelled an invasion, I doubt whether he would have received more exuberant or more heartfelt congratulations. The mortification of the vanquished made the triumph all the sweeter.

"I'll give you a rematch, my good fellow," he said condescendingly to the Aragonese, "but I'll give you the benefit of a handicap."

I should have preferred more modesty from M. Alphonse; I was almost disturbed by his rival's humiliation. The Spanish giant took the insult hard. I saw him pale under his tan. Looking sullenly at his racquet, he gnashed his teeth and then muttered in a voice choking with rage: "*Me lo pagarás!*" [You'll pay for this!]

M. de Peyrehorade's arrival interrupted his son's triumph. My host, greatly surprised not to find him supervising the harnessing of the new coach, was even more surprised to find him soaked with sweat and holding his racquet.

M. Alphonse ran to the house, washed his hands and face, dressed again in his new coat and patent-leather shoes. Five minutes later, we were on our way toward Puygarrig, with an entourage of all the town's tennis players and a throng of spectators joyously shouting. The powerful horses that drew us could barely keep ahead of those dauntless Catalonians.

On reaching Puygarrig, the procession was about to head for the town hall when M. Alphonse put his hand to his forehead and whispered to me: "What a blockhead! I forgot the ring! It's on the Venus's finger, devil take her! For God's sake, don't tell my mother. Perhaps she won't notice."

"You could send someone," I said.

"Bah! My servant stayed behind in Ille, and I don't trust anyone here. Twelve hundred francs in diamonds! That's too tempting. Besides, what would they all think of my inattentiveness? They would only mock me, call me the statue's husband.... But perhaps no one will steal it from me. Luckily, all my riff-raff fear the idol—they won't go within arm's length of it. Bah! It doesn't matter. I have another ring."

The two ceremonies, civil and religous, were performed with appropriate pomp, and Mademoiselle de Puygarrig, receiving a ring once the property of a Parisian milliner, did not suspect her husband of sacrificing a love-token. Then we sat down at table, where we ate, drank, and even sang, all for a long time. I suffered for the bride in having to bear with all the crude jokes erupting all around her, but she took it all in better stride than I could ever have hoped, and her embarrassment was neither awkward nor affected. Perhaps courage springs from a difficult situation.

Breakfast ended at God's pleasure; it was four o'clock; the men either went for a stroll in the park, which was magnificent, or watched the peasant girls of Puygarrig, dressed in their gala outfits, dance on the château's lawn. Thus, we passed several hours. Meanwhile, the women pressed round the bride as she showed them her wedding gifts. Then she changed her dress, and I saw she had covered her lovely hair with a cap and a hat adorned with feathers, for there is nothing a new wife does with such alacrity as putting on as soon as possible those articles of apparel tradition proscribes for maidens.

It was nearly eight o'clock when we prepared to return to Ille. But before we started, there was a moving scene. Mademoiselle de Puygarrig's aunt, a very aged and devout woman who had been like a mother to her, was not to accompany us to town. Upon our departure, she gave her niece a touching sermon on her wifely duties, which produced a torrent of tears, and interminable embraces. M. de Peyrehorade compared this separation to the rape of the Sabine women. At last, however, we got under way, and en route, we all did all we could to entertain the bride and make her laugh, but it was in vain.

At Ille, supper stood waiting, and what a supper! If the morning's crude jests had shocked me, I was even more taken aback by the double entendres and jokes aimed at the groom, but especially at the bride. The groom, who had absented himself a moment before sitting at table, was as wan as death and icily serious. One glass after another, he drank his old Collioure wine, which is almost as strong as brandy. I was by his side and felt duty-bound to warn him. "Watch out! It's said that wine...."

I have no idea what foolishness I uttered to keep pace with the other guests.

He pressed his knee against mine and said in a very low voice: "When we leave the table..., may I have a word with you ?" His solemnity surprised me. I looked at him more attentively and marked the strange alteration in his features.

"Are you ill?" I asked.

"No." And he resumed his drinking.

Meanwhile, amid the shouting and handclapping, an eleven-year-old child who had slipped under the table showed his accomplices a dainty pink and white ribbon he had removed from the bride's ankle. It is called her garter. It was immediately cut into pieces and distributed among the young men, who, in keeping with an ancient custom still practiced in some partriarchal families, made boutonnieres of them. This raised a blush up to the whites of the bride's eyes.... But her consternation reached its peak when M. de Peyrehorade, after calling for silence, sang some verses in Catalan—impromptu, he said. So far as I understand, their meaning was: "Pray tell, my friends? Has the wine I've drunk made me see double? There are two Venuses here...."

With a look of terror, the bridegroom snapped his head in another direction. It made everyone laugh.

"Yes," continued M. de Peyrehorade, "there are two Venuses under my roof. One I found in the dirt, like a truffle; the other, dropped from the skies, has come to share her girdle with us."

He meant to say "her garter."

"My son, make your choice—the Roman or the Catalonian Venus. The rascal chooses the Catalonian, and wisely. The Roman is black; the Catalonian, white. The Roman is cold, the Catalonian enflames all who approach her."

This caused such an uproar, such noisy applause and roaring laughter, I thought the ceiling would fall on our heads. There were only three sober faces at the table—the bride's, the groom's, and my own. I not only had a terrible headache, but also, for some unknown reason, a wedding always saddens me. This one, moreover, I found a bit distasteful.

The last couplets having been sung by the mayor's deputy—and they were very naughty, I must say—we went to the salon to enjoy the good-byes of the bride, who, it being almost midnight, was soon to be escorted to her room.

M. Alphonse pulled me into a window-recess, and avoiding my eyes, said to me, "Make fun of me if you want...but I don't know what I have...I'm bewitched! the devil has me!"

My first thought was that he believed himself threatened by the sort of misfortune spoken of by Montaigne and Madame de Sévigné: "The realm of love is full of tragic stories, *etc.*"

I thought accidents of that sort happened only to intellectuals, I said to myself.

"You have drunk too much Collioure wine, my dear M. Alphonse," I said aloud. "I warned you."

"Yes, possibly. But there's something much more terrible."

His speech was incoherent. I believed he was downright drunk. "You know, my ring?" he continued, after a pause.

"Ah, yes! Has it been stolen?"

"No."

"In that case, then you have it?"

"No...I...I can't remove it from the finger of that devil of a Venus!"

"Come! you didn't pull hard enough."

"I did...but the Venus...has clenched her finger."

He stared at me with a haggard look, leaning against the window-hasp to avoid falling.

"What a fable!" I said. "You pushed the ring too far. Tomorrow, try using pliers. But be careful you don't damage the statue."

"No, I tell you. The Venus's finger is contracted, bent; she has made a fist, understand? It appears she is my wife because I gave her my ring.... She refuses to return it."

I felt a sudden shiver, and for a moment I had gooseflesh. Then, as he exhaled a breath of wine fumes at me, all my emotion disappeared.

"The poor man is completely drunk," I thought.

"You are an antiquary, Monsieur," the groom went on in a lamenting tone; "you know these statues...could there be some spring, some devilish trick I don't know.... Would you go see?"

"Gladly," I said. "Come with me."

"No, I'd rather you went alone."

I left the salon.

The weather had changed during supper, and a driving rain was beginning to fall. I was about to ask for an umbrella when a thought suddenly stopped me. "What a fool," I said to myself, "bothering to verify the account of a drunkard! Moreover, he may be playing some nasty joke on me to set these simple rubes laughing. And the very least, I would get soaked and catch a bad cold."

From the door, I shot an eye at the statue, from which water was streaming, and then went up to my room without reentering the salon. I went to bed, but sleep was long in coming. Images of all I had seen that day formed in my mind. I thought of that lovely, pure girl given over to a drunken brute. "How odious is a marriage of convenience!" I said to myself. "A mayor dons a tri-colored sash, a priest a stole, and just like that the most virtuous girl in the world is delivered to the Minotaur! Two beings who do not love each other— what have they to say at such a moment, for which two lovers would give their lives? Can a woman ever love a man whom she has once seen act so crassly? First impressions are indelible, and, I am sure, this M. Alphonse will well deserve being hated."

During my monologue, which I have much abridged, I had heard much coming and going about the house, doors opening and closing, carriages driving away. Then it seemed I heard the soft footsteps of several women on the stairs heading toward the far end of the hall opposite my room. It was probably the bride's entourage, leading her to bed. Then they went downstairs again. Madame de Peyrehorade's door shut. "That poor girl," I said to myself, "how troubled and ill at ease she must be!" Ill-humoredly, I turned in my bed. A bachelor plays a stupid role in a house where a marriage is consummated.

Silence reigned for some time before it was broken by heavy steps climbing the stairs. The wooden stairs creaked loudly.

"What a clod!" I cried. "I'll bet he'll fall down the stairs!"

Everything became quiet again. I grabbed a book to change the course of my thoughts. It was a statistical report, embellished with an article by M. de Peyrehorade on Druid ruins in the Prades district. I dozed off on the third page.

I slept badly and woke up several times. When the cock crowed, it may have been five in the morning; I had been awake more than twenty minutes. Day was just breaking. Then I distinctly heard the same heavy steps, the same creaking of the stairs I had heard before falling asleep. That seemed peculiar. Yawning, I tried to divine why M. Alphonse was rising so early. I could imagine no likely explanation. As I was about to close my eyes again, my attention was again piqued by a strange tramping, which soon blended with the tinkling of bells and the noise of doors bursting open; then I distinguished some confused screams.

"My drunkard must have set a fire somewhere!" I thought, jumping down from my bed.

I dressed hastily and entered the hall. From the far end came cries and lamentations, with one piercing voice dominating all the rest: "My son! my son!" Evidently, M. Alphonse had met with an accident. I ran to the bridal chamber: it was full of people. The first sight to strike my eye was the young man, half dressed, stretched across the bed where the wood was shattered. He was livid and motionless. His mother wept and screamed at his side. A frenetic M. de Peyrehorade was rubbing his son's temples with Eau de Cologne and holding salts under his nose. Alas! his son had long since died. On a couch at the other end of the room, the bride was in a fit of horrible convulsions. She cried incoherently, and to robust servants were having a world of trouble restraining her.

"God!" I cried, "What has happened?"

I approached the bed and lifted the unfortunate young man's body; it was already cold and rigid. His clenched teeth and ashen face expressed the most chilling anguish. Obviously enough, his death had been violent, and his agony terrible. But there was no sign of blood on his clothes. I opened his shirt and saw on his chest a purple mark extending down his ribs and back. One would have said that he had been crushed by an iron band. My foot touched something hard on the rug; I stooped and saw the diamond ring.

I led M. de Peyrehorade and his wife to their room; then I had the bride taken there.

"You still have a daughter," I said to them; "you owe her your concern." Then I left them alone.

It seemed to me beyond dispute that M. Alphonse had been the victim of a murder in which the authors had found a way to introduce themselves at night into the bride's bedroom. The marks on the chest and their circular character greatly puzzled me, however, for neither a club nor an iron rod could have caused them. Suddenly I remembered having heard it said that, in Valence, the *bravi* used long leather bags filled with fine sand to cudgel those they were hired to kill. At once, I recalled the Aragonese mule driver and his threat; and yet I could not believe he would have exacted such terrible vengeance for a minor bit of fun.

I made my rounds of the house, looking everywhere for traces of a break-in, and found nothing. I went down into the garden, to see if the murderers could have entered there, but I found no clear sign. Besides, the previous night's rain had so saturated the ground that no footprint could have remained. Even so, I observed several deep footprints in the ground; they went in two opposite directions, but in the same line, from the corner of the hedge along the tennis court to the door of the house. They might be M. Alphonse's steps, made when he went to get his ring from the statue. On the other hand, since the hedge was less thick at that point than elsewhere, the murderers must have come through there. Pacing back and forth before the statue, I stopped a moment to look at it. This time, I confess, I was unable to contemplate its expression of ironic wickedness without fright. My head full of the horrible scenes I had witnessed, it seemed to me an infernal divinity, applauding the disaster that had stricken that house.

I returned to my room and remained there till noon. Then I went out and asked for news of my hosts. They were a little calmer. Mademoiselle de Puygarrig—I should say M. Alphonse's widow—had regained consciousness. She had even talked with the prosecutor of Perpignan, then in Ille on his rounds, and that magistrate had taken her deposition. He asked for mine as well. I told him what I knew and did not hide from him my suspicions about the Aragonese mule driver. He ordered his immediate arrest.

"Have you gotten anything from Madame Alphonse?" I asked the prosecutor when my statement was transcribed and signed.

"That unfortunate young woman has gone mad," he said with a sad smile. "Mad! Completely mad! This is what she told me:

"She had been in bed, she said, a few minutes, with the curtains drawn, when her bedroom door opened and someone entered. At that point Madame Alphonse was on the inside of the bed, with her face to the wall. Persuaded it was her husband, she did not move. A moment later, the bed creaked as if pressed by an enormous weight. She was greatly frightened, but she didn't dare turn her head. Five, ten minutes perhaps—she can't say exactly—went by. Then she made an involuntary movement, or else the other person in the bed did, and she felt the touch of something cold as ice—that was her expression. She squeezed closer to the wall, trembling in every limb. Shortly after, the door opened a second time, and someone entered, saying: 'Good evening, my little wife.' Soon, the curtains parted. She heard a stifled cry. The person alongside her in bed sat up and seemed to reach out. Then she turned her head...and saw, she says, her husband on his knees beside the bed, his head at a level with the pillow, clasped in the arms of a kind of greenish giant who was violently embracing him. She says—she repeated it twenty times, poor woman!...she says that she recognized...can you guess? The bronze Venus, M. de Peyrehorade's statue.... Ever since she made her appearance in town, everyone dreams of her. But to continue with the story of that unfortunate madwoman. At that sight she lost consciousness, and it is probable that she had lost her mind some moments before. She could not calculate for how long she had fainted. On coming to, she again saw the phantom—or, as she still insists, the statue—motionless, with its legs and the lower part of the body on the bed, the bust and arms stretched out, and, in its arms, her husband, also motionless. A cock crowed. Then the statue left the bed, let the cadaver fall, and exited. Madame Alphonse grabbed for the bell-cord, and you know the rest."

They arrested the Spaniard; he was calm, and he cooly defended himself with equanimity. Moreover, he did not deny making the remark I had overheard; but he explained it by saying that he had meant simply that, after a day's rest, he would defeat his vanquisher in tennis. I remember that he added:

"When he is insulted, an Aragonese doesn't wait for his revenge until the next day. Had I thought that M. Alphonse meant to insult me, I would have put a knife into his belly right on the court."

His shoes were compared with the footprints in the garden; his shoes were quite a bit larger.

To end the matter, the innkeeper with whom he lodged swore that he had passed the whole night rubbing and medicating one of his sick mules. Furthermore, the Aragonese was a man of good repute, well known in this part of the country, to which he came annually for business. So he was released, and with apologies.

I have forgotten the deposition of a servant, who was the last to see M. Alphonse alive. Just as he was going up to his wife, he had called the servant and anxiously asked if he knew where I was. The servant replied that he had not seen me. Then M. Alphonse sighed and stood more than a minute without speaking; then he said: *"Well, the devil must have taken him too!"*

I asked this man if M. Alphonse had on his diamond ring when he spoke to him. The servant hesitated before replying; at last, he said he did not think so, but then he had not paid much attention.

"If he had that ring on his finger," he added after a moment, "I would certainly have noticed it, for I thought he had given it to Madame Alphonse."

In questioning this man, I again sensed a little of the superstitious terror which Madame Alphonse's deposition had spread throughout the house. The prosecutor smiled as he looked at me, and I did not persist in pressing the point.

Some hours after M. Alphonse's funeral, I prepared to leave Ille. M. de Peyrehorade's carriage was to take me to Perpignan. Despite his feebleness, the poor old man wanted to accompany me as far as his garden gate. We crossed it in silence, with him, barely able to drag himself along, leaning on my arm. On separating, I cast a last look at the Venus. I foresaw that my host, although he did not share the terror and loathing she inspired among some of his family, would gladly rid himself of an object constantly reminding him of a frightful calamity. My intention was to convince him to place it in a museum. I was hesitating over bringing the matter up, when M. de Peyrehorade mechanically turned his head to where he saw me staring. His eye fell upon the statue, and he instantly burst into tears. I embraced him, and, without daring to utter a single word, I stepped into the carriage.

Subsequent to my departure, I have not had reason to believe that a clarification of this mysterious catastrophe will some day eventuate.

M. de Peyrehorade died a few months after his son. In his will, he left me his manuscripts, which I possibly shall publish some day. I found among them no article relating to the inscriptions on the Venus.

P.S. My friend M. de P. has recently written me from Perpignan that the statue no longer exists. After her husband's death, Madame de Peyrehorade's first concern was to have it melted into a bell, and in that new form, it now serves the church at Ille. "But," M. de P. adds, "it would seem that an evil fate pursues those in possession of that bronze. Since that bell has rung at Ille, the vines have twice frozen.

(Translated by Frank Gado)